CHICKEN CITY

Chris Brown

Published in 2024 by FeedARead.com Publishing.

A CIP catalogue record for this title is available from the British Library.

Set in 11pt Palatino and designed and artworked by Chris Brown and John Taylor.

I've lost a staggering amount of family, friends and acquaintances in recent years, from my parents Fred and Joan to my brother Mike and my brother-in-law Paul Curtis, who both passed away far too soon, you are sadly missed.

Many of the friends I've lost I've known since the 70s where I met them on the old Tote End at Eastville: Mark Alexander, Steve Bennett, Brian Bloodworth, Tim Blythe, John Bullock, Johnny Burge, Mark 'Bernie' Burnell, Pete Creber, Brian Daly, Glen Davis, Dale Dempsey, Bob Doling, Mike Easton, Jimmy Gilmore, Alan Gregory, Rob House, Bob Inker, Paul 'Wax' Johnson, Mike 'The Viking' Kaines, Chris 'Topper' Marden, Ian McDade, Des McKervy, Nigel 'Car Park Nige' Mogridge, Andy Molter, Graham Molton, Steve 'Boz' Perryman, Dave Phillips, Jimmy Robertson, Roy Savage, Geoff Shellard, Phil 'Shep' Sheppard, Tony Skuse, Steve Rudge, John 'Paddy' Ryan, Rob Wade, Brian 'Mr Tote End' Williams and sadly many others too numerous to mention.

There's also been two great losses on the Bristol music scene in recent years – DJ's Steve Ashby and Johnny Stallard, original Soultrain boys from back in the 70s have also sadly passed away, RIP soul brothers.

Chicken City is dedicated to you all, as well as my wife Carole and my family – Dan, Chloe, Amy, Max and Lily.

Life is way too short, make the most of it – it's not a dress rehearsal.

'They (who) seek to establish systems of government based on the regimentation of all human beings by a handful of individual rulers... Call this a New Order.
It is not new and it is not order.'

Franklin D. Roosevelt

Prologue

Summer 1969

The heat took its time to dissipate but at last, a cool breeze began to blow lazily across the sweltering city.

On a transistor radio somewhere in the near distance the sound of *Something in the air* faded in and out as a loon-panted, joint-smoking teenager tried in vain to receive a half decent signal from Radio Luxembourg.

The younger of the two lads crouched behind a bush and with annoyance noticed a mark on his new boots. He pulled the sleeve of his navy-blue Harrington jacket down into the palm of his hand and lightly rubbed the toecap to remove the blemish. A broad smile creased his face as the boots returned to their newly bought pristine state.

The youth, older and larger – if not wiser, crouched beside the boy and watched as the youngster carried out his cleaning task. His mother would be proud of him he thought. The youngster noticed the older lad watching him and grinned nervously, his friend returned a knowing smile and winked.

Thunderclap Newman's song bore into the boy's ear and brain. He found himself momentarily humming along to it – causing his friend to scowl at him in mild disgust.

'Fucking hippy crap,' sneered the youth.

Behind the two of them, a distressed bird, disturbed from finding its evening meal by the youths, screeched and departed noisily causing both lads to momentarily seek out the source of the commotion.

'Made I jump,' said the boy apologetically.

'An' I,' replied the youth, trying to put the youngster at ease.

'Nice song thrush,' said the boy.

'You what? You some sort of wanky twitcher?'

The boy felt embarrassed. Only a year or so earlier he would spend many an hour bird watching with his dad's old World War Two binoculars in one hand and a copy of *Encyclopedia of British Birds* in the other, but those days of innocent childhood were now long behind him.

Words were at a premium and the two of them quickly resumed their silent vigil. Five long minutes passed before the older youth spoke again.

'What you got?'

'What do you mean?'

'Tools, weapons – what you carrying?'

'Nothing,' replied the youngster, 'just my boots and my fists... you?'

'Same. That's all I need.' The older lad grinned.

The youngster nodded in agreement. While the older youth resumed his recce of the target, the boy surreptitiously studied him, taking in his features and his clothing – he was only just over a year older than him but physically they were so different.

He noticed his biceps taut against the short-sleeved blue windowpane check Ben Sherman shirt, while the skinny red braces holding up his immaculate olive-green Levi's Sta-prest set off and emphasised the older lad's physique. On his feet were well worn, but highly polished, 8-hole Oxblood Doc Marten 1460 boots.

The boy was jealous. He glanced down, somewhat embarrassed at his own uniform – the Millets-bought jacket, a world away from a real deal G9 Baracuta, the cheap Brutus shirt his mother had bought for him from Eastville market and the all-important footwear – just as polished, just as lethal as the youths DM's, but

Monkey boots somehow didn't have the cachet that his friend's boots had. He vowed that he would work as many spare hours as he could stacking shelves in the supermarket to pay for a pair of 1460's of his own – his dad had instilled into him what he called a 'Protestant work ethic' – he wasn't quite sure what it meant but knowing and admiring his dad as he did he thought it best that he adhered to it.

The boy was in awe of his older friend. His friend knew it, and in all honesty, he was a little embarrassed by the attention of the boy. But he liked him, he was a laugh – and a game young fucker, he would give him that.

He had seen him in action before and if things went well, he would see him in action again – soon.

Something in the air gave way to the sound of Desmond Dekker slaughtering the Queen's English with *Israelites*.

The older youth grinned inanely.

'This is more like it. Bit of reggae... I got this,' he smiled.

'So have I,' said the boy.

'Nicked it from Woolies,' said the youth.

'So did I,' said the boy.

They were both lying. The boy hummed along to the song for a few seconds.

'What's it about?' he queried.

'What?'

'This song – what's he on about?'

The youth shrugged.

'Fucked if I know, it's just some darkie singing about waking up in the morning and having baked beans for breakfast.'

'Oh,' the boy answered, still none the wiser.

The song thrush returned and set about extricating the remainder of his meal from the grass behind the squatting youths.

The youth nudged the youngster and nodded towards the public lavatory where two men entered simultaneously.

'Here we go, summat's up,' he said with a smile.

One was in his mid-forties, smartly dressed in an expensive casual suit and trilby hat while the other one was younger – much younger, and a bonus for the two crouching youths – a long haired hippy.

'We're in luck. Couple of homos and one of 'ems a fucking hippy – ace,' said the youth.

'C'mon then,' said the boy, 'what you waiting for?'

'Hold on a minute. I wanna catch 'em at it – see what they get up to.'

The boy felt repulsed as his mind's eye conjured up an image that he didn't really want to see.

'Well, I fucking don't,' the boy replied angrily.

The older lad was taken aback by the boy's forcefulness. It was not something he was used to – someone disagreeing with him, especially someone younger than him.

'Go on then, you get in there… have a pop. Let's see what you're made of.'

The boy rose and flattened the imaginary wrinkles in his jeans then straightened his Harrington before finally clenching his fists in readiness. The older lad nodded and motioned to him to move. The boy strode purposely towards the public convenience, every step towards it heightened his tension … and increased the smell of piss and disinfectant wafting into his nostrils.

At the entrance to the toilet he stopped and hesitated, he could hear them behind the locked door of the cubicle, heavy breathing and the sound of the movement of a zip caused him to catch his breath. He looked back towards his accomplice for reassurance.

The older lad nodded to his friend once more.

'What you waiting for… lost your bottle?' he said in a near whisper.

The youngster was no stranger to violence. He had indulged in random acts of casual brutality over the last year or so, but… this was different, he felt uneasy, perhaps even a modicum of sympathy for his potential victims. They weren't doing anyone any harm, they had never harmed him – did they really deserve the violence that his friend wanted to inflict on them? The violence that the youth seemed to think was both warranted and justified?

He turned back to the youth, shook his head and mouthed '*I can't*.'

The older lad showed his irritation and marched aggressively towards the boy.

'Fucking wanker,' he spat out as he passed him. 'Wait here then, give me a shout if anyone else turns up.'

The boy stared embarrassingly at his boots, his cheeks reddened to the colour of his friends DM's – it was an awkward trait of his that he'd endured since childhood. So much for being tough, he thought to himself, *can't even do a bit of queer bashing…*

'Come out you dirty bastards!' the youth shouted. Not waiting for any response, he kicked at the locked door causing it to shatter and crash off its hinges – it flew inwards and onto the hippy who was on his knees in the cramped cubicle.

The youth kicked out again, this time his boot came into contact with the hippy's head. The hippy slumped back as he tried in vain to grab the bowl of the toilet, his hand slid around the edge of the pan as his back crashed against the flimsy partition.

Standing back the youth took in the scene and surveyed the damage. He squinted in the gloom but failed to see the older homosexual who was cowering behind the unhinged door – all he could see of him was his Hush Puppy-clad feet beside the prostrate hippy.

'Come on you queer bastards, get out here so I can give you a proper kicking!'

He kicked at the broken door once more, leaving an imprint of the sole of his Doc Marten on the already scuffed paint, just above a crude drawing of an ejaculating penis and a phone number.

The younger boy stayed outside, booted but rooted to the spot, not wanting to witness the carnage that his friend was causing inside the Victorian public convenience.

Inside, the older lad turned his head to beckon to his friend.

'Oi, you gonna get in here or…'

His question was cut short by a lavatory chain as it smashed across his face, wielded by the now upright hippy standing wild-eyed in front of him. As the youth raised his arms to shield himself from another blow the hippy kicked out in retribution. He wore boots of his own and he was just as adept as the skinhead in the art of down and dirty street fighting.

He swung the chain once again and it wrapped itself around the youth's outstretched arm.

The skinhead fell to the floor, his face landing in a puddle of unknown substance. He let out a gurgled yelp as the hippy straddled him and set about punching him around the head and body.

Outside, the youngster heard his friend's plight. He suppressed his nerves and shame and ran inside, prepared and ready to help the older youth. He saw the back of the hippy who was still lashing out, his long hair swaying from side to side as he rhythmically punched the skinhead.

The boy grabbed the hippy's hair from behind with his left hand and pulled him back off of his friend; at the same time, he punched with his right hand to the side of the hippy's face.

He made contact – once, twice, the third punch connected with the hippy's nose, blood spewed out and mingled with his long, lank hair.

The hippy turned to face the boy, fists clenched, ready to retaliate…

'You!'

Chapter One

What if…

Friday 24 June, 2016

The people of Britain voted overwhelmingly by a majority of 82 per cent to 18 per cent in favour of leaving the European Union.

Steve Allen stared at the TV in wide-eyed bewilderment and disbelief.

'My God, what have we done?'

The present day

His eyes opened and he squinted at his phone in the morning gloom. It glared back at him from his bedside table.

Pressure Drop by The Maytals heralded the call.

He checked the time – it was six-twenty.

'What?' he grunted.

'I'm outside your gaff with The Professor. Why the fuck ain't you out here?' asked an irate Tony Preston.

'Uh, I didn't know you had a job for me,' he answered truthfully.

'Yeah whatever… hand off cock, hand on socks and move your fucking lazy arse. Pronto.'

The old Mondeo's rear door groaned open. He got in. There was a grunt and a poor imitation of some sort of false greeting from Preston – Steve responded in a likewise fashion.

'Where we going?' he eventually asked.

'Corby,' came the heart-stopping reply.

If there was a hell on earth, a place that the world had passed by, it was the small, deprived town in Northamptonshire known as Corby. A land of guttural, fading Glaswegian accents, derelict enterprise zones and choking fumes from a thousand lorry exhausts. He hated the place.

He propped his backpack against the window, rested his head against the makeshift pillow and drifted into a fitful sleep.

* * *

The tall, thin, bespectacled figure of Phil 'The Professor' Baxter nudged Steve in the ribs. 'Wake up sleeping beauty, we're here.'

Steve stumbled out of the Mondeo and stood in a pool of brown water and diesel. His backpack opened and the contents disgorged into the muddy puddle.

'For fuck's sake,' he cursed.

'Come on, get a wiggle on. The sooner we get in, the sooner we can get out of this shithole,' said Phil.

Steve fished out his meagre possessions from the murky water.

'I can't find my high vis,' he protested without a hint of irony.

Phil was already prepped and in standard trade plater mode: high-vis tabard on over a zip-up weatherproof jacket; backpack slung over shoulder containing sandwiches, flask, phone charger and newspaper; clipboard with ballpoint pen clutched in right hand while the all-important battered red and white trade plates nestled under his left armpit.

Phil grinned. 'You're wearing it you prat... not at the fucking races today are you?'

Steve didn't reply and merely stared blankly at his workmate.

'Come on Steve, it isn't that bad. At least we got a lift this time. Could've been worse, could've had to hitchhike,' said Phil with a forced smile.

If that was meant to have made Steve feel better, it didn't, not by a long shot.

They signed in at the security hut, showed their paperwork, then trudged in the morning gloom to the shabby Portakabin where another dozen or so bedraggled, miserable, pathetic, middle-aged men waited for their vehicles.

Steve slumped into an off-white plastic chair that had once adorned some chav's grubby patio while Phil sat opposite and immediately pulled out *The Guardian* from his backpack.

The other trade platers looked up and sneered before burying their heads in their mobiles, scanning the latest trashy updates from *The Sun* and *The Daily Star* websites.

In the rush, Steve had forgotten to pick up his Kindle. At least he could have lost himself for a while in a Michael Connolly thriller. He wondered for a moment what Harry Bosch, his favourite detective, was up to as he cleaned up the streets of Los Angeles. He cursed himself for his own aberration.

Steve looked over to his colleague who was engrossed in an article about the latest migrant crisis engulfing Europe. 'The Professor' as the other trade platers had dubbed him was, like Steve, a victim of circumstance.

He also once had a good career; teaching robotics at one of the London Universities, but long hours, stress and a failed marriage due to an affair with one of his pretty young students had taken its toll.

It transpired that he'd also been taking his work home with him – literally. His employers found out and he was dismissed quicker than you could say 'empty your drawers'.

His wife had kept the house in Ealing forcing him to move west where, with his tail firmly between his legs and his cock back in his pants, he sought refuge, solace and, most importantly, cheap lodgings with his ageing parents. Thanks to CRB checks though, what he couldn't find was a decent job, and like many fifty-something males he took the only job he could find – that of a grandly-titled Vehicle Logistics Operative, or trade plater as it was more commonly known.

Phil raised his eyes from his paper and looked over the top of his wire-rimmed glasses.

'Steve, seeing as we're up here early do you fancy taking in the Naseby battlefield? It's only down the road.'

Phil's clipped nasal tone irritated the rest of the inhabitants of the Portakabin. Sneers, jeers, farts and a mumbled *'posh twat'* echoed around the gloomy room that was now beginning to resemble a malodorous sauna.

All Steve could do was nod and smile lamely.

Not for the first time in the last few years he wondered how the hell his life had come to this.

Chapter Two

It was now raining stair rods. The two of them studied the inscription on the plaque in a revered, respectful silence, the only sound to be heard came from the incessant *caw-cawing* of a nearby murder of crows.

'Was it worth it?' asked Phil, 'considering the parlous state that Parliament is in today.'

He looked up and studied the hedgerows and the gentle slopes of the Northamptonshire landscape spreading out in front of him.

'Fifteen hundred dead in this battle alone you know, over a hundred thousand in the entire war. That was a huge percentage of the population – and for what? Four hundred years on and we've got a corrupt, cheating, lying bunch of charlatans whose only intention is to deceive the British people and to feather their own nests – frauds the lot of 'em.'

Steve didn't disagree but he was in no mood for a political debate. He had learnt over the years that on the political front at least, it was best to keep his mouth firmly shut.

'C'mon then, let's get back on the road.'

The two of them turned and trudged back along the muddy path to their parked-up Vauxhall Movanos.

Phil had pulled the short straw.

He had to deliver to Cold Meece, a place that more than lived up to its name: bleak, barren… and cold. Steve hated delivering to the huge ex-Ministry of Defence site in the heart of the admittedly beautiful Staffordshire countryside.

But then again, Steve hated delivering anywhere.

It wasn't so much the delivering, it was the not knowing where the onward journey would be – or even if there would be one – it might just be a terse '*make your way back home*' from his boss, the abrupt and boorish Tony Preston. But today at least, he had a return trip – drop off the Movano at a dealership in West Bromwich then '*get your fucking arse over to Erdington and take a Kuga down to Weston.*'

Result… of sorts. He knew the drill. Drop off the van, let the cheap-suited, brown pointed-shoed, dick-head of a junior salesman check it out, get the paper-work signed, blag a coffee and some digestives then walk to Black Lake, a small commuter station on the Midland Metro.

Catch the metro to Birmingham New Street, unfortunately having to pay, then a Litchfield Trent Valley train to the sprawling suburb of Erdington whilst staring out of the window and avoiding eye contact with the guard. Exit the station – luckily with no barriers – walk fucking miles in the drizzle, criss-cross busy streets and redundant canals, arrive and make small talk with another cheap-suited, brown pointed-shoed, dickhead of a junior salesman. Obtain keys and paperwork, check out car for scratches, kick tyres, blag more coffee and top-up the thermos, nick more digestives and fuck off. Not forgetting to fuel the car – they were always empty – *fucking car salesmen and their brown pointy-fucking-shoes.*

The rain was now of Biblical proportions. He rounded Spitfire Island as puddles the size of small lakes rapidly formed on the grey, pot-holed tarmac. He swerved, but couldn't avoid one hole that was filled with muddy water and a torrent of sludge flew upwards and over the tall, hooded youth who stood by the side of the road forlornly hitchhiking for a lift.

In his rear-view mirror, Steve could see the youth angrily gesticulate. The hand with the raised thumb quickly transformed to a hand with the middle finger pointing skywards. He thought for a second of driving on, but then remembered the many motorway junctions he'd miserably inhabited over the last year.

If not getting a lift was bad enough it was the numerous comedians who beeped their horns, slowed down then raised their thumbs and grinned idiotically as they drove away that really hacked him off.

He pulled in, leant over the passenger seat and pushed the door open. The bedraggled youth ran towards the vehicle, the hood of the sodden jacket pulled up in defiance of the elements.

'Sorry mate, I couldn't help it – where you going?' Steve shouted above the roar of the traffic.

The youth threw a backpack into the car then got in without answering, the hood of the soaking and muddied top finally came down and released a shock of long blonde hair.

Emerald green eyes focused on Steve angrily.

'Bristol, you bastard,' she said.

Chapter Three

They sat in silence. Steve shuffled awkwardly in his seat.

'Look I'm sorry, I didn't mean to splash you, I couldn't help...'

'Whatever.'

Steve noticed a slight accent, European of some sorts, he thought.

'I um... actually you're lucky, I uh – I'm going to Weston, I can drop you off in Bristol,' he stammered.

'Lucky?' she queried, whilst looking down at her wet clothing.

'You think, this lucky?' She raised her eyebrows, gestured at her top and muttered something in a language Steve failed to recognise.

'No, sorry I didn't mean that,' he said as he turned up the heater on the dash.

'Perhaps you should take that wet jacket off... uh, I'm Steve by the way.'

'Evalina, but people call me Eva.'

She nodded and unzipped her jacket then awkwardly leant forward and pulled her arms out of the sleeves.

Steve tried but failed to keep his eyes on the road as she peeled off the top revealing a tight white T-shirt. It too was as wet as the outer garment and Steve could clearly see her red, lacy bra through the T-shirt.

He averted his eyes to his right and felt a rush of heat around his neck, it burst up through his head and a bead of sweat formed on his forehead.

He wasn't sure, but this time he thought he heard a faint giggle.

'I suppose I should say thanks... for stopping, not for getting me wet.'

At last, her anger seemed to be subsiding.

'That's OK,' said Steve, 'I've done a lot of hitch-hiking myself, I know what a pain in the ar... sorry, backside it is.'

He definitely heard a giggle this time.

'Why you so polite Steve? Every Englishman I meet seem to be so... coarse?'

Steve, at last, thought it appropriate to make eye contact.

He glanced to his left and for the first time he studied her. She was bedraggled and wet as an otter's pocket and possessed a face that could stop traffic, but not on Spitfire Island on a wet Wednesday afternoon it seemed.

'Um, I don't know – just my upbringing I guess. I was always taught to respect women... Uh, so is that an accent I hear? Where are you from?' he asked.

'I come from Bajgora in Kosovo, it's just a small village, very beautiful.' She paused and looked at Steve.

'We... my mother and I, we had problems in Kosovo and we needed to leave urgently. I thought I was coming to England to study, but I get a job and just... stayed...'

Her voice trailed off. Steve detected sadness in her tone.

'Problems? What sort of problems?' He regretted the question as soon as he asked it.

She turned away from Steve, looked out of the nearside window and stared blankly at the dank and miserable landscape.

'I uh... I don't want to talk about it.'

'Sorry,' replied Steve, 'I didn't mean to pry... Where do you work?' he asked, but he was pretty certain he already knew the answer.

'I work in a food processing factory in Avonmouth,' she finally answered, 'it is horrible, I hate it.'

'Chicken City?' asked Steve.

Eva nodded and the silence returned. Steve wondered what kind of life she lived and why she thought that all Englishmen were coarse. He could tell that for all her giggles and her beauty she was troubled. She reminded him of someone from his past.

Steve gave out a false cough. 'Um, would you like some coffee? I've got a flask in my bag, it's on the back seat. It might warm you up a bit.'

She didn't respond but silently undid her seatbelt and twisted around towards Steve. Once again, her pert breasts caught Steve's eye. *For fuck's sake, keep your eyes on the road, she could be your daughter, your granddaughter even.*

Eva opened Steve's backpack, took out the flask and poured herself a hot, steaming coffee. She gripped the cup with two hands and stared into the distance through the windscreen, her mind elsewhere.

A minute or so passed, Steve thought it best not to query her anymore.

'Would you like some?' Eva looked towards Steve with doleful eyes. He nodded a yes in response. She drained the cup with relish then topped it up and passed it to him. He clumsily took it and their hands touched. He noticed her well-manicured hands and false nails.

'Sorry,' he apologised awkwardly.

She shook her head.

'Why you say sorry? You make me laugh... you're a nice man,' she giggled.

Her mood had changed once more, he hoped this time the troubled Eva had disappeared. She reached down into his backpack and pulled out a CD.

'Hey, let's put some music on!' She turned on the audio, took out the disc from its case and inserted it into the CD slot on the dashboard.

The Champion by Willie Mitchell blasted out through the speakers. Eva creased her brow and she looked at Steve questioningly.

'What's this? I never heard such music.'

'It's uh… Northern Soul,' replied Steve sheepishly, 'music from a long time ago, before you were born. But what the hell, I like it.'

Eva started nodding her head to the infectious beat. 'It's weird, but yes, it's good… when do they start singing?'

'They don't – it's an instrumental.'

The two of them started nodding their heads in rhythm, they looked at each other and smiled, the smile turned into a laugh.

Steve shook his head in disbelief. She winked at him and his heart raced, he turned up the volume as the rain drummed against the windscreen even harder as they headed in the gloom towards Chicken City.

Chapter Four

Five years earlier

'Would you like some more powder on your nose Mr Etchington?'

I'd rather have a bit more up my nose you little minx.

'Yes my dear, don't want the old schnozzle beaming like a Belisha beacon do we?' he grinned.

'There you go… perfect. Um, hope you don't mind, but can I take a photo of the two of us? I'll send it to my mum, she'll be well jel. She things you're lush!'

Etchington's grin grew wider. He resembled a Cheshire cat.

The young make-up girl leaned closer into him. Etchington could smell her perfume and feel her small but firm breast against his shoulder. She nervously looked around before she whispered in his ear.

'And we totally agree with your politics sir, you've got the backing of the nation. Send 'em back that's what we say.'

Another youngster arrived. Male, grey hoodie, scruffy Vans, headphones around neck, clipboard in hand.

'On in five Mr Etchington,' he said.

Etchington nodded. '*Cometh the hour, cometh the man*,' he said under his breath.

* * *

Philippa Bancroft, the uber feisty golden girl of *Newsnight* sat crossed-legged opposite Neil Etchington, the mature, poster boy of the far right and one of Britain's most eligible bachelors. She caught him admiring her legs, she was not impressed.

'Neil Etchington. Your rise in British politics has been nothing but meteoric... please tell our viewers a little about yourself. I understand you were in the Guards before you entered politics?'

'Good evening Philippa – do you mind if I call you Philippa?' Not that he waited for an answer.

'That's correct. I was in the Guards and served in the Balkans, I was part of KFOR, the NATO peace-keeping force. When I left the army, myself and some of my colleagues started up Solutio – we were part business, part think tank, part pressure group...'

'*Far right* pressure group,' leapt in Bancroft with an accusing tone.

'Well you might say that but we prefer to call it a pro-British, patriotic group – that doesn't make it far right.'

If only you knew – some of my close friends make Ghenghis Khan look like a lily-livered liberal.

'And your business dealings?'

'All above board if that's what you're insinuating... defence projects, construction, telecoms, logistics...'

'Arms deals?'

'Well, yes... as part of our defence projects and as I said all legitimate and above board.'

'And it's made you very rich?'

'We're a global enterprise, we employ thousands of people around the world and we pay a huge amount of tax and yes, I've done very well out of it thank you – we also export a huge amount therefore contributing to the wealth of this country and I support many, many charities. None of that is a crime is it?'

Philippa Bancroft visibly bristled.

Good answer old boy, she's reeling. God, she's very fuckable when she gets angry.

'Hmmm. So, you formed your England Unite Party in what... 2014? What made you get into politics?'

He hesitated for a moment, gathered his thoughts and stroked his handsome, chiseled chin.

'Just seemed a natural progression. Like a lot of people, I was fed up with the stale, grey political status quo in this country. I like to think we're representing the real citizens of this country, the people that made this country great, I intend to make it great once more. I want to look after the pensioners, the ex-service people, the families... hardworking people...'

'Not immigrants though, or refugees, asylum seekers or people of colour?'

Don't rise to the bitch.

'The colour of the skin is irrelevant, as long as people want to play by *our* rules and contribute to *our* society then they are welcome to stay but well... this multi-culturalism *thing* simply doesn't work.'

She shook her head but she sure as hell didn't want to go down that rabbit hole.

'Get on with it Pippa – ask him about this bloody plan of his!' yelled the producer in her ear.

'Yes well... so in the recent election your party got some 29 MPs, including yourself into parliament and now you find yourself in a coalition government with the Tory party – how's that going?'

'Very well thank you. Look, we have a lot in common – the Tory party are a broad church and there are very many who have welcomed us with open arms. I have large support within the Government for my plans which I'll be announcing in a white paper in the House of Commons next week.'

'Ah yes, I was getting on to that. So this *plan* of yours. Can you explain exactly how it's going to work?'

Here we go then, hit the bitch with some over-inflated figures...

'It's quite simple. We have over 100,000 people who are officially applying for asylum in the UK at present and that's not including the illegal immigrants who have slipped through the net. There are over 120,000 individuals in receipt of support, between 2015 and the present day we have offered a place to over 500,000 men, women and children who are seeking safety from around the world – and this is via the legal entry routes. Over 45,000 have arrived in boats across the Channel just this year… Quite simply, this situation is intolerable, this country is being swamped, we are full – enough is enough!'

'Yes, yes, yes – we're all aware of these figures but as I asked what are the details of your plans, your scheme. What exactly are you going to do about this *intolerable situation* as you call it?' She asked acidly.

'Yes, well I was just coming to that if you let me answer… as I said, this situation is intolerable and it simply can't continue. We, this government, our hard-working, law-abiding, tax-paying citizens are spending a fortune housing and feeding these so-say asylum seekers, nay *illegal* immigrants and for what in return? Absolutely nothing…'

Shit, don't overdo the hardworking people bit, rein it in old boy.

She interrupted once more.

'I would hardly call people – men, women and children who are escaping war and persecution, illegal immigrants… they are refugees who are seeking asylum surely?'

'Oh sorry, I didn't realise there was a war in France?' snorted Etchington as he looked directly into the camera.

'…because let's face it that's where they're coming from – across the Channel. Surely if they're really escaping war and persecution as you put it, they would stop in the first free country they came to? But no, they head to the UK for one thing and one thing only – our benefits system!'

It was getting heated.

'But...'

'Never mind "but" – that's a fact, so what my solution is...'

Damn, don't use the word 'solution', too many awkward connotations.

'What my proposal is, is to actually put these, uh, poor unfortunate people to work so that it actually benefits us all.'

'How exactly?'

She uncrossed her legs and leant forward. He could see down the top of her blouse... just a hint of ample cleavage.

Nice tits... but a bit old for me.

'We have a skills shortage in the UK – thanks to the debacle of Brexit.'

'So you accept Brexit was a debacle?'

'Not Brexit *per se,* but the way it was handled... Look,' he thrust out both hands, fingers splayed.

'Let's not forget that the good people of Britain voted 82 per cent to 18 per cent in favour of us leaving the EU. Whether you accept that result or not Philippa, we simply have to get on and deliver the mandate of the people. I'll be the first to admit that "Brexit *didn't* mean Brexit" and as for "Oven ready deal" – what the hell did he even mean by that? But well, Brexit can and *will* work – if we let it...'

'So you accept that Brexit hasn't been good for the UK?'

'No, not at all, but...'

'Do you accept that all Brexiteers are racist?'

'Don't be ridiculous.'

'But all racists are Brexiteers?'

'You are scraping the barrel Philippa, stop being so facile... so by your reckoning 82 per cent of those who voted in the referendum are racist – really?'

'No, that's not what I said...'

'Well, we're going around in circles but you need to accept the referendum result and move on and anyway we are not here to talk about Brexit… so, as I was saying… because of Brexit the UK lost a lot of key workers, I admit that. Yet here we are with an excess of fit young males, because the majority of these *asylum seekers* as you call them are fit, young males and *not* women and children contrary to what you and the rest of the BBC say Philippa – so let's face it the situation is only going to get worse – just last year we had the riot in Calais and the occupation of the Channel Tunnel which resulted in many, many deaths and now we have serious rioting in refugee camps in France and Italy and there's no sign of this disorder abating. The German Bundestag have announced that they're having a rethink about their open-door policy, and we know that these *refugees* will be heading to the UK instead. So yes, these people, these refugees, asylum seekers, *illegal* immigrants – call them what you will, we will put them to work, retrain them, *reeducate* them in our ways so that they become valid and valued members of our, *British* society.'

'I'm not sure I like the sound of this.' Philippa stated, eyes wide in horror.

'Well you might not but the inhabitants of our fair isles do. Desperate times call for desperate measures and I can assure you that when I've been on the doorstep talking to hard-working British people, this is what they've been telling me, they're not only fed up with these foreign…'

Damnit!

'… asylum seekers coming here for our benefits, they're fed up with the state of this country. Do you know I was in Bristol the other day…'

Checking out where we can put these fucking spongers.

'… and what a mess it is. The potholes, the litter and as for the graffiti – my God it looked like a cross between a third-world country and the Bronx. So first off, we'll get these poor, unfortunate refugees...'

Good, that's more like it, back on track.

'... out on the streets and tidying up our cities – they can fill in the potholes, pick up litter and get rid of the graffiti for starters and then...'

'Sounds like chain gangs.'

'Really Philippa. Chain gangs went back to prison and they weren't paid, fed and housed like we'll be doing with these poor people.'

Brilliant!

'But how exactly do you propose doing that, seeing as the Government has already taken over all the available military barracks and hotels – and I believe there's even talk of housing them in offshore barges?'

'Well that will never happen will it?... and anyway, this is what I've been coming to. We will build new towns for them, mini towns on the edge of our cities on old disused industrial areas and brownfield sites. They will be housed in comfortable purpose-built accommodation with their own schools and medical facilities and here's the crux of it all – we will build workplaces, factories, industrial units for them to work in *within* these towns. We will retrain them to produce goods that this country really needs, goods – and food – that currently we have to import.'

'Such as?'

'Well, clothing, microchips, electrical goods, mobile phones, laptops, electric car batteries – we'll even produce our own electric vehicles, a proper people's car designed by AI – and then of course there's food produce. Have you seen that ghastly sea of polythene in Almeria in Spain? Just so the EU can have tomatoes and strawberries all year round – and using slave labour housed in appalling conditions I'll have you know! Disgraceful, but we could build our own proper super greenhouses here, and the produce would be fresher seeing as it wouldn't have to travel thousands of miles – that will be great for our carbon footprint you know, so we'll also be helping to save the planet as well!'

'And how…'

Fuck her, keep it going, she's on the ropes.

'Then there's meat produce – chicken! Do you know that just this year we imported over 500,000 metric tons of chicken – that's ludicrous! No, all of this we can produce in the UK and these refugees can jolly well help us to do it. We'll pay them a decent wage of course and house them, but they'll be paying their way, so helping the economy – inflation will come down and there will be no more recessions. It's a win-win situation for us all!'

Fucking nailed it! Potholes sorted, inflation down, stopping the boats and saving the planet – you're a fucking genius old boy!

Philippa Bancroft was clearly agitated.

'Hmmm, what about the women and children, the mothers – how will they be looked after?'

We'll be sterilising the bitches for starters, don't want them banging out any more brown-faced little fuckers do we?

'As I said there will be medical facilities and schools. They will be adequately catered for. Our priority will be teaching them English and English history.'

She visibly groaned.

'That's a priority – really? And how about security – surely these *townships* of yours will need to be secure, policed in some way?'

If I get my way – which I probably will – they'll be surrounded by razor wire with armed guards patrolling 24/7.

'Well, it goes without saying that there will have to be… uh, yes some sort of security, but look they won't be prisons and the uh… residents will be able to come and go as they please.'

Will they fuck.

'And how will these townships get built, who will pay for them?'

'Ah – you remember the £350 million a week we used to pay to the EU…'

'Poppycock!'

'Yes well, OK, what with rebates it was about £250 million a week but whatever, it was still a huge amount and we'll be using some of that to pay for the build of these towns and of course we'll be using the refugees themselves to help with the labour, so costs will be drastically reduced and they'll end up paying for themselves within a few years.'

'I thought that money was earmarked for the NHS?'

'No, I never said that. You must remember I wasn't involved with the Government then but now my colleagues and I are part of the coalition Cabinet things will be done differently. We'll be more transparent, more honest and yes, when my scheme starts delivering, we will make it a priority that we'll inject the profits into the NHS. We'll give the people of Britain what they want and we really will *Take. Back. Control!'*

'Wrap it up Pippa, the fucker's winning,' sighed the producer, *'the switchboard's lighting up like a Christmas tree – they're all fucking agreeing with him!'*

* * *

'Well I think that went rather well don't you?' said Etchington as he took off his mic. Phillipa Bancroft tried her hardest to ignore him.

'For you maybe,' she reluctantly admitted.

He leant in and gave her a leering look.

'Philippa… I know it's a bit late, but I'm famished. Uh, do you fancy going for a bite to eat – my club is just around the corner and I'm sure they can rustle up something for the two of us, and they have a rather excellent Chablis in the cellar.'

She reciprocated and leant into him. She smelt gorgeous, he licked his lips.

'White van man and Primark woman might have fallen for all your bullshit and the red tops might think you're a smooth-talking maverick who shoots from the lip but me... I think you're a sleazy, racist cunt, now fuck off.'

* * *

Five months later the Home Secretary had reviewed and refined Etchington's plans and announced them in the House of Commons as a full-blown Bill under the title of 'Gainful Employment for Migrants, Immigrants, Refugees and Asylum Seekers (GEMIRAS) Act'.

Thanks to a sizeable majority for the Government, courtesy of Etchington's England Unite Party, Westminster rubber-stamped the Bill and fast-tracked it through Parliament quicker than you could say *'konzentrationslager'*.

* * *

The contract to run the mini towns unsurprisingly was awarded to Solutio and the first operation 'Solutio – Food Processing Division' was built in Avonmouth on the outskirts of Bristol on wasteland that was once one of the largest carbon manufacturing sites in Europe. It had been built in record time and as promised by Etchington it used much of the labour that would eventually work and live within its confines.

The plant would process, amongst other things, meat products – especially chicken – lots of chicken, on a massive, industrial scale. It was all going to plan, Etchington was like a dog with two dicks.

Many more towns were in the pipeline. The second of them, 'Solutio – Electronics Processing Division' manufacturing electric car batteries, microchips, electronic goods and mobile phone components followed in Birmingham, while a huge leviathan of a town housing some 30,000 people was being constructed on the outskirts of Glasgow. It too would process cheap food and electronics as well as manufacture affordable 'flat-pack' homes that could be erected quickly around the country to ease the spiralling housing crisis.

The fourth was to be built in Kent, near Dover and would consist of huge greenhouses and packaging plants to rival those of Almeria in Spain that Etchington had so graphically described. The Garden of England would now be transformed into the Greenhouse of England he claimed – *'Straight off the boats and straight to work!'* beamed Etchington on the announcement of its construction to the gathered fawning journalists. He had both them and the majority of the population eating out of his hand.

The inhabitants, the workers – the *'operamini'* as they were to become known – were paid a minimum wage in accordance with approved government guidelines and were housed in comfortable, clean tower blocks, collectively known as *'villatis'* that were segregated by ethnic origin so as to avoid any tension – not that the armed guards would allow anything to escalate that is.

Civil liberty groups around the world were horrified and naturally India, China, the United States and especially the EU were outraged by the plans, but as the UK had recently left the European Convention on Human Rights there was precious little anyone could do about it.

There was obvious home-grown opposition, but when potholes, graffiti and litter started to disappear and food, clothing, mobile phones and flat-screen TVs became cheaper, the indigenous population of Britain soon developed a severe case of moral amnesia.

Brussels and the rest of the world watched Britain's social experiment with a sense of unease, fear and maybe just a modicum of interest and envy.

* * *

Neil Etchington sat in his office aboard his ocean-going yacht, the '*Eostre*' – named after the Anglo-Saxon goddess of Spring and Rebirth – as it was moored on the Thames at Canary Wharf.

He eased himself out of his Elyium R aniline leather chair and looked west down the river towards Tower Bridge and the City, he allowed himself a self-satisfied smirk.

His public persona was of a charismatic and straight-talking populist, but in private he harboured darker thoughts and even darker intentions… his plan, his solution, his *final solution* was coming to fruition.

One day, he thought, never mind the people, the plebeians, it will be me, no-one else, just me, never mind them… *I really will take back control.*

Chapter Five

Back to the present day

The bright yellow glow from the multitude of phosphorescent lights on the horizon announced the presence of the giant food processing plant, officially known as 'Solutio – Food Processing Division' but to locals and inhabitants alike, more commonly known as 'Chicken City'.

The behemoth of a building and its accompanying workshops, warehouses, housing blocks, schools and shops housed and employed some 15,000 people, while a further 3,000 plus offspring attended the plant's onsite nurseries and schools. All of its inhabitants had come to the promised land of Britain for a so-say better life. It was hoped that the population wouldn't grow much further due to the fact that the women who worked there were forcibly sterilised after having a maximum of two children – not that the British public were made aware of this despicable act.

* * *

Eva had told Steve how she'd arrived from Kosovo with her mother four years earlier when she was just fifteen.

They had lived at various addresses in London for a year until '*they*' moved her to Chicken City when it first opened. Her mother also worked for Solutio, but they had been separated and she worked in Chip City in Birmingham.

Her mother had recently been taken ill and Eva had obtained a special visitor's permit to see her but Solutio had called Eva back prematurely as she was needed urgently at Chicken City to complete a special order. Unfortunately, she had little money so she had to hitchhike – that was when Steve had picked her up.

Special order to process a fucking chicken? You've got to be kidding, thought Steve.

Throughout the journey back to Bristol Steve thought Eva had been economical with the truth.

He'd heard stories about Chicken City and its inhabitants but like the majority of the native population, he preferred to close his eyes and ears to the rumours of exploitation, poor working conditions and even sexual and physical violence.

She'd told him that the inhabitants, the operamini, were in the main confined to quarters. They were allowed out occasionally for 'good behaviour', but as all of their passports had been confiscated there was little chance of them ever returning to their homeland – if they ever wanted to, bearing in mind that they were all migrants, immigrants, refugees or asylum seekers, or 'MIRAS' as they were all now collectively referred to thanks to Etchington's Bill.

When they did venture out, they had to be back at specific times, and if they weren't – well Solutio had ways of finding them she said. Steve could only imagine what those ways were.

But on the upside, they were well fed – *chicken mostly,* she said as she rolled her eyes – and she was able to send a little money back to her younger brother and sister who were living with their grandmother in Kosovo.

Her father, who had fought with the Serbian army against the ethnic Albanians in the late Nineties, had died of a heart attack just before they came to the UK.

'I'm, I'm sorry to hear that...' mumbled Steve awkwardly, 'but Kosovo was never in the EU and anyway the UK had left by then?' asked Steve, eager to change the subject away from the death of Eva's father.

'My mother and I... the Albanians in Kosovo got us fake Italian passports and visas so we could come to the UK legally. My passport says I'm Isabella Bettini, but I am Eva Petrovic,' she said defiantly.

'Albanians?' Steve assumed that was who Eva was referring to when she'd said *'they'*.

'Yes, the Albanian mafia – they run everything back in Kosovo – and now, well they run us,' she replied matter-of-factly.

So even if Solutio hadn't confiscated their passports, they would be of little use in trying to get back home, thought Steve.

They were trapped, stuck in Chicken or Chip City, and held captive by the Albanian mafia for the foreseeable future.

'Look,' Steve said, when they pulled up outside the gates, 'um, if you get another pass out of sorts, uh... give me a call.'

'Why?' asked Eva, coyly.

'Uh, nothing, sorry, I just...'

Eva laughed. 'I'm joking Steve! If I can I will... I promise.'

He pulled out his wallet and took out a business card. It wasn't his own, he hadn't had a personalised business card for several years now, it was his boss Tony Preston's, emblazoned with 'City Vehicle Logistics' in blood red type.

He turned the card over, fumbled for a pen in his jacket then wrote his address and phone number on the back. He handed it to her, but her eyes rested on his open wallet longer than they should've done.

'Oh, uh right... here, take this. Sorry, it's all I've got.'

He handed her two £20 notes, just over a half of what he'd earned that day.

'No, I shouldn't. You've already been too kind, but...'

'I insist.' He offered the notes once more.

She hesitated then nodded, took the notes and put them in her back pocket. She then exited the car and opened the rear door – she got back in, slid across the seat and began to undo the zip on her jeans.

'What the fuck are you doing?' Steve looked at Eva in horror.

'You want to fuck me, no?' she asked bluntly.

'*You what?*' Steve blurted out incredulously.

'No, no! That's not why I gave you the money. No – honest.'

Steve felt himself redden in embarrassment.

'Oh, Steve you're blushing... Sorry, sorry – it's just that I'm not used to, how you say... kindness. Every man I meet just want to fuck me.'

I'm not surprised.

It was Eva who was now embarrassed, she leant forward and kissed him on the cheek.

'Thank you Steve, like I said you're a good man. *Ciao!*'

Steve watched as Eva exited the Kuga and headed towards the entrance. He read the large sign that hung from the fencing: 'Gate 7B – Restricted access. Strictly no photography.'

Eva entered through a turnstile of sorts, all the time cameras and guards watched her every move – and his. She turned, smiled, waved then headed towards the brightly lit but grim buildings. It was still raining mercilessly as he pulled away. He wondered if he would ever see Eva again. He hoped so.

He rejoined the motorway and headed for Weston-super-Mare and yet another cheap suited, brown pointy-shoed salesman.

He struck lucky on the train back, head buried in a discarded *Guardian,* he avoided the gaze of the indifferent ticket collector. '*Always try and find a Guardian or Times,*' Phil had advised him on his first day, '*you'll look less like a fare dodger.*' It worked every time.

He alighted at Temple Meads then waited for a local train to take him to Lawrence Hill – a rundown and thankfully, a no-barrier station.

The walk back to his apartment took him through the grubby, graffitied and litter-strewn streets of the inner city. Discarded mattresses and fridges as well as numerous abandoned e-scooters impeded his progress while the sight and smell of excrement, both dog and human assaulted his senses. Not that it was any different from the rest of Bristol, it seemed the whole of the city was in a similar state and covered in graffiti and fly posters, while weeds the size of Triffids rose up through the cracks in the concrete and tarmac.

He passed a billboard promoting Solutio featuring a hotline to report graffiti and pot holes – it had been defaced to read '*FINAL SOLUTION*' and the words '*LIYING BASDURDS*' had been added by a passing budding, but illiterate graffiti artist.

'That Banksy has got a lot to answer for…' muttered Steve as he eyed up a road sign that was covered with undecipherable squiggles and unintelligible scrawls, 'and as for that 10 foot, he needs rogering with a 10-foot pole.'

Whereas the city once smelt of tobacco, chocolate and alcohol – thanks to thriving industries that had at one time been associated with Bristol's slave trade – it now smelt of cannabis, urine and spray paint. The city was a shithole, but it was Steve's shithole.

He stopped off at the Bahar Kitchen in 'Little Mogadishu', picked up his favourite mango chicken curry, some macsharo yariis and a couple of bottles of Warka Polish lager from the offy next door, so at least that was dinner sorted.

* * *

The years that had followed Kirsty's death, or *'Crazy cop Kirsty'* as Debbie, his ex-wife, called her had not been easy.

His redundancy payment from Pinnacle hadn't lasted as long as he'd hoped and his ever-decreasing pension pot was not worth cashing in. *Lamborghini pension my arse – more like a second-hand Skoda* he mused, which was as true as it was ironic as his top of the range Audi A7 had long gone and been replaced with an eight-year old Ford Focus.

On top of that, he was still bailing out Harry and stays at the Priory were not cheap, but at long last it looked like his son was pulling through and putting his drug habit behind him. The piercings and attitude had gone and he'd been clean for over a year, enabling him to get a job with Social Services, helping drug addicts get back on the straight and narrow. If anyone was qualified, it certainly was Harry.

Steve and Debbie had divorced three years earlier – it was inevitable following on from his involvement with Kirsty and all the grief that that had entailed. They'd tried to save their marriage, but they both knew it was a lost cause as it was pretty evident that Debbie was never going to forgive him, which Steve thought was a tad rich when he recalled the day when he caught her sucking the cock of Brad the Blindman in their marital bed.

Debbie had suggested marriage counselling but when they were asked to rate their sex life on a scale of one to ten and Steve's response being one, on the grounds that they didn't really have sex, but that he merely masturbated into her motionless body, did not go down too well – *like Debbie* – unless it was with Brad the Blindman of course.

But then it got worse, a lot worse.

Steve thought he'd noticed a hint of recognition between his wife and the counsellor when they entered the office, maybe even a slight frisson. Debbie had held on to the counsellor's hand just a little too long as they introduced themselves and at one stage, he even thought they were playing footsie under the table, but he'd quickly dismissed it as his overactive imagination going into overdrive.

Debbie admitted to knowing the counsellor when they left, saying that they'd met once or twice at Pilates classes, but when he came home early one afternoon to hear the familiar sounds of lovemaking coming from their bedroom once more, he knew that their marriage had run its course and it was finally time to call it a day.

The previous time he'd caught his wife in a similar position he found himself both disgusted and aroused in equal measures, but this time…

Sure enough, it was the counsellor – Felicity – that he'd found his wife *in flagrante* with, but it had still come as a bit of a shock, although it explained a lot of things about their relationship and at times, when he thought about it, it even raised a slight smile and knowing nod.

They'd sold the house and although he'd pocketed a fair wedge, the two-bedroomed apartment on the edge of the city centre had cost him more than he'd bargained for. His mid-life crisis of a decade previously resulted in the stereotypical desire to purchase a Harley Davidson but… the old skinhead in him drew him to a more practical scooter. Or so he thought.

He was soon to regret the decision as the small fortune he spent on an extremely rare but wrecked Lambretta TV175 Series 1 that he'd hope to restore, quickly turned into a very large fortune. He sold it six months later at a loss and rued the day he'd set eyes on the Milanese-built beauty.

Holidays to Jamaica, where he paid a long overdue homage to Prince Buster's Record Shack on Orange Street and a visit to Australia, to see his eldest son Sam, his wife and his new granddaughter Phoebe, had just about cleaned him out. He needed a job but at his age, employers didn't need him.

Trips to the Jobcentre on Stapleton Road proved futile. He pondered why they were called job centres, thinking *'waste-of-fucking-time'* centres more appropriate.

He sat on the deliberately uncomfortable chairs and waited for his name to be called when he would then be interviewed by a disinterested, acne-ridden youth by the name of Asif. How appropriate – *As if he'll find me a fucking job*.

'How about a postman?' asked Asif, 'we've got a temporary position just over the Christmas period.'

'Why not?' shrugged Steve, 'it's better than walking the streets.' Needless to say, he didn't get the job.

He received a paltry Jobseekers' Allowance for six months then faced the ultimate humiliation of a means test – the mighty, once proud Steve Allen, tested by some no-mark of a desk jockey just to get a few measly quid from the system he'd paid into for nearly five decades.

'Where do I sign?' he asked dejectedly.

Through a mate of a mate of a mate, he'd finally landed a job with City Vehicle Logistics, a vehicle movement company owned by Tony 'Punchy' Preston, a New Age football hooligan and senior member of the City Elite Squad, Bristol City's notorious firm, which annoyed Steve no end. But beggars couldn't be choosers, he constantly reminded himself through gritted teeth.

Previously he had a career where he hobnobbed with the cream of British business; he'd networked and attended one-to-ones to discuss strategies, challenges and ways forward. He could pick low-hanging fruit, take helicopter views and touch base with the best of them… now he was a nobody and, what's more, a nobody who worked for a City fan, but at least he had a job – if you could call trade plating a job. No sick pay, no holiday pay and no company pension, but the worst part was having to make his own way between jobs in his own time, at his own expense.

The job was never going to make him rich, in fact it only just about covered his bills, but it kept him off the streets, he joked to his mates and if truth be told, at times he actually quite enjoyed it.

He'd visited parts of the country he didn't even know existed and met people who made him laugh, smile and cry – sometimes all in the same day.

He'd been humbled by little old ladies who'd insisted on making him cups of tea, embarrassed by people who offered him a tip and thankful to others who'd driven miles out of their way to give him a lift to his destination.

He'd met people who barely had a penny and some who were millionaires; some who were famous – an Oscar-winner gave him a lift just outside of Luton – and some who were infamous… *'I've been inside for murder me, pal'* said a weaselly-looking lorry driver, who'd given him a lift from Bradford to Widnes.

The weasel also claimed to have been a friend of the Yorkshire Ripper and said he knew where the victims of the Moors Murderers were buried. Steve couldn't wait to get out of the cab and breathed a huge sigh of relief as he bid his farewell to the weasel.

That had not been one of Steve's better days.

He'd been mugged in Leicester, lectured by a Polish neo-Nazi in Market Harborough and drugged in Dorset by a wonderfully eccentric old hippy chick who'd talked to him through a stuffed rabbit that was mounted on the dashboard of her hand-painted VW camper van.

The rabbit was called Basil and the camper van was named Dave, she informed him – through Basil.

The hashish cake and herbal tea she'd given him caused him to fall out of Dave at a roundabout near Blandford Forum. He spent the afternoon lying on his back in a field of daisies, staring at the fluorescent coloured sky and laughing at the pink and orange striped sheep. To this day, he wondered how the hell he'd got back home.

Then, on one gloriously hot, sunny day in July, he met Nikki, an auburn-haired, forty-something beauty of a Sergeant Major's wife in Tidworth who answered the door mid-afternoon wearing just a bikini and a loose-fitting bathrobe.

'Mrs Baker? I'm Steve from City Vehicle Logistics. Could you sign here for your new Ford Puma?'

She glanced over his shoulder at the gleaming new car, but it barely registered. She was more interested in Steve.

'Call me Nikki. Would you like a cup of tea?' she asked with a devilish glint in her eye.

'Never refuse a cup of tea or the chance to have a piss,' Phil had also advised on Steve's first day, he was right – on both counts. *Or a shag,* thought Steve hopefully.

'I'd love one thanks – milk and no sugar.' *Better not mention the shag,* he thought.

Nikki ushered Steve in but she remained rooted to the spot. He brushed past as she made a grab for a framed photo of a fearsome, uniform-clad brute of a warrior that was perched on a nearby shelf. She turned it face down as she followed Steve into the hallway.

'Put the kettle on would you love… Sorry, I've been sunbathing, let me put on something more… appropriate,' she purred. Nikki exited the kitchen and ascended the stairs. Steve filled the kettle and opened cupboards looking for mugs. Taking two down, he heard her re-enter the kitchen behind him.

'Ah, you found the mugs,' she said, 'would you like some ginger nuts?'

He turned and dropped a mug causing it to shatter on the tiled floor. Apart from the chiffon scarf draped seductively around her shoulders she was entirely naked… and clearly a natural redhead.

Apart from a couple of sad one-night stands courtesy of Plenty of Fish it was the first sex he'd enjoyed since the death of Kirsty.

That had been one of Steve's better days.

Chapter Six

In all honesty the bachelor lifestyle suited him. His apartment was small but at least he had a balcony where he could sit with a glass of Malbec and watch the world go by whilst listening to the trains toing and froing from nearby Temple Meads station.

He had the obligatory cheap 42-inch flat screen TV – courtesy of Solutio – on which he at last could view programmes of his choice. No more depressing soaps and not a whiff of a dreary costume drama – it was now football, documentaries on World War Two tank battles and the occasional late-night porn.

The apartment was tastefully decorated in an IKEA blokey sort of way and as well as the TV he had a new state-of-the-art Bose sound system, shelves full of books – mostly Harry Bosch and Jack Reacher novels, military history and autobiographies – and racks of CDs and vinyl to house his ever-growing collection of soul, funk, reggae, ska and more recently, Northern Soul dancefloor fillers.

Framed posters of funk and ska gigs he'd attended and photos of his sons and his new granddaughter adorned the walls, whilst on a shelf in an alcove stood more photos – of his mother and father and his deceased dogs, his beloved Prince and Buster – the two Jack Russells who'd died after eating a diseased squirrel a couple of years back.

Pride of place in his apartment however, went to the 1959 Rock-Ola that had been bequeathed to him by the ex-love of his life, Kirsty. The bulky jukebox dominated the room and was always the centre of attention when friends visited, but he found it difficult to play any of the precious vinyl for fear of bringing back too many sad memories of a period in his life that he was desperately trying to forget.

There was one record however that had an extra special place in his heart – *Guilty* by Tiger on the Camel label. Like the jukebox it had been left to him by Kirsty and it sat proudly on display in a frame directly above the Rock-Ola, it was 'their' song from when they were teenage lovers and still bore the words written in blue biro: *'Kirsty Donohue loves Steve Allen – 4 ever'* that Kirsty had scrawled on the label when Steve bought her the record in the early 70s.

Truth be told he liked being on his own, although at times he did miss the company of the female of the species and he sometimes found himself chatting to Alexa on his Amazon Echo just to hear a friendly voice – even if like all females, she had to have the last word.

He did have some company, or rather company that sometimes graced him with its own presence. He'd always been a dog lover and hated cats with a passion – to him they were aloof, arrogant and untrustworthy – the complete opposite of canines, not to mention the fact that they always shit in his garden.

He adored his Jack Russells and was genuinely distraught when they'd died, vowing to never own a dog or get so attached to an animal ever again.

But he hadn't bargained for Derrick coming into his life.

Derrick was a coal black, short-haired Bombay cat that he'd found abandoned in a dustbin not long after he'd moved into his flat. It had half of one ear missing, was blind in one eye and walked or rather slouched with a distinct limp. It was rough, tough, ugly as sin and utterly devoted to Steve and, in response, Steve thought he was the coolest cat he'd ever met.

Derrick was like a miniature panther but if he had been a human, he would've resembled John Shaft or

Youngblood Priest and would definitely drive a flame-red mid-Seventies Cadillac Eldorado.

Steve had considered both names for the irascible moggy but in the end, he plumped for the name Derrick in homage to the nearly blind Jamaican original rude boy, Derrick Morgan.

Not that Derrick's disabilities seemed to hamper him in any way. Steve was convinced the cat possessed a sixth sense, he never bumped into anything and was as agile and cunning as a fox.

He ruled the roost and came and went as he pleased; when he did return after frequent and eventful nights on the tiles he would often have a new scar on his chiselled face and his limp resembled more of a swagger, at times Steve swore he even detected a smug smile about his grizzled fizzog.

Steve had read somewhere that if you wanted a dog, a cat or a monkey you really wanted a Bombay – and as a dog or a monkey for that matter were out of the question, then Derrick would have to suffice.

He'd also read that Bombays were outgoing, congenial and highly sociable cats that loved to be in the company of others… if that was the case then Derrick proved the exception to the rule and welcomed the rare visitors to his abode with a *'miaow'* that resembled a growl and a sneer that would put Billy Idol to shame.

Unlike Derrick though Steve rarely went out. In fact, he joked – to himself – that his bins went out more than he did these days. Luckily, he enjoyed cooking both for himself and the occasional guest but the plethora of takeaways and cheap cosmopolitan restaurants nearby more than met his culinary needs.

Steve liked living in the regenerated Dings. Back in the 1930s it had been one of Bristol's worst slum areas but the old back-to-back terraced houses had long gone and had now been replaced with private apartments and social housing, but as yet hadn't been repopulated with yuppies and students – which suited Steve no end.

Nearby Lawrence Hill housed the largest number of Somalians outside of London and the new influx of Syrian and Afghan refugees fleeing conflicts in their homelands made for an interesting and sometimes volatile mix.

The spare bedroom, which he needed for when Harry came to stay, which thankfully was becoming less frequent, doubled up as a gym. He had weights and a treadmill and a well-used punch bag hung suspended from the ceiling.

He had joined the local gym but when arriving home late from work he found a half-hour session on the punch bag ideal therapy for getting rid of tension and stress, but stress and depression were beginning to become distant memories for Steve.

Although he still had bad days whilst doing the driving job, they barely measured on the *'fucked right off'* scale that he regularly endured in the past. He still took statins for high cholesterol and aspirin to thin his blood but the anti-depressants and daily intake of Diclofenac and Ibuprofen had gone the same way as his ex-wife's collection of scented candles – in the fucking bin.

As well as his music he also had a collection of language CDs – he was currently learning French – which he would listen to on many a long, lonely car journey north when he couldn't stomach any more Radio 2 drivel and he considered himself way too old to be a Radio 6 music dad. In fact, he had started listening to Radio 4 more and was becoming addicted to *The Archers* and *Gardeners' Question Time,* even though he no longer had a garden, but strangest of all was his fascination with *Women's Hour* with its constant discussions about the menopause, sexual abuse and the sex trade.

He thought maybe at long last he was getting in touch with his feminine side but he also felt slightly grubby listening to it, like he was eavesdropping on private conversations between women which men should never hear. Then he would angrily snap out of it and query why there wasn't a *Men's Hour*, filled with discussions about football, fast cars and women with big tits.

* * *

Steve opened the door to his flat and waited for the usual loud miaow in greeting from Derrick, but it didn't come. He was probably out doing a deal or smooth-talking some hot Persian babe in an alleyway somewhere which caused Steve to smile wryly to himself at the thought of his feline flatmate.

A relaxing hot shower alleviated the knots from his shoulders and followed his sweaty session on the weights and punch bag.

He changed into a Diesel T-shirt and Puma tracksuit bottoms and admired himself in the mirror while waiting for the curry to warm up. The La-Z-Boy beckoned and a documentary on Channel 4 about great British castles caught his eye.

He devoured the curry along with a bottle of Warka then made a mental note to himself that the next time he had a delivery to Kent he would pay a visit to Deal Castle.

He woke with a jolt and a semi – a vision of Eva in a dripping wet T-shirt quickly disappeared from his mind.

'Eva,' he muttered to himself… 'what the hell are you up to?'

Chapter Seven

Tony Preston, or 'Punchy' as he was known to friends and enemies alike, was rightfully proud of the business he'd built up from scratch. His father and schoolteachers said he would amount to nothing and if he didn't watch out, he would end up inside.

They were right on one count, six months in Horfield prison for assault at a football match back in the Nineties may not have been enough to make him change his ways, but it certainly meant he would be a bit smarter and quicker on his feet when needs be.

He once worked as a fireman and on the side he delivered cars up and down the country for mates in the car business. He soon realised if he pulled a few strokes and cut some shady deals he could make more money at vehicle movements than he could at putting out fires and rescuing cats from trees.

In his younger days, he'd tried his hand at cage fighting but too many hidings as he aged made him call it a day. The crooked nose did nothing to disguise his good looks and his thick mop of dark hair still made him a bit of a ladies' man, even though he had been happily married to Charlie for twenty-plus years. They had two kids – a daughter, Abbie, aged seventeen, who was the light of his life, and a son, Lee, aged fourteen who, as much as Tony loved him, proved to be a disappointment to the rugged pugilist from south Bristol as he preferred the company of his own sex.

Tony had struggled with his son's sexuality, but he'd grown to accept it although he still found it difficult when his peers turned up at Ashton Gate with their mini-me 'hooli-sons' bedecked in Henri Lloyd and Stone Island, while Lee preferred more subtle clothing from the likes of Hollister and Gap.

Apart from the obvious football differences and over two decades in age, at times Steve and Tony got on surprisingly well. Tony knew of Steve's past and reputation and secretly admired the old terrace legend, even if he was from the other side of the divided city. He'd also heard how a few years earlier Steve had been involved with some heavy criminals and ended up with a bullet in his shoulder for his sins – it impressed Tony no end, not that he would ever admit it, well, not to Steve's face anyway.

While Tony was one of a new breed of cyber hooligan, Steve was strictly old school, a boot boy from north of the river who fought on the grim, concrete terraces in the Seventies and Eighties, when – he believed – there was a certain degree of honour and respect amongst his fellow thugs.

He and his mates, the Big Five and the rest of the Rovers' Tote End were tough, uncompromising but disparate battlers whilst Tony was a bona fide, card carrying – literally – member of City's well-organised and well-respected 'firm', who used the internet and mobile phones to arrange fights with other like-minded designer-labelled clad casuals. It was not a scene that Steve could either admire or embrace.

Tony had given Steve a hard time when he first joined his company, especially on a Monday morning if the results had gone City's way and not Rovers – which was more often than Steve cared for. Steve never bit – he had seen and done it all before, he'd earned his spurs and reputation before Tony was born and had nothing to prove to the young pretender.

The older City lads – the boys from the East End terrace who had battled with the Tote End for superiority on the streets of Bristol four decades earlier – had vouched for Steve and the Big Five, not that he needed anyone to stand up for him, he was more than capable of doing that for himself. He had a quiet, self-assured persona that intimidated Tony and a stare that rattled him more than he cared to admit.

Steve also recognised the signs – Columbian flu on a Monday and an irritability that lasted until Wednesday was something Steve was more than familiar with. But thankfully, like the football hooliganism, Class A substance abuse was also something Steve had long put behind him.

Apart from their penchant for marching powder and soccer violence, albeit Steve's from his past, there was something else that united the two – troubled offspring. But while Steve's boy, Harry, was at long last beginning to put his problems behind him, Tony's boy Lee was taking his first furtive steps into adolescent angst brought on by confusion over his sexual orientation… Tony Preston was not a happy man.

* * *

Tony picked Steve up just before seven. The two of them were heading to West Country Auto Care in Henstridge, Somerset, somewhere that competed with Cold Meece in the arse-end-of-nowhere stakes.

The surrounding villages were typical of that area of the country – pretty and well kept, some could even be described as chocolate boxy, but not in the wildest imagination could the huge, pot-holed, muddy field that passed for a car depot, be described as resembling the top of a chocolate box.

The only buildings on site was an 'office' – an old and overly warm and unwelcoming Portakabin, inhabited by foul-mouthed, ruddy-faced, scrumpydrinking locals – and a battered wheel-less caravan that had once offered Brummies a holiday home for a week in Minehead. It had been many years since it had stood on the Somerset coast and it now rather embarrassingly posed as a waiting room for the doleful drivers.

Toilets and washrooms were non-existent and a stagnant putrid pond of piss formed daily as a multitude of weary, middle-aged men with prostate problems relieved themselves after journeys from the four corners of the country.

'What's up?' Steve asked as soon as he got in the smoke-filled Astra. He had a sixth sense that told him things were not right with Tony – the fact that Tony had a face like a deflated balloon was also a bit of a giveaway.

'The usual,' Tony replied gruffly.

'Lee?'

Tony took a long drag on the last remnants of his cigarette – the first of many that day – then expertly jettisoned the burning stub out of the open window.

'Yep. Gone fucking missing again. Walked out two days ago after a row and we haven't heard or seen of him since. The wife's in bits.'

'Have you contacted the Old Bill?' asked Steve, showing genuine concern.

'Yeah, for what good it's done. Let's just say helping Tony Preston ain't high on their list of priorities – *the bastards.*'

Preston spat out the last two words with real venom – there was no love lost between Avon and Somerset Police and one of City's main troublemakers.

'I'm sure he'll turn up OK, we had the same problem with Ha...'

'Yeah, I know – with Harry, you've told me a million times.'

Steve nodded and held up his hands in apology. They drove on in silence until Tony broke the ice.

'He's done a runner before but this time he ain't phoned and we ain't got a clue where he is. No messages or nothing – in the past he's gone round his mate's but we've already checked and he ain't seen him for a while.... says he's been hanging around with an old foreign geezer... I'll tell you mate if some paedo has got his hands on him I'll fucking kill the nonce.'

Tony was shaking with rage, Steve actually did believe him when he said he would kill someone – he was certainly capable of it.

'The Old Bill said they'll put summat in the papers and on the telly but they ain't got the resources to search for every kid who's legged it. Just hope he turns up alright that's all.'

Steve felt reluctant to say any more. He could see the concern and anger in his face but more than that, he could see a bit of himself in his boss, Tony cared for his son more than he liked to admit.

* * *

Once he'd checked over the Hyundai – this time he'd drawn the short straw – he departed the compound like a cat with his arse on fire and headed for the delights of Grangetown in Cardiff. A place that brought back scary memories of violent Saturday afternoons from four decades previously, when Cardiff City's infamous Soul Crew took no prisoners.

This time, the trip to the Principality held no such terrors. It was an uneventful journey that took him north up the M5, over the Avonmouth Bridge and onto the M49 with its views of the industrial complexes on Severnside and the ever-expanding Chicken City.

His thoughts inevitably turned to Eva, he wondered if she would contact him and, if so, for what. Actually, he wondered what the hell he was thinking of, her in her late teens and him, well… he wouldn't see sixty again any time soon. He reassured himself that it wasn't sexual, but he was a sucker for a pretty face and a lost cause and Eva certainly ticked both of those boxes.

'And now it's time for Ten to the Top…'

'Wanna-fucking-bet!' he shouted out loud as he rummaged through his backpack on the passenger seat. He found the Northern Soul CD, dexterously opened the case with one hand and took out the disc. A rectangular, black piece of plastic caught his eye as it fell into the passenger floor well.

His brow furrowed in curiosity as he studied it, he leant over and down, grappling with the steering wheel at the same time. The Hyundai lurched to the left as he grabbed the rectangular object which drew a blast of anger from an irate Eddie Stobart driver on the inside lane.

'Fucking Eddie Stobarts – think they own the fucking road,' he muttered.

He held the memory stick between his thumb and forefinger, studied it and wondered how it had got into the CD case… it had to be Eva and it had to be deliberate, she must have wanted him to find it. But why? What the fuck was on it?

The car dealership in Grangetown was one of the better ones – the boss, Terry, recognised Steve and immediately gave him grief regarding Rovers' parlous state, which Steve thought was a bit rich coming from a swimaway Bluebird.

Steve grabbed a coffee and a packet of custard creams and scanned the *Daily Mail* while he waited for his paperwork.

He despaired at the headlines: increasing conflict in the Middle East and Ukraine, another ship carrying refugees from North Africa sunk in the Med, record numbers of small boats crossing the Channel and heading straight for the ever-expanding migrant cities and more rioting in European cities. He let out an audible sigh.

''Ere you go Gashead, you can get your sorry English arse back over the bridge now.'

Terry stood in front of him, paperwork in hand, pointed shoes on feet.

'I suppose you want a lift to Cardiff Central, butt?'

Normally Steve would jump at the chance of a lift, any lift, but Grangetown station was just a short walk away and it had no barriers – unlike Cardiff's main station – which was a trade platers' dream.

'Nah that's alright *butt*, I could do with the walk, if you know what I mean,' he answered with a wink.

'Tidy,' replied the ever-chipper Terry.

The local train was packed with gaggles of cackling mini-skirted Valley women, heading for bottomless brunches and shitloads of Prosecco in St David's Shopping Centre, which meant he had no problem in avoiding paying.

At Cardiff Central, he changed trains and got on the Portsmouth Harbour rattler that was already waiting at the platform. It was midday so he took a risk that it wouldn't be too busy and the discarded *Guardian* he found wasn't even needed as the disinterested ticket collector shambled up the aisle and only gave him a cursory glance.

He pulled his usual stunt at Temple Meads, dodging paying for a ticket and catching the commuter train back to Lawrence Hill. Before he knew it, he was back in his apartment eagerly anticipating what he was going to discover on Eva's memory stick.

He inserted the stick into his MacBook, clicked on the movie icon then watched in horror as it revealed its vile contents...

'Jesus H. Christ Eva, what the fuck?!'

Chapter Eight

Steve had lost his appetite. He pushed his microwaved ready meal to one side and poured the remainder of his Malbec down the sink.

He changed into a clean white vest and Puma tracksuit bottoms, donned his gloves and began pummelling the punchbag like he'd never hit it before.

His heart pumped and he quickly broke out into a fever-like sweat. The sweat stung his eyes and stained his vest, his taut chest threatened to burst out of the dripping wet garment, he exhaled loudly at each punch, *'Ugh, ugh, ugh… Arghhh!'*

A jolt of pain shot through his body. He grimaced and rubbed the spot with his glove where the bullet had passed through his shoulder some years previously.

The door buzzer startled him as it screamed like a banshee. Whoever it was with their finger on his entry phone was desperate to see him. He looked at the clock on the wall – it was nearly ten. He rarely had visitors these days and certainly not many at this time of night.

'Alright, alright I'm coming!' shouted Steve.

It was futile, knowing whoever was outside couldn't hear him.

He tore off his gloves, threw them to the floor and peered through the spyhole, the buzzer continued to scream incessantly. A distorted, unrecognisable face twisted from side to side on the other side of the door.

'Who is it?' asked Steve angrily.

'Steve, it's Eva – let me in!'

He opened the door but before he had the chance to speak, she pushed past him and entered his apartment.

'What? What's happening – what do you want?' Steve shouted in annoyance.

She stood in front of him breathing heavily.

'Have you a knife?' she screamed. Her face was contorted with fear.

'What? What do you want a ...'

Eva undid her jacket. She didn't stop there, she was wearing a buttoned blouse and she tore at it, sending buttons spiralling around the room.

'Whoa! What are you doing? What the fuck's going on?'

Eva shook uncontrollably and her breathing remained heavy. Distraught and clearly terrified she took deep breaths in an attempt to compose herself.

'Steve... please do something for me, get a knife – a very, very sharp knife, have you got one?'

'I, I've got a scalpel – is that any good?'

'A scalpel, what's a scalpel?'

He didn't reply but instead ran into the kitchen and scrambled around in a drawer for the elusive blade.

'*Fuck, fuck, fuck – where is it?*'

He rushed back into the lounge to a desk where his laptop sat, he opened the top drawer and found a bladeless handle nestling alongside a Rotring pen and a metal ruler – hangovers from his career in graphic design.

He then found a clean sterile blade hermetically sealed in a foil wrap. He ripped it open before expertly inserting it into the scalpel handle.

'This is the sharpest blade you can get, it's a medical knife, but what do you...'

He looked over his shoulder. Eva's blouse lay discarded on the floor, she stood in front of him shivering with fear, wearing nothing but a black bra and blue jeans.

'What the fuck!' Steve exclaimed.

'Steve, listen and listen carefully. I have a microchip implanted in my arm.'

She pointed at a small scar on the inside of her left bicep with her right hand.

'It's a GPS chip, they can track me,' she paused and breathed deeply again, 'I need you to cut it out.'

'A what?... who can track you?'

'I tell you later, but please you need to do it and you need to do it now!'

There were tears in her eyes. Her shivers were turning into convulsions.

'*Ple-eeeease!* I'm begging you!'

He led her into the bathroom and motioned her to sit on the edge of the bath. He hesitated.

'Are you sure about...'

'*Just fucking do it!*' she screamed.

Steve knelt in front of Eva. She raised her left arm, took his shaking hand and pressed his fingers gently on the scar. His eyes widened like a rabbit's caught in headlights. He could feel it, a small solid plate less than half an inch square.

His eyes met Eva's. She mouthed to him '*please*' but nothing came out. He grabbed a towel and laid it on her lap before picking up a sponge and giving it to her. Her brow furrowed questioningly.

'Put it in your mouth,' he said calmly.

She took the sponge and nodded to him to proceed.

He steadied his shaking hands and breathed out deeply, he felt for the chip once more then placed the sharp blade against her pale skin. She nodded again and he quickly drew the blade across the scar.

A muffled scream pierced the air as crimson blood spilt out, dribbled over the handle of the scalpel and down onto Steve's hand. The cut was good and clean, less than an inch in length.

Steve looked up at Eva, her eyes were full of tears as she started hitting the tiled wall with her fist. She spat out the sponge.

'*Out, out! Get it fucking out of me!*'

Steve placed the scalpel on the edge of the bath then without hesitation probed into Eva's bicep with the tip of his thumb and forefinger, Eva squirmed in pain and bit into her bottom lip. A sliver of blood formed in the corner of her mouth.

His fingers were too bulky and he couldn't get a grip on the device. He removed his finger and thumb and rubbed his forehead, a smear of blood appeared as if he himself was cut.

Eva sobbed uncontrollably. Steve stood and turned in anguish, his eyes widened as he remembered the tweezers in the bathroom cabinet.

He pulled open the mirrored door and found the small shiny implement. He turned and faced Eva once more then quickly inserted the tweezers into the still bleeding gash. He pulled and an inoffensive looking grey piece of plastic appeared firmly embedded between the prongs of the tweezers. He let out a long, low breath.

'Now get rid of it!... No, not in a bin!' she shouted as he headed for the kitchen.

'You need to get rid of it outside – *quickly!*'

Steve ran barefoot down the stairs then stood on the pavement looking around in confusion. He spotted a bus heading his way. The bus stop was some hundred feet away. He ran towards the oncoming bus and put out his hand.

'Single to the Centre mate,' he panted, then in an exaggerated movement he patted his pockets.

'Oh bollocks, forgot me wallet.'

The driver shook his head and rolled his eyes.

'Card only mate... OK I'll let you off. Just this once.'

Steve hadn't expected that answer – most bus drivers were jobsworths of the highest order, trust him to get the one decent driver in Bristol just when he didn't want one.

'Uh... on second thoughts, I'm alright mate.'

He turned to exit the bus then slipped the tracker into the waste ticket bin. He jumped off causing the driver to mutter a quiet but very distinct '*Wanker*'.

'OK, what the fuck is this all about?' Steve asked as he re-entered his apartment. Eva was still sat on the edge of the bath – she clutched a bloodstained towel to her arm.

He didn't give her a chance to answer.

'Come to think of it we ought to get you to hospital, you need stitches.'

'No, no – we can't, I have no records, you don't understand… I, I don't really exist. Please no Steve, they will try and get rid of me.'

'OK, OK…' he said as he held up his hands in submission.

He turned, entered the kitchen and returned with a first aid kit. He patched her up with sticking plasters, gauze and a bandage and at last the flow of blood seemed to be abating.

He was still kneeling on the floor in front of her when the severity of the situation at last hit him.

'Thank you,' she eventually whispered.

Her breasts were no more than six inches from his face – they were as perfect as the Venus de Milo's. He found himself unconsciously studying them.

He blinked and jerked his head backwards.

'Sorry, sorry, I uh… sorry, I didn't mean to,' he stammered and quickly got to his feet. He grabbed his bathrobe from the hook on the door and gave it to Eva.

'Here, put this on.'

She went to speak but he held up his hand.

'I'll make the spare bed up for you, you need some rest… we'll speak in the morning.'

There were a hundred and one questions he wanted to ask her, but now was not the right time. He made her a hot chocolate drink and gave her some Tramadol he had left over from when he'd been shot.

She took a bath and he changed her bandages somewhat embarrassingly. Her eyes began to glaze over and she mumbled incomprehensible words and phrases in a language Steve guessed was Serbian as the painkillers began to take effect.

He helped her into the spare bedroom, pushed aside the gym equipment and dropped her onto the bed. After pulling the covers over her he tucked her hair behind her ear before gently stroking her face until eventually sleep overcame her.

He momentarily stood in the doorway looking at her and wondered what the hell he'd got himself involved in.

Chapter Nine

'P/up transit from muller road and deliver to...'

He didn't bother reading the rest of the message on his mobile. He quickly responded:

'Sorry m8, been up all night with the shits, sick as a dog, no can do.'

A beep, beep heralded the inevitable response.

'Cock.'

The bedroom door opened behind him, Eva appeared and despite wearing Steve's oversized bathrobe she still looked stunning.

'Morning,' she grinned sheepishly.

'Morning? Is that it?'

'Morning *Bruce*.'

'Bruce? What, have you forgotten my name already?'

She walked towards him and ran her fingers through her long hair.

'No, it's just that last night – you, in your vest and muscles – and that scar on your face. You reminded me of Bruce Willis in *Die Hard*.'

Steve subconsciously touched the scar on his cheek, the scar that had been caused by a knife wielded by his old foe, Ewart 'Earl' Samson.

It was now his turn to look embarrassed although he wasn't entirely surprised. It wasn't the first time someone had said he resembled the sixty-something Hollywood star – before he had sadly succumbed to dementia. He motioned to her to sit on a stool at the kitchen breakfast bar.

'I'll fix you some breakfast and perhaps then you can tell me what the fuck is going on.'

Several cups of coffee and pieces of toast later – with Marmite, she liked Marmite – he still couldn't believe what he was hearing.

'So, this microchip inside you, everyone who works at Chicken City has one fitted, yes?'

'No, just the uh... chosen ones, like me, I guess. Everyone else has tattoos – barcodes.'

'Barcodes?' he queried.

'Yes, barcodes like here.'

She pointed at a barcode on the packet of muesli in front of her.

'I know what barcodes are, but why do people have them?'

'So the Albanians know who they are and who they belong to *duh*.' She answered as if it was the most obvious thing in the world.

'What, so every person there has been tattooed and they are owned... by who?'

'By whoever who has bought them. Everything and everyone has a price Steve,' she had reverted to his proper name, 'and when they are bought – or exchanged – the details get logged. The tattoos... they have a machine to do it, your arm is clamped in like this...'

She straightened out her bandaged left arm and turned it over, she then grabbed a fork with her right hand.

'Then it's tattooed here,' she motioned at her wrist with the fork.

'A machine does it?'

'Yes, they program it on a computer then *zzzzz, zzzzz, zzzzz* it goes...'

She dug at her wrist with the fork. Steve shook his head in disbelief. She relished telling him.

'Then others...'

She's grinning. She's actually fucking grinning. After last night's events she's actually enjoying telling me this.

'… others like me. We are the chosen ones, but me…' her eyes twinkled.

'I am the *special* one.'

'And what makes you special?' he asked.

'What do you think?' she hesitated.

The grin and the twinkle in her eye had now all but disappeared.

'Because I'm good at fucking,' she said in a near whisper as she lowered her gaze.

Steve was not entirely shocked by her answer.

He had known when he'd met her just two days previously that she didn't work in the factory and the video on the memory stick he'd found confirmed it. He wondered just when she was going to mention it.

'Well, I realised you didn't work in the chicken processing plant.'

'How come?'

'Uh, your hands… and your nails. They're too well manicured.'

She studied her own hands as if she'd never seen them before.

'And you're too smart to be just a driver Steve,' she replied.

If only you knew.

'Yep and you're too attractive to work in a chicken factory. OK, I get it – you're a…' he hesitated, 'prostitute?'

Eva looked horrified at Steve's accusation – but she didn't deny it.

'You're not the first sex worker I've known…'

He regretted it as soon as he'd said it and reddened in embarrassment.

Eva raised an eyebrow accusingly.

'Uh, I'm not entirely surprised… so the microchip with the tracking device, is so your "owner" can track you down if you go AWOL?'

'AWOL – what's AWOL?'

'Absence without leave – you've escaped, I presume, and you have no intention of going back?'

Eva nodded and slumped back on the stool.

'But what made you come here? What made you think I could help you?'

She screwed up her face.

'Because you told me to Steve, you said if I needed help, to contact you. You gave me your fucking address! So here I am!'

'Yeah but I didn't expect you to turn up within forty-eight hours screaming at me to perform surgery on you!'

He gathered himself.

'Sorry, I didn't mean it like that, I just...'

'No, it's OK. You are right.'

She pushed back the stool, got up and pulled the bathrobe tight to her body. She let out a small yelp of pain.

'I'll go – I'm sorry, I shouldn't have come. I get dressed and go.'

For good measure she added a theatrical, childlike '*Ow*.'

Steve stood and gently touched her arm.

'No, you can stay – for a while, at least until your wound has healed. Look, go and get dressed and you can tell me the rest, OK?'

Eva turned and hugged Steve, the smile returned in an instant. She kissed him on the cheek and Steve noticed how quickly her mood had changed again – it worried him.

'Thank you, *Bruce!*' She turned and playfully skipped her way back to the bedroom which worried Steve even more. She stopped abruptly and looked back at him.

'So, you find me attractive?' She smiled cheekily before closing the door behind her.

Steve shook his head and wondered once again what the fuck he had let himself in for.

* * *

The rest of the morning was spent filling in the gaps… it was not easy listening for Steve.

She reiterated the bit about coming to England with her mother four years earlier because of their 'problems', which again, Eva refused to elaborate on, but the move wasn't through choice.

They had been trafficked by the same Albanian gang who had arranged their passports, but they hadn't just arranged for Eva to leave Kosovo for the UK, they already had work lined up for her – she had been targeted for her looks – even at her tender age.

What else she told him made him feel sick to his stomach. The food processing plant really did exist and it did employ thousands of people who processed chicken, but it also processed people – lots of people who were employed in more clandestine activities – drug manufacture and prostitution mostly.

Within the factory and its environs were laboratories processing top-grade cocaine, heroin and other drugs that Steve had never even heard of, whilst cannabis plants were grown and cultivated in greenhouses the size of aircraft hangars. A multitude of brothels providing every form of sexual deviance known to man were also housed in the complex, some even underground – this was vice on an industrial scale.

Eva was indeed a 'chosen one' – as were all the girls and boys involved in prostitution within Chicken City. These were the recipients of the chips while the rest – the operamini – received the tattoos that bore a chilling resemblance to those that the Nazis inflicted on concentration camp inmates.

'But you've been saying you've been held prisoner, so how come you got a pass out the other day to see your mother?' Steve asked.

'How do you think?'

She pouted, pushed her breasts together with her upper arms then winced in pain.

'I told you, I'm not just a chosen one – I am the *special* one. I can call in a lot of favours, if you know what I mean,' she winked.

Steve nodded in sympathy but his face portrayed his disgust.

'Don't judge me Steve, you – you in your cosy little apartment.' She spread her arms out wide and looked around the room.

'I've had nothing but shit since I was born. My father is dead and I was brought to a foreign country against my will – and since then I've been forced to have sex with flabby, ugly old men on a daily basis and for what? A pittance which I send back to my brother and sister in Kosovo, so fuck you Steve, fuck you and your shitty fucking country!'

'OK, OK,' Steve held up his hands in apology.

They sat in silence for a minute or two.

'So, um, you escaping... how does this affect your mother... and your family back in Kosovo?' he asked.

'My grandmother died recently and my younger brother and sister have moved away to stay with an aunt – my mother's sister. I am hoping that the Albanians won't be able to track them down.'

I swear she said her siblings were living with her grandmother? Steve was already thinking her story was unravelling but he decided not to pursue it.

'Is that why you've left now?'

'Maybe – I've been planning it for a while, since my grandmother died. Then when you picked me up the other day, well it just seemed like a good time and you seemed to be the right guy. You know – someone I could trust.'

'And your mother?'

Eva shrugged and gazed at the floor. 'I don't know – she isn't chipped, she's just an operamini. I hope she can get out and maybe just slip away – there are ways and means,' she added as an afterthought.

So how come she managed to see her mother in Chip City if she was just an operamini? thought Steve.

Some things were not adding up and there was still no mention of the memory stick. Steve thought he would wait for Eva to bring it up. The images he had seen still indelibly printed in his mind.

'Hey Steve – can I watch the TV?' Eva asked.

Steve had little time for daytime TV and its diet of inane quiz shows and menopausal harridans – he'd had enough of it during his enforced period of unemployment.

He shrugged in a *'couldn't care less'* sort of way.

She launched herself onto the sofa, pointed the remote at the TV and tucked her long, lithe legs under her chin before wrapping her arms around them. She could have been any other teenage girl in Britain settling down to watch her favourite TV programme, instead of a trafficked sex slave from the Balkans.

'Do you watch a lot of TV?' Steve asked, curious to know more about her, not just about her life situation.

'I usually work all night so I only get the chance to watch TV during the day, I watch a lot of Netflix – oh and we have lots of old DVDs, mostly films from the Eighties and Nineties – that's why I like *Die Hard*,' she giggled, 'and guess what my favourite film is?'

Steve shrugged once more.

'*Pretty Woman!*... You can be Richard Gere and I'll be Julia Roberts!' She laughed out loud and fell sideways onto the sofa.

Steve looked at her in bewilderment. He was more confused about Eva now than he'd ever been. Her mature adult body hid a playful but emotionally scarred woman-child within. Having brought up two boys he wasn't sure how to react to her, she both excited and terrified him at the same time.

He was in the kitchen making her a sandwich for lunch – she asked for crisps and Coke, but he had neither in his flat – when she shouted out in excitement.

'Steve! Steve! On the news now!'

He ran into the lounge, a buttered knife still in his hand.

The perky, blonde newsreader continued with the news item '... the masked men boarded the bus on Baldwin Street at approximately ten forty-five last night and terrified the bus driver and passengers. They carried hand guns and according to eyewitnesses were clearly looking for someone.'

The local news programme then cut to the flabby-faced, animated bus driver who Steve had irritated the night before.

'Their car cut I up and then two blokes wearing masks jumped on. One pointed a gun at I and the other one searched me bus. They was looking for someone,' said the driver – an obvious owner of a GCSE in the bleeding obvious.

'Cheers drive,' said the interviewer in classic Bristolese.

'You so funny Steve – you stuck the chip on a fucking bus!' roared Eva.

She could barely contain her glee. She fell off the sofa and rolled around the floor in exaggerated mirth before a short, sharp stabbing pain in her arm quickly bought her back to reality.

'Ow, ow, ow,' she moaned as she curled up into a foetal position before the giggles returned once more sending Steve scuttling back to his chores.

'What is it now?' Steve shouted in irritation as Eva beckoned him once more just a few minutes later.

Eva was pointing excitedly to the TV.

'This boy on the TV, the police say he is missing... I know him, he's a new chosen one – they brought him in a couple of days ago.'

Steve's eyes widened as he recognised the photo of the fresh-faced, smiling, tousle-haired youth on the TV.

It was Tony Preston's son, Lee.

Chapter Ten

Besin Marishta swore and punched the office wall, the hammer blow from his huge hand formed a perfect fist shape in the plasterboard as well as making a framed photo of a red-shirted football team crash to the floor.

'You find me that *kurvë e vogël* and you find her quick... understand?'

His face was crimson with rage and almost matched the colour of the FK Partizani Tirana football shirt he wore under his ink-black Armani leather jacket. He walked menacingly towards two men in crumpled grey suits who were visibly shaking. The solid gold neck chains and bracelets he wore clinked and jangled with each step he took.

'I thought you two had bigger brains than these idiots.' He gestured towards two large gorillas that stood silently at the back of his office. They were both dressed similarly to Marishta but their black leather jackets were more Matalan than Milan and their jewellery more H. Samuel than Hatton Garden.

'*Besa! Besa! Besa!*' he shouted at the gorillas before looking back at the crumpled suits.

'Trust! Trust! Trust! – that is our Albanian code, they have let me down. These *idiotë të ndyrë* go and hold up a bus for fuck's sake!'

He rubbed the back of his head with his huge hand causing small bits of plaster to lodge like flecks of dandruff in his greasy hair. The two gorillas stifled a laugh.

'I pay you good money and you let things like this fucking happen?' he continued as a line of spittle dribbled on to his square, unshaven chin.

'Get out and don't come back until you fucking find her – and make it quick. He is coming next week and he will be, how you say... *pissed off*... if she isn't here. Now fucking get out of my sight.'

The two grey-suited men exited the room quickly and once the door shut behind them, they exchanged glances and exhaled deeply.

The older of the two men ran his hand through his thinning hair. He now regretted not taking early retirement when it was offered. But no, his missus had her eye on a villa in Spain – *stay on and boost your pension,* she'd said, which was why he was now sweating his cobs off in a gloomy corridor in the bowels of a huge factory in Avonmouth.

He was beginning to rue the day he'd been introduced to Besin Marishta, or *'I vogel' – The Tiny One,* as he was known rather ironically, in his native Kosovo; but the handshakes they'd exchanged confirmed to him that the Albanian was 'on the level' – one of us, the Worshipful Master had assured him.

Besin Marishta owned a thriving import and export-business and needed someone to act as a consultant for him on security for his various properties and operations scattered across Europe.

Being a successful businessman in his homeland as well as the UK also made him an ideal candidate to sit on the board of Solutio and act as one of their advisers, so everything seemed legit to Detective Sergeant Alan 'Tommo' Thompson of the Avon and Somerset police.

The fact that Marishta also headed up one of Europe's largest Organised Crime Groups who were responsible for the wholescale importation of both drugs and people into the UK was either unknown or conveniently overlooked by Thompson... and as for the fee that the Albanian 'businessman' offered – well it would've been rude not to.

Thompson recruited his protégé, DC Andy Bishop, to help him in his 'consultancy business' – it wasn't strictly illegal, but it was probably best to keep it from upstairs, Thompson had told the young Detective Constable with a wink.

Bishop was ambitious, fast learning and fit – he possessed a black belt in Tae Kwon Do – which complemented Thompson's thirty-odd years of dishing out kidney punches to West Country thugs and criminals.

The two of them made a formidable team, but right now, standing in a dark, deserted corridor outside of Besin Marishta's office in Chicken City, they felt anything but formidable.

Chapter Eleven

Steve came running into the living room on hearing Eva's high-pitched scream.

'What is it, what's wrong now?' he asked wearily, tiring of Eva's erratic and immature behaviour.

Eva pointed towards Steve's pride and joy – his jukebox.

'Th... that... what the fuck is it?' she stammered.

'It's a jukebox, or a Rock-Ola 1484 jukebox to be more precise, made in Chicago in 1959,' Steve replied with just a hint of pride in response to Eva's question, but he was mystified as to why it caused Eva such terrors, surely she had noticed it before, he thought.

'No, I know what a jukebox is, I mean that... that thing.'

She flapped her hand towards Derrick who was napping on top of the jukebox, blissfully unaware of the unfolding drama his presence had caused.

'Oh that... that's Derrick, my cat. Handsome devil isn't he?' answered Steve mockingly.

'He's harmless – well as long as you leave him alone that is. And whatever you do, don't try and smooth him.'

'Smooth him? What do you mean smooth him?'

'Er, stroke him, pet him. Sorry.' Steve admonished himself for slipping into his native Bristolese.

'Uh don't worry I won't,' she assured him as she warily approached the Rock-Ola.

'It's beautiful. The jukebox, not the cat. I have never seen anything like it – except on *Happy Days*.'

Steve smiled weakly.

'It was left to me by someone – someone who…' he trailed off. He thought it best not to go into details.

Eva eyed him coquettishly.

'Who Steve – a friend? A girlfriend… *wife*?'

'There's no girlfriend… or wife. There was uh… both, but no, not any more. Let's just say a friend, a friend who is no longer around. She died a few years back.'

'Oh, sorry.' Eva smiled an awkward apology. 'Kirsty Dono… *something?*'

'Uh Donohue… yes, but how do you know?'

Eva pointed to the framed record on the wall.

'So, she loved you… and you loved her, yes?'

Steve nodded. Eva sensed she shouldn't pursue it. She turned her attention back to the jukebox.

'Does it work, can I play it?' she asked.

Steve nodded. 'Sure. I don't play it too often these days. Go ahead.'

Eva studied the jukebox intently and ran her finger down the list of records whilst keeping one wary eye on Derrick who returned a stare of his own through his one good eye. Eva frowned and turned to face Steve.

'Is there nothing on here by Dua Lipa… or Rita Ora – I like her, she's from Kosova you know?'

'Yeah I know. Sorry but I haven't.'

'Why? Don't you like her, people say I look like her. What do you think?'

Steve shrugged.

'I suppose… a little.'

Eva thrust out her bottom lip in disappointment.

'You're, um… you're actually prettier than her,' he answered.

Eva beamed and turned back to the Rock-Ola suitably impressed, her frown returned.

'I know none of these songs.'

'Yeah, well they're all from my youth – a long, long time ago.'

Eva shrugged as she pressed a couple of random buttons. She studied the jukebox intently as it lit up, whirred and clunked – the record swivelled onto the turntable and the needle dropped into position. The crackles started and she responded by clapping her hands in joy.

Open the door to your heart by Darrell Banks, the tragic soul singer who had been shot dead by a policeman in Detroit in 1970, started playing. It was one of Steve's favourites, but unfortunately it was on Stateside and not on the rare London label which was worth a small fortune.

Eva moved her hips from side to side, she turned and took Steve's hand, he half-heartedly objected but Eva gripped his hands tightly and the two danced awkwardly to the Northern Soul classic.

She pulled him tightly to her body causing Steve to grimace. He could feel her young, firm breasts against his chest. He had not danced with a woman, certainly not a young woman as beautiful as Eva for longer than he cared to remember.

'Steve, you naughty boy,' she said with a giggle as he felt the blood rush around his body, causing his cheeks to blush and his loins to stir.

'Sorry it's been a long time,' he apologised for the movement in his trousers and shifted to a more comfortable position. He was eager to change the subject.

Steve breathed a sigh of relief as the record finished. He led Eva to the sofa eager to query her further about Lee, but her mind was flitting from subject to subject and she'd become preoccupied with the jukebox that dominated the room. She pressed another couple of random buttons.

The sound of *Dance Crasher* by Alton 'Mr Rocksteady' Ellis filled the room.

Eva nodded in approval.

She looked at Steve as if she was about to tell him something. He wondered if she was at last going to talk about the video, the video that had become a very large elephant in the room.

Eva reluctantly sat down. She was like a child in a sweet shop and keen to carry on exploring the room and its contents.

'So, this lad, Lee – you know him from Chicken City?' asked Steve.

'Well I don't really know him. He came in on Tuesday afternoon with some older men, he looked terrified. I worked until about two in the morning so I didn't see him again. I left at eightish to visit my mother, I stayed with her for a few hours and headed back... that's when you picked me up.'

She looked at Steve and smiled before continuing.

'When you dropped me back on Wednesday evening he was not around… we have a room and a gym where we chill, you know, hang out, but he wasn't there – maybe they put him straight to work, I don't know.'

Steve was disturbed by the formality of it all. Eva had said it so matter-of-factly in a way that made it sound so normal, but for her he guessed it was, it was her way of life.

'So how do you know him?' asked Eva.

'He's my boss's son. He's fourteen – he um, he ran away from home earlier on in the week, my boss – Tony – he's distraught.'

'He's gay, right?'

Steve nodded.

'They get a lot of young pretty boys like him. They pick them up off the streets and outside their schools. They start by giving them money, vapes and alcohol. Then they get them onto drugs, lots of drugs.'

It was a subject that Eva hadn't brought up before. Steve had already assumed, rightly or wrongly, that she was taking drugs of some sort, it might explain her irrational behaviour, although he'd been too pre-occupied removing the chip from her arm and then patching her up to notice any needle marks.

'So what are you going to do about him?' Eva asked.

Steve had thought of little else over the last few hours. How could he tell the police the whereabouts of a missing boy without implicating Eva?

She had already told him that senior police officers – and others in authority – were regular visitors to Chicken City. It was one of the things that Solutio had on the chosen ones, as well as the possession of their passports – fake or otherwise.

There were also the threats to their families, not to mention the implanted chips that tracked their every movement. All this meant that if Steve was going to expose Solutio and the fraud that was the migrant cities he had to tread very carefully and he needed help – a lot of help, but who he was going to get that help from he could only guess.

He stared blankly out of the window.

'Steve, I asked you a question, what are you going to do about him?' Eva repeated.

'I haven't got a fucking clue,' he answered bluntly.

Chapter Twelve

Steve used to love a Friday evening. In the past, Friday nights heralded the weekend and meant a night out on the lash with his old mates from the Big Five, the gang of lads that he had been matey with since his schooldays.

John 'JB' Burston was now debt-free and thankfully no longer beating up his wife Sharon, while Gerawzy 'George' Smolinski had not only given up sleeping with other women but also given up steroids, both the dealing and taken of them and at last had his volatile temper under control. Steve occasionally met the two of them for a pint or two in the Moon under Water but Pete McNulty had moved to his villa in Spain with his wife and troubled daughter so the regular meet-ups where they put the world to right had long gone.

They'd heard that Mike Cribb, the shamed and ex-communicated fifth member of the Big Five, who had turned out to be a paedophile, was out on parole but the likelihood of them all getting together and having a chat about old times was as likely as Rovers winning the Premier League.

This Friday evening however couldn't have been more different from those old beery nights. Instead of being out with his old mates he was stuck in his flat with a teenage Balkan beauty who had been trafficked to work as a prostitute in a factory in Avonmouth. *How the fuck had this happened?*

Steve prepared a lasagne for him and Eva, all the time she followed him around the cramped kitchen like an inquisitive puppy. She was full of questions and constantly pestered Steve asking him about his life,

Bristol – of which she knew very little – and his ex-wife and their two sons.

She knew there was someone else – the friend who'd left him the jukebox – but Steve always changed the subject when she'd asked about her. She had noticed the tattoos and the scar on his shoulder when he was removing the chip and she'd asked him about them but again he'd declined to answer. He was like a closed book and that made him even more attractive to her.

'You remind me of my father,' she said as she watched his every move.

Steve was not shocked. In fact, he had been expecting it.

'I thought it was Bruce Willis or Richard Gere?... Sure it's not your grandfather?'

She shook her head.

'No Steve, stop putting yourself down... my father was a good man too – and handsome.'

She touched his shoulder as he put the lasagne in the oven causing Steve to flinch and pull himself away from her.

'Don't,' he answered abruptly, 'it's not right.'

He hoped she was getting the message.

They ate their meal in silence. He'd opened a bottle of Pinot Noir – Eva had asked for vodka, but like Coca-Cola it was not a drink he was partial to and kept none in the flat. She accepted the wine and drank it with relish. She downed the glass in one and promptly fell asleep in front of the TV.

Steve scooped her up in his arms and carried her to the spare bedroom. She reciprocated by putting her arms around his neck and nuzzling into him causing Steve further discomfort.

'Goodnight papa,' she said in a whisper as he pulled the cover up over her.

Steve could do nothing but shudder inside.

Chapter Thirteen

He'd eventually found the card he'd been looking for just after one in the morning. It was in Kirsty's well-read folder in a black cardboard box binder alongside correspondence from the Inland Revenue and Debbie's divorce lawyer – coincidentally both demanding payments.

Seven hours later and after a fitful night's sleep he held the crumpled card in his hand. He rolled it between his thumb and forefinger and mulled over the implications of making contact with the person who several years back had tried to put him in prison.

'Alright squire, long time no hear from,' said the familiar voice at the end of the phone.

Simon Edwards had left the Serious Organised Crime Agency shortly after he'd put Vernon Lewis, Earl Samson and very nearly Steve Allen, behind bars. He'd decided to leave on a high and what's more the fallout from Kirsty's death and her sordid association with some of the top brass in the force had left a bad taste in his mouth.

Unlike the majority of retired cops who gravitated towards jobs in security, personal protection or the pub trade, Edwards invested in a shed load of fine art and opened up a small gallery in the quaint, sleepy town of Monmouth, which was just far enough west of the border to qualify him as a bona fide 'Taffy' in Steve Allen's eyes.

In truth Edwards had made a mistake. He was bored shitless and had already grown tired of the small town and its limited range of pubs, restaurants… and women, having already slept with all the eligible – and not so eligible – females in the surrounding area.

Since he'd stopped playing rugby there was little to keep him occupied and he began to rue the day that he decided to put his feet up and take it easy.

When he saw the name 'Steve Allen' appear on his mobile it was fair to say his heart skipped a beat or two, instantly bringing back memories of shootings, illegal Class 'A' drugs and hard-core gangsters – *God I miss those days*, he thought to himself.

'Hi Simon, er… how's it hanging?'

'To the left as ever, how about you?'

'Uh, fair to middling.'

The two lapsed into an awkward silence.

'OK pleasantries over squire, what can I do for you?' asked Simon Edwards at last.

'I've um, got a bit of a problem, wondered if you could help me out. Fancy meeting up for a beer?'

Edwards mulled over his answer.

'Only if you promise not to smack me in the mouth this time,' replied the Welshman ruefully.

Chapter Fourteen

It was a dull, grey cloudy Saturday morning. Previous Saturday mornings always meant the same thing, the eager anticipation of a football match in a few hours' time and a meet up with his mates. But the heady days of having a few beers and a tear up against the likes of Chelsea and Millwall had long gone.

Now… well he didn't even know who his once-beloved Rovers were playing, some nonentity outfit from the barren wastes of the North he pondered. Whoever it was, he'd decided he wasn't going to grace them with his presence, which pleased Eva no end.

Steve wasn't too enamoured with the thought of a shopping trip to Cabot Circus either but the constant whining from Eva had at last worn him down. He could see her point, she'd arrived with just a small bag of essentials – a change of clothes, some make-up and an old iPhone were the sum total of her belongings.

But she did have a shitload of money, nearly a thousand pounds in cash courtesy of tips from grateful punters – not to mention the forty quid she'd blagged off of Steve – much to his annoyance – and she was keen to spend it.

The stroll into the city centre didn't take too long; it was another reason why Steve had chosen the apartment.

They passed the Barley Mow in St Philips on the way, a place that Steve now liked to call his local. It ticked all the boxes for him as far as pubs were concerned and on the rare occasions when he did venture out, he liked to pop in the cosy hostelry to sample their ales and food, although he avoided the trendy 'craft' ales as no matter what they were called or what they boasted on the label – all tasted the bleeding same to him.

Not that he was a heavy drinker anymore. On his own admission Steve could be a bit of a pisshead in the past but his drinking had been curtailed somewhat in the last few years and in all honesty, he was feeling better for it. The regular workouts and the abstinence from Class A drugs had also had a positive effect and he was now fitter and leaner than he'd been since his thirties.

'Wow, you have a Harvey Nicks!' screeched an excited Eva. The nearest she had come to shopping in the last few years had been watching the QVC channel.

'Please Steve, can we go in? *Please?*' she whined as she grabbed his arm and pulled him in the direction of the plush store.

'All the clothes I have, they've been supplied by the Albanians and they make me look like a...' she hesitated, 'a whore.'

It was at that point that Steve spotted probably the last person on the planet that he wanted to.

'Steve Allen, you dirty ol' dog!'

The imposing frame of John 'JB' Burston stood directly in front of him, grinning lecherously from ear to ear. His wife – Sharon – stood impassively by his side. She eyed the two of them up and pulled a face as if she was sucking a lemon-coated razor blade.

'You kept this quiet you ol' fucker, talk about punching! Well are you going to introduce us or not?' JB's grin was growing wider by the second.

'Uh, alright John – it's not what it looks like,' Steve squirmed.

'This is Eva... she's a... friend. Eva, this is my oldest buddy JB, er John, and his wife – Sharon.'

JB held out his monstrously large hand, Eva took it, stood on her tiptoes and gave JB an awkward kiss on the cheek bringing an even fiercer scowl of disapproval from Sharon.

'She's foreign… uh from Kosovo,' said Steve lamely, which did absolutely nothing to ease the situation.

'No shit,' said a deadpan Sharon.

Eva stepped forward and tried to embrace Sharon who was having none of it.

JB had punched way above his weight when he landed the young, pneumatic Sharon but she was in real danger of being upstaged by the stunning – and much younger – Eva.

'Where did you two meet?' asked Sharon acidly, 'don't tell me – the Internet?'

Steve wished the ground would open up and swallow him.

'No, nothing like that… honest. Eva's just having a bit of a hard time lately. We met, uh… we met recently in work and I'm just letting her stay at my flat for a while until she gets back on her feet. We're not together or anything.'

He glanced at Eva hoping for some assurance.

'Are we?'

Eva pouted and slipped her arm between Steve's. It did nothing to convince JB – or Sharon – that Steve wasn't banging her left, right and centre.

Steve cleared his throat with a false cough and glanced at his Breitling Aviator, his cherished watch that he now only wore on special occasions.

'Blimey is that the time, look we'd better go,' he said as he anxiously tugged on Eva's arm.

'Yeah OK mate… tell you what give me a call. We haven't been out for ages, perhaps we could make it a foursome and go out for a meal or something?' JB said as he glanced at Sharon who replied with a '*you must be fucking joking*' look.

'He seemed like a really nice guy,' said Eva as they turned and headed towards Harvey Nichols.

‘If only you knew,’ muttered Steve.

A light meal and cocktails in Harvey Nichols, courtesy of Eva’s clients, proved entertaining as the young waiters, both male and female, vied with each other to serve Eva.

She responded by flirting outrageously at every opportunity, much to Steve’s embarrassment, annoyance and just a hint of jealousy. Eva demolished her lunch and drinks as if she’d never eaten in a top restaurant before – perhaps she hadn’t – wondered Steve, before she insisted on buying Steve a new Boss sweater despite his false protestations.

In honesty he was grateful, as buying new clothing, which had always been one of Steve’s favourite pastimes, had taken a back seat in recent cash-strapped years… he was now more of a Poundland man rather than the Fifty Quid Man that he had once been.

They arrived back at the apartment late afternoon, Steve exhausted and weary, Eva excited and bubbly. She was eager to try her new purchases on… again.

For all the hanging around in the stores and the untimely meeting with JB and Sharon, in truth Steve had quite enjoyed the afternoon.

Rovers had won, City had lost and Eva’s insistence on clinging onto his arm had boosted his ego and brought both admiring and envious glances in equal numbers from males of all ages, while women stared and shook their heads in disgust.

He’d half hoped to bump into his ex-wife, Debbie, and her partner Felicity, but in hindsight it wouldn’t have been such a good idea knowing as he did, that she would’ve been certain to tell their sons.

Steve smiled to himself at the thought of his bitter and twisted ex-wife as he nonchalantly looked through the spy hole in answer to the firm knock on the door. Bloody Jehovah’s Witnesses, he thought, nothing better to do on a Saturday evening.

Two stern-looking men in even sterner grey suits stood beyond his door, warrant cards in hands – Jehovah's Witnesses they weren't.

'Eva,' he hissed, 'get in the bedroom and stay there!'

Eva gathered up her bags, ran into her room and quickly shut the door behind her.

'Who is it?' shouted Steve, knowing full well what the answer would be.

'It's the police, can you open the door?'

He opened the door to reveal an old fox of a detective with a lived-in face, thinning salt-and-pepper hair and a scalp complaint. It looked like the weight of the world was on his drooping shoulders – as well as dandruff.

The other, younger officer looked the total opposite of the old fox, being broad shouldered, no-necked and in possession of a cold, unnerving stare that bore straight through Steve – not one to upset, he thought.

'Uh yes officers, what can I do for you?' Steve asked as innocently as possible.

'Just routine enquiries sir. I'm Detective Sergeant Alan Thompson and this is my colleague Detective Constable Andy Bishop.' He motioned towards 'No Neck' whose stare had shifted from Steve and re-focused on something behind him.

Steve gave a disinterested nod.

'We're looking for a runaway girl. A taxi driver reckoned he dropped her off outside these flats on Thursday evening. Have you seen a tall, slim, attractive blonde teenager in this vicinity – or do you know her?' asked Thompson.

Teenager. Steve momentarily let the word register.

'Er no, can't say I do,' Steve shrugged.

'Funny that – it's just that we have a photograph of her getting into your car, or at least getting into a car you were driving, on Wednesday afternoon.'

Bishop handed a folder to Thompson who opened it and took out a grainy colour print – he waved it under Steve's nose. Even with her hood up it clearly showed the sodden wet Eva getting into his Kuga at Spitfire Island in Birmingham.

'Oh her? Yeah, I remember now,' he stalled.

'I uh, gave her a lift back to Bristol. She was hitch-hiking and it was raining, y'know, really pissing down. I uh... felt sorry for her and yep, I gave her a lift back to the 'mouth – er, Avonmouth,' he said nodding his head rapidly.

'Avonmouth? Solutio's food processing plant by any chance?' asked Thompson. He produced another photo – this time clearly in focus and clearly showing Eva getting out of Steve's car.

Steve's face was also visible, as were the two twenty-pound notes Eva was stashing into her back pocket.

Fuck. Banged to rights, he thought.

'Uh it's not what it looks like,' said Steve sheepishly.

'Whatever,' replied Thompson impassively.

'Look I'm not interested in what you got up to with her, we just want to know where she is. You're saying that's the last you saw of her – you haven't seen her since? Not Thursday evening?'

'Thursday? No, no. Um... look, how did you track me down, I mean it wasn't even my car?' Steve was curious to know how they had found him.

'Nothing sinister sir, just an ANPR check on your trade plates – showed the car was in transit from a dealership in Birmingham to one in Weston-super-Mare, courtesy of...'

'City Vehicle Logistics,' chipped in Bishop.

'City Vehicle Logistics,' repeated Thompson. 'We contacted them, er... Tony...'

'Preston,' interrupted Bishop.

'Tony Preston,' said Thompson, giving his younger colleague an agitated glance, 'and he said you were the driver – so you can understand why we think you may know of this *young* girl's whereabouts.' He emphasised the word 'young'.

Cheers Preston, you arsehole – so much for not having anything to do with the Old Bill.

'Well I'm sorry but I don't know anything about her or her whereabouts. Like I said I gave her a lift, dropped her off at Chicken… uh Solutio, gave her forty quid as she said she was having a hard time – nothing else mind – and I haven't seen her since,' said Steve with a hint of irritancy.

'So, if you don't mind, I've got a lot on…' Steve made an attempt to shut the door, causing Thompson to agitatedly take a step forward.

'Would you mind if we came in and had a look around your flat sir? It won't take long.'

'Not without a search warrant you don't,' replied Steve.

'Something to hide sir? Like I said it won't take long.'

'Nothing to hide at all. I haven't seen the girl since Wednesday alright? Look, I know my rights, so come back with a search warrant and I might let you in.'

Steve slammed the door in their faces.

'Fucking arseholes,' he said to himself angrily.

He turned his back on the door, slid down it and slumped to the floor.

In front of him was the object that Bishop had obviously spotted – on a chair clearly in view was a shopping bag with '*Boux Avenue*' printed on it in bright pink letters.

'Bollocks' sighed Steve.

A muffled voice came from the bedroom. 'What is it Steve, have they gone?'

Eva emerged from her bedroom in a slinky black dress that left little to the imagination. She walked seductively towards Steve. Steve shook his head and exhaled deeply.

'Not now Eva – that was the fucking police, they're on to you… and me. They spotted that fucking thing.' He pointed in the direction of the lingerie bag.

'So? They might think you're a cross dresser,' giggled Eva.

'For fuck's sake Eva, this isn't a laughing matter! We have to get you out of here – and soon.'

'But Steve, I want to stay here with you, I'll be your Julia Roberts and you'll be my Richard…'

'For fuck's sake Eva – will you grow up!'

'OK, OK,' she held up her hands in submission, clearly hurt by his words.

'I go, tomorrow or maybe Monday – yeah? I go and stay with some custos – the guards – I know some who live on the outside. They owe me a few favours, if you know what I mean, seeing as I'm not good enough for you,' she sighed sarcastically.

Steve nodded wearily. He at last focused on what she was wearing.

His eyes widened in excitement.

'Well what do you think?' she purred, eager to take Steve's mind off the visit by the police.

'Christ Eva you look stunning, just amazing, but…'

Eva stood barely a foot away from him, he could smell the new perfume she'd just bought and that she'd applied liberally to her neck. Her piercing green eyes cut into him like a laser, her hair hung loose over her bare shoulders and she'd applied new make-up that accentuated her already high cheek bones.

The dress clung to every curve and finished way above her knees revealing toned legs that seemed to go on forever. She inched even closer in to him.

'Look Eva we have to talk.'

Steve's mind was in turmoil. Eva was fucking his head up, she was no normal teenage runaway and the visit by Thompson and Bishop had confirmed it – she really was the special one and someone desperately wanted her back. He eyed her up and took in every square inch of her beautifully formed body.

'This isn't right,' he squirmed.

'What isn't right? Don't you like me Steve, don't you find me attractive?'

'You know I do, Jesus any man would. You're off the fucking scale but we can't… maybe if you were twenty...'

He quickly did some mental arithmetic, '…forty years older, then yes, but you've got to get this out of your head, it's not going to happen.'

As much as I'd like it to.

She put her hand on his shoulder and leant into him.

'What is it Steve, are you gay?' she whispered in his ear.

'Is that why you stopped for me, you thought I was a young boy?'

'What? No! No fucking way – I'm as straight as they come it's just…'

'Ah, I get it,' she smiled wickedly.

'I have some little blue tablets – is that what you want?'

'No, no! I don't need Viagra!' he shouted angrily.

'Maybe something else then… how about cocaine?'

He paused and his eyes widened just enough for Eva to notice.

'You have coke?' he asked in a near whisper.

'Ah! I've found your vice! The chink in your perfect armour. Steve Allen likes the white powder!' She laughed out loud.

The last few days had been difficult for Steve. He'd been tempted by the seductress that was Eva, she was young, beautiful and witty in a childish way and up to now he'd managed to resist her and her charms.

But now it was his old mistress, cocaine, who was knocking on his door once more. The door, which he thought he'd shut firmly several years ago, was now unlocked and ever so gently opening in front of his eyes.

He shook his head in an attempt to snap out of it.

'I uh, used to – years ago… I dabbled,' he lied.

She closed her eyes seductively and drew her tongue across her top lip.

'I have some that will blow you away. They process it at Chicken City – it's the best you'll ever have.'

I doubt it, thought Steve as he remembered Earl Samson's Merck cocaine that he'd snorted with relish several years back.

'Do you know what really turns me on?' she purred, continuing before he had a chance to answer.

'I like to have a man – a real man, snort coke off of my tits before he fucks me stupid. Would you like to do that to me Steve, huh? Especially as this could be our last night together?'

Steve felt repulsed and excited in equal measures. Eva looked deep into his eyes, took his hand and led him to the bedroom.

Chapter Fifteen

'But Steve don't you want to stay here with me?'

Eva pouted at Steve as he put his North Face jacket on and gathered up his trade plates. He studied her and even with her bed hair and no make-up he had to admit he was sorely tempted. The tiny lacy red bra and knickers she was barely wearing didn't help things either.

'As much as I'd like to, but... I need the money and it's a straight return job, so it's a nice bit of bunce – sorry.'

'Bunce? What do you mean by bunce?' She furrowed her brow even more.

'Bunce... easy money. Look I shouldn't be too late, so just stay in and...'

'But I thought you wanted me to go?'

'Just one more night OK? I'm not working Tuesday so we can sort a few things out then. Just stay in and watch the telly eh? I got Netflix and there's some music and DVDs over there.'

He motioned to the CDs and DVDs neatly arranged on shelves in alphabetical order hoping to God that she didn't mess them up.

'And whatever you do, don't go out or open the door to anyone, alright?'

Steve was mindful of another visit from Thompson and Bishop.

The pout that Eva gave in response was enough to make her lips fall off her face. She tossed back her hair, stomped into the bedroom and slammed the door behind her, obviously still in a foul mood and angry with Steve for him spurning her advances on the Saturday evening.

* * *

He'd been sorely tempted. The offer of snorting coke off a naked girl's breasts, and not just any girl, but a stellar supermodel like Eva, had long been a fantasy of his. But his conscience had gotten the better of him and he'd pulled away from her just as she'd started unzipping the dress. His head had told him he'd done the right thing but his groin told him otherwise, he'd headed straight for the bathroom and behind the locked door he'd jerked off into the toilet instead, much to Eva's annoyance and his own disgust.

'You'd rather have a wank than fuck me! Are you fucking mad?' she'd screamed from the bedroom.

'I f-f-fucking must be,' he stammered as he shot his load into the pan with a loud gasp.

Eva had spent the Sunday sulking and pretending to ignore Steve like the love-struck teenager she was.

They'd barely spoken and when Steve received the text message from Tony Preston on the Sunday evening telling him of an easy return job to London he sighed in relief at the opportunity to get out of the flat and away from Eva for the day.

Or so he tried to convince himself.

* * *

Bunce? Did I say bunce? Fuck's sake it's a hundred quid for a day's work, Jesus I used to earn that an hour, he thought to himself as he started the Transit.

It was just before eight. He had to get the van to Barking in East London then get back across town to make a pick-up in Wimbledon. In the parlance of those Cockney geezers he had to jog on.

The drive east up the M4 was uneventful and even the clockwise journey around the M25 was easier than some previous stop/start journeys that he'd endured on what was at times Britain's longest car park.

The solitude gave him time to think things through, especially about the visit from Thompson and Bishop. He was still uneasy about them – and Eva for that matter.

Something didn't add up – especially when he mentioned to them about having to get a search warrant. In all honesty he thought they'd given up far too easily.

They knew he'd given her a lift from Brum to Chicken City – they had the photographs to prove it. But that had troubled Steve.

Two detectives had gone to a lot of time and effort to track down a teenage runaway.

Christ, thousands go missing every day – what was it that made Eva the 'special one'? How did they know to study CCTV footage of a roundabout with a Spitfire sculpture on it on the outskirts of Birmingham?

Then there was the taxi driver who reckoned he'd dropped her off outside his apartment. How had they found him? Steve was baffled – *they at least had enough to take me in for questioning,* he thought.

Then the penny dropped... *How the fuck could the Old Bill be investigating a missing person, who technically – according to Eva – didn't exist? Who the fuck reported her missing – Solutio? And to who? Avon and Somerset police?*

'Eva, get out of the flat now!' he shouted down the phone after her mobile answered with a cheery, 'Hi it's Eva, I can't take your call right now, please leave a message – *ciao!'*

He threw his mobile on to the passenger seat.

How could I be so fucking stupid? Thompson and Bishop weren't the Old Bill, or if they were, they were working for Solutio.

He arrived at Ripple Road in Barking just after eleven. He now had to get to Wimbledon and pick up a five-year-old Jaguar XF and return to Bristol, sharpish.

Underground trains via the District and Northern Lines took him to Tooting Broadway – sadly with the London Underground being less forgiving than the national railways, he had to pay.

His heart and lungs pounded as he ran virtually all the way. He took a short cut through Lambeth Cemetery before arriving at SW London Car Auctions, panting and sweating like a whore in a church.

'Been joggin' me old china?' asked the over-familiar young salesman.

But Steve had no time for pleasantries or even complimentary digestives. He did a quick check of the beast, kicked the tyres, exchanged paperwork and headed north through Wandsworth, crossing the Thames at Putney before getting on the A4 at Hammersmith and heading West.

The only thing that slowed him down was having to stop and fuel the Jag, it was running on fumes – *thank you, you pointy-shoed Cockney arsehole!*

He roared past the anonymous Berkshire town of Slough that could have been twinned with Corby and momentarily thought of John Betjeman's poem.

> *Come friendly bombs and fall on Slough!*
> *It isn't fit for humans now.*

He tried calling Eva once more. There was no response.

The big cat's three-litre turbo diesel engine roared into life as he put his foot down. It propelled him forward towards Bristol and, he hoped, back to Eva.

The police cars outside his flat and the blue and white striped tape tied to the railings signified that he was too late.

'Where is she? Where the fuck is Eva?' Steve screamed as he ran towards the two uniformed cops on duty outside the entrance.

He pushed them aside, ran up the stairs and burst through the damaged door of his apartment. A CSI in a white coverall was on her knees examining a large bloodstain on the floor. To the left of the CSI a startled plain-clothes officer turned and faced Steve.

'And who are you?' asked the stern-faced female detective.

'I'm Steve Allen and this is my flat – where the fuck is Eva?'

'This is your flat? In that case you're under arrest sunshine,' replied the detective grimly.

Chapter Sixteen

The four battleship grey walls of the Bridewell cell stared back at him mockingly.

This was not the first time that Steve had found himself in a police cell, but it was the first time he'd been arrested since the fight he'd had with his old adversary Earl Samson a decade or so previously.

He was still scarred from that event – literally, as the fight resulted in him not only being arrested but also being shot through the shoulder.

It might have been a relatively new building but below the reception area with its soft furnishings and multi-coloured walkways and flash, corporate graphics, it still had cells that were the same as a thousand others around the country. It reeked of piss and shit and it had the same crude, obscene graffiti and random 'ACAB' acronyms scratched on its walls.

The thin blue plastic mattress that sat atop a concrete base and the grey blanket draped around his shoulders did little to comfort Steve as he contemplated the dire predicament he now found himself in.

His previous, albeit brief incarceration was thankfully cut short by the intervention of Kirsty and her superiors but for obvious reasons that wasn't going to happen this time.

He sighed heavily, put his head in his hands and studied the white all-in-one paper coverall he was wearing. The hole in the toe of his sock seemed to emphasis his parlous state as the events of the last few hours reran and spiralled through his head as if he was binge-watching a series of bad boxed-set movies.

He'd told DS Mia Williams, the female detective who'd arrested him, everything.

Well nearly everything.

He'd told her how he first met Eva and most of what she'd revealed to him about what was happening within the confines of Chicken City.

He mentioned the chip in her arm and how he'd cut it out and put it on a passing bus, but the detective was unmoved – she rolled her eyes. She didn't believe a word of it.

'Look, Eva was terrified, she genuinely feared for her life!' he shouted in exasperation.

They hadn't even heard of an Evalina Petrovic and she certainly hadn't been reported as missing, which didn't surprise Steve in the slightest. What DS Williams did believe was that judging by the amount of blood in the apartment someone had been seriously assaulted and possibly even killed.

The police had received a call from a concerned neighbour at eight twenty-five, after they'd heard female screams and noise of a disturbance coming from Steve's flat. The neighbour eventually called the police an hour or so later after it had gone eerily quiet, but they'd been reluctant to.

'You know what it's like round 'ere. Thought it was a domestic,' they'd explained apologetically.

Steve had mentioned the two detectives who'd visited on the Saturday evening – Thompson and Bishop. He could tell from Williams' reaction that she knew of them, but Steve didn't know whether that was good or bad news; and then Williams hit him with the real bombshell – the discovery of thousands of obscene images of children on Steve's laptop.

Just when Steve thought it couldn't get any worse, it did.

'Who is this Mr Allen?' asked DS Williams as she placed an A4 colour photo on the desk in front of him.

Steve lowered his gaze and suppressed the urge to vomit.

'Any idea where this photo was taken?' she continued.

Steve shook his head.

'You don't know? Funny that because it looks very much like this is in your flat. Isn't that your jukebox?'

Steve nodded. The photograph showed a naked teenage girl bound hand and feet.

Her mouth was covered with gaffer tape and a knife was held threateningly to her throat – it was a wide-eyed and terrified Eva.

* * *

The cell door groaned and creaked open to reveal a large, bearded PC holding Steve's Timberland boots. He threw the boots at Steve then motioned him forward.

'Put your boots on, there's someone here to see you,' he said flatly.

Steve had used his one phone call to contact Simon Edwards who now sat in front of him across a cheap aluminium table. He'd hoped to be meeting his one-time love rival in a cosy pub somewhere over a pint, not in a police station over a Styrofoam cup of lukewarm tea.

Edwards had put on weight, grown his hair and sported a week-old beard that was a long way off from being fashionable.

His dress sense still hadn't improved and he obviously still had a penchant for Benson and Hedges, cheap aftershave and Mint Imperials. They shook hands out of politeness but not much else.

'Why, Steve?' asked Edwards after listening to Steve's account of events for the last twenty minutes.

'Why what?' replied Steve.

'Why do you do this? Why do you get involved with… with lost causes? Have you got some sort of death wish, huh? I mean last time it was Kirsty and we all know how that ended and now this… Evalina – if that's her name. What the fuck did you think you were playing at?'

'I wasn't *playing* at anything,' answered Steve angrily.

'I was trying to help, trying to help Kirsty and now I've been trying to help Eva, that's all.'

'Yeah right. The fact that this Eva has the looks of an Eastern European supermodel has nothing to do with it, eh?'

'Balkans,' Steve answered. 'Kosovo is in the Balkans.'

'Ever the fucking pedant,' replied Edwards, 'either way, judging by the photo she's a stunner so don't try and bullshit me that her looks have nothing to do with it.'

Steve didn't answer – deep down he knew Edwards had a point. Edwards shook his head.

'I dunno squire, this is deep shit you're involved in, but… I got to say I believe you. There's something fucking suspect about this Solutio group, I can't believe how the people of Britain have allowed places like this Chicken City to be built, to be honest. They're nothing short of slave labour camps. So, this story about its inmates being barcoded and even chipped doesn't surprise me at all. Things are changing in this country and I can't say for the better.'

He sighed and ran his hand through his greasy hair.

'I need to make a phone call.'

He pushed back his chair and got up leaving Steve to wallow in his own self-pity.

* * *

Over two hours had passed since Steve had been put back in his cell and he still hadn't been charged with anything – which he took to be a good sign.

He kept wondering how the hell anyone, whether it was Thompson and Bishop, or someone else for that matter, had accessed his laptop and uploaded the photos, including the one of a naked Eva bound and gagged, without knowing his password.

He also wondered what else the police might have discovered. He was soon to find out.

In a side room, not a minute's walk away from Steve's cell, G3 Fraser Winston of the National Crime Agency pored over Steve's statement, DS Williams' reports and a familiar dog-eared manila folder. Every few seconds or so he stopped, sighed, massaged his temple and scribbled notes onto the documents spread out on the table in front of him.

Simon Edwards leant against the wall opposite Winston. His arms were crossed and he remained silent, knowing full well it was not wise to interrupt his old colleague while he was working.

Fraser Winston was an ambitious and brilliant detective who Edwards had known since they worked together in the now defunct Serious Organised Crime Agency. SOCA had been superseded by the newly formed NCA in 2013, due in part to poor results and inter-departmental infighting, it was yet another reason that Simon Edwards had decided to quit and pursue a career in fine art.

Winston was junior to Edwards back then but Edwards knew the muscular, shaven-headed black detective from Bermondsey would eventually go on to greater things.

His rise in the fledgling NCA had been meteoric and Edwards had followed his career with interest ever since he'd left. If he'd been totally honest with himself, he would admit to being just a tad jealous of him.

Winston finally gathered up the papers and looked at Edwards.

'You reckon he's straight then?'

'Don't know about that, he's a bit of a rough diamond but yeah, he's legit.'

'But this trouble with Kirsty Clifton a few years back – Merck cocaine, guns, mixing it with the likes of Earl Samson and Vernon Lewis. I mean this bloke almost single-handedly fucked over the Premier League – what was that all about?'

'Think him and his mates watched too many Death Wish films in the Seventies that's all.'

Winston smiled broadly and exposed a set of perfect pearly white teeth and one solitary gold crown.

'OK let's go talk to Paul Kersey,' he said.

Edwards furrowed his brow. 'Who the fuck's Paul Kersey?'

'Charles Bronson's vigilante character – keep up squire,' answered Fraser Winston with a grin.

Chapter Seventeen

'I'm G3 Fraser Winston of the NCA, uh, the National Crime Agency… so you're Steve Allen? I've heard a lot about you.'

Winston held out his hand. Steve eyed it suspiciously before eventually taking and reluctantly shaking it. His grip was firm and hard. Steve felt a slight but distinct pressure on the top of his hand, truth be told it caused him some discomfort.

Steve raised an eyebrow.

'G3?'

'Uh yes. Think of me as a DI… Detective Inspector. G3 is what we're called in the NCA – don't ask,' replied Winston.

Steve instantly noticed the small diamond stud in Winston's left ear, his classy expensive Rolex watch and the small gold signet ring on the little finger of his left hand.

On his feet, but unseen by Steve, Fraser Winston wore a pair of black, handmade John Lobb Oxford Cap shoes, which complemented his expensive dark blue Armani suit perfectly. The suit was the sort that Steve himself would have worn a few years back. Steve admired his style if it was a little ostentatious for his liking.

Winston motioned Steve to sit. Steve knew it was an instruction, not a request.

'What did you mean when you asked DS Williams if she was "on the level"?' Winston asked before Steve had even taken his seat.

Steve shook his head slowly and shrugged.

'I wanted to know if she was a straight cop, I've met some bad 'uns over the years, some I don't trust, to be honest.'

He glanced at Simon Edwards who leant impassively against the wall.

'Like Thompson and Bishop?'

Steve nodded. Winston referred to Steve's statement on the table in front of him, Steve noticed certain words and lines had been highlighted bright yellow.

'You mentioned a "craft" knife?'

'Uh, yeah – that was when I cut Eva's... uh, when I removed the microchip.'

Winston nodded his head slowly before referring to the statement again.

'How about "squaring the circle" – what made you say that?'

'I don't know. Think I said something about me being in London when the flat was broken into, so how could you "square that circle"... Look, what the fuck's with all this third-degree interrogation?' asked Steve angrily.

Winston raised an eyebrow and smiled to himself.

'Ever been in the Masons Steve, or know someone who has been?' queried Winston.

Steve furrowed his brow.

'No, never... uh, a mate of mine was in it, he's a builder.' He remembered John Burston's brief involvement with the secretive movement.

'Name?'

Steve didn't answer.

Winston scribbled something on his notes then looked up and stared Steve straight in the eye.

'Hmmm... these expressions, they're all key words in the Masonic vocabulary, including third degree which you just mentioned,' he smiled once more before continuing.

'Seems odd you brought them up in conversation.'

'Pure coincidence – honest,' answered Steve truthfully.

'OK. I actually believe you – and your handshake confirmed it, but I had to check it out... You see Steve I've been investigating certain, shall we say rogue members of the Masons who are using the organisation to carry out various clandestine serious criminal activities, including amongst other things people trafficking for the sex trade – especially children.'

Steve was taken aback by his candour, but at last he thought someone was taking him seriously.

Winston turned and nodded to the bearded, uniformed PC who had been standing by the door. The PC exited the room then returned with a familiar-looking folder and a small, clear evidence bag.

He handed both items to Winston who put the folder on the table and opened the bag. Winston took out a small grey plastic rectangle and handed it to Steve.

'Do you know what this is Steve?' He asked.

Steve studied it intently. He screwed up his eyes in recognition and astonishment.

'Uh, it looks like the microchip I removed from Eva,' he answered quietly. 'Where did you get it?'

'That bus that was held up – the one where two masked gunmen got on – witnesses said they were looking for something... or someone,' he paused before proceeding.

'Well when a bus gets held up by masked gunmen in the centre of a city, especially in these troubled times, we, the NCA, get involved. My officers went over the bus with a fine-toothed comb and guess what we found in the used ticket bin? Yep, that little thing.' He pointed to the microchip in Steve's hand.

'So when I got the call from Simon I looked into what had been happening down here and when one of my colleagues mentioned the chip... Well I couldn't get here fast enough, so it looks like your crazy tale about chipped sex slaves and forced labour camps might just have a ring of truth about it.'

The sigh of relief that came from deep inside Steve was palpable.

'Take a closer look, Steve.'

Winston handed Steve a small magnifying glass that he'd taken out of his pocket. Steve took the glass and studied the chip. He had only seen it briefly previously and hadn't had time to take in the detail.

His eyes focused on a symbol etched into one side of the chip.

'It looks like a triangle with something at the top of it,' said Steve.

'Or a pyramid with an eye in it,' suggested Winston.

Steve felt his heart race. He looked up at the detective.

'The all-seeing eye of the Masons,' he finally said.

'On a GPS tracking device no less,' said Winston, 'appropriate don't you think? Here... how about this?'

Winston pushed an A4 sheet of paper across the table towards Steve. Printed on the sheet was the garish blue logo of Solutio that was becoming ever more omnipresent across the British landscape.

'Have a look at Solutio's branding – notice anything odd about it?'

'Hmmm, the ubiquitous and all too common Helvetica typeface – overly condensed and with piss poor kerning, but apart from that what about it?'

Winston raised an eyebrow. 'You what?'

'Nothing, I'm a... sorry, I used to be a graphic designer,' said Steve as an excuse for his pedantic behaviour.

'Take a look at the dot above the "i",' said Winston.

Steve had seen the logo many times in the past but thought nothing of it – apart from it being a particular poor example of typographic design that is.

'It's a triangle,' said Steve matter-of-factly.

‘And what’s another name for a triangle,’ asked Winston.

‘A pyramid,’ replied Steve with a knowing nod.

Chapter Eighteen

'OK let's talk about Eva,' said Fraser Winston after the PC returned to the room with a tray of tea and biscuits.

It seemed that Eva, the girl whose disappearance was the reason that Steve Allen was in custody, had been forgotten in the conversation.

'You say she has Serbian heritage and claims to have come from Kosovo four years ago with her mother?'

'That's right,' replied Steve, 'when she was fifteen. Her father had died of a heart attack and she and her mother had to get out because of certain problems, but she didn't tell me what the problems were. Her mother then obtained fake Italian passports and visas – in the name of...'

Steve hesitated as he tried to recall the name that Eva had mentioned she'd been given.

'Isabella something,' he offered with a shrug.

'She said someone in the Albanian mafia had arranged the passports and for them to get work here in the UK. As I said, she ended up working at Chicken City. Her mother also works for them but at the Electronics plant in Birmingham. Eva had been visiting her when I first picked her up. But you probably won't find records of the two of them anywhere – Solutio have confiscated their passports, it's like they don't exist.'

Winston looked up from Steve and nodded towards the bearded PC who turned and exited the room.

'Oh, they exist alright – I got the Border Force to check through their records from four years back and yep they show that they entered the country...'

He referred to his notes just as the PC re-entered the room. He handed two printouts to Winston, who took them without looking up.

'… in the March, in fact it was one of the last flights out of Pristina before the lockdown. It was just the two of them – Isabella Bettini and her mother, Giovanna.'

Steve nodded in recognition of the names.

'But as you rightly said, in reality Irena Petrovic, aged fifty-two and her daughter Evalina…'

He studied the printouts once more and exhaled deeply.

'… aged twelve.'

He stared at a horrified Steve and awaited his response. The blood visibly drained from Steve's face.

'Wait, what? No, no that can't be. She, she told me she was nineteen, nearly twenty – that only makes her…'

'Sixteen – just.' Winston finished Steve's sentence for him. Steve felt nauseous. Bile rose from his stomach and burnt the back of his throat.

'Steve, I have to ask. Have you been having sexual relations with Eva?'

Steve bit his lip and shook his head.

'No,' he answered. *But I came fucking close… literally.*

Steve studied his hands – they were shaking violently. Winston continued.

'OK, OK – well we'll move on for now. Whether she and her mother came here of their own volition or whether in fact they were trafficked we don't know. But whatever, it looks pretty evident that she's been working as a sex worker, no doubt under duress, and there's some sort of paedophile ring going on within Solutio, no doubt run by an Albanian OCG – then, of course, there's this other runaway you mentioned…'

He hesitated and referred to his notes once more.

'Lee Preston, who you said Eva identified as also being at the plant in Avonmouth… He's what?

Fourteen? All in all, it's a right can of worms you've uncovered.' He paused.

'How do you know this Lee Preston?' He took his eyes off his notes and studied Steve.

'I um, I don't... I know his father, Tony Preston. I work for him.'

'Bit of a coincidence?'

Steve shrugged once more and nodded in agreement.

'S'pose,' he muttered.

'Thinks of himself as a bit of a hard nut doesn't he?' He didn't wait for Steve to respond.

'Let's see,' Winston referred to his notes again.

'Been inside for ABH, quite a few arrests for football violence... known to deal in drugs. What else? Oh yeah, looks like he was involved with the EDL when they were active. Been filmed by our boys at some anti BLM marches a few years back. Another coincidence, Steve?'

'Uh, what do you mean – coincidence?' Steve replied, feeling uneasy with the direction the questioning was going.

'Oh, I don't know – birds of a feather and all that...' He studied Steve intently. His unblinking stare unnerved Steve.

'Football aggro, drugs, mixing it with the far right – sound familiar?'

'I don't like what you're implying,' replied Steve angrily, for once being careful with his words.

Winston shrugged. 'Not implying anything...what's up, have I touched a nerve?'

The younger Steve Allen would have reacted differently, but the older one had learnt his lesson. He was not going to react and take the bait.

'It was a long time ago,' he replied calmly.

'What was?'

'You know exactly what I'm talking about and I'm not going to play your mind games... I don't know where you're going with this, so just move on… like I have.'

Winston's stare remained fixed on Steve, his lips tightened like a taut rope. Steve reciprocated with an unblinking glower of his own.

Simon Edwards had witnessed the look on Steve Allen's face previously, just before he'd punched him in the mouth. Edwards took a step forward but he stopped as a grin broke out across Winston's face revealing his bright gold tooth.

'Good answer,' said Winston, his smile growing ever wider. 'It's all right Steve, I'm pulling your pisser.'

Steve – and Simon Edwards exhaled deeply in relief.

'Tell me, is Preston in the Masons?' asked Winston.

'Not that I know of… Look, what's all this about? Preston might be a bit of a wrong 'un but he's not involved in the Masons or what's going on in Chicken City for fuck's sake – I thought you were investigating the disappearance of Eva and Preston's son? Preston's not mixed up with any of this.'

'Probably not, but you know how it is, got to explore all avenues.'

'What, like the Masons? Are they mixed up in all this shit or not?'

'Dunno,' replied Winston truthfully. 'Criminals have long used legit organisations and companies to mask their activities. The fact that Masonic symbolism keeps cropping up in this investigation is not implying that the Masons themselves are involved – far from it. But some of those involved could just be using the networking aspects of it to mask their criminal acts. Which brings me on to this.'

He shuffled through the pile of paperwork on the desk and picked up the folder – the folder that Steve was more than familiar with. He cursed under his breath for leaving it out when he'd been searching for Edwards' business card.

'What's this?' Winston asked bluntly as he waved Kirsty's folder under Steve's nose.

'Where did you get that from?' asked Steve.

'In case you've forgotten, I'm asking the questions. But seeing as you're asking – your apartment... interesting reading.'

He opened it, flicked through and casually looked at random pages.

'Tell me, what is a sixty-something trade plater doing in possession of a detailed police file that lists some of Britain's top criminals and their activities?'

Winston looked up from the folder and fixed a stare on Steve who returned the stare with a shrug. The detective referred to the folder once more.

'Hmmm – there's a character in here who, from what I hear, you've crossed swords with in the past.' He gave a sideways glance to Simon Edwards who was busy studying a crack in the ceiling.

'Vernon 'Venom' Lewis, eh? A nasty piece of work, now thankfully locked up, due in no small part to your good self I believe.' He raised his eyes from the folder and gave Steve a sly wink before continuing.

'Guess what?' asked Winston, mischievously.

'Don't tell me – Lewis was a Mason,' replied Steve wearily.

'Bingo! But then you knew that didn't you Steve?'

Steve didn't answer, but he did – he'd read it in the very folder that Winston was now holding.

'And how about this one at the back, Ewart "Earl" Samson – what was he then Steve, an afterthought?'

He studied Steve again, awaiting a response. Steve remembered that Earl Samson wasn't in the folder when Kirsty had originally given it to him. He himself had added the photo of his nemesis, after he too, had been imprisoned.

'And there's two big red crosses over both of their photos. What's that about?'

Steve remained silent. He had no response to give to the questioning. Winston referred to the folder once more.

'Hmmm, let's have a look at some of the others, eh? These three look interesting… Ronald Terence McGuire, Paul 'Goldie' Godden and uh… Besin Marishta aka 'The Tiny One.'

Steve feigned disinterest but he was aware of all three – McGuire for his long-time involvement in gun-running that went back to his involvement with Loyalist paramilitaries in Ulster; Godden for his alleged participation in armed robberies and kidnapping dating back to the Seventies and Marishta for heading up an Albanian Organised Crime Group, an OCG whose chief interests were drug importation and distribution as well as people trafficking throughout Europe and the UK for the last two decades. But as with all of the men who found themselves listed in Kirsty's notorious file – there was not so much as a conviction for a traffic offence between them.

'What about them?' asked Steve, genuinely intrigued as to why Winston had picked three random names out of the folder that contained the cesspit of Britain's 'most wanted', but also most elusive, criminals.

'I was just wondering why their photos had been circled and this…' Winston pointed to a Cyrillic word with two exclamation marks after it, 'had been scrawled across their faces?'

Steve screwed up his eyes, genuinely intrigued. He had never met or heard of the three villains – apart from seeing their names in Kirsty's infamous folder – their paths had never crossed.

He shrugged.

'No idea. What does it mean?'

'Apparently it's Serbian… for bastards.'

Shit! Eva must have found the folder. She must know them.

'Well?'

'I can only presume Eva found the folder, recognised them and did it,' responded Steve, nonchalantly.

'Sure? Sure you didn't discuss it with her – were these three next on the hit list Steve?'

'Hit list? There's no fucking hit list. It was just something that…' he trailed off realising he had no excuse.

'If it looks like a duck, waddles like a duck and quacks like a duck…' said Winston.

The room fell silent – apart from the steady munching of a digestive by the PC the only other sound was that of the fluorescent lighting gently buzzing above their heads.

'Take a look at their involvements Steve. Who or what they are connected to.'

Steve took the folder and quickly read through the details that Kirsty had supplied with their photos – activities, both legal and illegal, were listed as were family details and known associates.

He knew it virtually off by heart, having read and re-read the details many times over the past couple of years. Sporting associations, political affiliations and charitable organisations – all meticulously researched and detailed by his former lover. Then he spotted it, first on Ronald McGuire's then Paul Godden's. He flicked through the pages and finally checked Besin Marishta – there it was plain to see. All three of them, prominent members of Masonic lodges – and in Marishta's case, the founding member of the first Masonic lodge in Kosovo.

'Masons,' said Steve, in a barely audible whisper.

Winston studied Steve who was rubbing his forehead in a vain attempt to dissipate the huge migraine that was brewing.

The near silence returned – the PC had at last finished his digestives and was busying tidying himself by flicking crumbs out of his beard.

Winston glanced at his Rolex.

'OK, I think we've heard enough to realise you're not directly involved in any of this. It's getting late so let's call it a day.'

He pushed back his chair and straightened up. 'You're free to go,' he said to Steve.

Steve let out a sigh of relief.

But it was only temporary.

'Uh, unfortunately there's something else,' he said.

He reached down into his sock with his right hand, causing the PC to momentarily take a step forward.

Steve revealed a small black rectangle of plastic with a metal tab on it – Eva's memory stick. He handed it to Winston.

'You might want to sit back down and take a look at this,' he said with a resigned sigh.

Chapter Nineteen

Fraser Winston, along with Simon Edwards and Steve, viewed Eva's video on a laptop in total silence.

It was evident to Steve that footage of a Member of Parliament having sex with an underage girl would prove to be as unpalatable to the British public as it was to him and if that MP happened to be someone as prominent as the perceived golden boy of the right, Neil Etchington, head of the Solutio group, then that news could rock British – if not world – politics to its very foundations.

Before Eva had disappeared that morning, she still hadn't mentioned the video to Steve, neither had Steve mentioned it to Eva for that matter.

He assumed that she'd wanted him to find it but he didn't know why she'd filmed it – presumably on her iPhone – or what she planned to do with it. But what was evident from the footage was that it wasn't a one-off. Etchington called Eva by her first name throughout and at one stage he even mentioned that he'd loved her from the first moment he'd set eyes upon her back in Kosovo.

A decade or so earlier he'd viewed similar footage of his lover Kirsty performing fellatio on Edwards, he glanced at the ex-cop wondering if he too was recalling the same video. He'd felt repulsed and disgusted then but this time he'd been shocked to the core when he first viewed footage of Eva and Etchington. The quality wasn't great but the ever-grinning Etchington could clearly be seen, as could the grimacing and tearful Eva. A date stamp from over a year ago when Eva would have been just fifteen was also visible, and at one stage another male joined them. He was large, imposing and, from his accent, Steve surmised of Balkan origin.

He finally turned and for a split second he faced the camera. Winston paused the video – Steve hadn't realised it when he'd first viewed it but he now recognised him from the photos in Kirsty's folder – it was Besin Marishta.

It was not easy viewing for Steve – or for the other two – and Steve could not watch it through to the end, he turned his head away and buried his head in his hands until Winston had finally agreed he'd also seen enough. Steve could see the anger and the revulsion in his eyes.

'I'm going to make these scumbags rot in hell,' he said as he slammed down the lid of the laptop.

* * *

'So, when are you going to raid Chicken City?' asked Steve, after the three of them had taken a break and gathered their thoughts.

Steve had presumed, incorrectly, that after Winston had viewed the footage, raids on Solutio's premises and mass arrests would be imminent – but he was wrong.

'That's between me and my superiors,' answered Winston curtly. 'I'm not at liberty to discuss it with a member of the public.'

'Don't tell me,' said Steve angrily, 'you need to review the situation – not in the public interest and all that?'

'Sorry Steve, but it's not as straightforward as just getting into my motor and heading down there with a shitload of officers and kicking the door in… this is obviously a very delicate situation.'

'Very delicate? For fuck's sake an underage girl has been trafficked to the UK and kept as a sex slave, she has been – and still is – being abused by a Member of Parliament and you're talking like you've just arrested a nun for shoplifting... Look what happened at Rotherham!' Steve protested. 'The abuse of those kids went on for years while the law and the authorities stood back and did fuck all!'

'This ain't no Rotherham Steve,' replied Winston angrily.

'No? Well it fucking looks like it to me.'

'This is way bigger than Rotherham. We've got to tread very carefully.'

'Yeah, and we know why you did what you did in Rotherham... and Oldham... and here in Bristol for that matter, don't we?'

Winston looked him in the eye.

'Don't go there Steve. Don't go involving race – or religion for that matter in this, it just won't wash. And anyway, I thought you'd said you'd moved on.'

'You fucking what?'

'Earlier... you said you'd moved on – from being a racist, I presume? Don't sound like it to me, all the old prejudices resurfacing are they? You know what they say about leopards and their spots.'

Steve jumped up from his chair, his fists clenched.

'Steve don't!' yelled Edwards, as he moved between the two of them.

'Don't you ever fucking accuse me of being a racist!' shouted Steve as Edwards placed his hand on his shoulder and motioned for him to sit back down.

Winston held up his hands in apology.

'OK, OK, chill. I was just making an observation,' he quickly pleaded, realising he'd made an error of judgement.

Even he had to admit that Steve had a point. The fear of adding fuel to the flames of Britain's incendiary racial and religious tensions had undoubtedly played a part in the child abuse scandals of recent years.

Steve exhaled deeply, regained his composure and sat back down.

'Well if race isn't an issue here, then what's the problem? I would've thought the authorities and the mainstream media would love to see the police smash a paedophile ring that *isn't* ethnically or racially motivated and what's more involves a prominent far right-wing MP – wouldn't you?'

Now it was time for Winston to bite his tongue and choose his words carefully. He decided that things were best left unsaid, unlike Steve who continued with his tirade.

'Y'know it would look great for race relations wouldn't it? Police smash white, right-wing middle-class paedo ring. The civil liberty groups will be jumping for joy – would make a change from all those headlines about Muslim grooming gangs wouldn't it?'

Like many occasions in the past Steve had let his emotions run away with him. It brought back memories of drunken Friday nights in the Moon with his mates, where they put the world to right and unhealthy prejudices reared their ugly heads above the parapets.

'You're forgetting something,' said Winston.

'What's that?' queried Steve.

'It looks like all this is run by Albanians.'

'Oh well that will really fuck around with the Home Office crime statistics won't it?' responded Steve sarcastically.

He shook his head in bewilderment, knowing there was no more to be said. He pushed back his chair, stood up and held out his hands in a *'you finished?'* gesture. All three of them looked at each other in silence.

'I've had enough. I need to get out of here,' Steve finally said.

'Uh Steve, you're not going to do anything stupid are you?' asked Simon Edwards, concern etched on his face.

'Stupid? Like what – get me mates together and go down the 'mouth and give someone a kicking?'

'You know what I mean,' answered Edwards.

'Just let us, I mean, G3 Winston handle this OK? We don't want you and your mates taking the law into your own hands again do we? Because we know what happened last time, eh?'

Steve stared at Edwards angrily.

'What, you mean like last time when somehow we managed to get a load of hard-core criminals locked up while the law of the land sat on their fat arses and did fuck all?' he answered bitterly.

'That's not what I meant and you know it,' replied Edwards.

'Whatever,' replied Steve wearily. He had grown tired of the argument. He made a point of looking at the clock on the wall.

'Look, do you mind if I go now, only I've got to see to Derrick.'

Winston had also tired of the proceedings, he too was eager to change the subject. He frowned and eyed up Steve curiously.

'Who's Derrick? I thought you lived alone?' he asked.

'I do. Sorry, it's my uh… cat.'

Winston looked puzzled.

'Derrick – odd name for a cat?'

Steve squirmed. He had an uneasy feeling how this conversation was going to end.

'Um yeah, he's named after Derrick Morgan, he's a…'

'Yes Steve, I know who Derrick Morgan is,' answered Winston wearily.

'How could I forget, Derrick is my middle name. Thank you, dear father.' He raised his eyes skywards – even though his father lived in a bungalow in Staines, Middlesex.

On his own admission Steve was a music Nazi, believing that his own taste in music was superior to anyone else's. He tried not to, but he often judged people by their musical tastes.

Ridiculously he reasoned that if they aligned with his own it often meant he could trust them, while if their choice in music happened to be different from his then he thought of them as inferior – it was just his own arrogant way.

He'd tried to be a bit more reasonable over the years and see other people's point of view – he was even prepared to listen to their argument in an unbiased way, but he would then agree to himself that in the end, he'd been right all along.

'You know who Derrick Morgan is?' Steve's pulse quickened.

'Are you a fan?' he asked like an excited teenager.

'You must be joking,' replied Winston mockingly, 'but my old man is. Used to play that *Seven Letters* and *Johnny Pram Pram* all the time. Drove me mad.'

He shook his head in recollection of his dad's music collection and many a Sunday afternoon listening to the sound of scratchy rocksteady 45's emanating from his ancient, huge gramophone.

'Oh,' said Steve dejectedly, 'it's just that I thought you might like…' he tailed off, realising his tongue was running away with him.

'What? Like ska and reggae? *Cos I is black?*' replied Winston sarcastically.

'No, I um…' Steve squirmed. Winston sensed his embarrassment. He had joshed with Steve enough.

'So, go on then, why did you name him after Derrick Morgan?'

'Uh, cos he's...' the words stuck in Steve's throat, 'uh black and nearly blind,' he replied reluctantly.

Winston snorted a laugh of sorts then a sly grin crossed his face.

'Well that's a relief, I thought you were going to say it's because he wears a pork pie hat.'

Steve sighed heavily and returned his grin.

At that moment he decided he quite liked Fraser Winston and that he was indeed someone he could trust, apart from the fact that he had very nearly accused him of being a racist.

'So, you don't like ska or reggae. What is it then? Don't tell me, I bet you're into drum and bass?'

Steve was eager to talk about his favourite subject – and it made a welcome relief from the horrors of Chicken City and the plight of Eva.

Winston didn't reply. He stared at Steve blankly.

Steve continued. 'Funk? R&B? I know... Dubstep.'

Winston shook his head and sighed.

'Oh, I get it. Being a bit stereotypical aren't we?' he answered.

'Eh?' replied Steve, furrowing his brow.

'If you're black it automatically means you like black music?'

'Uh, sorry, no, no I uh, I didn't mean it like that,' stammered Steve.

'I'm sure you didn't Steve... OK, so how come you're a fan of obscure West Indian music from the Sixties?'

Steve shrugged.

'Dunno, always have been, ever since my...' Steve hesitated knowing full well what response he would get as soon as he uttered the dreaded, almost taboo word.

'Ever since my uh... skinhead days.'

Winston raised an eyebrow.

'Skin-*head* eh?' He said it very deliberately, as if it was two separate words.

Steve could hear the accusatory tone in Winston's voice, but he wasn't going to rise to it, he remained silent. Winston sensed Steve's unease. He likewise thought it best not to pursue it, but the devilment in him couldn't resist...

'And how about you then Steve – these musical tastes of yours. What are you trying to do, overcompensate for past... *indiscretions*?'

It wasn't the first time the accusation had been levelled at Steve. It infuriated and annoyed him. Yeah OK... *maybe.*

'No!' he yelled angrily, 'and anyway – who's resorting to stereotypes now?'

Winston raised his hands in submission and smiled broadly.

'I'm winding you up. It's not a problem.'

But it could be.

'Coldplay.'

'You what?'

'I'm a big fan of Coldplay,' said Winston bluntly.

'You've got to be fucking joking,' replied Steve. With that his shoulders slumped and a slough of despondency once again engulfed him.

Chapter Twenty

Steve studied his dishevelled apartment. Dark, unsightly fingerprint powder patches covered the walls, doors and furniture.

The bloodstained rug and the towel he'd used to mop up after he'd taken out the microchip from Eva's arm had been removed, whilst various items including photos, books and Steve's precious music collection had been examined and, much to his annoyance, put back in their incorrect alphabetical order.

The door of his apartment had been destroyed and a temporary plain hardwood one installed in its place, whilst the locks had been damaged and replaced with inferior substitutes. The blood, of which there had been a great deal, was by and large now restricted to drops and splashes on the laminate flooring. He studied them and could only wonder what had become of her. He feared the worst.

He'd been released after it had become quite evident that his only 'crime' was that of harbouring a runaway teenage girl – and the fact that she had run away from what was almost certainly an industrial-scale illegal brothel of some sorts only served to confirm his innocence.

The thousands of images of child abuse and the photos of a trussed-up Eva that had been found on his laptop were proved to have been uploaded at precisely 11.08 am that day, roughly the same time that he'd arrived in Barking in London.

The salesman had already supplied an alibi for him and if that wasn't enough, the footage of him refuelling the Jag from the Hammersmith petrol station CCTV an hour or so later proved beyond doubt that he couldn't possibly have been in Bristol when Eva was seized – for once he thanked the bastard salesman and his brown pointy fucking shoes.

Fraser Winston had checked the station's log and, as expected, there had been no record of DS Thompson and DC Bishop making an official visit to Steve's apartment on the Saturday evening, which in Steve's eyes meant one thing – that they were undoubtedly mixed up in the day's events and somehow involved with Solutio. But to the powers that be it meant absolutely nothing at all.

Winston had agreed to keep an eye on the two of them but he thought it could be detrimental to the investigation at this point if they pulled them in for questioning. In hindsight Steve realised he had a point.

* * *

He'd managed to mop up most of what remained of the blood and he'd removed nearly all of the fingerprint powder stains whilst a final scan around revealed a photo of his mother and father enjoying the sun in Torquay had been disturbed. It wasn't quite horizontal on the wall – *not on the level,* he thought to himself.

He was busy straightening the photo when an unfamiliar voice from behind stopped him in his tracks.

'Steve… Steve Allen?'

A tall, blonde-haired female with impossibly high cheekbones and piercing green eyes stood in his doorway. Steve guessed she was in her mid-fifties but she could easily have passed for being ten years younger. The temporary door had not shut properly and it yawed open as soon as she'd pushed against it.

'Yes,' he replied, 'who are you?' But he was pretty certain he already knew the answer.

Irena Petrovic slipped off her navy-blue Puffa jacket before she collapsed in a heap on the sofa. The oversized jacket did nothing for her figure – neither did the baggy sweatshirt and nondescript jeans she was wearing.

She dumped a backpack and a huge Versace holdall – that initially screamed 'fake' to Steve – on the floor. She looked tired and puffy-eyed and the weight of the world sat uncomfortably on her deflated shoulders.

Steve handed Irena a steaming mug of coffee. She cupped it in both hands in exactly the same way as her daughter had. He couldn't help but study her wrists. Noticing they were free of tattoos, he wondered if, like her daughter, Irena had also been chipped.

What he did notice was a rather large, expensive-looking watch on her left wrist. It looked like a genuine Gucci and was at odds with her downmarket, dowdy attire.

A waft of expensive smelling perfume also lingered in the air – there was something incongruous about her that both intrigued and unnerved Steve.

'Irene's my mother's name,' said Steve lamely. Irena responded with a false smile and nothing much else.

'So, how do you know about me?' he continued as he eased himself into his La-Z-Boy, directly opposite Irena.

She coughed and cleared her throat.

'I've been talking to Eva – on her mobile – since you gave her that lift last week. She sent me your address.'

He'd wondered how she'd found him.

'She said you were a good man and that she liked you…' she smiled awkwardly.

'She told me you reminded her of Bruce Willis… I uh, must admit I thought you would be younger,' she said with a hint of disappointment in her voice.

Her accent was stronger than Eva's but her English was still good, he had not misunderstood her.

'Uh, sorry, but we um... we weren't, we aren't together. It's nothing like that,' he squirmed in his seat and felt himself redden.

'Oh, sorry, I didn't mean it like that. No, she said you weren't. She said that's what she liked about you, you didn't try to... how you say... take advantage of her like so many men have.'

She hesitated. Steve could tell this was difficult for her.

'She's very vulnerable, Mr Allen, she has had a very tough life.'

'Please call me Steve... I know, she told me, told me about her upbringing in Kosovo and what her life was like in Chick... the food processing plant.'

He stopped abruptly.

It suddenly occurred to him that perhaps Irena didn't quite know everything about her daughter.

'Don't worry. I know exactly what's been happening at... Chicken City as you call it. I, uh, I'm partly responsible.'

She put her mug down on the small table in front of her and wiped a tear from her eye.

'It was after we arrived from Kosovo, I, I had to do a deal with those...' she hesitated once more and shook her head.

'I had to do a deal with certain people to get us out. If we had stayed... well I don't know what would have happened. We came here to the land of honey and milk as you people call it and what happens... my daughter ends up as a sex slave!'

She finally succumbed and broke down, the tears flowed and she shook uncontrollably.

Steve handed her a tissue, she took it and momentarily held his hand. He thought about attempting to give her a hug but she made up his mind for him as she leant over and embraced him in her arms.

Steve awkwardly patted her back and mumbled something in an attempt to soothe her, but even he didn't know exactly what it was he said.

'Milk and honey,' he muttered, 'it's the land of milk and honey.'

Sometimes he hated himself for being such a pedant.

'Whatever,' she sighed as she dabbed her eyes and exhaled heavily. She gathered herself and gently pulled away from him.

'But, she's OK now yes? So… where is she? Where is Eva?'

Steve had assumed that Irena knew Eva had been abducted and that was why she was here in his apartment. It was only now that he realised she was unaware of her daughter's situation. She looked pleadingly into his eyes, searching for an answer.

'Eva, she's here with you? Just gone out to the shops yes?'

What at this time of night?

Steve slowly shook his head.

'No, she was… I'm sorry, but she's gone, it looks like she's back in Chicken City.'

Irena slumped back into the chair.

'But, but I thought she was here with you. She told me how happy she was – why did she go back?'

Steve thought about lying, thought it might be easier for Irena if she thought Eva had gone of her own accord, but he decided against it.

'Look, I don't know how or why it happened but it appears that someone has taken her back there, but…' he paused. Her tear-stained eyes studied his.

'But what?'

'But… I promise, I'll get her back,' vowed Steve.

But how? he wondered to himself.

Chapter Twenty-One

Steve looked at his watch – it was nearly nine. He'd slept like the dead only to be woken by his mobile blasting out *Pressure Drop*.

The screen showed it was an incoming call from Tony Preston – he had been expecting it.

'You fucking Gashead bastard!'

Steve had been agonising over phoning him to let him know of the whereabouts of his son, but Winston had advised him against it. Steve surmised by Preston's manner he now knew.

'Tony, I've been wanting to call you but the law told me not to.'

'Fuck the law and fuck you Allen! Don't you bullshit me. Not only did you dump that Jag outside your gaff without delivering it but you also knew about my boy and said fuck all! Typical fucking Rovers' cunt – how long have you fucking known?' he shouted down the phone.

'Couple days that's all – the law said to leave it in their hands and they would sort it.' He knew Preston wouldn't buy it one bit.

'Since when have the law sorted anything for me? Bastards just been round our house, told me about this place he's been spotted at but for whatever reason they ain't going to raid it yet – said they need more evidence, the cunts. They let it slip that it was you who told 'em. How come you fucking know eh?'

'It's a long story...'

'Yeah, well, I don't want to hear it, I just want to know where he is, so spill the beans arsehole – where is he?'

'I don't think...'

'I don't give a fuck what you think! Where the fuck is he? C'mon, I'm fucking waiting.'

'Tony don't do anything stupid. You can't just go down there and knock on the door and think they'll hand him over, it's like a fucking prison.'

'What's like a prison?'

Steve was fighting a losing battle. He let out a resigned sigh.

'Chicken City – same place I dropped that girl off... that's how I found out Lee was there, she told me. So now you know, you can tell me why *you* fucking grassed me up to the Old Bill.'

'What you on about? I ain't no fucking grass... and what's so special about this girl anyhow, they just said she was some runaway MIRAS?'

'You don't need to know and anyway who's fucking bullshitting now, eh? They came round here looking for her, said you told them I was the one driving the Kuga.'

'Yeah well they bunged me a hundred,' answered Preston matter-of-factly.

'Who did?' asked Steve, knowing full well that it had been Thompson and Bishop who'd paid him a visit and given him a backhander and not Winston from the NCA.

'The coppers who asked me about you dropping that bird off down the 'mouth – an old geezer with dandruff and his no-neck lump of a sidekick. Funny thing is, it weren't the same coppers who then visited me later and told me about Lee, that was some black geezer in a flash suit.'

It just confirmed to Steve that Thompson and Bishop were corrupt and working for whoever was running Chicken City, presumably Besin Marishta, and that Winston also knew. What Steve didn't know was what the enraged and volatile Tony Preston was going to do next.

'Look Tony, this place, this Chicken City – it's not just a prison, it's a fortress. You'll need a fucking army to get into it.'

'I can get a fucking army,' replied Preston ominously as he ended the call.

Steve put his mobile down then sniffed the air. He could smell fried bacon and eggs. It had been a long time since anyone had cooked breakfast for him – in truth he'd missed it.

He entered the small kitchen area and couldn't help but notice Irena had changed from her rather frumpy outfit from the evening before to a more flattering, figure-hugging sweater and matching short skirt. He quickly regretted only chucking on his old bathrobe.

Her freshly washed hair was piled high on the top of her head and held in place with a butterfly clip that exaggerated her already impressive height.

She resembled a statuesque, Balkan version of Amanda Holden, but with tits, no bottox and hopefully without the irritating laugh.

Her overpowering perfume almost masked the smell of the cooking. She turned quickly and caught Steve admiring her legs, causing her to smile coyly.

'Oh, hi Steve. I hope you don't mind. I couldn't sleep – this is what you have for breakfast, no?'

Steve quickly averted his gaze. 'Well no, not recently to be honest.'

'Oh sorry, you don't want? I was just trying to help.'

'No, it's fine. It's just I'm not used to it that's all,' he smiled weakly. Judging by the look of the cremated bacon Irena wasn't used to it either.

Steve filled the kettle for his morning tea while Irena returned to her task of incinerating the bacon.

'Thank you for letting me stay last night, you have been so kind.'

'That's OK, I'm just sorry Eva wasn't here for you.'

She nodded as if she understood the situation but the more they'd spoken the previous evening the more it was evident that she didn't.

Neither did Steve for that matter.

The two of them had stayed up until the small hours talking about Eva but Steve sensed that Irena was skirting some of the issues.

Certain things tied up but others just seemed to unravel like a ball of string. Steve had asked about her two other children and their home village of Bajgora in Kosovo. According to Eva it had sounded idyllic but Irena had merely shrugged and changed the subject.

She'd half-heartedly attempted to leave, saying she would book into a local hotel but Steve insisted she stayed and that she could sleep in the room that Eva had occupied.

It was late, Steve had argued and what's more she probably wouldn't be able to find anywhere suitable. Not that he had an ulterior motive, he tried to convince himself.

When Irena pushed open the door to the bedroom she froze. Seeing Eva's clothes and belongings were too much for her – she slowly closed the door behind her and Steve could hear her crying herself to sleep.

* * *

The bacon was burnt beyond recognition and the egg dry and crispy but it still tasted good to Steve, he was reluctant to admit it but it was nice having a woman cook him breakfast for a change.

He tried to convince himself that the fact that Irena was both beautiful and enigmatic had nothing to do with it, but he was only kidding himself.

'So, Steve, you have no wife – or girlfriend?'

'No, I'm divorced.'

Irena's eyes twinkled as she smiled beguilingly.

'Steve, there's something I need to tell you, about Eva. She's not been totally...'

She was interrupted by the sound of *Pressure Drop* emanating from Steve's mobile once more.

He picked it up from the table and studied the screen. It was not a number he recognised.

'Sorry, I just need to take this,' he apologised to Irena.

'Hello? Is that Steven Allen?' asked the vaguely familiar voice.

He listened intently but he couldn't process what he was hearing.

'Sorry... can you repeat that?'

'Dead?... But how?' His voice quivered.

He wandered around the room with the phone clamped to his ear, his face tortured in pain.

He staggered towards a wall, turned and slumped against it, the phone dropped to the floor as he slid down it.

Irena stared at him in open-mouthed horror.

'No!' She screamed.

Chapter Twenty-Two

The sombre, black, hand-made mohair suit beckoned once more.

In recent years it had been promoted from the back of the wardrobe, where it had hung rather dejectedly, to the front, alongside the immaculate classic Prince of Wales check three-piece and the edgy, brash iridescent blue and gold Tonic two-piece he'd had made by Marc Griffith in Soho.

He'd bought the Tonic suit on a whim – a rather expensive whim as it turned out – but the redundancy package and his proceeds from the sale of the house had turned him from a logical, pragmatic, sometimes frugal individual into a *'fuck the consequences, you're only here once'*, born-again skinhead – although to avoid confrontation he would often refer to himself as a 'suedehead' to the ill-informed.

Florsheim Wingtips, Bass and Loake loafers as well as real-deal British-made Solovair Oxblood full-grain eight eyelet boots had also featured in his short-lived spending spree.

Then there were the shirts. Off the peg Brooks Brothers, Ben Shermans, Fred Perrys and Mikkel Rude's vied with one pinstripe stunner he'd had made by Turnbull & Asser of Jermyn Street.

He had worn it just the once, on a disastrous date with a sixty-something leather-clad rock chick from the Forest of Dean, who'd spent the entire evening talking about her love for Jon Bon Jovi and who'd lied about her age and posted a photo of her younger sister on the dating agency website.

His eyes then rested upon the red Baracuta G4 Harrington jacket that Kirsty had bought him. He'd barely worn it since she'd died – the memories of her being too painful for him. He ran his hand around the distinct two-button collar then down the sleeve to the elasticated wristband. He sighed then turned his attention back to the sombre black two-piece.

Irena silently appeared behind Steve as he took his funeral suit out of the wardrobe. She looked over his shoulder at the stylish, colourful mod and skinhead inspired sartorial delights draped playfully on their hangers.

'Wow. Look at these clothes!' she exclaimed, startling Steve in the process.

'Are they yours?' she asked.

'Uh yeah, I uh… don't really wear them much these days,' Steve replied, somewhat embarrassed.

'Why not? They are beautiful – and so colourful. I've never seen clothes like them before.' She edged forward to get a closer look.

'You should wear them sometime.'

She rested her hand on his shoulder as she spoke, causing Steve to flinch involuntarily.

'Oh I dunno, don't really get the chance to,' he answered truthfully.

There was a time when he routinely wore Boss and Paul Smith suits to work and his best skinhead threads out on adrenaline-filled nights with his mates… but not anymore.

He smiled at the thought of him wearing his Tonic suit to work now – he couldn't imagine what his trade plating colleagues would make of it, let alone the residents of Corby or Cold Meece – and anyway it would clash with his high-vis jacket he mused.

'Well you should do. I can imagine you look so handsome in them,' she smiled at Steve.

Steve could feel himself redden once more.

He didn't answer. She then spotted his barely worn Solovair boots and she screwed up her eyes.

'And what are those boots for? They are so polished… but they look a bit – how you say – aggressive?'

Steve felt awkward and uncomfortable. The British subculture of skinhead was not an easy one to explain to some of his less enlightened countrymen, let alone a female ethnic Serb from Kosovo who had only spent four years in England.

'It's from my uh… days as a suedehead.'

'A what – what's a suedehead?' Irena queried.

'They followed on from uh… skinheads. I was a skinhead,' he answered apologetically.

'You were a skinhead? We have them in Kosovo – they are evil and racist, I not like them Steve – they are all Nazis. Are you a Nazi Steve?' She looked at him in horror.

'*No!*' answered Steve angrily.

'I'm not a racist and I'm not a Nazi – that's not what skinheads are about!'

He was exasperated. How often would he have this same argument, how often would he find himself having to explain the skinhead culture to the ignorant and the unenlightened? He'd lost count of the number of days that he had to defend the demonised skinheads in the past.

But today was not going to be one of those days – he had a funeral to attend.

Chapter Twenty-Three

The incessant rain and the low, dark clouds scudding over the horizon did nothing to lighten his mood. He felt cold drops of rainwater rhythmically drip down the back of his neck then run down the length of his spine. Another drop formed on the end of his nose, eventually falling off and adding to the ever-deepening puddle at his feet, which he studied as if he'd never seen rainwater before. Even at this dark time he silently admonished himself for the state of his Bass loafers. He looked around then quickly wiped them on the back of his trousers like a naughty, grubby schoolboy.

He hated funerals. The past few years he had attended far too many. From his old school mate Larry, who'd died from a heroin overdose and who'd very nearly made it to becoming the fifth member of the Big Five ahead of the cursed Mike Cribb, to his great friend and soul brother, Leon Campbell, who had succumbed to lung cancer a decade previously.

Then there was Gerry Fowler, a mate he'd known from the Tote End since the Seventies and who'd suffered in silence with depression and committed suicide by jumping off the Clifton Suspension Bridge one rainy Monday morning. And just six months previously he'd attended the funeral of his wayward old punk mate, Rob Sweet, who like many others, had let drink and drugs get the better of him.

Twelve years earlier he'd even paid his respects to Gary 'Bulldog' Rattigan, his one-time coke dealer who was there on that fateful day when Steve had been shot and Vernon Lewis and Earl Samson had been arrested by Simon Edwards and his team. Rattigan had been shot dead by one of Samson's cronies and to this day Steve was convinced if it hadn't been for Rattigan's actions, he too would've ended up on a cold slab in the morgue alongside him.

Undoubtedly, he would attend many more in the years to come – even more gloom descended and came to rest on his over-burdened shoulders.

Debbie, his ex-wife, stood impassively and reluctantly by his side. She was accompanied by their son Harry, who thankfully was now getting his life together and putting his own drink and drug problems behind him. Steve glanced at the two of them. They both returned awkward but sympathetic smiles that resembled grimaces with little warmth or emotion.

He returned his stare to the deepening puddle.

'Alright mate?'

He raised his eyes once more and saw the large frame of John Burston in front of him. By his side stood the shorter but just as broad Gerwazy 'George' Smolinski, the two of them immaculately turned out in matching dark overcoats, black suits and ties. JB's Crombie looked as sodden as he himself felt, both internally and externally. Steve thought the two of them wouldn't look out of place in a nightclub doorway, he half expected one of them to say '*No trainers*.'

Steve nodded. There was not much to say to his two old friends. They had known each other long enough to speak volumes to one another – without actually saying a word.

JB turned his attention to Steve's ex-wife and his son.

'Debbie, Harry.... Uh, ha, never thought of that before – you OK?'

Debbie's awkward smile returned. She stiffened as JB moved in and kissed her on the cheek causing her face to transform into that of a recently slapped arse.

'Alright Uncle John, Uncle George – keeping well?'

Harry was at last learning social niceties. A year or two earlier and all the two of them would have received would have been an animal-like grunt.

JB nodded and shook the boy's hand vigorously. He then turned his attention back to Steve.

'Good turnout… she is, she was well loved mate,' said JB with genuine sympathy.

Steve nodded again and at last succumbed to the raindrop on his nose, wiping it off with the sleeve of his Gabicci raincoat. The coat kept the rain out but the cold morning air had penetrated it and he eyed up JB's Crombie with just a hint of jealousy.

'I know… she, she wouldn't have liked the fuss though. You know our mum, never one to…' he trailed off as a late arrival caught his eye.

Like the rest of the mourners he had seen the car pull up earlier. He wondered who the owner was of the new, expensive silver SL class Mercedes.

A tall, powerfully built male in his early seventies exited the car. He opened and unfurled a gold-handled umbrella to protect his dark, sombre but very elegant suit.

The stranger wore a black Fedora hat under which thick, dark curly hair – looking like it had been regularly dyed – sprung out and hung down over the collar of a pristine, white shirt.

The dark, dismal day was momentarily illuminated as the wind caught the louche stranger's jacket exposing a bright red silk lining. A gold watch chain nestled in his waistcoat pocket and a small gold-hooped earring adorned his left ear.

The stranger strode purposefully towards Steve.

'Fuck me it's Beau Brummel,' said John Burston under his breath.

'Steven.' The stranger nodded and held out his hand in greeting.

Steve Allen first studied the extended hand and then the face of the stranger who was offering it. His eyes opened wide.

'I thought you were dead,' replied Steve coldly, leaving the hand hanging limply in the cold air.

The stranger withdrew his hand reluctantly and mulled over his response.

'Really Steven, here we are to say goodbye to our dear mother and you're still as disputatious as ever.'

Steve remembered how his brother always tried to outscore him. How he always had to prove his intellect as if it was some pissing up a wall competition.

'What the fuck do you expect?' replied Steve, slightly louder than he'd intended, causing the gathered mourners to desist from their small talk and shoot glances of disapproval at him.

Debbie eyed Steve with an air of disgust, the way she had done on many occasions over the years while Harry stood with his mouth agape, baffled by the events that were unfolding around him.

'What exactly do you mean by that?' asked his brother in hushed tones.

'You know what I mean… Christ, no-one's seen you for nearly fifty years. Fuck's sake you didn't even turn up for Dad's funeral so how do you expect me to react?'

'Very well Steven – you carry on believing that if it makes your petty little narrow mind feel better.'

Steve screwed up his eyes. His brother always liked playing mind games but this time Steve really couldn't fathom him out.

'Why, what are you trying to say?'

'For your information I was at father's funeral. Even if the old bastard did hate me and treat me like I was the spawn of the devil… but unlike you I don't bear grudges so I turned up to pay my respects, unseen by you and your oafish friends of course.' He glanced in the direction of JB and George.

'Oh, I didn't want to cause a scene so I slipped in to the back of the chapel and made sure I left before you came out, but I did catch up with mother.'

'That was good of you, what was that first time since…'

'I visited her more than you realised Steven, at least once a month I drove up from Brighton, sometimes I even stayed the night – and all this time you never knew I was being the dutiful son. Then of course there was the Facetiming, especially during Covid.'

Steve recalled the cheap Solutio laptop he'd discovered in his mother's bedroom when he'd cleared it out a couple of days earlier, he wondered then what the hell she was doing with it. He suddenly felt a wave of guilt engulf him.

'I um, I don't know…'

'What to say? That's a first. You always had an opinion about everything – even if it was often wrong.'

'But I…'

Steve's brother held up the palm of his hand to stop him continuing.

'Oh no need to apologise Steven, I've got used to dealing with prejudice and narrow-mindedness over the years, it would just have been nice if it hadn't come from my own flesh and blood.'

He lowered and shook his umbrella with a flourish, deliberately aiming at JB and George. The two cursed under their breath and stood aside as Steve's brother brushed past, releasing a waft of expensive eau de cologne as he did so.

'Come on my little brother, we need to pay our respects to our mother.'

Kenneth Allen, in the words of his father, was as 'bent as a nine-bob note'. He'd left home after a beating by his father shortly after he came out to his shocked and distraught parents.

Steve, of course, already knew his elder brother's secret – ever since the sordid incident in the public toilets on that hot summer's evening in 1969. Steve was just as upset as his parents – up until that day he had worshipped the very ground he walked on. It had been another five years or so before Kenny told his parents of his secret and Steve hadn't seen his older brother to this day.

Since their father died Steve had noticed birthday and Christmas cards from Kenny proudly displayed on the mantelpiece of their mother's home but when he'd queried her about them, she merely shrugged and changed the subject claiming she didn't know the whereabouts of her eldest son. It was a secret she had taken to her grave.

* * *

'Still not fussy about the company you keep then Steven?' said Kenny as he stared at JB accusingly. It was a rhetorical question – he didn't wait for an answer.

'And you John, still attempting to beat up young queer lads in public lavatories?'

JB studied his pint in silence – even after all these years the guilt of some of his behaviour back in his young skinhead days still haunted him.

'What's up John? You were always the loquacious type, cat got your tongue?'

'It was a long time ago Kenny, we all made mistakes,' JB answered bluntly.

'Mistakes? Is that what it was? ... The only mistake was that I happened to be someone you knew and that I fought back. If I had been a stranger tell me, what would you have done?'

JB didn't respond, the bottom of his pint looked even more interesting.

'I'll tell you shall I? You – and my sweet little brother here – would probably have beaten me senseless, perhaps to within an inch of my life. Then who knows how my life would have turned out? And what would you have done it for? A laugh? To teach me a lesson? To cure me of my homosexuality? Or was it just for your own self-gratification... or, even worse, was it to prove your own masculinity, prove to your mates how hard you were, prove that by beating up homosexuals you couldn't possibly be like them... queer, gay, a poofter? Which when you think about it is ridiculous isn't it? All that homo-erotic violence...'

Steve squirmed.

'What's up, have I touched a nerve Steven, a bit close to home?'

Steve responded with a drop-dead stare. Kenny Allen continued with his tirade.

'Christ if there was ever a fashion that was as queer as a clockwork orange it's got to be the skinhead movement. All that butch behaviour and hanging around with your hard mates, ooh I'm getting all excited just thinking about it... You all thought you were so tough didn't you with your boots and your knuckle-dusters and God knows what else? What did you think that sort of behaviour would achieve, hmmm? Well I'll tell you what it achieved... a big round fuck all. Whether you were out queer- or paki-bashing or fighting amongst yourselves, you just proved yourselves to be what you were, still are – a bunch of Neanderthal losers.

'Look at you – what a depressing group of bitter old men you've become – just like our father, Steven. The apple didn't fall far from the tree in your case that's for sure.'

An awkward silence followed that was finally broken by John Burston.

'I ain't bitter.'

'Oh it speaks – thought you'd lost the power of speech, go on then John, pray enlighten me.'

'Look, I know we did some bad things back then, but I wouldn't have changed it for the world – I had a great time and made some great mates.'

He cast his eye over Steve and George who sat impassively opposite him.

'And anyone who got a slap off us back then was fair game, uh – usually.'

'Fair game? Fair *fucking* game? I was a mixed-up teenager having issues with my sexuality. How the fuck was I fair game?'

'Yeah, well sorry, you were one of the exceptions.'

'Please John don't, your compassion is killing me,' replied Kenny sarcastically as he took another sip of his gin and tonic.

Apart from a Matt Monro song playing reverentially in the background and the muted small talk of the grieving, the pub was calm and respectful. As a wake this was not one of the better ones thought Steve.

Mrs Holloway, the neighbour who had phoned Steve after she'd found his mother slumped dead in her hallway from a heart attack, caught Steve's eye.

'Nice spread,' she mouthed shortly before sinking her dentures into a salmon and cucumber sandwich. Steve smiled weakly and nodded before studying his brother and his mates around the table. He cleared his throat.

'So what have you been up to for these past fifty years – apart from staying in touch with your mother but totally ignoring your brother?' Steve asked acidly.

'Don't expect me to rise to that, but since you ask…' Kenny leant forward and crossed his legs, causing Steve to squirm. He could tell his brother was now in full flow, this could take a long time, he thought.

'Well, I've been living in Brighton since God knows when. Lived in Amsterdam for a bit after father kicked me out – don't know why, just as intolerant there as in the UK back then to be honest.

Anyway, long story short, met a guy in the early eighties, Sam… Sam Shapiro. We lived together until three years ago – until he died.'

Steve looked up and screwed his eyes in faint recognition of the name.

'No, not AIDS, a motorcycle accident, before you ask,' added Kenny.

'We had, well I still have a profitable antique import and export business and a specialist clothing shop. Doing very well thank you – and that's about it. He was my – God I hate the expression – Civil Partner. We were hoping to get married but well, sadly he died so we never got around to it.' Kenny was clearly upset by the memory of it all.

'Uh, sorry to hear that… Sammy Shapiro? Where do I know that name from?' asked Steve.

'When I first met Sam in Amsterdam he was a struggling tattoo artist, this was uh… early Eighties. Of course tattoos weren't as *de rigueur* as they are now, this was the days when only punks, sailors, bikers and criminals possessed them.'

Steve nodded his head knowingly then subconsciously rubbed his ancient 'Big Five' tattoo on his left shoulder with the palm of his right hand. JB and George noticed and the ghost of smirks formed on their faces. They also possessed the same crude, blue-inked tattoos.

'He was a genuine artist, producing freehand masterpieces when others were just getting pathetic Mum and Dad and leaping tigers about their person.'

Steve squirmed even more – he possessed both.

'Then through word of mouth his reputation started growing. Rock musicians, actors, all sorts of celebrities began visiting him and having beautiful freehand works of art done. But then… well AIDS reared its ugly head. The old prejudices came to the surface again and no-one, but no-one wanted a tattoo from a queer, irrespective of how good they were. Sammy became disillusioned, we got into antiques and he never did a tattoo again, well apart from one or two on me of course – you know, just to keep his hand in. Sammy kept producing designs though – I've got loads of his work, shame really, he could've made a fortune.'

'I've heard of him,' said Steve.

'I read an article in *The Guardian* a year or so back. Come to think of it, it might have been when he died? Wasn't he known as Sam from the 'dam?'

Kenny smiled and nodded.

Steve continued. 'They were saying his work was ground breaking and a big influence on today's free-hand artists – isn't there a famous one in Holland...?'

'Jay Freestyle.'

'That's him,' nodded Steve. 'Unbelievable work.'

Kenny downed the remainder of his G&T in one and licked his lips.

'My round I think,' he said as he took a new fifty-pound note out of his monogrammed leather wallet before heading to the bar.

'Well that's a turn up for the books mate,' said JB to Steve as soon as Kenny was out of earshot.

'You're telling me. Must admit at one time I thought he might be dead. It was only when those cards started appearing that I realised he wasn't. All these years he's been visiting Mum and sending her money. Fucking hell what a prick I am. Tell you what, I can still remember that day in the bogs in the park – makes me feel sick.'

'What, that your brother's queer or that we gave him a hiding?' asked JB.

'Gave him a hiding? If I remember correctly it was you who came off worse. Big JB done in by a queer hippy – took you a while to live that down at the youth club... And anyway, are you serious about me feeling sick because I got a poof for a brother? Fuck's sake JB, haven't you moved on? Thought we were over all that behaviour and those narrow-minded attitudes.'

'Yeah, yeah – sorry mate,' said JB.

'And it's gay,' interrupted George.

Steve and JB stared at George with furrowed brows.

'Poofs – they don't like to be called queer – they're gay. Except they can call themselves queer… I think. Bit like blacks calling themselves…'

'Yeah alright George, leave it out,' said Steve as he shook his head. He glanced towards Harry who sat quietly nursing a pint of Thatchers. His son was both enthralled and disgusted by the conversation between his father and his mates – and up until now, his unknown uncle.

'Hold up, he's coming back,' said JB. He awkwardly smiled as Kenny returned with a tray of drinks. Kenny placed them on the table and the others took them eagerly.

'Uh… cheers Ken,' JB raised his pint glass and looked at him quizzically.

'Ken, I hope you don't mind me asking… but what made you turn…'

Before JB had a chance to finish his question, Kenny rounded on him angrily, his face incandescent with rage.

'What made me turn? What, you think it was a choice? Like I woke up one morning and decided to be gay? It doesn't fucking work like that, you're born gay, it's not something you decide to do, like what pair of fucking socks you'll put on. For fuck's sake… just when I was beginning to think you lot had changed – I don't fucking believe it!'

Steve shook his head in shame as he shared his brother's anger. His face demanded an apology from JB.

'Uh, I was going to ask what made you turn from a mod to a hippy,' replied JB sheepishly.

It was now Kenny's turn to be embarrassed.

'Oh, uh sorry… I, uh assumed…'

'That's alright Ken, apology accepted.' There was a faint hint of sarcasm in JB's voice.

George rolled his eyes and smirked.

'Seriously Ken, what made you change? I mean you were an ace face on the mod scene weren't you? Always used to wear the top gear from London, and you had that cracking Lammy didn't you, what was it?'

'SX200. And before that I had an LI Series 2,' replied Kenny wistfully.

'All the whistles and bells – literally. Not to mention more mirrors than an Amsterdam brothel, whiplash aerial, fox tails, air horns – you name it, I had it.'

JB let out a low appreciative whistle and nodded in agreement.

'So, like I said what happened?'

Kenny topped up his glass with tonic then loosened his tie.

'Well, by sixty-six the mod movement was over – in London anyway. You remember I used to go up most weekends, do a bit of shopping in John Stephen's and The Ivy shops… I had loads of mates up there, we used to have good fun, go to blues parties, go to see bands, that kind of thing… but the whole mod thing, you know modernist, stylists, it had somehow lost its kudos, lost its individuality – it had been taken over by the masses in their parkas and desert boots. I guess it had been ruined by its own success. And then of course we were always pushing the boundaries, always looking for something new – that was the real essence of mod. So those boundaries, those borders – well they were there to be crossed, to be broken – so we started experimenting, experimenting with our sexuality, our fashion, oh and drugs, especially the drugs,' he said with a wink as he took another sip of his drink.

Harry's eyes widened, he leant forward not wanting to miss out on any detail. Steve looked at his son and considered asking him to leave, but realised it might be some sort of education for Harry, and for himself for that matter.

'So yeah, we started looking beyond the horizon. We'd always been influenced by America, especially with the Ivy League fashion from New England, but then we started being drawn to California and the early hippy movement – its freedom and its free-spirit attitude, so us more *avante-garde* mods latched on to it. It was exhilarating and exciting… liberating even.'

He paused for effect.

'And then of course, the younger mods, the ones who were drawn to the aggressive side of it, the side that I, and my friends totally abhorred – all that fighting at Margate and Brighton, well that was just barbaric and nothing to do with being a modernist, just something the *Daily Mirror* latched onto and sexed up. Anyway… yes, the younger mods – they veered off towards the harder edge of it and rejected the direction us original mods were heading in. They embraced that aggressive side and exaggerated it – the Fred Perrys, the Ben Shermans – all typical mod clothing as you know, they then became the, what did they call them…?'

'Hard mods,' answered Steve.

His brother screwed up his nose as if there was a bad smell under it.

'Hmmm, yes, the so-say hard mods – an oxymoron if I've ever heard one. They added the boots, the braces and yes, I guess the attitude and became what you lot turned into… fucking skinheads. And us, us more enlightened and educated ones became hippy. Simple really John – even for your tiny mind to grasp.'

JB smiled awkwardly as if he understood.

'But,' Kenny continued, 'funny thing is, I've gone back to my roots. That clothes store I own in Brighton – we sell retro mod and I'm almost embarrassed to say it, skinhead gear. It's going down a storm, making a mint out of it to be honest – selling it to born-again originals as well as new-age mods and skinheads. You boys must come down some time – what is it you oiks say? I can do mates' rates.'

Kenny winked at his nephew. Harry responded with an awkward grin. At last it seemed that they had all come to an understanding, they exchanged uncomfortable glances and sat in silence for a while.

Can't get used to losing you by Andy Williams came to an end. There was a slight pause before *Goodnight Irene* by The Weavers started. The two brothers looked at each other with moist eyes.

JB smiled then raised his glass to the others. 'To Irene Allen,' he said cheerfully.

Kenny made a point of clinking his glass with his young brother.

'To Mum,' they both said in unison, 'we'll see you in our dreams.'

Chapter Twenty-Four

It had been nearly a month since Eva had disappeared from Steve's apartment and Irena had turned up.

Luckily Steve had managed to clear up all traces of blood from the rooms before she'd arrived so she was blissfully unaware of any injuries her daughter had obviously sustained.

The discovery of Eva's mobile under her pillow also slightly eased her mother's fears. At least it explained why she hadn't returned any of her calls since the Monday morning, but equally it made her fear the worst, as like every other teenage girl in the country, Eva wouldn't go anywhere without her precious phone.

Steve had seen an article on the *Bristol Live* news site regarding a visit to Solutio's food processing plant by Neil Etchington – he presumed that this was what Eva had meant by the 'special order' she had to process.

There were photos of the MP with his trademark sickly grin giving the thumbs up whilst surrounded by weary-looking operamini and the grandly titled Chief Executive Officer of the plant – Besin Marishta. Steve felt physically sick.

He made a call to Fraser Winston but it went unanswered.

He then phoned Simon Edwards.

'The NCA are on the case,' said the concerned Welshman.

'They are monitoring the plant and they can categorically state that Eva is safe.'

How they knew, Steve could only guess, but it placated him – for the time being.

'Promise me Steve,' Edwards had pleaded, 'do not get involved. This is bigger than you can imagine.'

Steve wasn't sure exactly how it had happened but Irena had made herself at home, which if he was honest with himself, he was more than happy with.

She'd offered to leave but Steve insisted, a little too hard he conceded, that she should stay. As much as he liked having his own space and no scatter cushions or scented candles cluttering up the place, he missed the company of a female and the incessant chatter about nothing in particular that seemed to be the trait of virtually every woman he'd ever known… but Irena was different, very different.

She was witty, practical and highly intelligent and apart from being a disaster in the culinary department pretty damn near perfect – she also had money, lots of it, it seemed and as much as Steve objected, she was more than willing to pay her way.

The fact that she was an older version of Eva, albeit possessing a few extra pounds, silvery flecks in her hair and one or two wrinkles, was not lost on Steve. He was beginning to fall for her charm – and she knew it. But there was one thing he was absolutely certain of – if she worked on an assembly line manufacturing microchips for mobile phones, his cock was a kipper.

She fussed over Steve, especially after he had returned from his mother's funeral. She comforted and soothed him, brought him tea, sat him down and massaged his tired, aching shoulders. She washed his clothes, did his ironing and cleaned the flat from top to bottom.

On the downside she cooked incessantly – badly admittedly, but on the upside she made him smile, and that was something that a woman hadn't done for Steve for a very long time. She would brush past him and smile seductively which caused his heart to race and his loins to stir and on more than one occasion she appeared from the bathroom with just a small towel wrapped around her svelte body. She would giggle and apologise profusely causing Steve to avert his gaze and mumble apologies of his own in embarrassment.

Their relationship was purely platonic he kept telling himself… but he knew it was only a matter of time, the clock was ticking.

As the weeks went by, they slipped into some sort of normality that resembled cosy domesticity, at times they even forgot about Eva's predicament until one evening Irena opened up a little bit more about their life in Kosovo… and then she dropped the bombshell.

'Steve, I have to tell you something, something about our previous life.'

Steve looked up from scouring the Situations Vacant pages on various websites on his phone. He'd heard nothing from Tony Preston since his '*I can get a fucking army*' phone conversation – he presumed he was no longer employed as a vehicle logistics operative – not that he lost sleep over it.

Irena poured out a glass of Kosovan Stone Castle Pinot Noir wine that she'd picked up in the local Lidl. She handed it to Steve as she sat beside him on the sofa. He took the glass then motioned for her to continue. He took a sip and nodded in approval.

'We didn't live in Bajgora, it's mostly full of Albanians, we lived in Pristina – the capital. My dead husband's family come from Bajgora. His mother, Eva's grandmother still lives there.'

Steve stared at her open-mouthed.

'So, her grandmother hasn't recently died?'

Irena lowered her head, not wishing to make eye contact with Steve.

'No – and there's no aunt or younger brother and sister. I have no other children, I didn't have her until I was forty, that's why Eva is so precious to me. Sorry but she's made it all up. She can be a bit of a what is it … fantasist, I guess it's her escape uh… mechanism?'

She looked at Steve for support before continuing. 'And I haven't been entirely truthful either.'

She raised her head and took a deep breath.

'Although I was only in my twenties, I was a senior lecturer in Electrical and Computer Engineering at the University of Pristina. I took after my father, he was also an expert in the same field while my mother taught advanced mathematics. My husband, Dragan – as Eva truthfully told you, was a Major in the Serbian Army. We had a very comfortable life and although we Serbs were in the minority, we got on okayish with our Albanian neighbours. Of course, all that changed after the war of 1999.' She paused and took a sip of her wine.

'Yes, Eva told me. She said her father had been in the army but he died of a sudden heart attack just before you came to the UK,' said Steve.

'Uh, let me get to that. As you probably know, NATO troops, including a large contingent of British forces, have been involved in peace-keeping duties since then. One of the officers – Neil Etchington – became friendly with my husband.'

'Neil Etchington? The member of the cabinet?' queried Steve as he tried to feign all knowledge of him. He desperately tried to control his emotions, not wanting to give away the fact that he had seen footage of the MP having sex with her daughter.

'Yes, him,' she replied angrily before continuing.

'He had been serving in KFOR and my husband was on a joint committee of Albanians and Serbs who were working on the early stages of what became known as the Normalisation Agreement.'

Steve nodded as if he knew what she was on about. He didn't.

'So, as I was saying, Etchington and my husband worked together – in fact they became friends. And over the years he became a frequent visitor to our house. Long after his involvement in KFOR had finished he would still visit, right up to five years ago, uh, just before I came to the UK with Eva. At first, he came around for dinner with Dragan but then he started visiting on his own. He um... he took a, shall we say, an unnatural interest in Evalina... I just thought he was being kind. He brought her presents and sweets that sort of thing but I realised it was getting uh... unhealthy.

'I told my husband about it but he said I was imagining things, then one evening Etchington let himself into our house. Dragan was still in work and I was preparing dinner...'

She hesitated once more and took a large gulp of wine before continuing.

'I heard a noise upstairs and called out Eva's name but she didn't answer, as I went out into the hallway Etchington was coming down the stairs. He had been in Eva's bedroom. She was only... eleven,' she said in a near whisper.

She lowered her gaze then wiped a tear from her eye. Steve took her hand and held it in his before awkwardly kissing the top of her head. Irena composed herself before continuing.

'Of course I phoned my husband. He went after Etchington and attacked him. He very nearly killed him, but Etchington had friends in high places – he still has. There's one friend in particular, an animal called Besin Marishta, he was in the Kosovo Liberation Army. You won't believe this but he is now running Chicken City.'

Steve shrugged and shook his head. He was keen not to let Irena know that he was fully aware of who the Albanian gangster was – he had known ever since Kirsty had given him the notorious folder several years previously.

'The Albanians, they hated Dragan for his involvement in the civil war. My husband, I'm sorry to say took part in the massacre of Albanians at Račak – not that the Albanians knew, they would have killed him before if they had. But then Etchington told Marishta about his involvement in the massacre and well, he and his thugs didn't take much persuading… they beat him to death, set fire to his body then buried it somewhere in a forest outside of Pristina.'

She looked up at Steve who returned her gaze with a look of horror.

'Your husband was murdered?'

Irena nodded.

'I presume you went to the police? The authorities?'

'The authorities? *Jesi li lud!* No Steve, we couldn't. You don't understand, we Serbians were in the, what is it… *minority* in Kosovo. At that stage the Albanians hated us, especially anyone who was involved in the war like my husband. They and Etchington, they said we had to keep quiet or they would kill us as well – in the end they forced us to leave Kosovo. They told us they could get us jobs in England. So, they sorted the passports – the fake ones – and they trafficked us here, and ever since then that bastard Marishta has had his claws in us.'

She could no longer hold back the tears. She broke down and sobbed uncontrollably, not for the first time in the last week or so Steve put his arms around her to console her. She reciprocated and held him tight to her body. She raised her head and Steve wiped a tear from her eye, Irena forced a smile and nuzzled closer into Steve until their faces touched.

He gently kissed her on the cheek causing her to sigh gently. Their lips met and Steve kissed Irena with a passion he hadn't felt for several years.

Irena pulled herself away, took his hand and stood up.

'Come on,' she said as she led him towards his bedroom. 'I need you to make love to me.'

This time, unlike when her daughter had made the same offer, Steve didn't resist.

Chapter Twenty-Five

He woke the following morning to the sound of Irena lightly snoring beside him. He studied her as she slept, gently pulling the sheet up so he could take in her full impressive body. He was not disappointed.

She looked as good now as she had done the night before. He kissed her on her bare shoulder then sniffed and inhaled the seductive scent of a woman. Irena murmured in appreciation, rolled over and faced Steve.

'Tea?'

She nodded and smiled. Steve returned her smile as he wondered at the ordinariness of it all.

He'd heard his mobile notifying him of a text message the previous evening, just as he was on his vinegar stroke. He cursed but was too far immersed in the moment to let it bother him. Irena likewise was reaching a noisy climax, panting and moaning furiously as Steve shuddered and came inside her.

He put the kettle on then picked up his iPhone and read the message. It was from Tony Preston – *not a fucking job, not now for fuck's sake…*

'Get yer arse over to the eagle 2morro nite at 8 – we got summat big on and bring as many of yer fuckin gashead mates as you can. Were gonna need em.'

He read it again just to be sure – it definitely said *'were gonna need em'* and not *'you're gonna need em'*. Preston was semi-literate; Steve had received enough of his garbled texts in the past to know he meant *'we're'*. Either way it didn't sound like he was inviting him over for cocktails and canapes – not to The Eagle anyway.

'Fuck.'

Irena sat bolt upright in the bed.

'What is it Steve – is it Eva?'

Steve turned to face her. The bed sheets had dropped down to reveal her impressive, voluptuous breasts.

'Uh no, it's uh, nothing for you to worry about.'

'Good, in that case, forget the tea and get back into bed,' she said as she threw back the covers.

It was an offer too good to turn down.

* * *

Julie Smolinski looked over the top of her reading glasses and cast an accusing eye at her husband as he tied up the laces of his Doctor Marten's.

'How come you're wearing your boots?' she asked, with just a hint of concern.

'Just felt like wearing them that's all,' he lied. Something told him they might be needed.

'Where is it you're going again?'

'I told you, I'm out with JB and Steve for a pint,' he responded wearily.

'Hmmm, apart from his mum's funeral you've hardly seen Steve over the last year, so what's up?'

The memory of her husband's affair with her ex-friend Karen Cribb was still fresh in Julie's mind. They had made up but she questioned him incessantly whenever he ventured out without her.

'Dunno love,' he answered truthfully.

The call he'd received that morning from Steve was as unexpected as it was baffling. Steve wasn't one to exaggerate and if he said he needed a favour then George knew he needed a favour.

In fairness George knew he had a lot to thank Steve for. It was Steve who'd eventually made George face up to his steroid problem – 'problem' being an understatement – he was both addicted to them and dealing in them. George was still into his strict gym regime and since he'd taken early retirement from Aeroengine International he'd spent even more time working out, but this time without the intake of creatine and steroids that had at one time so dominated and plagued his life.

The anger management sessions that George had attended, also brought about by Steve's concern over his old mate, had worked wonders and the one-time ticking time bomb was now more chilled than a polar bear's bollocks.

The mongrel that he and Julie had rescued from the Dog's Home, again on Steve's advice, had been a godsend and he and his wife spent many a blissful day just enjoying each other's company whilst walking the scruffy but loveable mutt in the nearby parks and woods.

George knew he'd had a close call.

The disastrous affair with Mike Cribb's alcoholic and unhinged wife very nearly cost him his marriage and he was damned if he was about to put it in jeopardy again.

He kissed his wife tenderly on her cheek as he left, ever thankful for the second chance she'd given him.

'Don't wait up,' he said with a meek smile.

'Oh, I will, don't you worry,' she replied – Julie Smolinski had still not quite forgiven her errant husband.

It wasn't just George Smolinski getting the third degree from his partner. Two miles away John Burston was beginning to appreciate what the inmates of Guantanamo Bay had gone through…

'So you're out with Steve Allen?' asked Sharon. She had her arms folded tightly across her ample chest – JB knew this was a bad sign.

'Yes,' he answered bluntly.

'And who else?' she hissed.

'Just George… I told you, Steve phoned and said he fancied a beer.' He glanced at his watch.

'He's picking me up in five minutes – so give it a rest Shaz.'

'Give it a rest? I'll give you give it a fucking rest… I'm telling you John Burston, if you're up to something I'll fucking swing for you – and if it involves that… that internet scrubber of his, you'll be a dead man, hear me?'

Hear you? Think half the fucking street can hear you.

'Yes love… Look, her name's Eva and he didn't meet her on the internet OK? He'd just been letting her stay at his drum for a bit and if Steve says there's nothing going on between them then I believe him. It's pretty obvious she's got more baggage than an airport carousel and on top of that he's old enough to be her father… fuck's sake he's old enough to be her grandfather – and anyway she's gone, moved out. He told me today.'

But what Steve hadn't told JB was that Eva had been abducted and he certainly hadn't let on that he'd been helping the police with their inquiries – again.

Sharon screwed up her eyes.

'Hold on a minute, you said that he'd only asked you out for a drink – you didn't say you spoke.'

Women – why do they always speak in riddles?

'What do you mean, "you didn't say you spoke"? What do you think we did, made sign language down the fucking phone to each other?' replied JB sarcastically. He regretted it immediately.

Sharon's nostrils flared in anger.

'Don't you come the smart arse with me John Burston… what else did he fucking say then?'

JB sighed. 'Not a lot, just that she'd moved out.'

'And?'

'And he said her mother's moved in,' he muttered under his breath.

'Are you fucking serious! Her mother?' Sharon screwed up her eyes once more.

'What's she like then… the mother?'

'Dunno, but Steve reckons she's a proper SMILF.'

'Don't you mean MILF?'

'No,' said JB with a grin, 'she's a Serbian Mother I'd like to…'

'You fucking bastard,' said Sharon as she punched her husband's arm playfully, causing JB to falsely howl in protest.

'How old is she?' Sharon continued with her interrogation.

'Think he said she was a bit older than you,' replied JB with a hint of a smile, hoping this would placate Sharon.

'Well he'll be shagging the arse off her then,' said Sharon triumphantly as the *beep-beep* from outside heralded the arrival of Steve.

'Right, I'll be off then,' sighed JB, relieved that his ordeal was finally coming to an end.

'OK hun, have a nice time. Oh, and give Steve my love,' said Sharon with a self-satisfied smirk.

JB opened the front door, shaking his head in bafflement as to how his wife's moods could swing like a pendulum in the space of a minute or so. He was also trying to fathom out whether he'd actually won or lost the argument with his aggravating but loveable wife.

He got in the car and was immediately greeted with an 'Alright JB?' from both Steve and George.

'Alright lads?' responded JB.

'Shagged the mother yet, Steve?'

Steve rolled his eyes. 'Very funny… now then lads, have you got your passports?'

'Passports?' queried George.

'Yep – we're going south of the river.'

'Bollocks,' responded George and JB simultaneously.

* * *

The Eagle stood at the end of what was once a rank of shops that had been built at the same time as the surrounding council estate. Where at one time butchers, green grocers and bakers served the local community now just a Polski Sklep, a kebab house, a vape shop and a bookies plied their wares.

This was one of Bristol's most notorious estates and The Eagle one of its most notorious pubs, it was the kind of place you wiped your feet on the way out and if anyone shook your hand – which was unlikely – you checked that they hadn't nicked your watch. It was a City pub. In fact, it was City's main pub. Steve and his mates would be as welcome as farts in spacesuits but he knew he couldn't turn the invite down – not if he wanted to show his face on the streets of Bristol again.

Tony Preston had instructed him to bring his 'Gashead' mates, who now consisted of just John Burston and George Smolinski. There were others but he knew that none of them would venture to The Eagle, not unless they were really mob-handed and that was as likely as a meth-head winning a smile of the year contest.

It was hard enough to get his two best mates to agree to accompany him, but he could be a persuasive bastard and in all honesty the two didn't want to let him or the blue side of Bristol down… or see him in intensive care for that matter.

They parked up opposite and viewed the pub through the steamy windows of Steve's Ford Focus. The pub was decorated with England flags, bunting and banners taunting the 'Blue Few' as the Reds liked to call them. Steve had always argued that they might have been few in numbers but they more than made up for it in loyalty, if not to their club then certainly to each other.

Steve looked at his two mates and let out a deep breath.

'Come on then us merry band of the "Blue Few", let's see what this Shithead Preston has got to say for himself.'

'I got to be honest mate, I don't like this one fucking bit,' said JB. He wasn't scared – apprehensive maybe, but never scared.

'Same here,' said George, 'you sure it ain't a set up? You know what these wankers are like, they're sketchy as fuck. I mean they still point at aeroplanes in the sky for fuck's sake.' He gave out a nervous laugh.

'I've told you it'll be alright. Like that beer we had with them the other Christmas – they were sound then weren't they?' replied Steve, trying his hardest to reassure his mates.

'Yeah, but it was still a bit iffy, could have kicked off at any time – especially when Bob threw that sausage roll at one of their old boys,' said JB.

Bob Humphries was an old Tote Ender like them, a couple of years younger but just as experienced. He was always up for a laugh and didn't mean any harm by launching the pastry at Terry 'Trouble' Duggan, one of the respected old East End boys. But some of the City lads had taken it the wrong way and for a moment the Mexican standoff threatened to escalate into a full-scale brawl. Steve managed to placate the gathered clans and an uneasy truce ensued.

Steve half smiled as he remembered the event, it was meant to be a bit of a 'pow-wow', just a bunch of old lads having a chat about their past battles and conquests but the ill-feeling was still there, simmering just under the surface even after all these years.

They stopped outside the imposing pub – a typical estate inn, built in the early Fifties, The Eagle had seen many fights and even a couple of deaths over the years. It was constantly in the news, mainly for drug dealing and stolen goods, but the most depraved event happened a few years back when an illegal dogfight took place in the yard at the back, resulting in the pub shutting for a while. The new owners promised to clean it up and start afresh – they'd failed miserably.

A huddle of youths dressed identically in black hoodies and three-striped tracksuit bottoms stood outside The Eagle leaning against their bikes. The smell of full-strength cannabis hung in the air.

As the three walked towards the entrance the youngsters remained rooted to the spot like week-old chewing gum stuck to the pavement. Steve nudged one aside, the rest begrudgingly followed. A tan and white Staffie growled an unfriendly greeting.

'Can you smell dirty, stinking gas?' smirked one of the track-suited youths to his toothless, tattoo-necked mate. They both looked like they were participants in the Jeremy Kyle show from several years back.

JB fixed his stare on the youth.

'No, but I can fucking smell shit.'

The youth's smirk turned into an awkward sneer as he averted his gaze.

A handwritten sign taped on the cracked window of the door caught George's eye. It read 'No shoplifters'.

He let out a derisory snort. 'That's alright then – murderers and druggies are welcome, just no shop lifters.' The three of them smiled weakly but it hardly lifted the mood.

'Come on then, let's do it,' said Steve as he pushed open the scuffed, heavy door.

A blast of Terry Hall singing *Ghost Town* hit them as they entered, seemingly the whole pub stopped talking and turned as one, the loud and boisterous conversations abruptly ended and fifty-plus pairs of eyes studied the strangers. Actually, it was forty-nine and a half pairs as one unfortunate punter had lost an eye in a brawl the previous year.

'You fucking made it then – got to be a first.'

Tony Preston ambled towards Steve, one hand thrust deep into his Armani jeans pocket, while the other clutched a pint of wife-beater lager. A just visible joint was tucked behind his ear under his Henri Lloyd cap. He cast a caustic and disparaging eye over JB and George.

'OK so you bought a couple of old geezers from Dad's Army but where's the rest of your mob?'

'Er… this is it,' replied an embarrassed Steve. 'This is John and George.'

'John and George? Where's fucking Paul and Ringo?' asked a grinning Preston.

'Seriously,' he continued, 'is this all you got?'

'It's all we need,' replied JB, a little too quickly for Preston's liking.

'You fucking reckon?' fired back Preston.

Pleasantries over and pints bought by Tony Preston, Steve was eager to find out why they had been summoned.

'So what's this all about?' he said as he sipped his Guinness in the absence of a decent pint of ale.

'My boy Lee… seeing as the Old Bill ain't bothering to get him from that Chicken City – we fucking will,' replied Preston bluntly.

'And how are you going to do that – seeing as Chicken City resembles a fortress?' asked Steve.

Preston ran his tongue over his top lip.

'We got contacts ain't we? Everyone knows us around Europe. We've got links with teams in Holland, the Czech Republic and we even know a few of the fucking Kraut firms.'

Steve didn't or couldn't disagree – it was like a gathering of international Facebook chums when City played. He momentarily thought of whom Rovers had links with. There was Sabadell, the Catalonian team who lived in the shadow of their near neighbours Barcelona – who shared the same distinctive blue and white quartered shirts – and he knew a few lads who went to St Pauli, the anarchistic and down-at-heel Hamburg club, who like Rovers shared a passion for skull and crossbones and all things pirate.

Then there was a couple of Scottish clubs who had a 'soft spot' for that wee Bristol Rovers Football Club aka The Gas, but that was about it, hardly enough to set the elite world of Euro hooliganism on fire. But it had always been about that with City – numbers. Never mind the quality feel the width, he thought.

'Firms?' asked Steve.

'Yes firms, you know – crews, mobs, ultras – something your tinpot club have never fucking had.'

JB took a pace forward. Steve put his hand across his chest to stop him.

'And?' Steve continued.

'And I've been asking questions. Turns out the bloke who runs this Chicken City shithole is some greasy Albanian... Besin Marishta. They call him The Tiny One... he's a known old hoolie on the Euro circuit, main man of FK Partizani Tirana ultras in Albania apparently.'

He was talking to Steve as if he himself was a 'main man' in the hooligan world – he wasn't, and in truth all the talk of firms and ultras bored him shitless.

Steve rolled his eyes. *Fucking get on with it.*

'And?' he repeated.

Preston sensed Steve's irritation.

'Look old man, you're in my pub, on my turf, and in case you haven't noticed you're surrounded by my mates. So less of the attitude – *right?*'

Steve was aware of South Bristol's finest head cases eyeing him and his mates up. Preston had a point. Steve shrugged and swallowed both his Guinness and his pride.

Preston continued. 'So... I've got word to him... about my boy. He's agreed to hand him over.'

'Good news,' answered Steve with a palpable sigh.

'Yeah but there's a catch – he wants an *ustawka* in return.'

'A what?'

'An *ustawka*,' interrupted George, 'you know – those organised fights that they have in forests in Europe. They mad fuckers in Poland started it – it's all over YouTube, you must have seen 'em?'

Steve shrugged once more and shook his head.

'See – ol' Captain Mainwaring in the DMs knows what I'm on about,' said Preston.

'They all meet up, hundreds of 'em, no weapons involved – that's the rule – just a good ol' tear up like you old fuckers used to enjoy. You're always banging on about it... "in my day we used to scrap with just our fists and our boots". So here's your chance to prove how hard you really are... or are you just a bunch of Rovers' pussies?'

'You fucking what?' said JB, who up until now had been uncharacteristically quiet.

Preston turned to JB and stared at the big man.

'I said here's your chance to prove how hard you are. I've heard nothing but how tough you old skinheads were back in the day – not just from you lot but our old bastards as well...'

He nodded in the direction of Terry Duggan, the recipient of Bob's sausage roll and Alan 'Spike' Smith – two of City's old boys who Steve and the others used to cross swords with back in the Seventies. They sat impassively at the bar, nursing pints of rough cider, looking a tad sheepish.

Steve nodded at them. They returned his nod in mutual respect.

'And do you know what?' Preston continued, 'I think it's all bollocks, I don't think you ever had a firm. The famous Tote End? Don't make me fucking laugh, just a bunch of dirty fucking pikeys, same as your

G-Force these days – you had nothing then and you got nothing now.'

If that mythical pin had descended to the beer-stained floor at that moment everyone would have heard it.

'So,' Preston continued, 'have you lost your bottle? Gone all soft in your old age? I reckon you lot are just a bunch of fucking chickens.'

He thrust his elbows out at right angles, puffed out his chest, stuck out his arse and strutted around the bar, all the time making a *pa-wock, pa-wock, cluck-cluck-clucking* sound.

Preston's mates erupted in maniacal laughter.

He returned, stood menacingly in front of JB and poked him in the chest with his outstretched finger. JB momentarily flinched causing Steve to grimace. JB had had enough – he edged ever closer to Preston.

Preston responded and raised his head up to meet JB's. The two of them had their noses within inches of each other.

'What's up old man – scared?'

'Easy, easy,' said Steve aware of the eager, volatile audience who were hanging on every word. Apart from the constant ringing of bells and blips from the ubiquitous fruit machine the pub had suddenly gone very quiet.

JB chewed the inside of his cheek and screwed up his eyes.

'Scared? I don't know the meaning of the word and I'll tell you something else… I've shit out bigger turds than you, you fucking scumbag… I'll show you how soft I've gone in my old age shall I?'

JB's huge head went around to the side of Preston's. Preston didn't budge.

'I'll rip your fucking ugly mug off your shoulders and shove it up your spawny Shithead arse if you call me scared again,' he whispered menacingly into Preston's ear.

'Fucking bollocks,' muttered Steve.

He clenched his fists and threw a sideways glance to George who cracked his knuckles in anticipation.

Preston kissed his teeth, grinned and gave a playful punch to JB's huge bicep.

'That's the spirit big fella... game fucking on. Now then, whose round is it?'

Chapter Twenty-Six

Irena patiently waited for Steve's return. She busied herself flicking through cookery books and tidying the flat while randomly choosing music from the Rock-Ola.

Like her daughter she had never heard of most of the records but there were several that she found herself humming along to and that caused her feet to involuntarily tap along to the infectious rhythm, taking a particular liking to Steve's Tamla Motown and old soul collection.

She smiled at the lyrics of *My Girl,* Otis Redding's version of The Temptations classic and Marvin Gaye's *Wherever I lay my hat, that's my home* – hoping that the two tracks might just be a sign of things to come, unlike *First I look at the purse* by The Contours which caused her to turn her nose up in mild disdain.

Raising her eyes from the jukebox she found herself looking at the same framed record, *Guilty,* that Eva had studied several weeks earlier. *Who was Kirsty?* she pondered and not for the first time, but then her mind switched back to her daughter...

Although Steve had assured her that everything would be all right and that the police were on the case, she was still concerned and worried about Eva, even though Irena Petrovic knew exactly where she was.

She once again called up the app on her mobile. It was evident that Eva had been fitted with a replacement chip – there it was, a reassuring red glow emanating from a pin located in a huge building on Severnside – Chicken City.

She was back.

She'd also seen the article about Etchington's visit to the plant, she knew that meant one thing – he would be spending time with her daughter or the special one as he liked to call her.

Considering the circumstances and how vulnerable Eva was, it was probably best that she was in Chicken City. Irena knew that she was such a valuable asset to Solutio that they wouldn't dare harm her, not physically anyway.

The barcode tattoos had been a prototype, they had worked well for registering the comings and goings of the operamini – where they originated from, their date of birth, who *owned* them, but that was about it.

What Solutio – with the tacit approval of the British government really wanted was to be able to track them, track their movements, track their location and track who they were meeting, and in real time.

What George Bush dubbed 'The War on Terror' in the aftermath of 9/11 spawned the 'Politics of Fear', causing governments worldwide to introduce ever more draconian measures and restrictions that would have been deemed totally unacceptable in more peaceable times.

In a quirky irony, the more the terrorists attacked, the more the people of Britain seemed willing to give up their freedom. It needed just one more outrage, one more bombing on the streets of Britain, one more brutal killing of a soldier or one more massacre on the streets of a European city… just one more atrocity and then they would act.

They knew one day it would come and when it did the Government and the Secret Intelligence Service would be ready and act in a way that the British people would find strangely palatable. They would give up their freedom, give up their individual identities and allow themselves and their children to be chipped – and there would be precious little that any civil liberties group could do about it.

The GPS tracker had worked well and Irena and her team had at last developed a rechargeable battery that ensured a lifetime of power, the movement of the body alone was enough to keep the tiny unit charged. But there was one small problem with the chip – it could be removed – as Steve had proved all too well.

The next hurdle they had to overcome was how to ensure it couldn't be removed. It was tricky but they knew they could do it, they had tried various options – from tiny barbs that would tear into the flesh if the chip was moved, to toxins that would be released if the device was tampered with, but the team thought the best option was simply to find a location in the body that caused irreparable damage if surgery was undertaken – like *close to the heart*, something that Irena knew only too well. It was something Irena and her team had been busy working on.

If only Eva had been more cooperative, if only she'd been able to blank out her troubled past like her mother had. She'd tried....

She'd even convinced herself that her family had lived in the rural idyll of Bajgora, a place that she only knew from visits to her grandmother's small farm when she was young. What's more she had even managed to convince herself that her father really had died of a heart attack and not of something far more sinister.

But the defence mechanism occasionally failed, as it had done the previous month when she woke in the early hours sweating and screaming, knowing that she just had to visit her mother.

She'd bribed the guards with sexual favours and blagged a lift from one of the custos to her mother's home in Birmingham, a home that was not within the confines of the villatis but in a comfortable and expensive apartment that overlooked Pype Hayes Park in Erdington, where her mother, unlike her, was free to come and go as she pleased.

Irena had comforted and calmed her daughter, but then as often happened in the past Eva became hysterical and attacked her mother before smashing up her flat and fleeing out into the pouring rain and the desolation of Spitfire Island, where she optimistically stuck out her thumb hoping for a lift out of there.

As ever Eva would show remorse once she returned to the confines of Chicken City. She had phoned her mother and apologised but this time she was adamant, she was going to get out and at last she'd found someone she knew she could trust and who would help her.

'He looks like Bruce Willis,' she had told her mother. 'He will help me *majka*. Help me get out of this fucking hellhole that I'm in – that *you* put me in!'

For once Irena believed her troubled daughter. Eva was not the only one who was remorseful, her own mother who had treated her so badly since their arrival from Kosovo had finally broken down and faced up to her terrible treachery. She also needed to get out of the trap that they were both ensnared in and she also had to face up to another fact – she'd finally met a man she could really love.

* * *

'Did you have a good night out with your friends?' asked Irena as Steve entered the apartment after dropping JB and George off back to their homes and their wives. She helped him off with his jacket and kissed him on the cheek as she did so. Steve smiled contentedly.

'Friends? Oh yeah… not sure you could call it a good night – eventful maybe,' he replied recalling the evening's events.

'Oh OK, have you arranged to meet them again?' she asked as she fussed over him.

'Yeah,' replied Steve wearily, 'we're going for a jolly in the woods next week.'

Chapter Twenty-Seven

To all intents and purposes it looked a suitable setting for a battle. An imposing, three-turreted Gothic-style castle stood atop a high, landscaped mound whilst a lush verdant field surrounded it, which itself was enclosed by a heavy wooded area. Not that it was a real castle, just a folly – built in 1766 for the pleasure of John Harford, the wealthy merchant and owner of the Blaise Castle Estate in the north west of Bristol.

Steve knew the woods well – it was only a mile or so from his childhood home in Southmead and as a lad he spent many a hot summer's afternoon exploring the woods and catching sticklebacks in the stream with his brother Kenny.

There were two paths leading up to the field from the woods through which the two armies would approach; Tony Preston's motley allegiance of battlers from the West and Besin Marishta's Albanian custos from the East, no vehicles could get within a mile of the battlefield.

It was dusk. A dank fog descended giving a suitably dark atmosphere to the scene.

'This is fucking mental,' said George as they trudged through the woods. He looked around him and studied the assortment of thugs, bruisers and general dross of the football hooligan world making their way up the hill.

'Is this for real? I mean, what the fuck are we even doing here? I thought we'd put all this shit behind us yet within ten minutes we're going to be scrapping with a load of gyppos – and for what? To rescue some

Shithead's gay lad from the clutches of an Albanian warlord… you've got us into some scrapes Allen but this one takes the fucking biscuit.'

Steve Allen had heard it all before, but even he had to admit that this scene was out of the top drawer of surreal situations that they had found themselves in over the years. Before he had a chance to answer JB interrupted.

'Yeah well, I ain't having no Shithead accusing me of being chicken – could be a laugh anyway, as long as no one gets hurt.'

'No one gets hurt? Are you fucking joking – have you seen this lot? And I can only imagine what these Albanians are going to be like – it's going to be like that battle in Lord of the fucking Rings,' wailed George Smolinski.

'Oh stop your moaning – I thought you Polaks invented all this anyway, you ought to be in your fucking element,' JB retorted.

'Can I remind you that my old man escaped from Krakow during the war so he could fight the Nazis and that I was born here, you ignorant fucker.'

'Whatever,' JB muttered as he trudged up the hillside towards the castle he had also known since his childhood.

Yet again Steve was indebted to his two oldest mates, but this time there was to be no direct result at the end of it – apart from the freeing of Preston's son this would not lead to Eva being released, she hadn't even been part of the equation.

But Steve did feel guilty about the situation, even though he played no part in it. This time, if it was up to him, they wouldn't be where they were now, wouldn't be tramping through the woods at dusk to have an organised fight – an *'ustawka'* – with a mob of hooligans from the Balkans, but JB had not backed down, no-one could get away with accusing him of being scared, and certainly not someone from the red half of Bristol.

Tony Preston had thrown down the gauntlet and Steve, with JB's and George's help had picked it up, but the three of them wouldn't be enough.

Besin Marishta had been strict about the rules of engagement – one hundred of your best men, he'd said, no more no less. No weapons, and if anyone is knocked unconscious you help them, it will be a fair fight and at the end they will shake hands – that is how we do it in the Balkans, he had boasted.

He had even agreed that whatever the result, and usually there was no winner or loser, he would personally hand over Lee to Tony Preston no question – he was a man of honour and his word was his bond.

Steve had wondered why the fuck just those two couldn't have a fight and settle it like men but it wasn't to be – and that's why now, at six o'clock on a dismal Thursday evening in early spring he was part of a group of men who were heading up a hill in north west Bristol to fight with one hundred Albanians.

You couldn't make it up, he thought.

For all of Tony Preston's boasting about how he could raise an army in practice it wasn't quite that easy – his recruitment campaign fell a long way short. The call to duty had been answered by just over sixty of his mates, including some who were prepared to travel from Plymouth and Portsmouth. The hooligan grapevine buzzed with the news, but few so say comrades in arms of Preston's rose to the challenge – least of all from City's old enemies like Rovers and Cardiff City, a hundred? Preston would be lucky if he had seventy in total – he feared the worst.

Steve had appealed to some of the retired old Tote End boys and the more game, if naturally suspicious, youngsters from Rovers' G-Force. The Gas youngsters had enhanced their reputation somewhat in recent years and earned more respect from the City lads than they had enjoyed for many a year, especially after one notable occasion when G-Force managed to catch out the City lads in their own backyard which brought out a declaration from one CES veteran that indeed 'the war was over'.

'Why the *fack* should we 'elp them bastards out *moi san*?' asked Callum 'Dyer' Burrows, who had recently been given the nickname by his piss-taking G-Force buddies.

Burrows, as well as being a die-hard Rovers lad was also a big fan of West Ham United, and although the thirty-four-year old scaffolder was a born and bred Bristolian his accent morphed into that of a pie 'n' mash chomping Cockney the more he ventured up to see the Hammers, which to date, was precisely five times.

Burrows walked the walk and talked the talk, he also wore the gear, and after purchasing a light beige trenchcoat similar to that worn by Tommy Johnson in *Football Factory*, he acquired the name Danny Dyer and the sobriquet stuck.

'Dyer' admittedly had good credentials and came from good stock. Steve knew his dad, Frank – he was a tough old greaser back in the sixties and seventies and one of the founding members of the old Tote End.

Sadly, Frank was now suffering from motor neurone disease and Steve hadn't seen him for years, he felt a pang of guilt and chided himself for not visiting the old boy. He added to his ever-growing list of things he had to do before it was too late.

Steve had to concede that like his dad Dyer was a game fucker. He had the neck and attitude of a bull mastiff and was none too happy about being asked by Steve to join Preston's 'band of brothers'.

'If I have to explain it you wouldn't understand,' replied Steve, knowing full well that it was a throw-away line that didn't have any meaning or significance whatsoever. Dyer screwed up his eyes.

'Don't give me all that pony *moi san*. Just 'cos you lot been cosying up with them wankers recently don't mean us young 'uns 'ave to.'

Steve knew he had a point – there was a definite schism in the ranks between the old boys and the young lads on both sides of Bristol's football divide.

The younger lads had little time for the likes of Steve and his mates who had put their differences with City's old East End boys aside and who now enjoyed pre-Christmas drinks with each other whilst back-slapping and reminiscing about the 'good old days'.

'You got a short memory old man. They've always been *Barney Rubble* and it wasn't that long ago they were setting fire to our stands and attacking our players on the pitch, not to mention 'aving a pop at us when we was outnumbered five to one.'

Steve held up his hands in submission.

'Alright, alright – I know where you're coming from, but look if you change your mind it's next Thursday, up…'

'Yeah, yeah, I *facking* know all about it, but it ain't 'appening. *Fack* their spawny red arses OK?'

* * *

The clearing was eerily quiet as they approached.

On Tony Preston's instruction they fanned out in a long, thin line either side of him, he looked around and gave encouraging nods and winks to his cohorts. *If only those Gashead wankers would have turned up*, he thought.

He hated to admit it but he knew that Rovers' youngsters could make a big difference. As it was, they were at least twenty short – he cursed the absentees under his breath.

'Alright lads?' Preston nodded to those nearest to him. He nervously rolled a cigarette between his fingers and the rapid chewing of the gum in his mouth exaggerated the fact that he'd recently snorted several fat lines of Columbia's finest.

'You all know the score. This ain't gonna be pretty but it should be fair, I know we ain't got the numbers but we're Bristol...'

'And Pompey.'

'Yeah, all right – and Pompey.'

'Don't forget us Janners.'

'OK, OK, and-you-fucking-Janners…' he replied in a machine-gun style staccato.

'Now, where was I? Oh yeah we ain't got the numbers thanks to those Gas wankers letting us down,' his eyes darted in the direction of Steve, 'but we're all game lads, so we're going to give these gyppos a taste of fucking English knuckle and boot, alright?'

It was hardly Churchillian pondered Steve, but it served a purpose he guessed.

'So when it all kicks off, we hit them hard and we hit them…'

Preston was distracted by a noise in the woods to his left. He wasn't the only one who heard it.

The others looked around towards the direction of the commotion. The echoes and thuds were getting louder, it was a definite sound of footsteps walking and crunching through the undergrowth, branches and twigs could be heard snapping and breaking, there were muffled voices in the shadows.

They all squinted in the gathering gloom.

It couldn't be the Albanians, thought Preston, they're meant to be coming from the opposite direction.

'Alright Preston – 'eard you might be needing a 'and from the mighty G-Force.'

Out of the woods appeared Dyer Burrows and twenty-plus other lads, mostly in their twenties and thirties. At the back were half-a-dozen older men, Steve recognised them instantly, it was Bob Humphries – this time without a sausage roll – and some other old Tote End boot boys that he knew from back in the Seventies.

'Better late than never,' said Preston sarcastically.

'You're lucky we made it at all,' sneered Dyer.

'If I 'ad my way we wouldn't 'ave bothered, but well... we 'eard your boy was mixed up with some paedos, and I fecking 'ate paedos more than I 'ate you Shitheads so 'ere we are. And anyway, without us, you'd be *facked*.'

'Oi, fucking shut it, you're the one that looks like a paedo in your fucking flasher's mac,' replied Ryan Jackman, an eager young CES member who'd recently gone toe-to-toe with Dyer outside a city centre night-club.

The younger lads had yet to indulge in the mutual respect that the older ones enjoyed. The two stepped menacingly towards each other.

'Fucking leave it out,' said Preston, 'tonight we put all that shit behind us alright? We're all together... Bristol united, alright?'

'And Pompey.'

'Yeah, an' Pompey... an' you fucking Janners,' said Preston wearily.

'Now shake hands... all of you!'

The G-Force members warily approached their long-time adversaries. Dyer held out his hand to Jackman who gingerly shook it.

Preston produced a baggie of coke from his back pocket and sprinkled a small amount of powder onto the back of his hand.

'Here you are, have a fucking bump and shut the fuck up.'

He offered the powder to Jackman who snorted it with relish. He then repeated the ritual with Dyer. Steve looked on with wide eyes and involuntarily licked his upper lip. JB noticed and shook his head in disgust as a warning to his old mate.

'Don't,' said JB bluntly. Steve guiltily looked away.

'Cheers *moi san*. You're alright for a Shithead,' said Dyer with a wink to Preston.

Steve caught Burrows's eye.

'Alright Callum, uh, Dyer. Glad you could make it… been meaning to ask, how's your old man?'

'Died two nights ago,' replied Dyer flatly with no emotion.

Steve was struck by Dyer's bluntness and the guilt of not visiting Frank Burrows before he passed away once more consumed him.

'Sorry about that, I don't know what to say. I should've…' Steve's grovelling apology was cut short.

'What the fucking hell is that?' said a voice from further along the line.

Steve turned and looked towards a youth who was pointing anxiously across the clearing.

Through the gloom a bright red flash of light could be seen. A lone figure held a flare aloft – he was clad all in black and a menacing balaclava covered his face – he resembled a bizarre, sinister Statue of Liberty.

A low, deep chant started from a still unseen group behind the masked figure… *'TEE-RA-NA! TEE-RA-NA! TEE-RA-NA!'*

Steve glanced at his mates stood either side of him. JB bit his bottom lip in excitement whilst George nervously cracked his knuckles. It was left to Preston to break the silence, he took a step forward from the gathered mass around him and put both arms in the air…

'You're gonna get your fucking heads kicked in!'

The others joined in with just a hint of a smirk and the notorious chant from several decades earlier echoed around the woodland.

The Tirana ultras responded by emerging from the woods causing Steve and the others to stop in their tracks.

They were uniformly dressed in black or red sweat-shirts, many emblazoned with Eighties-style Lonsdale or Everlast logos, it appeared Stone Island had yet to find its way to The Balkans. Virtually all of them wore peaked caps or balaclavas and the scarlet red and yellow shirt of FC Tirana was also on show as were matching scarves tied around their faces in a menacing fashion.

'Fucking 'ell – and we thought you Gasheads were a bunch of scruffy bastards! Fucking Lonsdale? My Staffie sleeps on better labels than that!' said a Paul and Shark-clad CES youth.

'Yeah well, it's always been about fighting gear for us, it ain't a fucking fashion show you Shithead fuck boy,' responded an agitated G-Force youth who'd turned up straight from the building site wearing a paint-spattered Alpha Industries MA-1 flying jacket and work boots.

'Will you lot fucking leave it out!'

Preston was growing impatient with the bickering of the youngsters. He had set himself up as the General and although grateful for the mob that had turned up to fight his cause he was becoming increasingly annoyed at the ill-discipline all around him.

'If you lot can't put club loyalties aside you can fucking jog on. In case you've forgotten we've got a scrap to get on with here.'

He motioned towards the Tirana ultras who had now fully emerged from the woods and who massed in a long black and red line some one hundred yards away.

'Fuck me it's like something out of Zulu,' said George to Steve. He had been uncharacteristically quiet up till that point, but he was not exaggerating, thought Steve.

Preston piped up once more. 'Look you fuckers we all need to stick together. No giving it large then doing a runner – this lot might look like they've just raided Primark but we know they're up for it. But they ain't got no fighting history like we have – us English invented football hooliganism. We got a long and proud history and we ain't gonna let a bunch of fucking pikeys get one over on us, 'right?'

Preston looked around for reassurance.

There was half-hearted nodding and murmurs but Steve inwardly groaned. He and the others could feel and smell the fear. He was out of his comfort zone; he hadn't been involved in events like this since the incident with Lewis and Samson several years previously and nothing on the scale of this since the Eighties. He was now in his sixties and although fit and still capable of looking after himself, fighting of this magnitude was something he'd thought he'd long put behind him.

Preston continued with his rallying call.

'Let them come to us. You old 'uns need to conserve your energy,' he looked towards Steve and grinned.

'Leave it out,' interrupted JB, 'I don't need no Shithead telling me how to fight alright?'

Preston nodded. Deep down, he knew that the likes of John Burston and Steve Allen knew the score – they had earned his respect.

'OK mate, I'm just saying for the benefit of the young 'uns… pick out your man and go for 'im, get him down, give him a kicking them move on to the next one and the next…'

And the next, thought Steve. Although he knew that thanks to Burrows's G-Force and the old Tote Enders turning up their numbers had swelled, it still looked like they were outnumbered. But this was it, there was to be no turning back, a battle of epic proportions was about to happen in his backyard with no Old Bill around to stop it and he was to be part of it, part of the first *ustawka* to be fought in Britain.

His mouth was as dry Prince Andrew's armpits. He could feel his heart thumping in his chest and his veins popped in his forehead like bursting balloons at a New Year's Eve party. He started to shiver uncontrollably and his hands began to shake. Truth be told he was close to shitting himself.

The red flare arced towards them. It twisted and spiralled in the dark evening sky and left a trail of thick red smoke behind it. It landed on the damp grass in front of Preston and fizzled out with a whimper, it had been a signal for the ultras to advance. The black and red line moved forward as one. They quickened their pace.

Steve inhaled deeply and clenched his fists. The adrenaline kicked in. His eyes focused as best they could in the gloom and he fixed his stare on a short but stocky ultra with close-cropped dark hair who was marching purposely towards him.

He needed to focus. Not just his eyes, but also his mind. He needed to feel revulsion, disgust and loathing. He needed to hate.

He thought of Eva and what had happened to her…

The ultras' pace quickened.

The one Steve had concentrated on became aware of Steve's stare. He reciprocated and his eyes bore into Steve. The two of them locked onto each other, everyone and everything around them became a blur.

The advancing ultra's eyes widened. His pace slowed ever so slightly, imperceptible to those around him but Steve spotted it. In that split-second Steve knew he had his opponent beat.

The first punch, when it came, connected with Steve's left cheek. It hurt, but it would have hurt more if Steve hadn't had sidestepped to his right. As the ultra connected with his right fist Steve swung and rabbit punched his opponent to the base of his skull, Steve had known to his cost in the past that punches like this could hurt like fuck and at worse, do irreparable damage to the spinal cord – not that he aimed to do so. Luckily for the ultra, the punch simply disorientated him enough to make him stumble like a Saturday night drunk.

Steve followed up with a left hook to his face – the hours on the punch bag had paid off. He was quicker with his fists now than he had ever been. He punched again powerfully with his right and followed up with a quick jab from his left. The young ultra raised his arms, both in defence and in a desperate attempt to attack.

He swung his right arm and his large fist connected with the side of Steve's head, now it was Steve's turn to stagger. He felt his legs buckle slightly and the ultra lashed out with a kick, but it was weak and only connected with Steve's side, it was enough to jolt Steve into a powerful reaction. He stood upright and raised both clenched fists.

For the first time the two men stood upright and faced each other like two pugilists in a ring. Steve lunged with his right. The ultra blocked it. Steve jabbed, once, twice with his left – this time the ultra didn't react quickly enough.

Steve punched again with his right and connected with the ultra's undefended face, his nose split like a ripe tomato.

He flailed frantically with his right arm, Steve took a step back and easily avoided it, he then hunched down and responded with two punches to the ultra's stomach. The ultra slumped down onto his knees and looked Steve in the eyes, blood poured from his split nose and his cut lip, he nodded in recognition to his opponent. He had been defeated. Steve was the victor.

All around the fighting continued. Steve couldn't take it in, couldn't focus. Moaning, groaning and battered men lay all around; others hobbled away back to the woods before slumping to the ground to nurse their wounds. He saw Dyer Burrows come to the aid of

Ryan Jackman who was struggling to see off a much larger opponent than him.

Burrows sideswiped the ultra causing him to yelp out loud, Jackman seized the opportunity and with one quick jab to the jaw the Albanian fell to the ground in a pitiful, defeated heap.

George was to the left of Steve. He was on his back while a masked colossus straddled him and pummelled at his face, if Steve had noticed his friend's predicament he would have helped, but he staggered away oblivious to it.

JB fared better. He had already knocked out one opponent with a single punch and was now battling away with an altogether more spirited foe who matched him blow for blow.

The scene was chaotic and brutal yet at the same time exhilarating. Steve wandered around aimlessly and casually threw a lazy punch at a fleeing ultra; he then felt a kick to his back. He spun around, planted his feet and punched out – once, twice at a new but already bloodied adversary. The wild-eyed and long-haired opponent was more wily than the previous one, he shook off the punches as if they had been delivered by a toddler and arched back his head in a motion that was all too familiar to Steve.

The crunch of forehead onto nose when it came was devastating, Steve stumbled backwards at the impact of the head butt, he clutched at his nose with both hands in a desperate attempt to stem the blood, but he failed and the warm, crimson liquid spurted through his fingertips.

Steve fell on to his back still holding his nose whilst his opponent towered over him and glowered – his glower slowly turned to a maniacal grin, he held out his right hand and Steve reluctantly took it with his own bloodied palm, his opponent pulled him up and slapped him on the back.

'Hey old man, you punch hard, very hard – on another day you would have knocked the *dreqin e ndyrë* out of me. Here...'

The Albanian offered Steve a checked bandana that he'd pulled from his jeans. Steve took it and pressed it against his nose as he muttered a half-hearted 'thanks'.

'It looks like it's coming to an end.' The ultra motioned with an extravagant wave to the dying embers of the battle around him.

Steve squinted and peered through the descending gloom – the battle was indeed ending. All around were youths and men shaking hands and slapping each other warmly on the back, others lay prostrate on the ground, some moaning and writhing in pain, others being tended to by both friend and foe.

Of all the bizarre situations Steve and his mates had found themselves in over the years, this surely ranked as one of the weirdest.

'*I vogel* won't be happy.'

The ultra pointed towards the large frame of Besin Marishta who was on his knees in the middle of the field. Stood over him was an enraged and badly beaten Tony Preston who was motioning to his bloodied opponent to get up.

'Who?' asked Steve as he mopped at his bloody nose.

'*I vogel* – Tiny One. Besin Marishta – he is our leader, our top cat.'

Steve recognised the name instantly. 'You mean top dog.'

'Dog, yes, he top dog – he not normally get beat, he very tough man.'

Steve inched closer to get a better look at the Albanian, the madman who had caused Irena and Eva so much pain.

He sidled up to Tony Preston, who it looked had won his personal feud with Marishta. It was hardly surprising considering the circumstances, Steve thought. He had seen Marishta before, not in the flesh but in photographs in Kirsty's infamous folder, the one that Eva had scrawled over. He'd also seen him in Eva's video, his thoughts turned to her. He wondered if the evening's events would make her whereabouts any clearer, or perhaps make her predicament even worse.

Preston lunged at Marishta and grabbed his throat with his left hand. He raised his clenched right fist and aimed it menacingly at his foe's face.

Steve instinctively moved forward to back Preston up. His movement drew an agitated glance from the battered Albanian.

'It's alright Allen I don't need your help, I've got this,' said Preston without taking his eyes off of Marishta.

'Where's my fucking son? You stick to your word you fucker… where the fuck is he?'

The Albanian raised his hand and clicked his fingers. From the woods behind him two men appeared, between them stood a scared-looking foppish youth.

'*Dad!*'

Lee Preston broke away from his two guards and bounded towards his father in exuberant leaps. Tony Preston released Marishta and turned to face Lee. His overjoyed son leapt into his arms and they hugged joyously.

'I knew you would come for me, I just knew it!' Lee said gleefully.

'Course I would son, wouldn't let my best mate down now would I?' He embraced his son and kissed him on the forehead.

'Now come on, let's get you home – you OK?'

Lee nodded half-heartedly. The two of them walked back past the still kneeling Marishta with their arms around each other, both with absurd grins on their faces.

'Uh sorry dad, I've forgotten something.'

Preston looked at his son quizzically.

Before he had a chance to question him further his son spun around and confronted his captor. Marishta rose to his feet, his large frame towered over the approaching youth.

'What do you want boy?'

'Nothing, I just wanted to give you something.'

'Give me something? Like what?'

Lee Preston swung his leg back and delivered a perfect kick to Marishta's groin.

'*This!*' he shouted triumphantly.

The Albanian let out a low, deep groan as he slumped back down into the mud of Blaise Castle once more – the battle was over.

* * *

'My god! What fucking happened to you?' Irena studied Steve's battered faced as he entered the apartment. She looked at him with genuine concern then gently cupped his face with her hands.

'It's nothing – just had a slight disagreement with someone,' answered Steve, not wishing to discuss the evening's events.

'Eva? Was this anything to do with Eva? Please tell me she's OK?' She pleaded with hope in her eyes if not in her heart.

'Sorry, I uh, no, not entirely, but I'm pretty certain that the people I had… the disagreement with, know of Eva's whereabouts. But I'm sorry, I don't know what more I can do to find her.'

Irena looked at Steve, disappointment etched on her face.

'Steve, it's not a case of finding her – we know where she is, she's in that Chicken *fucking* City, it's a case of getting her out!' screamed Irena.

There was something about her reaction, just a little bit too exaggerated he thought. If it wasn't for Irena, Eva wouldn't be incarcerated in that hellhole, he was sure of that.

He wondered about questioning her but then thought better of it. He was not in the mood for a row with the unpredictable Irena; he just wanted a long soak and his bed – with or without the company of the Serbian beauty.

'Look, it's in the hands of the police – we have to trust them. We all know where she is and we have to let them handle it – they will, in time,' he said acidly.

He had been warned off, not only by Simon Edwards but also Fraser Winston. They had both told him straight – don't try any heroics like he'd tried a few years back, these villains make Vernon Lewis look like a petty shoplifter.

If he and his mates tried anything this time there was only two places they would end up – prison, if they were lucky, or on a mortuary slab if they weren't.

'But when Steve, when will I see my little girl again? Tell me, I need to know?'

Steve shook his head slowly. 'I'm sorry… I honestly don't know. But right now, I need a soak.'

* * *

Steve drew the line at scented candles but he was partial to the Australian Seamoss Hydrosoak that his son, Sam, had sent over to him for Christmas, he smiled to himself as he remembered the card with the message *'Get in touch with your feminine side Dad!'* written inside it.

He ducked his head under the steaming hot water and let the stress-relieving bath oils go to work, it was one of life's simple pleasures that he'd got used to since he'd reverted to bachelor status.

He raised his head above the waterline and let the hot water trickle over his closed eyelids and gently soothe the cuts and abrasions on his face.

The unseen hands that touched his neck as his head emerged from the water made him initially recoil in mild shock, but he soon relaxed as Irena expertly rubbed and massaged his aching shoulders.

'Someone's stressed,' she whispered in his ear. The gentle, caring, sultry Serbian was back.

Steve didn't reply. He just let out a low contented moan in approval.

Irena moved her hands over Steve's toned physique, lingering momentarily on the angry circular scar on his left shoulder blade. She studied the wording that Steve had had tattooed around the almost perfect circle of the exit wound.

'I've been meaning to ask…'*Makes you stronger'*?' she queried as she traced the blue inked words with her finger.

Steve took her hand and moved it to the entry bullet wound on his chest that lined up perfectly with the scar on his back. In the same italic script Irena read the words '*What doesn't kill you…*'

'An old war wound,' said Steve, anticipating Irena's obvious question.

'I've been involved in a war Steve, it looks like it was caused by a bullet?' queried Irena.

'It was,' answered Steve matter-of-factly. 'I'll tell you about it some time.'

He couldn't see her face but he sensed that she nodded understandingly.

Her hands slipped down from his shoulders and continued to knead and rub his muscular biceps and forearms. They then moved across to his chest, tracing the outline of the now faded '*Mum & Dad*' tattoo on his right chest, she then did the same to the leaping tiger artwork on his right shoulder and the old, faded and barely legible *'Big Five'* ink just above the bullet wound.

'You like your tattoos – no?'

'Um, I guess. Haven't really thought about them.'

'All you Englishmen, you are so tattooed. Some are horrible. But yours… make you look sexy,' she purred, 'uh apart from that one on your backside – what does it even mean – *"100% GAS"*?'

'Oh that… uh, lads' weekend away in Benidorm. It's my football team, Bristol Rovers. We're known as "The Gas",' he replied sheepishly.

A boyish grin spread across his face at the memory of him, JB, George and Pete McNulty having the cheap tattoos done for a drunken bet several years previously.

Irena shook her head mockingly then leant forward and kissed Steve on the back of his neck, she moved her hands further down his body, her tongue traced slowly across his neck then up to his ear. She nibbled his lobe gently.

Steve groaned slowly and instinctively arched his back as Irena's right hand moved further down his body to seek out his now erect penis. She stroked it several times then stopped abruptly causing Steve to moan in disappointment, but his frustration didn't last as he soon surmised she was gradually moving around the room.

He slowly opened his eyes to see a naked Irena stood at the foot of the bath.

'I join you… *no*?' she asked seductively, her accent highlighting her sexiness.

He had to admit, that like her daughter she was stunning.

She had full, round breasts, an hour-glass figure that wouldn't have looked out of place on a woman half her age and cheekbones you could balance a pencil on.

Her nakedness confirmed that her shoulder length blonde coloured hair was natural.

He smiled and nodded.

Like I'm going to say no.

Chapter Twenty-Eight

Fraser Winston stared at his laptop screen then back to the raft of paperwork on his desk. He ran his finger down one sheet of paper then picked up a highlighter pen and started marking the page. He turned over the page and repeated the process on yet another sheet.

Is this what it has come to? Filling in spreadsheets and ticking boxes These are real people – real children with real names, but all they've been reduced to are an Excel spreadsheet with a tick against the level of abuse.

After several minutes he threw the highlighter pen onto the desk, exhaled deeply, tilted his head back and rubbed his unshaven chin.

He looked around at the certificates of merit on his wall and the photos of him and Carleen beaming widely at a multitude of presentation ceremonies. It was his boasting wall and he was rightly proud of it. He then fingered the diamond stud in his left earlobe, a habit that his wife always noticed he did when things worried him.

He looked at his Rolex. It was nearly one in the morning, Carleen and the kids had long gone to bed.

'I'll be up in a minute love,' he'd said as she kissed him on his forehead. But the two of them knew he wouldn't.

He thought of Marcus and Clarissa in their beds just feet above his head – they were of the same age as some of the victims he'd been reading about. He felt sick to the stomach at the reports he'd been reading, not just tonight, but the previous night and for far too many nights that he cared to remember.

This was child abuse on an industrial scale, up there and beyond Operation Yew Tree and Operation Fairbank – the list was never ending. Then there were the locations: Rotherham, Rochdale, Oldham, Sheffield, Oxford – it seemed there wasn't a city or town in the country that hadn't been affected and stained by child grooming, abuse, rape and trafficking.

And now Fraser Winston and his colleagues were involved in the latest investigation, grandly named Operation Waffle, but this inquiry didn't stop at the White Cliffs of Dover, it stretched across the Channel and bore into the very depths of the European Parliament in Brussels.

Then there were the perpetrators of the evil acts – the businessmen, the high court judges, the doctors, the teachers, the so-called celebrities, the politicians – Jesus there were even accusations by one individual of active VIP paedophile rings within the royal household.

And it went back decades – people know about this, thought Winston, know about the abusers who committed the vile atrocities. People – lots of people covered the crimes up. The more important the abusers and the higher up they were in the echelons of British and European society, the more a veil was drawn over their vile deeds.

He hated to admit it, but he could even see the Met had suppressed evidence – and for what reason? Were high-ranking officers involved in paedophile rings? Even ex-Prime Ministers were aware of the abusers, yet they chose to ignore or worse, cover up the allegations. Maybe even the current one knows?

So what the fuck can I do?

He and his colleagues, the one's he'd worked with for several years and who he trusted implicitly had escalated their findings up as high as they could. They'd waited for the response, waited for the signal for their investigations to step up a notch, waited for the green light, waited to start raiding properties, waited to start making arrests. And still they waited – the silence was deafening. How many times had he heard the same old excuse?

Not in the public interest – he was sick to the back teeth of not in the public fucking interest.

It was time to make a decision and fuck the consequences. He and his team were going to act and act soon – the group known as Solutio was going to get hit and he was going to hit it with the biggest hammer he could get. He would wipe the scum off the face of the earth and nothing – or no-one was going to stop him.

Not in the public interest – my fucking arse!

* * *

'Simon? It's Fraser Winston, sorry to bother you at this ungodly hour but I need your advice.'

Simon Edwards rubbed the sleep from his eyes, furrowed his brow and stared at his phone as if he could see the chiselled ebony features of his ex-colleague's face looking back at him.

'Go on,' he answered, genuinely intrigued.

'I don't know what to do. I've got evidence, masses of evidence – in fact I'm suffocating under the sheer weight of it.'

'Evidence of what?'

'Wholesale child abuse and people trafficking on an industrial scale – it's like a major import/export business. I've got names, sworn statements, photographs, video footage, DNA evidence – you name it, I got it.'

'And?'

'And I don't know what to do next. It's like I've hit a fucking brick wall. I've sent requests in triplicate, ticked every box, followed procedures and shown due diligence in everything I've done. I've crossed t's and dotted i's until I'm blue in the fucking face – but nothing… I know there's kids being held against their will and being forced to perform disgusting acts with… well, all sorts of scumbags, all over the country – and that group Solutio are no better than the Cosa Nostra. They're just a front for a multitude of nefarious activities with links to Masonic lodges in Britain and Eur…'

'And therein lies your problem,' said Edwards abruptly.

'The Masons?'

'Of course. You've known all along haven't you? I was there when you revealed the connections between Solutio and the Masons to Steve Allen and I know why you tried to paint them in a good light.'

'You do?' Winston shifted uncomfortably in his seat.

'Of course. You of all people know how the Masons are involved in all this, you know why all this is being suppressed. It goes right to the top, so you either sit on your hands and shut up, or…'

He hesitated.

'Or what?' asked Winston.

'Or you pull your Masonic finger out of your Masonic arse and do something about it.'

'Such as what?'

'Well, that's the sixty-four-thousand-dollar question squire… Do you take it to the Home Office? The Secret Service? The PM? I don't know, maybe you already have. You got to go with your gut feeling, but of course you take the risk of breaching the Official Secrets Act. But then again you know what they say about the Official Secrets Act don't you?'

Edwards didn't wait for a response.

'It's there not to protect secrets, but to protect officials… You're a logical and pragmatic detective Fraser. It's what makes you what you are. But for once don't go with your head, go with your heart… that's the only advice I can give.'

'But they've told me it's not in the public interest to pursue this,' pleaded Winston.

'To coin a phrase squire, they would wouldn't they? But it's nothing to do with what's in the public's interest – it's what's in *their* interest... whoever *they* are.'

There was a moment's silence, neither of them sure of how the conversation was going to end.

Edwards finally spoke once more. 'Tell me Fraser, have you heard of Edmund Burke?'

'Uh yeah, an MP wasn't he? Back in the eighteenth century?'

'Yep, that's the fella, for Bristol as it happens. He was a great orator and one of the things he once said was "the only thing necessary for the triumph of evil is for good men to do nothing".'

'And?'

'And you're a good man... and I don't think the likes of you, or Steve Allen for that matter, are the sort of men to do nothing. Goodnight.'

Edwards didn't give Winston the chance to ask any more questions. The phone went dead.

Winston put the mobile back in his pocket. He fingered the diamond stud in his ear once more then the small gold signet ring on his little finger. He twisted the front around and studied the pattern on it – the unblinking all-seeing eye stared back at him impassively.

Truth be told, he had a lot to thank the United Grand Lodge of England for. He was one of only a handful of black Masons in the UK and he saw himself as a pioneering ground-breaker.

He was ruthlessly ambitious and always prepared to push boundaries and if joining the Masons gave him the perfect opportunity to smash those glass ceilings and advance his career then so be it.

To his surprise he had experienced little, if no prejudice, no bigotry and no ill-feeling. In fact, he was welcomed with open arms and he revelled in the camaraderie and fraternity that the admittedly secretive, but not secret, society brought to his life. But he had to admit that once or twice he'd wondered if, like the abused children he'd been investigating, he himself was not just another box-ticking exercise and merely a desperate example of tokenism.

But there was one thing he was convinced of, contrary to what Simon Edwards thought, the insidious Solutio group was *not* directly linked to, or operated by the Freemasons.

His investigations had concluded that although there were undeniable links between certain individuals who were in the Masons there was nothing that actually implicated the Masonic movement itself.

There were no conspirators within the fraternity, no criminal brotherhood and no evidence of a cover up. The guilty parties were using the Masons as a conduit, a cover for their nefarious acts and abusing the secret symbolism for reasons known only to them, perhaps their own private little joke he mused.

But then again…

Perhaps Edwards was right, perhaps the Masons were involved and they were controlling Solutio. Perhaps his own involvement with them was blinding him to the obvious – maybe he himself had to take off the Masonic blindfold, imaginary or real, and open his eyes.

Winston was convinced of one other thing though – there was undeniable government involvement, but at what level he could only guess.

Someone within the Government was behind the microchip implants, of that he was sure.

He just had to find out who.

Chapter Twenty-Nine

Carleen groaned and kissed her teeth as her husband's mobile woke her from her slumber. Fraser Winston did the same. He had only slipped into the marital bed some four hours earlier. He gently let go of his wife's warm, soft breast, rolled over and sleepily fumbled for the phone on the bedside cabinet. It was five-fifty a.m.

'What?' he growled.

'Sorry to bother you boss but you know we've been keeping an eye on Thompson and Bishop?'

'Uh-huh.'

'Well, we've just found them half buried on the beach at Clevedon with their throats cut.'

Winston sat up ramrod straight in his bed, his eyes ablaze.

'Please don't tell me their tongues have been cut out?' He shook his head as he spoke.

'Yeah, how did you guess?'

The soft thud of the mobile phone as it hit the carpet caused Winston's long-suffering wife to curse the day her husband joined the police force.

'I've got to go to work,' he said with a palpable sigh.

* * *

Winston entered the temporary tent that had been erected around the deceased officers' bodies. He had seen many horrific sights over the years but this ranked up there with the worst.

He recalled what Simon Edwards had said to Steve Allen in the aftermath of Eva's abduction – an abduction that in Steve Allen's eyes had been perpetrated by the two men whose mutilated bodies he was now studying.

'You and your mates aren't going to do anything stupid are you?'

He dismissed the thought immediately. From what he knew of Steve Allen he was capable of many things, but murder was not one of them, but then again he also recalled Edwards *'good men doing nothing'* speech – he inwardly shuddered.

Judging by the lack of blood around the bodies the two of them had been killed elsewhere and then dumped and partially buried on the shingle and pebbles of the North Somerset beach, just a stone's throw away from the elegant Victorian pier.

Winston studied their contorted faces and the gaping wounds in their necks. Their mouths were agape and bloodied and as he had correctly surmised, devoid of their tongues.

'So how come you knew their tongues had been cut out?'

G4 Daniel Britton stood with his hands immersed deep into his dark blue padded Barbour jacket, a similarly logo'd peaked cap was perched on his round, closely cropped head. Like Winston he was unshaven and bleary eyed.

He studied his boss's weary face, eagerly awaiting a response.

'It relates to a Masonic oath that new members have to swear to regarding maintaining lodge secrecy. The so-say penalty for revealing Masonic secrets is, and I quote – "having my throat cut across, my tongue torn out by its roots, and my body buried in the rough sands of the sea at low water mark, where the tide ebbs and flows twice in twenty-four hours, should I ever knowingly violate this my Entered Apprentice obligation."'

'So the two of them were Masons? Christ, it don't sound a barrel of laughs does it boss? And there was me thinking they were just upmarket Rotarians,' snorted Britton in response.

'It's purely symbolic. Masons who do break the code of secrecy are generally just reprimanded, suspended or kicked out,' explained Winston.

'So no tongues cut out then?'

'No tongues and no throat cutting.'

'Been studying them a bit have you boss?' queried Britton.

'You could say that... Now where can I get a coffee?' he asked as he took a packet of Ibuprofens out of his pocket.

Winston now knew one thing for sure, he was going to raid Solutio as soon as he was able – with or without authority from above.

He wasn't going to sit with his finger up his arse, as Edwards had put it, while the situation grew worse by the day. Not that it could get much worse – children kidnapped and held against their will for sexual abuse, people trafficked and forced to work in labour camps – and now the murder of two cops, irrespective of whether they were bent or not, was a step too far.

These bastards were going to pay, and if these bastards were Masons, MPs or his fellow cops it was irrelevant, he was going to get them.

A young PC entered the tent and handed Winston a mug of coffee, he took it gratefully, swallowed the tablets and washed them down with the murky liquid. He grimaced.

'Dan, I can trust you, yeah?'

'Course you can boss. Why do you ask?'

'I need to get a squad of good men... and women together – all armed. I can authorise...' he corrected himself, '...I can get firearms and a chopper if needs be. Are you in?'

Dan Britton had worked under Fraser Winston for two years; he admired him and would trust him with his life. He had never queried his boss's motives before and he wasn't about to query them now… but he had to ask.

'Uh, what do you mean am I in? This is legit yeah? You've authorised it with the Super?'

Winston shifted his weight uncomfortably.

'Not entirely… he knows what we've been investigating and he knows what I want to do, but… for whatever reason he's reluctant to authorise any further action.'

'Hmmm, have you taken it further – gone to Citadel Place?'

'All the way up, right up to the Director General – and there's only one other person I can go to after her.'

'The PM?'

'Exactly, but I especially don't want to go there.'

Dan Britton knew there was no point in pursuing the questioning of his boss, it was clear that some things were best left unsaid.

'But it's still part of Operation Waffle, yeah?'

'Operation Waffle? Fucking good name for it – that's all that's happening – waffle. No, let's just say the waffle has been put on the back burner.'

'So this is an undercover, off the record operation – like what they did in the Sweeney?'

Winston nodded, but he failed to raise a smile.

'OK, count me in – uh, who else is involved – CEOP, Special Branch?'

Winston hesitated, he knew good men and women in both outfits but he was unwilling to ask for their help, fearful of who or what they may be connected to. He had to keep this operation as tight as a duck's arse.

'Nah, this is on a need to know basis, but I'll be calling in a few favours. I'll give Chloe Curtis in the

Birmingham office a call and I've got some bods on the outside who can help as well. If I can get this sorted in the next couple of days we should be able to start knocking on doors early next week.'

He glanced at Britton. Winston could sense his concern.

'Don't worry there'll be no comebacks, no fears of breaching the Official Secrets Act if that's what you're thinking – far from it. After what's happened in recent years with the Met and South Yorks forces suppressing evidence of paedophile rings in the establishment and the like we'll be thought of as bloody heroes – trust me.'

Who am I fucking kidding?

Chapter Thirty

Steve was hoping that with Lee Preston's release from Chicken City following the *ustawka* in the woods he might be able to learn something from his father about the whereabouts of Eva.

Steve had phoned and asked Preston but he was given short shrift.

'Yeah, Lee said he'd seen her,' Preston replied bluntly to Steve's question.

'And?'

'And what?'

'And what about her – did he speak to her, was she OK?'

'Didn't say. Just said that she was as fit as a millionaire's racehorse, and…'

'And fucking what?' asked Steve impatiently.

'And that if he wasn't gay, he would sling one up her… he said even Graham Norton would turn for her.'

* * *

Steve could sense Irena's impatience. He tried to placate her with suggestions of going out – visiting the shops, having a drink or just a walk around the Centre but she wasn't interested.

She'd admitted she wanted to see more of the sights of Bristol but at the moment she had only one thing on her mind – apart from the occasional picking of random songs on the jukebox and passionate, energetic sex – she was totally preoccupied and obsessed with getting her daughter released from Solutio's grasp.

It was understandable, but then again Steve couldn't help but think if it wasn't for Irena she wouldn't be in there in the first place. He was reluctant to broach the subject with her though, he was becoming both weary and wary of her mood swings – one moment she would be throwing saucepans around the kitchen whilst cursing in incomprehensible Serbian expletives and the next she would be lunging at Steve and tearing his clothes off demanding wild sex. He could cope with the latter but the former was making a fucking mess of his apartment.

'Steve, I fucking fed up! You promised me you would get Eva back to me, but you not do anything!'

She waved an already battered saucepan frantically in front of him. He placated her and gently took the pan from her shaking hand.

He knew he had no words that would pacify or comfort her, he took her in her arms as once again she sobbed uncontrollably at the thought of her absent and troubled daughter.

Eventually, her sobbing subsided. He looked into her puffy, red eyes.

'Come on,' he said, 'no objections. Get your coat on, we're going out.'

* * *

She'd compromised with him. She would go out for a walk around the Harbourside if he wore the colourful clothing she spied in his wardrobe – *but not the boots Steve, I not like the boots.*

He reluctantly agreed, he'd not worn the classy, but confrontational skinhead clothing for some time and, in all honesty, he now felt ill at ease with the fashion that had once defined his generation.

Instead of his Solovair boots, he wore his highly polished oxblood Bass loafers, complete with attention-seeking Blakeys, while he gave his Turnbull & Asser handmade pinstripe shirt only its second ever airing.

A pair of slimfit, pale blue dogtooth-check trousers complete with frogmouth pockets, courtesy of his brother's Brighton retro clothing store and Kirsty's red Harrington finished off the classy, sharp ensemble.

Steve had originally suggested a stroll around the Downs and over the Clifton Suspension Bridge but Irena had wanted to see the City Centre and the Harbourside with its bars, museums and motley assortment of old and new boats, ships and assorted watercraft. He'd hardly visited the revamped and restored old dockland area of Bristol since the death of Kirsty and he approached the area with a sense of apprehension and trepidation.

Irena hooked her hand around Steve's arm that itself was thrust deep into the pocket of his jacket. She looked up and studied his chiselled, scarred and gnarly face and smiled with pride. They made a handsome couple, Steve was aware of admiring glances from young and middle-aged males of the stunning Serbian on his arm while Irena noticed not just women but men eyeing up her partner – the women for his looks and the men for his stylish threads.

Bristol had always been an edgy, rebellious and subversive place – Steve often put it down to the heavy consumption of cider within the city. He was reminded of its unruly history as they passed by the empty pedestal where the statue of Edward Colston, the seventeenth-century slave trader, once stood before it was unceremoniously dumped into the nearby harbour following the Black Lives Matter protests of 2020.

They then strolled through to Queen Square, the elegant Georgian quadrant that had been the scene of violent riots in 1831 when drunken rioters burnt nearly a hundred buildings to the ground and looted the cellars. Order had eventually been restored when the

Third Dragoon Guards drew swords and attacked the rioters. Dozens were killed and in the ensuing trials four were sentenced to death and hundreds imprisoned.

At one time the square had also housed many of the slave traders who had made the city so wealthy. According to the history books that Steve had read at school, slavery had been abolished in 1807 but now, over two hundred years later, he knew different.

'You're quiet,' said Irena, aware of his sudden sullenness.

'Eh... uh yeah, it's just all this history. Bristol has got such a dark and shameful past. The guilt lies heavily on our shoulders. We all like to think those days have long gone, but well – it's still happening isn't it? Modern-day slavery, right under our noses and the majority of the population just seem oblivious to it all.' Steve sighed loudly.

Irena motioned Steve to sit on a bench.

'You think you British have a what is it – *monopoly* – on shame and guilt? You've heard of the Barbary pirates yes and the slaves they captured from all over Europe?'

'Of course.'

'Well then, don't knock yourself out and anyway you don't have to lecture us Serbs on the history of slavery.'

Steve creased his eyes. *'Beat yourself up'* he said under his breath before asking 'what do you mean?'

'Us Serbs – people from the Balkans. You know we're all descended from Slavs yes?'

Steve nodded. He did, but he wasn't sure where Irena's history lesson was going.

'And you know where the word slave comes from?' She didn't wait for Steve to answer.

'It's from us, the Slavs. We were the original *robovi* – slaves, taken by Spanish Muslims in the ninth century and we're still being taken now – nothing has changed in over a thousand years!'

Steve wasn't sure about the 'original slaves' bit but he wasn't in the mood to argue. He knew his history and was fully aware of how it had been distorted and rewritten over the years to fit the narrative. They got up from the bench and headed for the Harbourside. For a moment Steve thought about imparting his knowledge of the city's bloody and shameful past to Irena but the nearer they got to the quayside the more reticent he became.

He glanced to his left at the Shakespeare pub and recalled the meeting he'd had there with Kirsty, when they'd met for the first time since they'd split up all those years previously. Kirsty had been his first love. He'd loved his wife Debbie and he'd been grateful to her for giving him two fine sons, but he knew deep down that Kirsty had always been the one for him.

He turned back and took in the beauty of Irena, his heart danced. Like Kirsty she turned heads wherever she went. Helen of Troy may have launched a thousand ships but Irena could make a pub full of pissheads miss their mouths with their pints. If ever there was someone who was going to get him over Kirsty, it was Irena. He smiled to himself contentedly but remained silent as they crossed the road and the vista of the waterfront opened up in front of them.

In the eighteenth century the only vessels in the harbour would have been slave ships heading for the West Coast of Africa to collect their wretched and terrified cargo on their way to the West Indies or the Americas. Or they would have been newly arrived ships unloading cocoa, tobacco and sugar – all goods that contributed to the wealth and prosperity of the city, but now just yachts and pleasure craft of all shapes and sizes filled the docks.

A trio of gaily-painted boats filled with excited and gawping tourists – most of whom were blissfully unaware of the city's dark history, chugged past them on their way to cosy tea gardens and welcoming waterfront pubs and bars. A young girl, seated on the lap of her protective mother on one of the passing ferryboats, smiled and waved energetically at Irena. Irena beamed and returned her wave enthusiastically.

Steve remained unmoved and Irena sensed his unease. The hurt and pain of the loss of Kirsty was still raw and etched in his memory like a freshly inked tattoo.

'What is it you say, a penny for your thoughts?' She looked at him with concern in her eyes.

'It's nothing... just got some bad memories of this area that's all,' he said as they approached the spot where his former lover had fallen to her death.

He looked up at the penthouse apartment – there were plant pots and new items of furniture on the balcony. He wondered if, like the tourists, the new residents were oblivious to the tragic history of their surroundings.

Irena creased her brow.

'Bad memories – of what, or is it who?... *Kirsty?*' she asked.

Steve guessed that like her daughter, Irena had spotted 'their' record with its crude but truthful message scrawled across the label. He hesitated and gathered his thoughts but reasoned it best not to tell Irena about his previous love.

'I don't want to talk about it... let's just say you're not the only one who's had a tragic past.'

Irena squeezed Steve's arm tightly.

'Who was she Steve? Your former lover – you not tell me about your past? You like a book that's closed.' She looked at him questioningly.

'And that *closed book* is going to stay that way,' replied Steve bluntly.

He quickened his step and tugged at Irena's arm.

'Come on,' he said, 'the pubs are open.'

Chapter Thirty-One

Fraser Winston expertly adjusted the straps of his Kevlar jacket then checked the rounds in his Glock pistol. Dan Britton took it as a sign to do the same with the Heckler & Koch semi-automatic submachine gun he held across his chest.

'You alright Dan?' asked Winston. 'It ain't too late to back out you know.'

'No worries boss. Looking forward to nicking a few nonces to be honest,' replied Britton, a little too enthusiastically for Winston, who tutted and shook his head.

'Dan this ain't a few *nonces* and these Albanians are organised criminals, almost definitely armed and with military training not like those wet wipe Hellbanianz wannabe gangsters in East London. You've seen the reports – this Besin Marishta commanded a bloody army back in Kosovo. We also know Etchington is back here and he has a military background. They ain't no mugs so don't go thinking we're up against Jimmy *fucking* Savile and his perverted mates.'

'Sorry boss,' replied Britton sheepishly. 'Uh… when's the balloon going up?'

Winston checked his Rolex. 'Oh six hundred hours – twenty minutes' time.'

They sat in the back of an unmarked battered dark blue Transit – along with eight other similarly armed, battle-fatigued members of the National Crime Agency, all of them willing volunteers and hand-picked by Winston.

Parked at strategic points around the vast processing plant in Avonmouth were eleven other similar vehicles

– all containing well-trained and well-disciplined NCA officers of varying ranks. A hundred or so miles to the north a comparable collection of officers headed up by G3 Chloe Curtis sat armed and ready outside of Solutio's microchip plant on the outskirts of Birmingham; they too studied their watches and nervously checked their firearms in eager anticipation.

Winston had been busier than usual in the last few days, but his hard work had paid off. He had to tread carefully and be wary of who he spoke to but the trust and admiration of his colleagues up and down the country stood him in good stead. They had seen the evidence and read his reports and they too had wondered and queried the inactivity from on high. They did not require a lot of persuasion.

From inside the van the low *whump, whump, whump* from the rotors of the approaching Eurocopter EC 135T belonging to the NPAS could be heard. It heralded renewed activity from the occupants of the vans who were all eager and keen to engage in the greatly anticipated raid. Winston eyed his watch once more then pressed a button on his Tetra police issue mobile phone.

'Alpha Group... *Go! Go! Go!*'

The chopper descended until it was barely twenty feet above the ground. Two thick nylon ropes dropped down from either side of the craft and four black-uniformed and heavily armed NCA officers expertly slid down and planted their boots on the grey tarmac within the compound. Within seconds the officers had surrounded the main entrance and forced the two startled guards to the ground.

G4 Johnny 'Shirley' Temple, the officer in charge of the four-man Alpha Group pressed his stubby-nosed Glock to the back of one of the guard's head.

'Police! *Bëni ju flisni anglisht?*'

The terrified guard crooked his head around and squinted at Temple.

'You f-fucking what?' he stammered.

'I said do you speak Eng…. Forget it. I thought all you lot were Albanians?'

'Not me, me babber, *El Dub* born and bred.'

'El Dub?' asked Temple. 'Where the fuck's that?'

'EL Dub – Lawrence Weston mate.'

Temple allowed himself a wry smile at the reference to the sprawling nearby Bristol neighbourhood.

'Good. Now open the gates will you – *mate*?'

Twelve sets of gates opened simultaneously as the guard pressed buttons on the panel in front of him.

The awaiting vans accelerated through the gates and quickly disgorged their occupants who met with little resistance from the occupants of the gatehouses. Within minutes all of the guards were prostrate on the ground with their hands cable-tied behind their backs.

'Nice one Shirley,' said Winston as he patted Temple on the back, 'now let's go for the big guns.'

Winston activated his phone once more.

'OK all units – good work. Now enter and sweep as instructed… and the units entering the villitas take extra care, there's gonna be women and kids in there – copy?'

A chorus of 'copy' chattered over the phones.

The officers fanned out and headed for the locations that they'd all been previously briefed on. 'Enforcer' hand-held battering rams lived up to their name and smashed through locked metal doors or took them off their ineffective hinges.

Winston referred to his iPad and studied the layout of the building as he entered the huge hangar-like structure.

He and his team – Temple, Britton and the rest of Alpha Group – semi-crouched and scampered through a small, unmanned reception area which resembled a thousand other nondescript receptions in factories and offices across the country – an MDF desk, a filing cabinet and coffee machine were positioned in one corner, whilst cheap prints of faraway exotic landscapes adorned the walls. Two faux leather chairs were positioned either side of an Ikea coffee table on which sat a dog-eared and ancient copy of *World Poultry* and week-old newspapers.

Winston opened the heavy double doors that led directly to the factory floor. In front of him startled workers – the operamini – stood rigid and resembled grossed-out mime artists in blue, blood-stained overalls, hairnets and white boots.

They abruptly ceased their work and stared incredulously at the armed officers. The clanging of machinery, conveyor belts and squawking chickens competed with the sound of recorded muzak blasting out from numerous unseen speakers.

The stench of dead and decaying poultry and of unidentified chemicals permeated Winston's balaclava. It invaded his nostrils and mouth, causing his stomach to tighten as he barely controlled the urge to wretch.

The floors were awash with blood, guts and shit of which he presumed, and hoped, were of avian origin – the decapitated head of a recently deceased bird stared up at him mockingly.

Fraser Winston approached one of the workers who, due to the overalls and facemask, was of undeterminable sex. He lowered the mouthpiece of his balaclava.

'Do you speak English?' he barked in a desperate attempt to be heard over the cacophony of noise.

The figure nodded.

'Take your mask off,' he ordered.

The figure removed its headgear and mask – it was a female in her twenties – she had huge, dull, impassive eyes, bad skin and looked severely undernourished.

She stared blankly at Winston, he was reminded of the haunted images of concentration camp victims. He felt a pang of guilt for shouting at her.

'What's your name?' he asked, deliberately and slowly.

'Hyiab.'

'Where are you from Hyiab… originally?'

'I, I from Eritrea,' she answered, her voice quivered with fear.

'OK Hyiab, listen to me. We're police officers and we're here to help you – all of you. We are going to get you all out of here.'

He motioned with his hand to the rest of the cavernous factory. He then noticed for the first time that the vast majority of workers were totally oblivious to his and his officers' presence and were carrying on relentlessly with their mundane tasks of killing and plucking.

'We are looking for Besin Marishta – do you know him?'

Hyiab's eyes widened in recognition of the name, she looked even more terrified. She nodded once more.

'We know he's in this building – can you tell me where?' asked Winston.

'He still sleep,' she answered coldly, 'we never see him until late, he lazy shit.'

Winston glanced at his watch – it was six-fifteen. Chicken City was a twenty-four operation – twenty-four hours of electro-shocking, decapitating, hot water scalding, feather plucking, gizzard wrenching, shit removing, cleaning and packing – all to satisfy the ever-increasing demand for takeaway tower burgers and Friday night kebabs.

'Can you show me where he sleeps?'

Hyiab nodded, turned and led Winston towards the far end of the building.

The officers trooped in line behind their boss and walked past endless rows of workers slaughtering endless rows of chickens.

For a fleeting second, the regimented lines of opera-mini stopped and watched the officers as they filed past – with a look of both fear and indifference on their faces, then like automatons they turned back to the production lines and continued with their task of ending the lives of thousands of chickens.

In a side room watching their every move on CCTV and through a two-way mirror were two armed-guards – custos. One, shaven-headed, bull-necked and as angry as a drowning wasp in a Summer pint of cider, glanced sideways towards his concerned colleague.

'Phone him now!' he barked.

Besin Marishta cursed as his phone woke him from his slumber. He switched on a lamp and fumbled for his mobile phone on the bedside cabinet, knocking off a baggie and spilling its content of white powder as he did so.

'What the fuck do you want?' he grumbled into his mobile.

In an instant he sat upright in his bed. A bead of sweat formed on his forehead and ran down his fleshy, flushed face.

'How the fuck did they get in here?'

He didn't wait for a response.

'Stop them – now!'

Marishta threw back the black and gold duvet and eased his massive bulk off of the mattress. Two fifteen-year old girls, who had been sharing his bed, embraced and comforted each other under the garish cover.

He grabbed a silk kimono from the floor and put it on, embroidered across the back was the legend '*Tiny One*'.

He strode across the room, a room that was as large as it was tasteless.

A profusion of fake animal skins, chrome fittings and geometric patterned wallpaper assaulted the senses – as did the smell of stale cannabis, lubricant and sex. He cursed as he trod on a large, shiny multi-pronged vibrator.

A black vinyl covered padded door leading from his bedroom beckoned him. He opened it and peered into the darkness.

'Etchington! Fucking move – we've got visitors!' he bellowed into the gloom.

A startled Neil Etchington, dishevelled and bleary-eyed, stared at Marishta.

'Wha… who issh it?' slurred Etchington. He tried in vain to focus but his pupils were constricted to the size of pin pricks.

'Never mind – just get the fuck out of here!'

Etchington fell back onto the bed, his eyelids slammed shut.

Beside Etchington lay a bruised, but still beautiful young girl. Her emerald green eyes widened and a gentle smile crept across her exquisite face.

'It's Steve – he's come for me,' whispered Eva quietly to herself.

Chapter Thirty-Two

Dan Britton slumped to the ground as if he'd been hit with a baseball bat between his shoulder blades.

He'd simultaneously heard the crack and felt the thud as the bullet slammed into his back but his Kevlar vest had proved as efficient as it always had. He felt winded but nothing else, he'd had heartburn from late night curries that had been far worse.

The rest of Alpha group dispersed, crouched and took positions as they had practiced many times in the past.

Around them terrified operamini screamed and ran for cover leaving a multitude of reprieved and hapless chickens to squawk and flap on the hooks that pierced their bloodied feet.

Another shot rang out, hitting a carbon dioxide cylinder that was propped up against a nearby wall. The cylinder erupted with a loud hiss and steaming gas gushed out with a piercing high-pitched whistle, the cylinder fell to the ground then spun on its axis like an oversized Catherine wheel.

'You alright Dan?' shouted Winston above the discord that surrounded them.

'Not even a flesh wound boss,' grinned Britton.

Winston activated his mobile phone.

'Beta Group, we've come under attack from armed custos, gimme a sitrep.'

Beta Group were raiding a similar-sized building adjacent to the one Alpha Group were in. The phone crackled in response.

'Same here gaffer, one of our guys wounded but we're OK… looks like we've kicked the hornet's nest.'

Winston was worried. The last thing he wanted was a firefight with the custos with so many innocent operamini around.

'How many are you up against Mac?' shouted Winston into his phone.

G4 Kevin McNaughton, Beta group's commander, did a quick count in his head.

'Six or seven – they came out of one of the side rooms, must have spotted us on CCTV... trouble is there's operamini between us and them, bit of a stalemate at the moment.'

'Yeah ditto,' answered Winston. He had to make a quick decision.

'Mac – are you able to safely withdraw?'

'Withdraw? Uh, yeah guess so – there's exit doors to our left, we can easily get to them.'

'OK, exit as soon as you can then enter the building we're in. Come in the same way that we did. The custos will be directly in front of you, there's only two of them – they'll have their backs to you, just get them to surrender then clear the building – copy?'

'Copy gaffer – see you in five.'

The double doors burst open and as predicted by Winston, McNaughton and his colleagues caught the two custos unawares.

'Armed police! Drop your weapons – now!'

The two startled custos had no option. They did as they were told and simultaneously raised their hands above their heads. They were quickly bundled to the floor and handcuffed with black cable ties.

'All clear gaffer,' McNaughton signalled to Winston who promptly ordered his officers to proceed to the large door at the far end of the factory. All around them operamini scattered and made for exits as directed by the advancing Beta Group.

'Cheers Mac. Now revert back to the original plan, get back in and do the business... but be careful.'

Winston and the rest of his group stealthily made their way to the back of the factory. As they did so they heard the deafening sounds of exploding thunder flashes from the adjacent building as McNaughton and his men swept through the building with military efficiency. They quickly reached the door and Winston signalled to an officer carrying the heavy 'Enforcer' to move forward.

'Careful,' said Winston, 'they'll be on the other side and almost definitely armed.'

The officer moved forward and swung back the menacing battering ram.

'Hold on a minute,' said Winston as he stepped towards the door and tried the handle – it opened with a creak. He turned to the officer and winked.

Winston warily pushed the door open unsure of what he might find inside the darkened room, he switched on his powerful Lenser torch and the room was immediately flooded with crisp, white light…

Shelves full of boxes, packaging material and plastic barrels of cleaning fluids and chemicals lined the walls. Carbon dioxide cylinders were stacked haphazardly in one corner. In another corner a metallic contraption with tubes, belts and straps sat bolted to a workbench; electrical cables linked the contraption to a desktop computer adjacent to it.

Another door led off to the right, Winston indicated to his men to enter it. They found a near identical room – similarly furnished, similarly nondescript, it also housed the same contraption as in the previous room.

'It's just storerooms boss,' said Britton, stating the obvious.

Again, a door led off to the right… they swept through five rooms in all – all featuring the same shelving, furniture and contraptions. The last door was marked 'Fire exit' – Winston pushed the bar below the sign, the door opened outwards and daylight flooded in, he walked out and blinked as the early morning sun penetrated his visor.

He looked around at the environs of the complex – operamini wandered around as if in a daze while recently liberated chickens pecked at non-existent specks of grain.

Winston looked to his left and smiled approvingly as black-clad NCA officers escorted custos with their hands on their heads to waiting vans. He congratulated himself that the operation was looking like it was going to plan… except for one thing. *Where the fuck was Besin Marishta?*

Winston caught up with Hyiab and started hurriedly questioning her again. She was now more relaxed as the realisation that at last, some sort of freedom for her and her colleagues might be on the horizon.

'Are you sure Marishta's bedroom is where you said it is?'

'Yes, we see him going through that door at night – and he comes out in the morning so it is bedroom, no?'

Winston liked her logic. He removed his helmet and balaclava and studied Hyiab sympathetically.

'Hyiab, have you ever been in there yourself?'

'Yes,' she said, 'just once, when I first arrive. To have this done…'

She rolled up the left sleeve of her overall and revealed a black-inked barcode tattoo on her wrist. It was barely visible against her dark skin. Winston sighed and nodded his head in recognition and disgust.

'OK I understand, but you haven't ever been into Marishta's private rooms… his er… actual bedroom?'

She shook her head – almost in shame. She then looked around.

'But she has.'

Hyiab nodded towards a young, sultry, dark-haired teenager who was leaning against a wall casually smoking a cigarette. She had pulled down the top of her overall and it flapped in the wind around her waist.

She wore a grubby, bloodstained, tight-fitting T-shirt that, underneath the blood spatters, carried a sparkly Chanel logo.

As Winston approached the girl, she seductively blew a cloud of smoke in his direction. He stifled a cough then noticed the only flaws in her beauty, the barcode tattoo on her arm and her yellow, crooked teeth.

'I'm Fraser Winston of the National Crime Agency… the police. Do you speak English?'

She nodded, causing her large hooped earrings to swing in unison. Her dark brown eyes stared unblinkingly at the detective.

'Look you're not in any trouble. We're here to help you – help you all get out of here. But I need to ask… have you ever been into Besin Marishta's, uh… private rooms – his bedroom?'

'What if I have?' she answered with a thick, exotic accent.

'Nothing, nothing – I just need to know where they are exactly.'

She dropped the cigarette to the ground and stubbed it out with her boot; she even managed to make this mundane task seem sensuous. He suddenly felt uncomfortably hot and it wasn't just his body armour that was making him hyperventilate.

'At the back of the factory, in the storerooms. Past the tattoo machines,' she answered flatly.

'You've been there – yes?'

'Yes, he took me there and fucked me – many times he fucked me.'

Winston was shocked by her cold candidness.

'Uh… OK, but can you tell me where exactly?'

The girl's eyes widened. It was her turn to be embarrassed.

'I uh… I don't know if I want to tell you,' she stammered.

'Please, it's really important,' implored Winston.

The girl hesitated. Winston motioned to her to continue.

'Uh, OK… he fucked me in the arse, he said I looked better from behind… the bastard.'

'*Shit!* No, no… sorry, I didn't mean it like that!'

Winston heard a stifled laugh from one of the officers behind him. He shot an angry and irritated glance over his shoulder.

He turned back to the girl then rubbed his brow in a vain attempt to hide his embarrassment.

'Sorry I meant whereabouts in the building… *shit,* sorry.'

The girl let out an audible sigh.

'No, sorry my mistake… what is it you say? It got lost… no?'

'No, I mean yes… lost in translation. Sorry, what's your name?'

'Ligia.'

'Where are you from Ligia?'

'Romania, I am Roma gypsy.'

'Have you family here Ligia?'

'Yes, my mother work here. And I have brother and a sister here as well… I hate it, we all hate it.'

'I understand. Look, like I said we'll get you all out of here,' he said truthfully, but in all honesty, he didn't know what would happen to the inhabitants of Chicken City, but that was for others and not him to sort out at a later date.

He was just going to ensure that the hellhole would get shut down, or at least repurposed and rebuilt, sooner rather than later.

'So, you work in the chicken processing plant, yes? And the rest of your family, do they do the same work?'

'My mother does, but my brother and sister are in the chemical plant.'

'The chemical plant?' he queried.

'Yes, unit four – over there. That's where they process and package the drugs.'

She pointed towards a huge, blue, hangar-like building some half a mile from where they were to the northern edge of the complex. Winston knew Gamma Group had been designated to sweep through the building – he reached for his Tetra phone.

'Gamma Group come in... Micky, can you give me an update.'

The phoned jumped into life, a crackle preceded the voice of G4 Michaela Dobson.

'Alright boss... yeah all good. Seized the building... Got at least a dozen guards in custody and we're getting the operamini out into the open... You'll never guess what they're making in this place guv.'

'At a guess I'd say some sort of pharmaceutical cocaine?' answered Winston with an air of resignation.

'Yeah, not to mention the heroin, cannabis and loads of other shit ... uh, how did you know?'

'Just a hunch.'

'Yeah and shitloads of the stuff. Ain't seen anything like it since that fact-finding tour of Columbia a few years back. This makes Escobar's operation look tinpot – there's enough drugs here to sink a fucking battleship, uh and there's something else.'

'What is it Micky?'

'There's loads of young women – and men here. Think they're all prosti... sorry, sex workers. Uh, slaves even. Fucking loads of slimey punters as well.'

The news hadn't surprised Winston, he sighed and wearily turned his attention back to Ligia. He looked at the barcode on her wrist.

'Ligia, I see you have a tattoo – do you have anything else, have they inserted something into you?'

She twisted her arm around and studied the tattoo as if it was the first time she'd ever seen it.

'No. I am just an operamini, everyone here all have the tattoos… well apart from the chosen ones.'

'The chosen ones? Who are they?'

'The ones who are young, very young – even younger than me. They are chosen, chosen for their looks and for their… skills. Is that what you say?'

Winston nodded knowingly.

'Marishta said I would be chosen but I wasn't. He said he didn't like my teeth, the fucking bastard. He got nerve, the fat fuck. But I'm glad though, they just fucking machines, young fucking machines and they not tattooed but they are… they have things put inside them, what do you call them?'

'Microchips?'

'Yes, they have microchips inserted in them… here.' She pointed to the inside of her upper left arm.

Winston grimaced then slowly nodded and thought of the conversation he'd had with Steve Allen less than a month ago.

* * *

At first he'd doubted what he'd heard. Doubted that anything so barbaric could be happening anywhere in the world, let alone Britain. He had doubted that the slavery existed within the migrant cities, doubted that they had been set up and funded by the Government, but they had and people in power in this country were behind them.

And who had the Government awarded the contract to to run the migrant cities? Etchington's Solutio.

And who had Solutio employed to run the migrant cities? The very same Albanian Organised Crime Group who also smuggled the refugees and asylum seekers across the Channel in small boats.

Every problem has a solution, thought Fraser Winston, he had to concede it was a brilliant business model. *It was pure, evil genius.*

Some of the very same people who had democratically been voted into power and who claimed that they would categorically 'Stop the boats' were now responsible for the trafficking of people into slave labour camps as well as the monitoring and microchipping of people as if they were no more than pet dogs.

Then there was the manufacture and distribution of illicit drugs on an industrial scale and the tacit knowledge of sexual exploitation of children.

Paedophile gangs operated in all corners of society, but as he had been told on more than one occasion, it was not in the public interest to prosecute them – and if the Crown Prosecution Service thought that, who was he to argue? *Who was he?*

He was Fraser Winston of the National Crime Agency, that's who he was... husband and father to two beautiful children and he was going to argue, argue with whoever the fuck he wanted, whatever the consequences.

* * *

'Here it is.'

Ligia had led Winston and his officers back into the building and they were now in one of the storerooms that they had previously visited. She pointed triumphantly at an insignificant panel on the wall.

Winston and his men hadn't noticed it when they had previously searched the room, it being just a set of fuses, switches and random meters busily rotating and whirring like a million others around the country.

'That button there – press it,' she said.

Winston stepped forward and pressed the large green button. Almost immediately a motor hummed behind the panel and a previously unseen door sprung open revealing a set of well-worn metal steps that descended into a darkened room.

'What the fuck? A secret room... Jeez, it's like a fucking James Bond movie.'

Dan Britton stood open mouthed at the entrance to the subterranean room. He switched on the flashlight mounted on his Heckler and Koch semi-automatic and peered into the darkness.

'There's a light switch on the wall,' said Ligia with a wry smile.

Britton sheepishly felt for the switch and flicked it on. The room became bathed in a cold, bluish light – in front of them could be seen exercise bikes and weights.

'It's a gym – they like the chosen ones to keep fit. Over to the right there is a sauna and tanning room and that door over there...' Ligia pointed directly in front of her.

'...that leads to a corridor with the chosen ones' rooms leading off of them, they will probably be locked. At the far end of the corridor is a door leading to Marishta's rooms... I show you, yes?'

'No, you stay here. It could be dangerous from here on – thank you Ligia, you've been a great help,' said Winston as he motioned for her to leave.

She turned and left, then looked over her shoulder at him. 'Be careful, he's a fucking animal.' She spat out the words with venom.

Alpha Group led by Winston descended the stairs and swept through the empty gym before opening the door leading to the corridor.

At the end of the corridor Winston could see one single door as described by Ligia – Berishta's rooms. Along the two side walls were twenty-four numbered doors, twelve on each side – it reminded Winston of some of the cheap hotels he had stayed in over the years.

'We'll check these rooms later Dan, first priority is to…'

BANG! … BANG!

The sound of two loud gunshots rang out from the direction of Marishta's room. Winston nervously glanced at Britton before running towards the door without hesitation, he kicked at the heavy steel door but it refused to budge.

'Enforcer now!' he shouted.

The thud as the heavy enforcer smashed against the door was almost as loud as the gunshots, there was a slight movement but nothing more.

The officer swung again – *Boom! … Boom!*

'Sorry boss… it ain't moving, fucking thing's like Fort Knox.'

'OK step down,' said Winston with a resigned sigh.

'Any ideas?' he asked of no-one in particular.

There was no answer.

A door slowly opened behind him.

A young girl dressed in baggy floral pyjamas stood bleary-eyed in the middle of the corridor. She was clutching a raggedy but obviously much-cherished, teddy bear.

Winston guessed she was in her early teens, the same as his own daughter. Her hair was strawberry blonde and either fashionably unkempt or looking like she had just got out of bed. Winston guessed the latter. She looked tired.

She was pretty, achingly pretty, he thought.

'What's happening?' she asked innocently as she rubbed the sleep from her eyes.

Winston took a step towards her, causing her to take a pace back. She held onto the doorframe as if seeking reassurance and protection.

'Don't worry – we're the police, we're here to help you. Is there anyone else in the room with you?'

She shook her head.

'Uh... no, I had a night off last night. I wasn't booked in with anyone,' she answered matter-of-factly in a polite, soft West Country accent.

A night off from what? Winston dreaded to think.

'What's your name?' he asked.

'Rebecca. What's yours?'

'Fraser. I'm Fraser Winston.'

'Nice to meet you Fraser Winston.' She looked around at the other officers and took in their uniforms and weapons.

'I heard a bang about twenty minutes ago and then I just heard another two. Has someone been shot?' she asked with no emotion.

Winston and the team had only heard the two shots, according to Rebecca another shot had rung out previously, Winston was visibly worried.

'Uh we're not sure – the shots came from this room,' he motioned towards Marishta's door.

'Do you know who's in there Rebecca?'

'Uh huh... it's Besin Marishta's private rooms. He's with Laila and Yasmin, they're sisters – twins. And I think Evalina is in there with that Etchington – the *cunt*.'

* * *

Eva sat, partially naked, on the edge of the bed toying with a small, dull black pistol.

She began to run the short, stubby barrel up along her long legs.

For just a second or so she hesitated as the gun reached her genitals before she then moved it up and circled it around her exposed breasts.

She raised the gun to her neck, then up around her chin and finally up to her open mouth. The barrel was still hot. She licked the tip of it and tasted the bitter, acrid cordite.

Her lips seductively encircled the hard shaft of the pistol. She closed her eyes and smiled.

'Come on Steve, I'm waiting,' she gently whispered to herself.

Chapter Thirty-Three

Steve had at last woken from his slumber. He sensed Irena had been studying him for some time.

He'd slept like the dead, his head was still muzzy and his mouth was as dry as a camel's hoof. The six or seven pints of Timothy Taylor Landlord and the couple of St Lucia Chairman's Reserve Spiced Rum night-caps he'd consumed the previous night had been responsible. The day had progressed into the night and it turned out to be a long and memorable one.

After a couple of drinks in The Shakespeare they headed to the famous Old Duke in King Street where his favourite local funk and soul outfit The Soul Strutters, performed a typically blistering hot and sweaty set culminating in *Move on up*, Curtis Mayfield's ground-breaking masterpiece. Irena had been well impressed by the band's performance, unlike Steve's when they eventually fell into bed in the early hours.

'What?' asked Steve gruffly.

'Nothing,' replied Irena. She too felt just as groggy but at least Steve's previous day's sullenness appeared to have been forgotten. A twinkle appeared in her eye.

'Well, how do you fancy making up for last night?' she asked with a wicked grin.

At times Steve loved Irena's bluntness.

She slid her hand down under the duvet in the direction of Steve's groin.

Her smile grew even wider.

'I take that as a yes,' she purred.

* * *

Fraser Winston had to admit defeat and make a call. *How the fuck could I have overlooked this?* he asked himself.

He had plans of the buildings and layouts of Chicken City and studied them until he knew every door, corridor and room – apart from the surreptitious cell-like rooms beneath the building that is.

His crack squad of hand-picked confidantes and confederates had been beaten by a locked door, a door that no matter how many times they'd battered, refused to budge.

He knew that Besin Marishta, Neil Etchington, Evalina Petrovic and at the very least two other young girls were on the other side of the door, although following the gunshots he had no idea what condition they were in, or whether they were even dead or alive.

The search of the other rooms that led off the corridor had been more rewarding however, not that Winston and his colleagues felt rewarded in any way, repulsed more like.

His team were now busy processing the contents and the inhabitants of the rooms – the chosen ones… and their abusers, who were now being led away in various states of undress.

The call Winston had reluctantly made was to his enraged superiors, but he fronted them, took the threats of sackings with a pinch of salt and vowed to bring the fuckers down if they even had a hint of what was really happening in Chicken City.

'Alright, alright – I'll live with the consequences, yeah I know, on my head be it. Just get me an EXPO team down here and make it quick.'

* * *

A team of Explosives Officers carrying heavy backpacks eagerly approached Winston.

'Eddie Flanagan from Avon and Somerset. What's want doing boss?' asked a tall, rangy, padded-up officer as he unloaded a string of det cord from his backpack.

'I need this door opening,' replied Winston, 'and please tell me you can do it.'

Flanagan studied the door.

'Easy as having a piss in a shower boss, so yep should be able to get the bugger open in a jiffy,' said Flanagan in a thick Yorkshire accent.

Within minutes the door was ready for breaching. Flanagan produced a loudhailer drawing quizzical looks from Winston.

'Better tell whoever's on t'other side to take cover.'

'Uh right, yeah guess so,' nodded Winston.

Flanagan approached the door, put the loudhailer to his lips and cleared his throat.

'If anyone's in there take cover. I'm going t' blow fuckin' door!'

He winked at Winston who smiled nervously. Winston guessed Flanagan wasn't too hot with his communication skills but he didn't have to worry about his ability to open a locked door as it exploded with a dull, loud thud.

Easy as a piss in a shower indeed, thought Winston.

The heavy door fell into the room in a cloud of grey smoke. Winston tentatively entered and swept the room with his gun as the smoke cleared.

'Armed police, get on the floor now!'

The rest of Alpha Group filed in behind him.

Beams of light from a dozen Lenser torches pierced the acrid gloom. The room was still and eerily silent.

'Don't think there's anyone in here guv,' stated Dan Britton as he peered into the darkness.

'Hold on a minute…'

Winston approached a huge bed that was positioned on the far side of the room. His eyes were drawn to a Masonic painting hanging above it showing The Square and Set of Compasses.

Under the duvet on the bed was a large lump that quivered violently as they approached. Winston motioned to his men to surround the bed. They edged forward with their guns at the ready and took aim at the quaking mound.

'Come out with your hands up!' shouted Winston.

The duvet slowly moved.

'Please don't shoot!'

The two sisters – Laila and Yasmin, raised their hands and stared in terror at the officers.

'It's OK, OK,' said Winston in hushed tones, 'we're the police – you're safe now.'

Before he had a chance to placate them further a single shot rang out from behind a black padded door behind them.

'Jesus, not another fucking room – this is like Alice in fucking Wonderland,' said Britton as he began to tire of their predicament. He hesitantly approached the door and removed his helmet. He put his ear up against the door then turned to his boss.

'I can hear someone snivelling, sounds like a bloke. What's reckon guv? One shot… always sounds ominous to me.'

'Try it, but be careful,' replied Winston.

'No shit,' said Britton under his breath as he turned the handle. To his relief the door wasn't locked – he gingerly eased it open.

Unlike Marishta's room this one was bathed in a warm, almost soothing glow.

A dozen lit scented candles surrounded a large sleigh bed that was positioned against the far wall. The flickering light drew Britton in. There was someone, female he thought, sat upright on the bed.

He approached the bed with his gun raised. He could now see that the figure on the bed was definitely female, apart from a pair of black knickers she was naked. Her breasts glowed and shimmered from the light of the candles while her long blonde hair cascaded down over her bare shoulders.

She too had a gun in her hand. It was pointing away from Britton towards a cowering figure huddled in one corner of the room.

Britton averted his gaze from the girl and studied the trembling figure in the corner. As his eyes grew accustomed to the light, he could make out it was a grey-haired male, possibly in his fifties.

He was completely naked and blood oozed from an angry wound in his abdomen and another one in his right shoulder. He shook and whimpered uncontrollably as tears rolled down his blood-splattered cheeks.

Fraser Winston looked over the shoulder of Dan Britton. He recognised both the teenage girl and the middle-aged male instantly from the video.

'Hi Eva. I'm Fraser Winston. This is my colleague Daniel Britton, we're the police… we're here to help you. Can you put the gun down please?'

Eva's wide-eyed stare remained fixed on the bloodied male, as did the gun she was aiming directly at his head.

'Where's Steve?' she asked without blinking.

'Steve? Steve who?' replied Winston, although he knew exactly whom she was referring to.

'Steve Allen, he is my *boyfriend*. Get him here now or Etchington gets his fucking brains blown out.'

'Eva, I need you to put the…'

BOOM!

Eva fired off a shot without hesitation. It missed Etchington's head by an inch and the plaster behind him shattered into a hundred pieces.

'Don't fuck with me – I'm an expert shot, I was taught by my father and have handled guns since I was five. The next shot will take his fucking head off. Now get me Steve Allen!'

* * *

'Now it's your turn,' whispered Irena as her head disappeared below the covers.

Steve lay on his back with his eyes closed. He rolled his tongue over his lips and savoured the distinct sour taste of his lover as she reciprocated below the duvet.

'Oh my fucking ... *GOD!*' he groaned. 'Jesus fucking H...'

The familiar sound of *Pressure Drop* by The Maytals rang out once again from his phone on the bedside cabinet.

'*You got to be fucking kidding!*' screamed Steve.

The classic tune continued incessantly.

'*Mwicch id ufff!*' came a muffled sound from under the sheets.

'What?'

Irena's furious head appeared. '*I said switch it off!*'

Steve leant over towards his mobile and glanced at the screen. His eyes widened as he saw the name Fraser Winston appear on it.

'Whoa, hold on Irena – it's the police!'

He grabbed the phone and pressed the answer button.

Irena scrunched up her eyes as she read the anxiety etched on Steve's face.

'OK, OK got it... yeah I'll be ready!'

He put the phone down.

'What? What is it... Steve tell me? It's Eva yes?'

'Yes. Now get dressed. The police will be here in five minutes.'

Chapter Thirty-Four

Steve and Irena were greeted by a nervous and weary-looking Fraser Winston at the main entrance to Chicken City.

He'd just come off a debrief call with his NCA colleague Chloe Curtis – the raid on Chip City in Birmingham had been a great success and thankfully, unlike the operation in Avonmouth, hadn't resulted in any casualties.

It too had unearthed similar-sized drug factories and brothels as well as a laboratory where the GPS microchips were being manufactured and a state-of-the-art print factory where forged passports and visas were being produced.

Winston had removed his helmet and body armour and stood dejectedly with his hands on his hips.

As they approached, he put out his hand and greeted Steve with a firm handshake. Steve noticed the familiar pressure – he was still sounding him out.

'This is Irena... Eva's mother.'

'Ms Petrovic – pleased to meet you.' Winston gently shook her hand.

'You have found Eva, yes?' pleaded Irena.

'Yes we have, but sorry, we need to move quickly. Have you been brought up to speed?' he asked.

'No more than what you said on the phone and that you've found Eva and she's in some... uh, some sort of delicate situation,' replied Steve.

'Delicate situation? Uh, yeah.' He didn't want to alarm either of them.

'I guess you could say that... please, follow me.'

They trooped through the building flanked by armed officers. All around them newly arrived police liaison officers were comforting frightened youngsters – both male and female – with blankets draped over their shoulders and cups of tea in their hands.

Steve studied them as he passed. He guessed they were the chosen ones and without exception they were young, attractive, bewildered and terrified.

Next, a group of around twenty adult males and a couple of women, mostly in their fifties and sixties, some even older, approached them. Armed officers escorted the group whose heads were bowed and their hands cable-tied behind their backs.

As Steve passed them, he thought one or two looked familiar, he had seen their faces somewhere before.

And then it dawned on him – *Kirsty's folder...* Ronald McGuire and Paul 'Goldie' Godden dejectedly slouched past.

They gave him a curious, cursory look as he studied them intently.

'This is for you Kirsty... and you Eva,' he said triumphantly as they shuffled towards the waiting police vans.

Then another familiar face, one he'd seen many times on the TV, caught his eye.

'Fucking hell, is that...?'

Winston raised his hand instantly and motioned for him to be silent. 'Yes – but not a word. You haven't seen anyone, right?'

Steve nodded. He'd got the message loud and clear.

* * *

'I've got to warn you Steve. I think she's on something,' said Winston as he helped Steve into a Kevlar vest.

'On something. Like what?' Steve stared at Winston.

'Fuck knows, take your pick. They've got a lab here straight out of Breaking Bad. All the usual shit plus they've got the Syrian refugees making that captagon and kids from Thailand producing ya ba – the madness drug and if that shit hits the streets, *Jeez* – don't bear thinking about. There's also a cannabis factory the size of a football pitch.'

Steve shook his head and looked around nervously, wary that Irena could overhear them.

'Uh, where's Irena?' he asked Winston.

'Don't worry about her, she's in a mobile ops unit drinking a hot cup of tea with a bit of luck.'

Steve nodded. 'Uh, what makes you think Eva's on something?'

'What do you think… erratic, irrational behaviour, OK this isn't your normal every day situation I admit. A beautiful, sixteen-year-old Kosovan girl sat half-naked on a bed pointing a gun at an MP that she's already taken two lumps out of… but, well, we've tried negotiating with her and one minute she seems to be coming round, she's even smiled at us a few times and then… she just glazes over and fixes her stare on Etchington. It goes right through you, chills you to the bone.'

'Tell me about it… look it goes without saying she's one fucked-up kid. But whatever happens in there don't shoot – either her or me, OK?'

'We'll try not to,' said Winston with a nervous smile.

'Steve, one other thing. She starts rambling as well. I mean she's been on about you since we found her. You know, uh… she's called you her boyfriend and says she wants you to…'

'Yeah, OK, I can guess what she's been saying… but I'm not and uh… I haven't, right?'

'OK, yeah I believe you. But y'know, she says that's the only way she'll come out. That's why she's put all the candles around the bed. She says she wants you. Uh... then she's mentioned a Bruce – *who the fuck's Bruce?'*

'Bruce Willis. She reckons I look like him... like in the *Die Hard* movies,' squirmed Steve.

'Uh, *riiiight,'* Winston creased his brow and tried to get the image of a sweaty Steve Allen in a white vest out of his mind.

'Whatever. Look, she's also mentioned her father. This isn't easy to say... she's saying you, Bruce... uh Willis and her father, all in the same breath. It's like she's morphed all three of you into one man, what's that about?'

'I dunno... look she fantasises over Bruce Willis and, yeah, me as well, I guess. And she was obviously very close to her father before he died.'

Winston nodded.

'Yeah she said he taught her to shoot – and it looks like she's an expert shot, so be careful.'

'Oh I will,' replied Steve as he pushed open the door.

'Good luck Steve... or should I say *"Yippee Ki-yay, motherfucker"*?'

Steve rolled his eyes then entered the room. He took a moment to take in the scene then recognised the décor and the sleigh bed from Eva's video.

Directly ahead of him sat crossed-legged on the dishevelled bed was Eva. Her right arm was outstretched and clenched in her hand was a small, black handgun. Winston had told Steve he thought it was a Beretta 950 – not overly powerful but at close range, lethal.

Around the bed, on the floor, were the lit candles. They flickered sensually and gave off the only light in the room. They smelt of cinnamon and vanilla and momentarily reminded Steve of his ex-wife Debbie and not in a good way. His heart skipped a beat as he once again took in the magnificence of Eva's near naked body.

Directly opposite the bed, slumped against a wall in a pool of ever-expanding blood was a naked and bloodied Neil Etchington. His arms hung limply by his side and one leg was bent up under his body at an acute angle. He was barely breathing.

'Steve! Steve! You've come for me – I knew you would!' She was as excited as a five-year-old on Christmas morning.

'Hello Eva,' said Steve in a soft, calming voice.

'Yes… I promised I would. So here I am. Now come on, put the gun down, let them treat Etchington and let's just get out of here.'

The smile dropped from Eva's face in an instant. She kept the gun aimed at Etchington, but her stare was fixed on Steve.

'Who? Who did you promise – n, n, not me?' she stammered.

It was only at this point that Steve realised Eva had no knowledge of him meeting her mother. It was Irena who he'd made the vow to, the vow to find her daughter.

Steve hadn't seen Eva since the morning of her abduction from his apartment. He knew she was fragile and he knew he had to be careful with his words. He was also unsure and wary of the true relationship between Irena and her daughter.

'I made a promise to myself Eva, I promised myself that I would find you.'

It seemed to be the right response. Eva nodded. She was placated… for now.

'Now please, either put the gun down or hand it to me.'

'Come here first Steve. I need you. I need you to give me a hug… I've missed you.'

'I've missed you too Eva,' he answered.

Steve edged closer towards the bed. She still had the gun aimed at Etchington but her smile grew wider the closer he moved towards her. He was now just a few feet from the bed.

He noticed a small cotton pad on her inner left arm.

'The bastards have implanted a microchip again,' said Eva in response to his stare. She then furrowed her brow on spotting the Kevlar vest.

'What are you wearing?'

'Oh this?' He looked down and studied the body armour that Winston had made him wear.

'Sorry. I said it wasn't necessary but they insisted I wear it... just in case there were others in here. You know, Besin Marishta... uh, where is he by the way?'

There had been no mention of the Albanian gangster, not by Winston nor Eva. His absence had been overlooked by the immediate situation with Eva.

'Who cares?' she shrugged.

'The fat fuck has gone... but I gave him a new arsehole before he went,' she laughed.

'Now come here Steve I need you.'

Steve took another step forward and edged to the side of the bed. She patted the mattress with her one free hand.

'Come on, sit down.'

Steve did as he was told, mindful of the gun in Eva's right hand, still aimed unwaveringly at Etchington.

As well as the patch on her left arm Steve also noticed an ugly wound, some two inches long on the inside of Eva's right leg. It was red, angry and looked like it had been recently stitched. It was some way off healing.

'What happened to your leg?' he asked, genuinely concerned.

'This?' She glanced down at the wound.

'That was those bastards who took me from your apartment. When you went off to work instead of staying with me.'

She stared at him accusingly before continuing.

'One of them... the older shit, he said he needed me to bleed a lot. He wanted it to look like a murder scene, said he would get my fucking boyfriend – *you* – locked up for my murder.'

Steve squirmed at the reference to him being her '*boyfriend*'. He then recalled the amount of blood in his apartment, he felt sure at the time that she had indeed been killed.

'And the sick fucker made me strip off,' she lowered her gaze 'and the younger one...' she said in a barely audible whisper, the memory still painful for her. She gathered herself before continuing, tears welled up in her eyes.

'... the younger one, he put tape over my mouth, a knife to my throat and then... he raped me. They took pictures of me and put them on your laptop. The older one then stabbed me in the leg, all the time he was laughing, telling me how easy it was to find your password if you knew where to look.'

Steve felt sick to his stomach – and guilty for leaving her in his apartment alone, knowing that Thompson and Bishop were likely to return.

She came to me for refuge and ended up being raped.

Steve grimaced at the thought of the photos, the photos that unknown to Eva he had already seen.

'Eva, I'm so sorry, I don't know what to say...I uh, I've seen the photos... and there's something else I've seen.'

'What?'

'The video.'

'What video?'

'The one on the memory stick that you put in the CD case the first time we met.'

'Oh.'

Eva's eyes became vacant. She stared off into the distance in thought. Steve could see she was visiting a bad, dark place in her mind.

There was something that had been baffling Steve.

'Why did you put the stick in the CD case Eva? I don't get it, you filmed it on your phone didn't you? You had my number, why didn't you just send it to me?'

'All I can do with that shitty phone is take photos and videos and make calls, *duh*. You think they would give us access to the outside world? I loaded it up on the stick using one of the laptops they use for the tattoo machines. I had it for a while, I was just waiting for the right time and right person to give it to.'

Steve gave an understanding nod.

'So you wanted me to find it, you wanted me to see it?'

'Of course. I wanted you to see what that fucking animal has done to me.' She motioned to the barely breathing body of Etchington once more.

'It was my, how you say, insurance. I thought that one day I would end up dead in Chicken City. I needed to give the video to someone I could trust. I thought I could trust you Steve.'

'You can Eva. I'm sorry, I shouldn't have left you alone that morning,' said Steve in a near whisper.

She shook her head and refocused on Steve in the gloom. Her mind was now back in the present.

'But at least *he* had them killed,' she said with a ghost of a smile.

Steve eyes widened. 'Who had who killed?'

'Etchington. He got Marishta to kill those two bastards for what they did to me.'

She didn't give Steve the chance to process what she'd just told him. Her mood was changing again. She stared at him angrily.

'I not like you with that vest on. You think I'm going to shoot you? Take it off.'

'But I . . .'

'Take it off now!' she screamed, causing Steve to flinch. Her eyes blazed.

He undid the straps and pulled the vest up over his head causing his T-shirt to ride up. Eva stroked the side of his body with her free hand. He involuntarily recoiled.

'What is wrong Steve? I can't work you out. I know you want to make love to me but you are acting so cold. You not like my body yes? Am I not beautiful?' She pushed out her breasts and giggled.

'Of course you are Eva, but… you are so young. You lied to me, you told me you were nearly twenty, but you're only just sixteen, aren't you?'

'So? What difference does it make? Most men like me because I *am* so young – like that bastard over there.'

She nodded towards Etchington once again.

'But I'm not like most men Eva – that's what you said before. That's why you said you liked me, because I didn't take advantage of you.'

'But you're not taking advantage of me like those animals. I'm willing with you Steve…' she said coquettishly.

'Have I told you that you remind me of my father as well as Bruce Willis?'

Steve winced but didn't answer.

'Come here,' she whispered as she reached out for his hand. He flinched and pulled away.

'I said come here or I blow your fucking head off – and mine!' she screamed as she pointed the pistol away from Etchington and directly at Steve's head.

In the next room watching through a hole he'd had drilled through the door was Fraser Winston.

He gripped his pistol, inhaled deeply and weighed up the situation. It was not looking good.

By the look of Etchington he only had a short time to live and with a gun at Steve Allen's head he wasn't faring much better.

If Winston kicked the door in, she would shoot, both Steve and herself, he was sure of that – and that would mean he had two dead civilians and possibly one dead MP to deal with.

If he wasn't already up shit creek with his superiors he surely would be then. He waited.

Eva leant into Steve and nuzzled her face against his, playing for a kiss. She moved her mouth up and lingered for a second on the scar on his cheek before continuing to his ear. She nibbled at his lobe. All the time she kept the pistol pointed unwaveringly at Steve's head.

Steve squirmed and spoke through gritted teeth. 'Eva stop. This is wrong. You're only sixteen and I'm in my sixties... *it's fucking sick.'*

Eva laughed and ignored his pleas.

Her tongue probed his ear then it moved down his jawline to his chin while her left hand caressed his body and slowly moved down to his groin.

'Ooh, that's better,' she said with a smile.

Steve closed his eyes as Eva traced his chin with her tongue.

She moved her mouth up to his and bit hard into his lower lip causing Steve to wince in pain. He felt a trickle of warm blood run down his chin and the familiar coppery taste once more filled his mouth.

Eva smiled wickedly then licked at the blood as it dripped down his jawline.

She stopped abruptly.

Steve could feel her breath against his face. His heart hammered in his chest like a jackhammer as she dug the barrel of the pistol into his forehead.

'I can smell something,' she said, quietly and precisely.

Steve remained silent. His breathing quickened. She sniffed long and hard around his mouth.

'I can smell perfume.'

His heart raced even more.

'I can smell my mother's perfume.'

She sniffed again, longer and harder. She then licked around his bloodied mouth.

'And I can taste something. I can taste… *woman.*'

She pulled her face away from Steve's and studied him intently. She held the gun firmly against his temple as Steve's blood dripped from her own mouth. She wiped it away with the back of her hand.

'You've been with my mother,' she stated, slowly and deliberately.

'Look Eva it's not what…'

'I'm not good enough for you but my mother is?… *For fuck's sake you've been fucking my mother!*' she screamed hysterically.

The door crashed open with a loud crack as Winston kicked it in. As Eva momentarily flinched at the sudden noise Steve swung his right arm up against hers, causing the gun to fire off a wild shot as it flew out of her hand and smashed against the adjacent wall.

'Eva put your hands up!' shouted Winston as he pointed his Glock at the panic-stricken Eva. Four other officers stood behind him, all armed and all with their guns pointed at her.

'*She's unarmed! Put your fucking guns down and get out of here!*' bellowed Steve as he took Eva in his arms.

'But we need to…'

'*NOW!*' shouted Steve as he glared at Winston.

He and his fellow officers slowly lowered their guns and backed out of the room.

Steve stroked Eva's hair then gently kissed the top of her head. Eva's body responded with fit-like convulsions and animal-like wails.

She gathered herself and looked up at Steve with tear-stained eyes.

'You betrayed me,' she sobbed.

Chapter Thirty-Five

'What the fuck kept you?' said a crimson-faced and sweating Besin Marishta as he heaved his corpulent body onto the back of the black Jaguar XK saloon.

The black-suited driver turned around and eyed up the kimono-clad Albanian over the top of his Brunella Cucinelli sunglasses.

'Traffic – the place is heaving with wooden tops,' he said with a sneer. 'If it wasn't for the Government plates I wouldn't have got through.'

He looked around, beyond Marishta. His eyebrows knotted.

'Where the fuck is Etchington?'

'Fuck knows. I told him to get out quick but he didn't move. Think the prick must have taken some sort of shit. He was with his Serbian bitch and judging by the shots I heard he might be dead.'

'Oh well, that might not be a bad thing,' replied the driver.

Marishta let out a large groan as he shifted position awkwardly on the black leather seat.

'What's up with you?' asked the driver.

'The bitch shot me in the arse,' replied Marishta, pain clearly etched on his face.

The driver's sneer turned into a sly grin, he threw a tracksuit over his shoulder at the Albanian.

'Well try not to get blood on the seats. Now put this on and keep your big fat head down.'

Chapter Thirty-Six

The strong, black coffee that Steve sipped did nothing to alleviate his pounding headache.

He sat on a bench in the mobile operations unit with Irena by his side. She clutched his arm tightly but he was in no mood to reciprocate.

'Why won't they let me see her, Steve?' She studied him intently but he ignored her and looked straight ahead at random photographs and aerial shots of Chicken City stuck on a whiteboard on the opposite wall.

'They have to debrief her,' he answered flatly.

'I don't understand, she has done nothing wrong.'

Apart from nearly killing a Member of Parliament... But she was right. She had done nothing wrong.

Eva had been abused and trafficked into a miserable life of sexual exploitation, while physical and mental abuse had occurred on a daily basis. She had been plied with drugs and subjected to God knows what to pleasure manipulative and exploitative men, men just like Steve. He felt ashamed and disgusted to be a male.

'You alright Steve?'

He snapped out of his thoughts and looked up to see the imposing figure of Fraser Winston standing in front of him. He was chewing gum and fiddling with the diamond stud in his left ear. He looked nervous.

'Yeah, couldn't be fucking better,' answered Steve sarcastically.

Winston stopped playing with his stud and smiled unconvincingly at Irena.

'Look, it's just a formality. We have to question her, she's with well-trained female officers. She's in no trouble, well not *real* trouble, but… well there's still a couple of questions we need answering.'

'Such as?' asked Steve.

'Well for one, we found another hidden door. It led into a tunnel that went all the way out of the plant and exited into the scrubland opposite… We think that's how Besin Marishta got out, but we found blood in the tunnel. Looks like Eva may have shot and wounded him.'

'Pity,' said Irena flatly.

'Pity she shot him?' queried Winston.

'No, pity she didn't kill the fucking animal.'

Steve and Winston found it hard to disagree.

Steve furrowed his brow.

'Any idea where Eva got the gun?'

'Yeah, she told us Marishta had a whole arsenal of weapons in his room – we've found at least a dozen in there – Uzis, Kalashnikovs, you name it we've found them. She managed to steal a Saturday night special and keep it under her mattress, just waiting for the day she was able to use it – turns out it was today.'

Suddenly the door of the mobile operations room burst open. Dan Britton, looking anxious and breathless, stood in the doorway.

'Guv – we've got a situation developing, you'd better come quick.'

Britton led Winston back through the factory into the bowels of the building where they had first begun their search for Marishta's private rooms.

A crowd of blue-overalled operamini blocked their way as they tried in vain to enter one of the storerooms at the back of the building.

Winston turned to Britton. 'What is it? What's going on down there?'

'The workers, the operamini, they've captured some of the guards. We think they're using those tattoo machines on them.'

'*Jeez*. Come on, we need to get down there.'

He turned to the officers lined up behind Britton.

'Draw your batons, we have to get them out.'

Britton hesitated. 'Uh, why guv?'

'*What?*' Winston bellowed in response.

'Don't mean to question you guv, but me and the others… well, you've seen the conditions these poor sods have been forced to work in – and the lads who raided the villatis – their accommodations. Well they said they were like pigstys, ten people including kids in a room that was meant for four, filthy conditions – infested with rats, the lot. And do you know what else they've found?' He didn't wait for his boss to answer.

'A clinic of sorts where they've been sterilising the women – forcibly by the looks of the fucking restraints. Sorry guv but you can't blame them for well… wanting to take a bit of revenge can you?'

Winston was stunned into silence.

'Are you disobeying orders Britton?'

'Uh, no, not really – we just…'

'Good. Then in that case… go and get me a cup of coffee will you?'

'Sure boss – two sugars?' he answered with a smirk before scurrying off.

Winston turned and pushed through the crowd, he was reluctant to admit it but he was eager to witness the bizarre spectacle unfolding before his eyes.

In front of him, in a corner of the room, two burly male operamini had pinned down a bloodied and terrified-looking long-haired custo.

He was naked apart from his underpants and was lying on his back with his head clamped rigidly into a bizarre looking leather and metallic device.

His arms were stretched out wide and held in place by the two workers while another two female operamini held firmly on to his legs. The surreal crucifixion symbolism was not lost on Winston.

Protruding from the device which encircled the custos's head were cables and tubes – the cables were attached to a laptop and the tubes went into a reservoir filled with black ink.

Another operamini dressed in a black hoodie stepped forward and flicked a switch on the device causing it to hum into life. He tapped the keyboard and with a theatrical flourish and cheers from the baying crowd pressed the '*Enter*' button.

Winston watched as the device began to buzz, the hooded operamini pressed another key on the laptop and unseen needles inside the device moved into position. They slowly lowered and came to a halt within just a few millimetres of the custo's forehead. The operamini once again pressed more keys as if he was spelling out something and he pressed '*Enter*' once more.

Judging by the screams coming from the custo the needles had come into contact with his flesh and the tattooing process had begun.

Winston had tattoos of his own – his wife and both of his children's names in scrolls encircling a heart on his left chest and '*Ordo ab Chao*' in italic script on his right bicep. It was a Masonic motto meaning '*Order from Chaos*', which, when he'd had it done some two years previously somehow seemed appropriate.

He would be lying if he said he didn't find the process painful but it was of his own volition and he knew that it was something he would cherish and treasure for the rest of his life… something that could not be said for the screaming custo as the word '*BASTARD*' was crudely tattooed across his forehead.

Unknown to Fraser Winston, Steve Allen stood behind him watching the unfolding drama in wide-eyed fascination – and interest.

Chapter Thirty-Seven

Thirty-six hours after the raid on Chicken City, Fraser Winston found himself in the headquarters of the National Crime Agency in Citadel Place, South East London.

He'd been told to bring everything he had on Operation Waffle – files, tapes, videos, hard drives – they wanted the lot. He'd thought about going straight from the operation still wearing his battle fatigues – just to make a point, but in the end, he decided against it. He'd antagonised his bosses enough in recent weeks so the sight of him in his black, bulletproof body armour probably wouldn't do his cause any good – like he fucking cared.

He'd had many meetings with the Director General before and always got on well with her. She was honest, straightforward and backed her officers to the hilt, but he knew that this time he'd overstepped the mark and she wouldn't be as welcoming or accommodating as she'd been in the past.

He knocked on the office door and waited for the familiar soft Home Counties accent to answer with her usual warm greeting…

'Uh, who are you?' asked Winston on entering the office. 'Where's…?'

'She's unavailable,' came the curt reply.

There were two of them. One roughly the same age as Winston with glossy, floppy flaxen hair and steely, blue eyes and a similar, but much younger, version. They were dressed in expensive dark grey suits, handmade shoes and identical pale blue and white striped ties and judging by their hairstyles they obviously frequented the same Curzon Street barber.

The two of them possessed firm, unnerving handshakes that Winston was more than familiar with. He took an instant dislike to them.

'Sit down Officer Winston,' said the younger one, in an Oxbridge accent that was as highly polished as his jet-black brogues.

Winston bristled. He was primed and up for an argument.

'I'd prefer to stand thanks,' he replied stubbornly.

'You know why you are here don't you?' continued the young suit.

'To be honest, no,' replied Weston, his anger rising. 'Look… who the fuck are you?'

'You don't need to know,' came the response from the older suit, 'let's just say the DG – your boss – answers to us.' He glanced at his younger colleague and smirked.

You smug bastard. I'd like to wipe that grin off your face.

Ten minutes later and Winston was spent. There had been no niceties, little dialogue and certainly no reasoning or debate. They had no desire to listen to Winston's side of the story – he'd disobeyed orders and ignored the instructions of his superiors, end of.

'But two officers – admittedly bent officers – have been murdered. Their throats cut and their bodies dumped on a beach. Surely we had to act after that?' pleaded Winston with an air of exasperation.

'People exploitation on an industrial scale? Human trafficking? All with the tacit approval of the Government,' he continued.

The suits exchanged glances and remained silent.

'Child abuse – paedophile gangs?'

'Illicit drug manufacture and distribution?'

'Routine microchipping of teenagers as if they were runaway dogs?'

The rhythmic tick-tock of a mahogany Victorian timepiece on the wall was the only sound in the room.

'Flogging dodgy chicken after its "sell-by" date?'

At last one of the suits – the younger one, who looked as if he had yet to master the art of shaving, spoke.

'That's e-*fucking*-nough… You know the challenges confronting us and by us, I mean the Government, Officer Winston. Yet you deliberately disobeyed orders. You knew the consequences of all this, it's not in the…'

'Yeah, I know, not in the public fucking interest… How many times have I heard that?' replied Winston wearily.

He creased his eyes and recalled what Simon Edwards had said to him.

'Have you heard of Edmund Burke?' he asked with an air of superiority.

The young suit rolled his eyes and sighed.

'I studied politics at Oxford, old bean, so of course I have. Would be a tad remiss of me if I hadn't… I guess you're referring to the old "*good men doing nothing*" tosh – really?'

Winston felt deflated. He finally succumbed and slumped into a nearby leather wingback chair.

The young suit motioned to the pile of evidence that Winston had brought with him. It stacked up in an R-Kive storage box over a foot high on the desk.

'Look, we know what's been happening within Etchington's migrant cities. Let's just say they haven't been playing by the rules, eh? Not really cricket is it? Perhaps they did need reining in a bit…'

'Reining in a bit?' Winston interrupted, 'they're not a bunch of unruly schoolkids for fuck's sake!'

'We know, Officer Winston, which is precisely why we had to tread carefully – with them and shall we say their um *clients.* We were going to take care of it, all of it, until you acted all gung ho and went in with all guns blazing... literally.'

Winston eyed the suit up and down. He was stiffer than a shop window mannequin and had Bullingdon Club running through him like a stick of Blackpool rock.

'Take care of it? How?'

'We have our methods. But look...' the young suit smiled and perched himself on the edge of a highly polished walnut desk that dominated the room. At last it seemed like he was becoming more conciliatory.

'This not in the public interest – it's real, genuine. Take the clergy... and I don't just mean ours.'

'What's *ours* when it's at home?' asked Winston screwing up his eyes. The young suit's face flushed like a schoolboy caught masturbating in the dorm.

'The Establishment... C of E. Then there's the Catholic priests, dare I saw it there's probably even some Jehovah's Witnesses we could implicate... but we're not. Think about it, the good name of the church, all churches and all religions for that matter, well they would just be destroyed. And as for the MPs who may be – how do I put it – caught up in this sordid little affair...'

'*Sordid little affair?* This ain't another Profumo for fuck's sake! There are people – children – who have been trafficked here then microchipped and abused by God knows who and from what you've been saying people in the Government knew all about it. So don't talk to me as if it's a another case of an MP caught shagging his secretary while fiddling his expenses!' screamed Winston.

The other suit – who, up until now had remained silent, touched his colleague's arm, gave a small but discernible shake of the head and took a pace forward. Winston couldn't help but notice he walked with a distinct limp in his right leg.

'War wound old boy – Afghanistan,' he grimaced as he noticed Winston's gaze fall upon his damaged limb.

My arse – probably fell of your polo pony, thought Winston.

'Look I'm sure you thought you were doing the right thing – some sort of noble crusade, but it's nothing for you to get concerned about. This um, microchipping for instance… you of all people can surely see the benefits of it?'

Winston's jaw dropped as he stared at the suit incredulously.

'What do you mean, *you of all people* – and what do you mean by benefits?'

The senior suit sighed with an air of resignation. He motioned for his young colleague to move from the desk and he repositioned himself onto the vacant space, squirming in discomfort as he felt his associate's warmth penetrate the seat of his trousers. He clasped his hands together in front of him, his fingers forming a steeple.

'You are an exemplary officer in the NCA, Fraser – do you mind if I call you Fraser?'

He didn't wait for a response.

'You have arrested and put many, many criminals in their rightful place – behind bars. Thanks to literally hours of sheer hard work and good old coppering you, and officers like you, have arrested and locked up thieves, rapists, murderers… even terrorists, but at what cost hmmm? Hours and hours, days even, of trawling through PNC records, staring at endless mug shots, fingerprinting, collecting DNA evidence, liaising with other units. Thank God for HOLMES Two, eh?' His lip curled up in a forced smile.

HOLMES Two was an IT system used by the British Police to investigate major incidents – Winston had used it on many occasion, and thought it a godsend.

'Sorry, I don't follow,' said Winston.

'Look. What if there were a simpler way, hmmm?... Tell me Fraser, what do you think of ID cards?'

Winston pushed out his bottom lip and considered his response.

'Uh yeah, thought it was a good idea to be honest. Would have been a big help to us, shame the Human Rights lawyers got their way and kicked it into touch.'

The senior suit smiled broadly.

'Precisely old boy. So in this day of more troubled times, terrorism and the like – it's amazing what the people of Britain would agree to. Do you get my drift?'

His smile turned into a sick, smug grin.

'Not sure that I do,' answered Winston.

'Politics of fear old boy – seeing as you like political quotes here's one from Tricky Dickie Nixon: "*people react to fear, not love*". In other words, convince the people of a perceived threat, whether real or unreal and you can push through all sorts of rules and legislations that you couldn't in, shall we say, more peaceful times.'

'Such as?'

'The aforementioned ID cards for starters, which if I'm not mistaken just a minute ago you seemed to be in favour of. But of course, we've moved on from 2006 when the proposal was thrown out of Parliament... Who needs physical ID cards when you can have state-of-the-art electronic digital ones?'

Winston remained silent whilst he gathered his thoughts. He hated to admit it but it was slowly beginning to make sense to him.

'So the microchips – that's what they are – ID cards?' answered Winston.

'Bravo old boy. Well, ID cards with all the whistles and bells... still in the development stage of course but what with the help and co-operation of some uh... volunteers, we should be perfecting them in the next year or so.'

Winston pictured Eva in his mind's eye. *Hardly volunteers,* he thought. 'Then what?'

'Then we will introduce them as a major advance in the fight against terror and organised crime and have them implanted into everyone over the age of sixteen and eventually… every new-born child.'

Winston's eyes opened wide in horror.

'We can then keep track of everyone's movements and their whereabouts from the cradle to the grave. No more wannabe terrorists swanning off overseas and joining some fanatical jihadi group and of course, the benefits are huge. It's not just the tracking capability – we'll be able to upload information, so we'll have everyone's DNA and blood group on record, just think how easy it'll be to track down murderers and rapists! Everything about them logged in a central computer. The benefits to the Government and all hard-working, law-abiding citizens will be immense… do you have children Fraser?' He knew he had.

Winston nodded.

'Ever lost them when out shopping… on the beach maybe?'

Winston didn't respond but his blood ran cold as he recalled the time when they had lost Clarissa in the crowd in Covent Garden one Christmas – the memory of the sheer terror he felt at the time made him feel sick.

'Imagine the ultimate horror for every parent – their precious child goes missing, or worse, they're abducted. But, of course, if every child was microchipped with a GPS tracker they could instantly be traced – how wonderful would that be?'

Winston sprang up from the chair.

'Wonderful? You've got to be fucking kidding! This is something out of… I don't know, it's like some sort of Nazi ideology. What do you think you're creating… a New *fucking* Order? The people of Britain would never stand for it!'

'*Au contraire*... a beheading of a soldier on the streets of Britain, a mass attack on London by jihadi terrorists, a bombing of a concert hall, yet another Muslim paedophile ring. How about a co-ordinated mass uprising of ungrateful MIRAS and the shooting of a much-loved and well-respected MP within our wonderful migrant cities *à la* Chicken City?'

He looked at his colleague and winked. The young suit responded with a loud guffaw.

'You'd be surprised at what the populace of this country will agree to after a few more atrocities and outrages.'

Winston shook his head in disbelief. Could it be that by raiding Solutio's processing plants he had inadvertently played right into their hands... whoever 'they' might be. Maybe his actions had actually set the wheels of this heinous process in motion?

'So are you saying that all of this – Solutio, the food processing plant and the rest of the migrant cities, they're just a front for developing and implanting the microchips into the inhabitants of Britain?'

'No, no – not at all old boy. Even you have to admit that these cities have been a huge success? I mean, how much has the cost of mobile phones and what are they called, KFC bucket meals, come down over the years – and I bet you're loving a family visit to Nandos these days eh?'

He laughed and winked at his colleague once more.

'*You fucking what?*' shouted Winston angrily.

The suit had realised he'd overstepped the mark and held up his hands in mock surrender.

'Sorry, sorry Fraser... uh no, the microchip has turned out to be a rather convenient by-product of it all. Those clever scientists in the Balkans have been looking into it for donkey's years. You know what they were like with all their ethnic cleansing – any excuse to make it easier to sort out the wheat from the chaff as it were. Anyway, we've just embraced their technology and taken it a stage further – you know those Albanians were looking at barcoded tattoos first? Talk about bloody primitives!'

Winston was furious at the slur but he let it pass. He unconsciously toyed with his earring and paced around the room as he recalled seeing the tattoo machine in action the previous day.

'And Etchington – what's his role in this?' he eventually asked.

'That ghastly pervert?' The senior suit shook his head.

'Yes, well, that's where it all went tits up. Seemed like he was kosher at first – should have known, went to bloody Cambridge didn't he? But no, his idea – Solutio and their cities seemed perfect. I mean this bloody MIRAS problem isn't going to cure itself is it? And after those illegals took control of the Tunnel the other year… well we couldn't let that happen again could we? Held the bloody country to ransom didn't they?'

Winston recalled the events of six years previously when thousands of migrants camping in Calais rioted, attacked French border guards and seized the Channel Tunnel.

Eventually the army were called in and over 100 migrants and 18 troops and border guards were killed after a three-day battle. It was one of the events that led to Etchington getting a position in the Government and the rise of Solutio – and the eventual launch of the migrant cities. Winston felt himself reluctantly nodding in agreement.

'But well, like communism – works in theory but there's always someone who wants to stick his snout further into the trough isn't there? Etchington, that Albanian thug Marishta and his cronies – well they just used it for their own deprived sexual perversions. Of course, word got out in the paedophile network and it brought every miscreant out of the woodwork wanting to sample the goods on offer, at a price of course. Fucking animals all of them.'

Winston at least felt satisfied that he was hearing some reassuring truths.

'You mentioned Besin Marishta, somehow he managed to escape yesterday – any idea of his whereabouts?' asked Winston.

The two suits exchanged glances before the older one replied.

'Hmmm, bit of a fly in the bloody ointment, isn't he? But don't you worry – we'll take care of him.'

'Really? How?'

'Like my colleague said we'll take care of him and all of the rest of this shitstorm – that's all you need to know,' replied the older suit with a hint of irritation.

Winston got the message. He was not going to pursue it. He tried a different tack.

'Uh, there's something else… what about the Masons? What's their involvement in all this?'

The older suit threw back his head and let out a loud guffaw.

'Really this is all getting a bit tiresome old boy. Masons – the age-old bogeymen and high priests of conspiracy theories rear their ugly heads again! You'll be asking about their involvement in the Jack the Ripper murders next… come on Fraser, you're one of us – *you're on the level* – you know the score,' he said with a wink before continuing.

'Total smokescreen. Etchington and Marishta just got carried away with Masonic symbolism and totemism. Yes, they're in the Masons but they'll soon be blackballed and thrown out, that's assuming Etchington pulls through of course – so don't you worry. I can categorically state that all of this has absolutely nothing to do with *us* Masons.'

Winston shifted his weight uncomfortably at the use of the word '*us*' but he was undeterred, he continued with his questions.

'What about the murders of Thompson and Bishop? That had all the hallmarks of a ritualistic Masonic punishment.'

'Precisely… ritualistic, that's all it was, carried out by Marishta's goons by the looks of it. We hear the two of them were getting cold feet about their involvement in it all. Sounds like the Albanian got wind of them thinking of reporting his operations to their superiors, for what good it would have done. And as for their deaths… yes, bit of collateral damage unfortunately, and of course they did overstep the mark a tad when they recaptured that escapee… but well, perhaps they shouldn't have sampled the goods.'

'Two deaths – collateral damage? And as for the *escapee*… she was one of the ones who'd been micro-chipped. She'd been trafficked as a child sex slave for Christ's sake! She has a name you know… Evalina Petrovic. She's just sixteen and been in Etchington's clutches since she was a little girl. For your information she's now having intensive psychotherapy – she's going to be scarred for life!'

He suddenly reflected on what he'd just heard, his eyes widened in horror.

'What do you mean by *"sampled the goods"*?' He was unaware of what Eva had told Steve regarding the deaths of Thompson and Bishop – unlike the two suits. The older one was visibly agitated.

'Like I said, they overstepped the mark before they took her back to her um…'

'Prison. You're looking for the word *prison*,' answered Winston angrily. He was getting nowhere, but he was like a dog with a bone.

'Hold on a minute… you said, *"for what good it would have done"* when you mentioned Thompson and Bishop reporting it to their superiors. What did you mean by that?'

The senior suit reddened, glanced at the clock on the wall and cleared his throat.

'Yes well… golly is that the time? Look old boy we must be running along but why don't you toddle off back to the West Country and your lovely family and take a bit of time off? Reflect on what we've told you and keep mum eh?' He tapped his nose and smiled.

Winston sighed heavily. He knew he was pissing in the wind. He was not going to get any more answers… *'Bit of time off' – sounds like a suspension,* he thought.

'And what if I don't?' he asked.

'Well, you know there's already a bloody great D-Notice slapped all over this don't you – I mean, have you seen today's papers?'

He picked up a sheath of newspapers from the desk and waved them in front of Winston.

'See… Fleet Street has already bought into it.'

'Insurgents in riots at Migrant cities' read the headline in *The Guardian.*

'The bloody *Guardian* of all papers!' grinned the young suit.

'Send 'em back!' preached the *Daily Mail.*

'Ungrateful MIRAS!' screamed *The Sun.*

Winston dejectedly shook his head.

'According to the media,' continued the older suit, 'the rioting was caused by insurgents hell-bent on causing trouble and it had to be suppressed by our heroic police officers – that's you old boy.' He winked yet again.

'And Etchington being shot – how's that being reported?' Winston rubbed his brow. He had the distinct feeling he was beginning to lose the argument.

'Oh, don't worry we won't implicate… what's her name… Evalina. I'm sure we can come to some sort of arrangement for the poor girl. No, Etchington was shot by some dreadful jihadist sympathiser who had infiltrated the MIRAS. He managed to wound a heroic and popular member of Parliament whilst he was on a fact-finding mission – talk about biting the hand that feeds you. Perhaps the Government will have to look into introducing some tougher measures – you know what they say Fraser, every cloud has a silver lining, what?'

The young suit laughed out loud and rubbed his hands in childlike glee as Winston turned and dejectedly left the room.

'Oh Fraser… one other thing.'

'What?' asked Winston without bothering to turn around.

'Leave your warrant card and security pass at reception there's a good chap.'

It was definitely a suspension.

As the door closed behind Winston the younger of the two suits raised an eyebrow and looked at the older one questioningly.

'Well? Do you think he bought it?'

'Wouldn't trust the oik as far as I could throw him,' replied the older one as he stood up and straightened his tie.

'Make the call.'

Chapter Thirty-Eight

It was quite evident to Fraser Winston that the previous day's events had been distorted to bring ever closer the introduction of microchip ID cards – and in some way he felt responsible for it.

The irony of it all was that the public would agree to even more stringent security measures the more their freedom was perceived to be threatened. *The politics of fear indeed*, he thought.

Despite everything he'd just been told, he thought that for the first time in a while he could sleep soundly in his bed in the arms of his loving wife, while his two children could sleep soundly and safely in theirs.

The operation might not have gone entirely to plan but at least he and his colleagues had been responsible for the freeing of thousands of modern-day slaves and dozens of young sex slaves from what was nothing more than enforced labour camps and brothels.

His conscience was clear. He had done the right thing, irrespective of what it would do to his career prospects or those of some of his superiors.

Could they say the same – were their collective consciences clear? *Not in the public interest?* How could the freeing of thousands of exploited people and the exposing of possibly hundreds of paedophiles, abusers and people traffickers not be in the public interest?

And it wasn't just the perpetrators of the evil crimes they had found on the day. As well as Neil Etchington – now grimly clinging onto life in a secret private hospital in Sussex, there were several other *honourable* Members of Parliament, four high court judges, two senior police officers, one member of the royal household, a couple of so-say national treasures and more head teachers and members of the clergy than you could shake a bottle of Rohypnol at – and that was just for starters.

The numerous records, memory sticks and hard drives they had discovered yielded enough names, addresses and video footage to jail so many politicians and perceived pillars of society that the Government would have to build more prisons just to house them.

But… where that evidence that he'd handed over to the two Bullingdon suits would end up, he could only guess.

And then he thought – *has anything really been resolved? Thousands freed? Freed to go where?* For now, they would be staying in their accommodation – the villatis – within the townships.

Emergency teams were being moved in and the deep cleaning of the housing blocks was about to start while field kitchens and thousands of tents were also being deployed.

Emergency supplies that normally would be sent to disaster sites in third-world countries were also about to be delivered. *Third-world countries*, thought Winston, *who's the bloody third-world country now?*

But all of these measures were just temporary – he knew that. The real issue of resolving not just Europe's, but the world's, immense mass migration and refugee crisis was obviously not Fraser Winston's. Better men than he would have to figure that one out.

The only thing necessary for the triumph of evil is for good men to do nothing, he thought to himself, not for the first time.

'At least I bloody did something!' he shouted as he glanced in his rear-view mirror.

He momentarily studied his reflection then switched on the ignition, totally oblivious to the black

Jaguar XK behind his BMW that simultaneously pulled away as he headed back to his home and his loving family in the Cotswolds.

* * *

The sun was low in the sky as he joined the elevated section of the M4 at Chiswick together with thousands of others heading out of the capital, all rushing like lemmings to get out of the city at the end of the working day.

For a moment he'd thought about stopping off in his old stomping ground south of the river and looking up a few old mates… but then thought better of it.

The phrase *'the other side of the tracks'* could have been penned for Fraser Winston. He had now crossed over those tracks, but most of his friends – ones he had known from schooldays and who he'd gone to watch the Lions with on many a Saturday afternoon, had stayed firmly where they were, while his parents had long moved out to a cosy bungalow in Staines.

He glanced at his Rolex. He really ought to go and visit them but he knew his mother would only fuss over him, tell him he was losing too much weight and force patties and dumplings on him until he was fit to burst, while his father would just sit there as he always did, staring at the TV whilst kissing his teeth and shaking his head at everything his son said.

Or worse, he might start playing his collection of old Derrick Morgan records.

No, he would leave it for a while, pop up and see them with the kids in a few weeks' time. After all, he would have plenty of time in the near future to do all the things that he hadn't managed to do in the last few years.

Yes, he would make a day, maybe even a weekend of it. Take Marcus to Millwall to cheer on the Lions, even though his son would rather go to watch the Arsenal, whilst the girls gave his credit card a severe bashing in the West End.

He would make up for lost time and be the dad and husband that his family deserved, perhaps the suspension – as long as it didn't last too long – wasn't going to be a such a bad thing after all.

His phone rang through the in-car Bluetooth system. It interrupted Chris Martin singing *Fix You*.

It was Simon Edwards.

'Alright Fraser – how did it go?' he asked bluntly.

'Uh, hello boss... sorry, Simon. Uh, didn't get to see the DG, saw a couple of suits from the Home Office instead. Fuck knows who they were, but well, like we thought. I've been suspended.'

'For how long?'

'Didn't say – indefinite leave.'

'So what are you going to do about it – appeal?'

Winston mulled over his response. He hadn't given it much thought, he was more concerned with getting back to his family, truth be told.

'I dunno. The two suits were pretty adamant about it all. To be honest it could have been worse, I could have been sacked there on the spot. I mean, deliberately disobeying orders – fuck's sake they could have thrown the book at me. Look the bottom line is we've freed thousands of poor sods and the migrant cities are going to be cleaned up – and Etchington's going to be off the scene for the foreseeable future. Alright, some scumbags are going to be let off the hook but I don't think they'll be up to their old tricks for a while, and as for that Marishta lowlife, well, I haven't got a clue where he's gone... uh, you still there Simon?'

Edwards let out an audible sigh.

'Yeah, yeah – how about the Masons? What's their involvement in all this?'

Winston responded with a harsh, derisive laugh.

'Masons? You've really got it in for them haven't you? Red herring Simon, tenuous link that's all – move on.'

'Yeah well you would say that wouldn't you? I can't believe what I'm hearing from you to be honest, sounds like you're wimping out squire,' snapped Edwards.

Winston bit his lip and hesitated before answering. He angrily flipped down the sun shield in a vain attempt to stop the sun shining in his eyes.

'That's easy for you to say, you're retired – got your big fat pension to live off ain't you? I still got the wife and kids to look after don't forget.'

Winston fumbled in his glove compartment for his Aviators.

Edwards' disembodied voice crackled through the speakers again.

'OK, OK, but look, if you're not going to do anything about it, how about getting some stuff out on social media eh? No-one needs to know it's you, trust me, this story needs to be out there. You'd make a great whistleblower… Steve Allen knows someone on Fleet Street, they'd love to expose all this…'

'There's a D-Notice on…'

Winston winced as a high-pitched metallic screech came through his speakers and filled the car with a sound that made his gold tooth vibrate.

'Si… Simon – are you there? … Hello… *Hello?*'

He glanced at the audio controls and pressed aimlessly at random buttons as the ear-shattering sound continued.

The sun broke through the clouds once more. He looked back up through the windscreen and the piercing bright light momentarily blinded him.

He squinted, looked away and tried to shield his eyes whilst all the time the noise that now resembled a mutant animal-like scream engulfed him.

As he shunted into the Renault Traffic in front of him his head shot forward then ricocheted back like a whip.

It wasn't a huge impact but it was enough to make the airbag inflate and the efficient German technology came to his aid causing him to sigh heavily in relief. The airbag did its job perfectly as his head rocked forward once more and impacted into the soft, almost comforting pillow.

The collision however was just enough to make him grip the steering wheel a fraction too hard, which in turn caused the vehicle to veer to the left after the impact… straight into the path of an undertaking Sprinter courier van.

The van slammed into his front nearside, sending the BMW spinning back around the way it came. It careered across two lanes of fast-moving traffic and hammered into the central reservation in a hail of grit, sparks and debris.

Bouncing off the barrier the battered car then spun furiously and narrowly avoided a black Jaguar XK that had come perilously close to it.

The driver of the Jaguar adjusted his sunglasses, put his foot down and accelerated away from the mayhem whilst Winston's BMW came to a sudden halt in the middle lane of the motorway where it faced the wrong way into the oncoming line of speeding traffic.

The metallic screeching had at last stopped, only to be replaced by the soothing tones of Chris Martin's voice coming through the speakers once more.

Fraser Winston raised his bloodied head from the soft, comfortable airbag just in time for his eyes to focus on the Scania 44-tonne truck as it ploughed headlong into his BMW.

Chapter Thirty-Nine

Steve had to pinch himself, still not quite believing that he'd managed to filch one of the tattoo machines from under the noses of the dozens of police officers who had been guarding Chicken City on the day of the raid.

He had phoned John Burston asking for a lift for him and Irena, as no offer from Fraser Winston's team seemed to be forthcoming.

As JB pulled up Steve noticed the unguarded and unlocked police Transit van in the parking bay. Not one to look a gift horse in the mouth, he opened the back door, leant in and with the help of his best friend hauled out the unit and deposited it on the back of JB's flatbed before covering it with a tarpaulin.

Thirty minutes later they were unloading the machine into JB's lockup in Easton, as yet Steve was unsure of what to do with it, but something in the back of his inquisitive and ingenious mind told him that there was something to be made of it.

'You might get twenty quid for it down the scrapper mate,' offered JB as he studied the contraption with an air of puzzlement. He shook his head and not for the first time he questioned his mate's sanity.

'Mate – this time next year we could be millionaires,' said Steve in an exaggerated Cockney accent. He winked at his friend, but not in his wildest dreams did he think that statement would one day come true.

Not that Steve Allen was a dreamer. He was a pragmatic, practical problem-solver and not someone who was usually attracted to flights of fancy but… something had connected deep inside him.

Maybe after over a decade in the wilderness – with numerous part-time and low-paid jobs, not to mention the acute sense of under achievement – something at long last was beginning to click.

Not that he believed in the astrological mumbo jumbo that his ex-wife Debbie avidly studied each day, but perhaps it was a genuine moment of meaningful coincidence – perhaps the stars and planets really were aligning and at last Steve's life was going to change for the better.

Those astrological bodies had started to shift into position when his brother came back into his life at his mother's funeral. The brother who he now conversed with on a regular basis and who surprisingly and fortuitously had a stash of priceless original body art and who had first planted the seed in his mind about the automated tattoo machine.

Stars, fate or synchronicity – whatever it was, Steve took advantage of the situation and grabbed it with both hands, literally, when he unexpectedly came across that unlocked police van in Chicken City.

The purloined tattoo machine sat in JB's lock up for a month or so before Steve paid it another visit.

He plugged it in, switched it on and watched in awe as it hummed into life. The screen blinked enticingly, begging him to press its keyboard. But it was as crude as a Grimsby fishwife, it needed refining, it needed someone to rebuild it and breathe new life into it, it needed a Formula One mechanic to transform it from a second-hand Skoda into a front of the grid Ferrari.

It needed the Professor.

'The Professor' – Phil Baxter, Steve's trade plate colleague from City Vehicle Logistics, who in reality *was* an actual Professor and in robotics of all things. *Well you couldn't make it up,* thought Steve.

* * *

'Phil? It's Steve Allen. Ditch your trade plates – I've got a *real* job for you.'

The Professor stood forlornly at the exit of Newport Pagnell's service station on the M1 as he took the call.

He clutched his trade plates in one hand and a pitiful handmade cardboard sign with '*Anywhere but Corby*' scrawled across it in the other. His mobile phone was balanced somewhat precariously under his unshaven chin.

It was sheeting down and the rain had penetrated right through his grubby and well-worn Patagonia jacket. An Eddie Stobbart 12-wheeled artic roared past sending a huge wave of oily, putrid water in his direction.

'When can I start?' he asked as he wiped his dripping nose with the back of his hand.

* * *

Steve and his brother Kenny, JB, George, Phil and Irena stood in front of the contraption in JB's lockup and stared at it in total silence.

Steve cleared his throat and for ten minutes attempted to explain his vision... he wanted to develop and produce an automatic tattoo machine that could be programmed to deliver skin art of the highest calibre from a library of templates.

Kenny rolled his eyes.

'But dear brother, one of the basic appeals of having a tattoo about your person is that it has been handcrafted by an artist, they instil part of their own DNA into it, it's part of their...'

'Bullshit,' said Steve bluntly as he interrupted his brother. 'Sorry Ken but that might be true for the likes of your um...'

'Partner? Boyfriend? Still having problems with my homosexuality little brother?' said Kenny acidly.

'No, you know I haven't. What was I saying?... Oh yes, your partner Sammy Shapiro. Yes, that might be true of the likes of him.'

'Rest his soul,' said Kenny.

'Yes, rest his soul... and other true artists around the world, but even the ones who excel at their art but who can't hold a candle to the Jay Freestyles of the world have up to a year's waiting list. I'm telling you, this is one of the few markets in the world that hasn't been brought into the twenty-first century through automation. It's ripe for exploitation.'

Phil, who until now had been silent, stroked his chin in thought.

'Sorry, I just don't get it. You're proposing that this... device will be able to produce freehand work?' he asked, creasing his brow.

'Not freehand, but exact duplicates of the work of the very best tattoo artists from around the world. Currently anyone who wants a tattoo is restricted by one thing – geography. You're restricted by your locality, OK if you've got a few bob you can schlep up to London or maybe over to Europe to get a decent bit of ink but imagine if that tattoo artist could come to you – courtesy of a remote machine based in your neighbourhood tattoo parlour.'

'But these artists – the real top dollar ones, they wouldn't allow their work to be plagiarised like this surely?' queried Phil.

'Who said anything about plagiarism? This wouldn't be copies of these artists' work it would be their *actual* work, produced under licence and copyrighted by them. They would earn commission each time their tattoo was reproduced. These tattooists who are restricted to performing their art by their location would be producing skin art all around the world – they could earn a fortune without even lifting a finger. You telling me they wouldn't jump at it? And as for the punters – why be restricted to some grubby tat from a back-street tattooist when you could be inked by one of the world's best?'

The six of them exchanged glances. JB studied his collection of crudely inked and leeched out tigers and daggers on his forearms and shook his head in bewilderment. Steve could tell none of them were convinced.

'I do not know Steve, an automatic tattoo machine? Sounds a bit rabbit-brained to me,' said Irena.

'*Hare*-brained Irena – and anyway it's not, but the real USP of this…' said Steve as he reverted back to his sales-speak vocabulary.

Irena furrowed her brow even deeper.

'Unique selling point,' continued Steve, 'the real USP of this machine is not that it's automatic or that it can reproduce thousands of tattoos from a library of the world's greatest tattooists…' He deliberately paused to ramp up the effect.

'The machine would have a multitude of needles… imagine it, five needles, five times as quick, ten needles, ten times as quick. These works of art…'

He held up a sheath of print outs of Sammy Shapiro's work.

'…they take hours and hours, days, weeks even to produce. This device will revolutionise the tattoo world and make us a fortune.'

He pointed towards the sorry collection of metal, leather and flexible pipes that made up the machine that not long ago sat in Chicken City scratching crude barcodes onto the puny, sallow arms of wretched migrants and refugees.

John Burston was now utterly convinced his best friend was as mad as a box of frogs.

Chapter Forty

'Steve, it's your brother... Ken. I, uh, wondered if you fancied going out for a drink one night, uh, tomorrow night actually. Eight o'clock in the Gin Palace... there's something we need to talk about.'

Steve played back the message just in case he hadn't heard it right, but he had – the Gin Palace, *fuck it's as camp as a row of tents in there,* he thought.

The Palace Hotel, as it was officially known, was a beautiful but somewhat shabby old Victorian pub within walking distance of his flat, so it least he didn't have to drive. His brother sounded agitated and he obviously needed to talk – but about what Steve could only guess.

* * *

He'd tried on his Harrington jacket but the colour, on his own admission, was a tad loud. He then tried his weathered Orvis leather jacket but that, matched with his suede Timberland boots together with his unshaven, bristly chin just screamed '*Gay Bear*'.

He shaved, without putting on any aftershave then decided on his Trojan Records T-shirt, Levi's jeans – that thankfully weren't too tight – and a pair of navy-blue Adidas Hamburgs that he'd bought after being goaded by the younger G-Force lads at the football. He'd barely wore them, still not entirely convinced of the senior casual look.

It was a cool, damp evening that warranted a hooded jacket so he played safe and put on his old black zip-up North Face jacket that had served him so well in his trade plating days.

He'd been in the Gin Palace a few times in the past, mostly for a couple of cheap pints before seeing some old funk or reggae band at the nearby Trinity Hall with JB and the other lads. It was always welcoming and upbeat with never a hint of trouble and the distinct sloping floor added to the quirkiness of one of Bristol's most famous gay haunts.

'Hello stranger! What brings you in here?' shrieked an excited voice from behind as Steve ordered a pint of Butcombe ale. He turned to see a face that he vaguely recognised but for the life of him, he couldn't think of where from. He screwed up his eyes and trawled through his memory bank…

'Sorry, I, I… do we know each other?' Steve stammered in embarrassment.

'Ooh you tease, it's Roger! We met in the Shilling a few years back. You and your mates were in a bit of a pickle – don't you remember?' asked the Crimplene trouser-suited stranger.

Steve studied the baby blue outfit. It was like something his mother would have worn in the sixties, he presumed Roger was being ironic, or wearing it for a bet maybe.

How could I forget? Steve recalled the evening when he and the rest of the Big Five had a run in with some racist bonehead skinheads in Tricky Dickies in Denmark Street.

They had won the battle but they sought refuge, bruised and battered in the Queen's Shilling – like the Gin Palace, a well-known gay pub in the city centre. Roger had lent a sympathetic ear and a warm shoulder to Steve that evening and slipped his number on a scrap of paper into Steve's pocket.

Steve had found the note later, smiled to himself – and promptly thrown it away.

'Rog! Yes of course mate. How's it hang... going?'

Steve offered his hand. Roger took and held on to it just long enough for Steve to feel uncomfortable.

'I just knew you were one of us – took your time mind, you never did give me a call you bitch!' squealed Roger as he playfully punched Steve's arm.

Steve could feel himself redden.

'Eh?... No! I'm not gay for fuck's sake! Uh... not that it's a problem. I mean, if I was it would be OK, it's just um... I'm er, waiting for my brother. He... he's one of you. I mean he's gay! Fuck me it's hot in here!'

Steve unzipped his jacket, pulled at the neckline of his T-shirt and blew heavily onto his chest. He desperately looked around for his brother, hoping he could extricate himself from the situation which grew ever more humiliating by the minute.

'Really?' replied Roger with a raised eyebrow, 'so that's why you're promoting gay condoms on your T-shirt is it?'

Steve stared down at the orange and black Trojan logo although he had seen it many times before. *Not a-fucking-gain* he thought, recalling the quizzical looks he used to get on dress-down Fridays when he worked at Pinnacle.

'What this? Have you never heard of Trojan Records? It's a ska and reggae record label for fuck's sake!'

'Of course it is honey, of course it is... Now what's a girl got to do to get a drink around here – I think you owe me one, don't you?'

Roger didn't wait for an answer.

'I'll have a voddy and tonic – and make it slimline, I'm watching my figure, sweet cheeks,' he winked as he sashayed away to a vacant seat.

He sat, crossed his legs and patted the seat next to him just as Kenny pushed open the door of the pub. Steve zipped up his jacket tight to his chin and smiled at his brother, his sigh of relief was palpable.

'Thank fuck,' said Steve to himself as he waved energetically as his brother entered the pub.

Kenny shook out his umbrella, put it in a stand by the door then acknowledged Steve with a slight nod before sidling up to his younger sibling.

'Why the fuck did you want to meet in here?' whispered Steve out of the corner of his mouth as Kenny took off his trademark Fedora and placed it on the polished oak bar.

'Why not?' replied Kenny tersely.

'Well y'know, it's um…'

'Gay? Like me? Now can you get me a gin and…'

'Oi! Are you two-timing me?' came the shrill shout from behind the two of them as an irritated Roger drummed his fingers on the table.

Kenny turned and smiled as Steve ordered the drinks.

'Oh hi Rog. Sorry, this is my brother Steve. Don't worry he's straight – at least I think he is,' grinned Kenny.

'I wasn't talking to you, you slag!' replied Roger with a mischievous smile.

'Come on, park your arses over here and we can have a cosy little threesome.' He patted the seat enthusiastically once more.

'Uh maybe later Rog, I need to chat with my brother first,' said Kenny as he placed Roger's vodka and tonic on the table with a flourish, 'but don't you go anywhere, we'll catch up later… honest.'

He blew Roger a kiss, Roger responded with a heavy sigh and a ferocious batting of his false eyelashes. 'Men!' he groaned.

'You know Roger then?' asked a curious Kenny as the two of them took their seats in a quiet corner of the pub.

'Not really,' responded Steve as he took a large gulp of his Butcombe.

'Let's just say he helped me and the boys out a few years back... we had a scrap with some racist boneheads. They'd picked on George Smolinski, it was a bit nasty to be honest – don't get me wrong we gave the fuckers a right hiding but a couple of the lads took a bit of a kicking. We were with the women – it was when I was with Kirsty,' he added ruefully.

'Anyway, we managed to get the women off home but the law were on to us – we legged it into the Queen's Shilling to clean up and...' he hesitated.

'And what?' asked Kenny as he raised an eyebrow.

'And we made out we were... *gay*,' he coughed.

A smirk crossed Kenny's face.

'*We?* What even JB?'

Steve nodded. 'Oh yes, even JB. Think Rog and his mates were quite taken with the big fella to be honest.'

Kenny's smirk grew into a hearty grin.

'Oh, I would have paid good money to see that!' he roared.

'So what happened next?'

'Nothing really. The law came in and took a sniff around but they were looking for five middle-aged thugs giving it large, not some gay old queens on a night out,' he laughed.

Kenny rolled his eyes and shook his head in disbelief at the thought of John Burston making out he was homosexual, he vowed to himself to give him a hard time next time he saw the avowed homophobe.

'So what's this about?' asked Steve nervously before taking another large gulp of the Somerset-brewed ale.

Kenny cleared his throat and gathered his thoughts before responding.

'Uh, it's about Harry. You know he's been in contact with me, don't you?'

Steve did know. Kenny had been staying at an old acquaintance's house in Clifton for a while – catching up with some old friends, he'd said – and meeting new ones, thought Steve, judging by his conversation with Roger earlier.

He knew that Harry had taken to his previously unknown uncle after their first meeting at his grandmother's funeral. Steve had welcomed it – thinking it good for his once-troubled son to build a relationship with his intelligent, colourful and liberal-minded brother. They were worlds apart but then again, there seemed to be something that united them, some sort of connection. *Free spirits* thought Steve.

'Yep, it's good. I'm glad you and him have been talking. Perhaps he has been stifled a bit… y'know what with my… uh, perhaps jaundiced view of life.'

Steve was careful with his words, but on his own admission he had been overly strict with his wayward son and now in hindsight he thought maybe he could have handled him better.

Kenny was offering Harry a different perspective on life and it seemed to be working. Harry seemed happier and more settled in his life than he'd ever been in the past – and Steve was thankful to his brother for that.

'Jaundiced? Hmmm, that's one way of putting it I guess,' replied Kenny as he sipped on his G&T before continuing.

'Look, from what I gather he's always been a bit… *different*?'

Steve nodded in agreement.

'Certainly from his brother. He's told me that he never got into football like Sam did. He never went to the Rovers with you, never… embraced laddish behaviour, shall we say?'

'Well, he was a punk for a while,' replied Steve, remembering the time a few years back when Harry lived in a squat on Stokes Croft and got involved with a group of anarchists.

He'd been arrested during the protest riots against a new Tesco store but Kirsty had pulled some strings and he'd been let off with just a slap on the wrist.

'And of course, he got involved in drugs which led him to a spell in Horfield unfortunately – but he seems to have put all that behind him now. Looks like he's turning his life around…' Steve smiled to himself.

'All he needs to do now is find himself a nice girl and things will be hunky-dory…'

Steve's smile quickly disappeared as the sudden realisation of the situation hit him. His eyes narrowed as he studied his brother's blank expression.

'He's gay isn't he?'

Kenny nodded. 'Is it a problem?'

Steve exhaled deeply and gathered his thoughts, he'd he lying if he'd said the thought hadn't crossed his mind. The shyness, the awkwardness as a young teenager in the company of girls, never wanting to join in with games with his older brother but preferring to stay in his bedroom as a recluse, usually with his head buried in a book. He'd always been a bit more thoughtful, sensitive even.

Then there was the rebellious streak that manifested as an anarchistic, drug-fuelled punk – and all the time the absence of female company. But he was never – Steve mulled over the thoughts in his head – he was never effeminate.

He then reflected on the fact that his wife, his brother and as it turned out, one of his son's were all gay. He shook his head and inwardly smiled.

Steve glanced around the pub. His gaze fell on a rugged twenty-something with a chiselled chin who stood at the bar nursing a pint of Thatchers. He was built like a brick outhouse, dressed in scruffy overalls and looked as if he'd come straight off a building site. He was making small talk with a smartly dressed, earnest-looking office worker next to him.

His gaze then fell upon Roger who was now surrounded by a gaggle of men and women – all of them deep in loud, humorous, animated conversation.

Steve smiled to himself and dismissed the prejudiced, stereotypical, homophobic thoughts that he had in his head.

'No, it's not a problem,' he replied truthfully.

'Good,' said Kenny as he took out his pocket watch and glanced at it, 'because he'll be here in a minute with his partner… Adam.'

As if on cue, Harry Allen entered the pub. His head was bowed and he looked nervous. Behind him stood another young man – tall with a long blond fringe that obscured his pale-blue eyes, he too bowed his head as if in embarrassment.

Harry gazed around the pub and caught his father's eye, causing him to smile anxiously. Steve nodded and returned his smile, which triggered his son to visibly sigh in relief.

* * *

After the initial clumsy introductions and occasional awkward silences, the evening went surprisingly well – much to everyone's relief.

Harry had met Adam in a bar one evening. He worked in IT, lived with his parents in Henleaze and drove a battered old Mini with a Union Jack on the roof.

He liked cooking, drinking real ale and was also a part-time DJ with a penchant for Seventies funk – he couldn't make up his mind whether his favourite record from that era was *Change* by Donald Byrd or maybe *Wipe your feet and dance* by Wee Willie and the Winners. Steve was impressed, the boy had immaculate taste.

But there was one small problem, Adam was a City fan. Steve joked with him – he could handle his son being gay, but he wasn't too happy about him going out with someone from the 'dark side'.

* * *

They left the pub on closing time and said their good-byes. Steve faced Adam, the two of them grinned and awkwardly shook hands, which then transitioned into a full-blown man hug. Kenny and his nephew did the same before the backslapping spread to all four of them.

'Oi, do you fucking mind you faggots?'

Steve turned to see two young men stood side by side. They were about the same age as Harry and Adam, but that was all they had in common.

They were well built and looked as if they spent as much time in the gym as they did injecting steroids. They carried non-existent medicine balls under their armpits while their fists were balled and ready for action. Near identical tribal tattoos were visible on their pumped-up biceps that bulged angrily against the capped sleeves of their taut T-shirts.

Before Steve could answer, Kenny stepped forward and put a hand on his brother's shoulder.

'Now now chaps – no need for the crass insults, we don't wish to make a scene do we?' said Kenny quietly but firmly.

'And who the fuck are you – Gary fucking Glitter?' asked the larger of the meatheads as he took a step towards Kenny.

Steve could see the meathead's eyebrow ring glint in the streetlight as well as the anger and hate in his eyes, much like he had in himself at the same age.

The meathead approached Kenny menacingly and continued with his insults.

'You two old fuckers ought to be locked up... Wassup, not happy shagging each other, you gotta pick up two young batty boys like them 'ave you?' He nodded towards Harry and Adam who were cowering against the wall of the pub.

'It's not like that,' said Steve as he squared up to the thug.

'This is my brother and that's my son.' Steve motioned towards Harry.

'Jesus that's fucking sick – what kinda weirdos are you for fuck's sake?'

The meathead spat out the words angrily before raising his clenched fist so it was within inches of Steve's face. His accomplice stepped forward and did the same to Kenny.

'Look we don't want any trouble,' said Steve as he held up his hands in submission.

'Tough!' said the thug as he cocked his arm back ready to throw a punch.

Steve readied himself, instinctively bent his legs, crouched and quickly changed his stance to take the impact and then react with swift, hard punches of his own. The punch that he expected never came, instead the meathead let out a yelp and his balled fist quickly transformed to a flat palm as he put his hand to his face as the razor-sharp blade slashed at his cheek.

The thug screamed then studied the smear of blood on his palm. '*What the fuck!*'

Steve fired a startled glance at his brother.

Kenny smirked and flashed the blade once more. This time, he ran it down the thug's chest and stopped at his crotch. He gave it a small but energetic poke.

'You and your friend should spend less time at the gym and more time working on your personalities – now run along before I cut your tiny little dick off, there's a good chap.'

The meathead took a few steps back then motioned to his mate to move, they turned, ran and disappeared into the damp night.

Kenny nonchalantly returned the long blade into the sheath of his umbrella while Steve stared at him open mouthed.

'Did... did I just see you nearly stab a man?' asked Steve incredulously.

'Not at all little brother – just making the streets a little more shipshape and Bristol fashion that's all. Now who's for a nightcap?'

Chapter Forty-One

The most difficult part had been creating the needle head so that it followed the contours of the body in the same way that a skilled tattoo artist's hand did. It needed just the right amount of pressure to ensure the needles penetrated the skin, but not too much to actually cut into the flesh.

Phil relished the challenge and with Irena's help he worked wonders and eventually created tiny, ultra-sensitive sensors that worked perfectly – the device was nearing completion.

They'd tested the machine time and time again on pork shoulder joints that JB had 'borrowed' from a mate down the abattoir. When they'd finished experimenting JB took the joints to a nearby shelter for the homeless where 'tribal tattoo pork and mash' became a firm favourite with the grateful vagrants.

The next stage was to make a flexible head and restraint of sorts, something that was comfortable and pliable and not like the rigid metal and leather contraption that the Chicken City version had. It also had to be big enough to comfortably accommodate a full-grown male body to enable the needles to tattoo torsos and not just inside wrists and forearms as before.

It needed so much crafting, retooling and re-inventing that at times they thought they would fail. They rebuilt, restructured, reprogrammed and worked long into the night. They swore, they shed tears and they fought, but on a warm summer's evening some nine months after Steve had first purloined the device from Chicken City the machine was finally ready.

They had all contributed. Phil's obvious skills in robotics, Irena's electrical and computer manufacturing knowledge and George's engineering and welding capabilities, while JB seemed to be able to get his hands on just about anything the team wanted – within reason.

Kenny, now known to all and sundry as D'Artagnan, supplied his deceased partner's artworks as well as substantial funding while Steve played his part by obtaining a high-res desktop scanner from a supplier he knew from his graphic design days and most importantly, in his opinion, he designed the logo.

Steve cracked open a can of Thatchers Gold cider in celebration and let the golden fluid fizz and spill over the prototype machine.

He raised the can in his right hand and put his left arm around the smiling Irena.

'I name this beautiful creature Evalina,' he beamed proudly.

'Evalina!' they all repeated.

George eventually broke the silence. 'Well?'

'Well what?' asked Steve, but he knew full well what George was alluding to.

'Well, who's going to be the first? We need to try it on one of us and not just legs of fucking pork.'

They all looked at each nervously. Eventually JB spoke.

'Go on then, in for a penny in for a pound.'

The others all breathed a sigh of relief as JB started undoing the belt of his jeans. Irena gave him a startled look.

'Sorry love but it's the only part of my body I ain't got any ink – think I got a gap on the back of my thigh somewhere… or you can do summat on me arse.'

He dropped his jeans to the floor. Irena squirmed.

'There you go.' He pointed to a nine-inch square bare patch of flesh on the back of his left leg.

Five minutes later JB was lying face down on the padded bench, his leg firmly strapped in place.

He'd chosen a stunning snarling wolf's head from Sam Shapiro's portfolio of work that had already been scanned, digitised and stored in a library on Steve's laptop.

The process was surprisingly easy. Steve registered the positions on the back of JB's thigh that corresponded with co-ordinates on the master artwork file. He sprayed JB's flesh with Lidocaine, cleaned the needles with sterilisation solution then aligned the head just above the area to be tattooed.

'Ready?' Steve asked JB.

JB gave a thumbs up.

'Go for it mate.'

Steve pressed a couple of buttons on his laptop. The machine burst into life with a loud buzz and the needle head lowered into position – the process had begun.

Steve started the stopwatch on his phone. Eleven minutes and twenty-five seconds later the tattoo was complete, much to JB's relief.

He admitted the pain threshold was high due to the fact that more needles were in use but this was more than compensated by the short length of time that the process had taken. Steve wiped down JB's thigh with an antiseptic tissue and they all stared at the fresh tattoo in awe.

Staring back at them with bright yellow eyes was the head of a ferocious snarling wolf, every hair, every whisker, every minute detail was perfectly replicated – an exact rendition of Sam Shapiro's artwork that hadn't seen the light of day for nearly four decades.

'*Holy shit!*' exclaimed Steve.

* * *

Nearly one hundred miles away in Hampshire, Evalina Petrovic was relaxing by the side of a pool of a well-known spa resort, glass of Veuve Clicquot in one hand, iPhone in the other.

Ever since that fateful day in Chicken City, Eva had been cared for and looked after by the authorities, much to Irena's chagrin.

Following an initial debrief from Fraser Winston and his team Eva had been whisked away and ensconced in a private rehab centre in Wiltshire, courtesy of the Government.

Her mother had initially fought tooth and nail to be reunited with her daughter but eventually, after many heated conversations with Steve she begrudgingly and reluctantly accepted the decision and after just a few months even she had to concede that the intensive counselling and psychotherapy that Eva was receiving on a daily basis, was beginning to work.

As a relief from the sometimes harsh and intrusive counselling she would often be rewarded with a weekend stay at the luxury spa resort where she swam, worked out in the gym, ate good healthy food – but not chicken – and blagged the odd glass of Champagne from the besotted young male staff.

Eva took a sip of Champagne then watched with interest the video that her mother had sent her of the debut of 'Evalina' – the tattoo machine that bore her name.

She smiled broadly then gasped in delight and wonder at the sight of the stunning artwork on the back of JB's leg.

Eva thanked her mother, smiled then blew a kiss into the phone before bellowing *'Ciao mama, speak to you soon – love you!'* as she had done nearly every day for the past nine months.

Opposite Eva on the other side of the pool, relaxing on a sun lounger was a tall, elegant slim woman in a gold one-piece swimsuit, bright red Louboutin sandals and slicked back grey hair.

She raised her eyes from her copy of *Vogue*, peered over the top of her Gucci sunglasses and watched the animated Eva with interest. She then picked up her iPhone and dialled a number.

'Bonjour Charles, it's Esther. I think I've found her.'

Chapter Forty-Two

Eight months later

The multi-millionaire entrepreneur screwed up his eyes and gave a sideways glance to his fellow Dragons. He then stared back at Steve inquisitively.

'So, you're trying to tell me that *this*... this contraption could give me a return of two point five million in two years?'

'At least,' said Steve with an air of confidence.

'There are over ten thousand tattoo artists in the UK alone and good, seasoned artists earn over fifty K a year, that's...'

'Five hundred million,' answered the Dragon as his eyes lit up in excitement.

Steve's pitch had been near perfect. Years of experience of delivering punchy presentations to stoney-faced and underwhelmed ad men had served him well and the thousand pounds he'd spent on the male model who agreed to have his chest tattooed in real time was well spent.

The tattoo, which matched anything produced by a skilled and experienced tattooist, took just twenty minutes to complete and the Dragons watched the process in open-mouthed incredulity.

It was a risk but it paid off.

Sammy Shapiro's intricate and beautiful illustration of a Japanese Ryu dragon had been an inspired choice and the Dragons were suitably impressed – none more so than the waspish and normally stony-faced Dragoness who could barely contain her excitement when the model stripped off his robe to reveal his gym-honed torso.

Irena, who stood by Steve's side throughout the pitch, provided the eye candy for the male Dragons – and much to Steve's relief, the expertise and knowledge of how the machine actually worked.

The two of them formed a formidable team, they'd expertly wound the Dragons in and Steve relaxed knowing an offer would be forthcoming. He was not to be disappointed and the unedifying sight of all five Dragons battling with each other to get a piece of the action made compulsive TV viewing.

The offer on the table was exactly what Steve and Irena had asked for, they had not given so much away so that they would lose control of the business but it was enough to get valuable expertise and financial backing to see their dream come to fruition.

The two of them mulled over the offer, not wanting to seem overly keen. They falsely consulted with each other as if they were debating whether to accept the offer or not, but it was a done deal, they both knew it. Steve had reeled in the Dragon he wanted, the ruthless and driven publishing and telecoms tycoon.

Finally, Steve took a step towards the towering, multi-coloured sock-wearing Dragon.

'I think we have a deal,' he grinned as he shook the Dragon's outstretched hand.

Chapter Forty-Three

The following year

Simon Edwards woke early on the Sunday morning and raised his pounding head from the kitchen floor. A crusty, dried piece of pizza stuck to his cheek like a leach – he peeled it off, sniffed and inspected it, then ate it like the miserable dog that he'd become.

He dragged himself up then looked around and cursed at the accumulated rubbish. The sink was full to overflowing with a multitude of dirty, greasy pans soaking in putrid dishwater while the filthy work surface was covered in detritus of all descriptions.

He gazed at the walls that were covered in photos, Post-it notes and newspaper cuttings – mainly relating to allegations of police cover-ups, shootings and conspiracy theories from around the world.

He straightened a photo of the twin towers and repositioned another one of a shadowy figure stood on a grassy knoll in Dallas, Texas. He made a promise to himself that he would start tidying up the place… tomorrow.

Rummaging through the clutter he swore as he tripped over a discarded bottle then smiled at the realisation that it contained a few mouthfuls of Scotland's finest export. He bent down to pick it up then lost his balance and fell to the floor once more amongst the discarded takeaway boxes and chip wrappers.

Through his drunken stupor he managed to focus on the precious bottle. He reached out once more, grabbed it and with shaking hands, undid the top and put the bottle to his lips. The fiery liquid eased down his throat and briefly gave him respite from his demons – the demons that had arrived and not left him since the death of his friend and one-time colleague, Fraser Winston. The death that haunted him every day without fail.

* * *

Carleen, Fraser Winston's widow, had assured him that it wasn't his fault. It had been a freak accident – the low-setting sun had blinded her husband while he'd been distracted – and he was driving at over ninety miles per hour, she'd been told by the investigators.

But Simon Edwards knew different. It wasn't the fact that he'd been speaking to Winston on his mobile moments before the crash, it was the fact that he'd harassed him into doing something about the case he'd been investigating, the case that his superiors had told him to drop.

He'd actively encouraged him to disobey orders – *'pull your Masonic finger out of your Masonic arse and do something about it'* he'd said. Well, he had – and look where it had got him, decapitated and burnt to a crisp in the middle lane of the M4.

It played on his mind every single day of his miserable, wretched life. His art gallery business had gone tits-up, he'd been barred from every drinking establishment in Monmouth and the few friends he'd had ignored his calls and disowned him.

He'd put on weight, was smoking heavily and was a shuffling, shambling mess and a far cry from the alert, fit and ambitious young cop that he had once been.

He had one person in his life that he called a friend of sorts – Steve Allen, but unfortunately for Simon Edwards the friendship wasn't being reciprocated.

Steve had grown tired of the late night and early morning phone calls from the inebriated and resentful

Welshman, phone calls in which he ranted about the latest government-backed infringement on civil liberties and attacks on human rights.

Then there were the conspiracy theories – from MI6 being involved in the death of Princess Diana to the Covid pandemic being a worldwide hoax that would lead to a New World Order coming into effect, influenced and controlled by the Illuminati and the Freemasons of course.

* * *

Full of self-loathing, he raised himself up and crawled into the living room – 'living' room being the operative word judging by the state of the carpet and the furnishings.

He cleared a pile of old newspapers and empty high-strength lager cans from a battered, urine-stained armchair and slumped into it before rummaging down the side of the chair. He found the remote and turned the TV on. He tuned into Sky News as he always did then stared at the TV in open-mouthed disbelief.

Forty odd miles away across the Severn, Steve Allen was sleeping soundly in his bed. He awoke with a start as his mobile once again played the first few chords of *Pressure Drop*.

He didn't have to look at the screen – there was only one person who phoned him at this hour on a Sunday morning.

'For fuck's sake Edwards, do you know what time it is?' said Steve angrily.

Edwards ignored the question.

'You've gotta do something about this squire,' he drawled.

'Do something about what? What are you fucking on about now?'

'The news – they're setting the wheels in motion.'

'Who? What wheels?'

'The powers that be… the Government, the Masons, whoever. It doesn't matter precisely who, but it's happening.'

'Will you stop talking in fucking riddles – what's happening?'

'It's on the news now. MI5 have foiled a triple-pronged terrorist attack on Buckingham Police, 10 Downing Street and the House of Commons – and get this, the perpetrators have been linked to an Asian paedophile ring…'

'Don't tell me,' Steve interrupted wearily, 'I suppose these paedophiles are all MIRAS who came across the Channel in small boats.'

'Probably,' answered Edwards.

'What do you mean probably? You're sounding like a *Daily Mail* reader!'

'That's not *me* talking. You know I don't believe that crap, that's precisely my point – it's the Government propaganda machine swinging into action – if, and it's a big if, there's any truth in this whatsoever then what's the betting that the next thing we hear is COBRA are having an urgent meeting and they'll be bringing in drastic new measures to combat terrorism and Asian paedophile rings?'

Steve groaned 'But…'

'Never mind "*but*". Think about it – they wouldn't take action against all those white, upper class paedophile rings, you know the ones that Fraser Winston was investigating with all the MPs, vicars and prominent businessmen involved, but they'll act against the Asian ones – strange eh?'

Steve conceded he had a point.

'Sorry,' replied Steve, 'but I don't see where this rant is leading, it's just the same as all your other rants to be honest.'

'What do you mean rants?'

'You know what I mean – all your bloody conspiracy theories, Illuminati, Masons, Men in Black – you'd make a bloody good Hollywood scriptwriter…'

Edwards interrupted.

'What do you know about the Men in Black?'

'*Nothing!* I don't… I was joking.' Steve stifled a laugh.

'Well don't, it's no laughing matter, it's fucking true I tell you. Can't you see – all of these events, it's the politics of fucking fear! Look how they pushed through the Surveillance Bill the other year, the Government can access all your internet history and view every website you've ever visited, not to mention every phone call and text message you've ever sent – all on the pretext that it's for our own safety! Christ I can't believe how gullible the British people have been!'

Steve reluctantly found himself nodding in agreement. Edwards continued with his rant.

'They've just been waiting for the next big thing to happen so they can push through even more drastic measures, and this is it! If it's happened at all that is. I wouldn't be surprised one little bit if all this shit has been made up. What's the betting this is a false flag operation eh?'

'A what?' queried Steve.

'False flag operation – don't tell me you've never heard of them, Steve?' he didn't wait for an answer.

'Covert operations conducted by governments or even private organisations – they're designed to deceive the public in such a way that the operations appear as if they've been carried out by other entities – such as terrorist groups. It all makes sense, then like I said, they'll push through drastic measures and you know what those drastic measures will be don't you? Yep, *your* fucking microchips. They're going to microchip the entire population – just you wait and see… *You were right all along!*'

Steve sighed in exasperation.

'Give it a fucking rest will you? And anyway, what if you're saying is true, what the fuck do you think I can do about it?' he pleaded.

'Well put your big boy pants on and talk to that newspaper mate of yours – the one who exposed the use of Merck in the Premier League, I mean that all worked out OK didn't it? Once they ran the story, social networks went into meltdown. This would be the same. It would all be exposed as a huge hoax perpetrated by the Government without anyone being incriminated… what was his name?'

'Barry Mason. And no he can't help, he's moved on – he keeps alpacas up in the Cotswolds and anyway, what's the point?' answered Steve as he rubbed his eyes and looked at his watch – it was just after six.

'What's the point? What's the *fucking* point? Am I hearing this right? Is this the same Steve Allen who took on a couple of major league drug barons and the football establishment – not to mention the City bankers?'

'Yes, and I got the scars to prove it – literally… Simon, that was a lifetime ago and things have changed.'

He glanced at Irena who was now awake and looking at him grumpily through bleary eyes. The bottle of Chateauneuf-du-Pape and Balkan vodka she'd polished off the night before was now not doing her any favours. He kissed her shoulder in assurance, got out of bed and shuffled into the bathroom.

'Look, all this came about through Eva and Chicken *fucking* City,' said Steve as he sat down on the toilet. He rubbed his stubble and mulled over his response…

'Thanks to Fraser Winston and his colleagues Chicken City and Chip City have been exposed for what they were. They've now been sorted, cleaned up and the residents are free to come and go as they please. They live in clean accommodation and they're getting a decent wage. Admittedly Solutio are still on the scene but I get the feeling that won't be for long, and at least that shit Etchington's been confined to a wheelchair for the rest of his life. On top of that a major Albanian OCG has been smashed and best of all, for me, Eva's made a new life for herself and if you must know, I've never been happier with my life than I am right now. So, the thought of me getting mixed up in all that shit again doesn't really appeal – got it?'

'Yeah, like you said, thanks to Fraser Winston – who now happens to be fucking dead!' shouted Edwards down the phone.

'*Whoah!* Now hold on – that was an accident.'

'Accident? No it fucking wasn't, he was murdered. I'm telling you I was talking on the phone to him at the time. It was when I mentioned your name and going to the press and the like that the interference came on the phone and the next thing I know he's fucking toast. And anyway, are you forgetting the fact that when Eva came to you she was fucking chipped? Hmmm? And we all know that this is where it's going don't we? They're going to chip us all, I tell you squire it's going to be a New World Order – is that what you want, eh?'

Steve was exasperated. It was like listening to a scratched record.

'Since when have you been a member of Liberty, eh? Never thought of you as being a guardian of civil liberties. Remind me you were in SOCA weren't you?'

'You what? What's that got to do with anything? I'm from the fucking valleys, my old man worked down the pits, so don't go querying my left-wing credentials squire. Just 'cos I was a copper don't make me a fucking fascist!'

Like being a skinhead never made me a racist, thought Steve. He squirmed and mumbled an apology of sorts.

'I've always been on the side of the law,' Edwards continued, 'and I've always distinguished between right and wrong – thought you did as well, it was one of the things I liked about you to be honest. And so did Fraser for that matter – he fucking trusted you!'

Steve could feel Edward's anger and resentment across the ether. It pricked Steve's conscience. If he was honest with himself, he was uncomfortable about the situation but he didn't want to admit it. He remained silent.

'What's up Steve? Lost for words? Truth hurts doesn't it? I'm telling you this is it, this is the one they've been waiting for and they'll be microchipping the population sooner than you can say *"Big Brother"*. But don't worry about it squire, as long as you can cosy up to that beautiful missus of yours and you can live in that cute little cottage then everything's going to be OK… *Sorry I fucking bothered you!*'

Simon Edwards hung up with his words ringing in Steve's ears. Steve stood up from the toilet and took out two high-strength Ibuprofens from the bathroom cabinet. He swallowed them then studied his reflection in the mirror and delved deep into his soul.

The hard man of the streets and terraces had long gone, he had no urge to take on the world and the one-man vigilante of old had confined his baseball bat to the back of the wardrobe alongside his bovver boots. His prejudices and phobias had dissipated along with his cocaine habit and his addiction to prescription painkillers and anti-depressants.

The angry, mixed-up, bitter middle-aged man of old had been replaced with a mellower, softer, chilled-out version – and in all honesty he felt better for it.

He re-entered the bedroom and looked around the tastefully decorated room and the expensive soft furnishings. His gaze fell upon Irena who had dozed off again. She was sleeping contentedly in their oversized bed with its thousand thread-count Egyptian cotton sheets and its winter snow goose down pillows. He brushed the hair from her face and once again admired her finely chiselled features and those immaculate cheekbones.

Even hungover and dishevelled she looked stunning. He allowed himself a slight, smug smile as he reflected on the past few years – it only seemed like yesterday that he'd been standing on motorway sliproads desperately hitching for lifts to godforsaken hellholes in the middle of industrial England. He thought of the scary neo-Nazi Polish truck driver, the wonderfully mad hippy chick and her stuffed rabbit and his smile grew to an expansive grin as he remembered the curvaceous Nikki and her awesome ginger nuts.

His life had certainly changed, and for the better, he thought. He had made his peace with his brother Kenny and his relationship with his son Harry was better than it had ever been – due in no small part to Steve finally accepting his son for what he truly was – different.

His friendship with his mates John Burston and George Smolinski was stronger than ever – all three of them had recently visited Pete McNulty in Spain and they'd laughed out loud as they recalled their adventures and mishaps from their youth over too many San Miguels and sangrias.

Pete and his wife had been delighted to see them and the sun had worked wonders in easing Steve's aches and pains. He looked and felt better than he'd done for many a year and to top it all, Steve had a woman in his life who although had quirky, odd and at times baffling ways – especially in the kitchen – was a joy to be with.

At long last, life was looking good for Steve Allen.

Then of course there was Eva. The sad, mad and utterly beguiling Evalina who finally seemed to be getting her life together. He corrected himself, she was not just getting her life together, she was having a ball.

The year of intense therapy, help and support that Eva had received from certain sympathetic – or perhaps, guilt-ridden – individuals in the Home Office had worked wonders.

The fact that those individuals were desperate to keep the real reasons behind the raid and the subsequent omnishambles away from the public's eyes may have had something to do with the way they dealt with Eva. They treated her with compassion and empathy – rather than charging her with the attempted murder of a well-known and much-loved Member of Parliament.

She had been transformed. She was still fragile and subject to intense mood swings – like her mother – but the damaged, broken youngster had been put back together and her demons had been well and truly exorcised.

Eva was now a confident, beautiful sassy young woman and thanks to Esther Katz, the talent scout for a global modelling agency who had spotted her at the health spa, she was now a top international model. It was hardly surprising, she turned heads wherever she went – as Steve Allen knew to his cost.

His gaze moved away from Irena and he studied the copy of *Vogue* that rested on the bedside cabinet.

He smiled – staring back at him from the cover with those stunning emerald eyes under the headline '*The Special One*', was the bewitching and beautiful Evalina. Like Chicken City, Eva had been rebuilt and reinvented... she was indeed 'The Special One'.

In the short time she'd been modelling Eva had amassed a small fortune. She'd insisted on giving a sizeable chunk of that money to her mother and Steve and, with the cash that was beginning to come his way from his ever-expanding tattoo machine empire, an empire that thanks to pre-orders and a franchising arm that the wily Dragon had suggested, he and Irena were able to purchase the stunning cottage in Frenchay on the outskirts of Bristol, that they now lived in.

It needed work – a lot of work, but with the help of his good mate JB, the detached eighteenth-century, walled gardened house was beginning to look like the sort of home that he and Irena had dreamed of.

Irena was like a kid in a sweet shop, but even Steve had to admit she had an eye for detail and what with weekly visits to John Lewis it meant the furnishings and décor were tasteful and of the highest quality. He felt truly blessed.

He considered sliding back into bed and cosying up to Irena but she was sleeping soundly and he thought it best not to wake her, knowing full well that if he put his arm around her and gently hugged her, she would stir and the inevitable energetic sex would happen, and following the conversation with Edwards he wasn't really in the mood for it. He didn't quite believe he would ever have a thought like that. He smiled to himself once again.

The phone call from Simon Edwards had troubled him but he tried to put it to the back of his mind. He knew what the inebriated and disturbed Welshman was saying was true, that the Government were indeed paving the way to have the microchips introduced, if not in response to the latest terrorist threat, then in response to the next one – but what was he supposed to do about it? If it hadn't been for him, the two migrant cities might never have been raided and reformed. He accepted there had been casualties and some of the paedophiles and child-traffickers had no doubt escaped, but at least the migrant cities were now genuinely in government control and they seemed to be working – for now.

He felt uneasy that Solutio was still in operation – albeit in a much improved and restructured format with a new board of directors, but at least Etchington and Marishta were off the scene and for that he felt partly responsible – and proud.

He hadn't felt a great deal of remorse for the deaths of Thompson and Bishop either. Why should he? They knew what they were involved in and they were as corrupt as their paymasters. They'd tried to frame him for a murder, a murder that had never even taken place and worse of all they had assaulted and raped Eva, so had he any sympathy for their demise? *Had he fuck.*

Fraser Winston's death was different, however.

If, and it was a big if, what Simon Edwards had claimed was true then yes, it pricked his conscience, but where was the proof? He himself had been blinded by the early evening sun on many occasion when he'd left London and headed back West, so it was highly likely that an agitated and distracted Fraser Winston had crashed and been killed due to his own actions.

Perhaps it was a way for Simon Edwards to ease his own conscience, knowing full well that he had been partly responsible for his friend's death. After all it was Edwards who had phoned Winston and badgered him into pursuing the Government – or at least certain rogue members of the Government and, in his twisted mind, the guilty and out-of-control Masonic movement.

What was it Edwards had said? *'It was when I mentioned your name and going to the press.'*

Steve suddenly felt a cold shiver run down his spine.

Why had he mentioned my name?

He put it to the back of his mind. It had been nearly two years since the raid on the migrant cities and if there was going to be any repercussions against him and the part he played – albeit minor – then surely something would have happened by now… *wouldn't it?*

Chapter Forty-Four

He wandered downstairs in his shorts and a monogrammed 'SA' towelling bathrobe that Irena had bought for him the previous Christmas, she had a matching 'IP' one – he secretly hated it but she thought they looked classy and tasteful… and who was he to argue.

He filled the kettle and put it on the hob of the AGA then rummaged through the cupboard looking in disdain at the collection of Earl Grey, pure green tea and Croatian chamomile in front of him. His sigh turned to a triumphant smile as he spotted the familiar red box of Typhoo tea bags tucked away at the back.

He made a brew in his 'No. 1 Bristol Rovers fan' mug, took a chocolate digestive out of the biscuit barrel then turned around to survey the carnage.

Irena had assured him it would all look perfect when it was finished – she wanted it to look like the homes in *House & Garden*, although she was a tad disappointed that the cottage didn't have a thatched roof, as when she was a young girl, she thought all English people lived in thatched cottages.

But… in the meantime it looked like a bombsite and he was beginning to rue the day he'd asked JB to extend the cottage and give them the kitchen that she'd yearned for – although why she wanted a large kitchen complete with a central island and the latest AGA stove when she could barely boil an egg was beyond him.

JB may have been a master builder but he was one unorganised, untidy bastard when it came to working – all around lay power tools of various descriptions as well as hammers, chisels, saws and screwdrivers.

Steve took in the scene and shook his head. Thankfully it was Sunday, meaning they'd get a day's respite from the incessant hammering, drilling and general disruption that had filled their days for the last couple of months.

JB had worked late the evening before and his tools lay strewn across the work surfaces and floor. His wife Sharon, who had taken to Irena much more than she had to Eva had also come over and the four of them enjoyed an Indian takeaway, too many red wines and vodkas and a night's reminiscing while the jukebox played away in the background.

Steve rubbed away a patch of sawdust from a grimy window and looked out into the garden. The sun was breaking through the early morning mist and a squirrel busied himself burying nuts in Steve's lawn.

'You just wait you little bastard,' muttered Steve as he thought of the new Jack Russell puppy that he would be getting in two weeks' time. He'd already thought of a name for him – Otis.

He'd vowed to himself that once he moved out of his flat and into a house with an enclosed garden, he would get himself a new dog, but only the one this time. Prince and Buster had been dead for a few years now and although he missed the energetic, mad double act he knew that just the one canine would be enough – and besides, it had been hard enough to persuade Irena to have a Jack as what she'd really wanted was a Bichon Frise.

'Over my dead fucking body,' said Steve under his breath as he wandered into the thankfully still intact living room.

He turned on the TV and switched to the Sky News channel. The news was dominated by the storylines that had been breaking all night and reaffirmed what Simon Edwards had told him earlier – that MI5 and the authorities had foiled a triple-pronged terrorist attack on Buckingham Palace, 10 Downing Street and the House of Commons.

As Edwards had also mentioned there was talk of links to Muslim paedophile gangs and the screen was ablaze with red 'breaking news' banners whilst a plethora of easy-on-the-eye blonde news reporters named Kelly or Jackie interrogated so-say experts and right-wing politicians for their views on the latest terrorist outrage.

COBRA – the sexily-named crisis response committee that in reality stood for the more mundane 'Cabinet Office Briefing Room A' had indeed been summoned by the Prime Minister for an emergency meeting and the TV talking heads were already speculating on what extreme measures were about to be unleashed onto the people of Britain – one had even suggested the introduction of a modern, state-of-the-art electronic ID system.

They had been primed, the groundwork was being prepared – the clock was ticking.

It appeared that Edwards was right.

Steve had felt a gun pressed against his temple before, when he was in Chicken City sitting nervously on Eva's bed. But he hadn't expected to feel the barrel of a handgun pressed against his head while he watched Sky News whilst sipping Typhoo tea and nibbling on a chocolate digestive.

Chapter Forty-Five

'Where the fuck is she?' Besin Marishta whispered menacingly in Steve's ear.

He said it in a manner that was as cold and as hard as the pistol that he held. Steve felt Marishta's warm breath on the back of his neck, his halitosis and body odour combined to emit a smell that was as rancid as a month-old kebab.

'Who?' replied Steve. He tried to say it as calmly as possible but it came out as no more than a high-pitched screech.

'You sound scared Mister Allen and there was me thinking you were some tough guy – and you know who I'm fucking talking about.'

Steve stared unblinkingly at the TV screen.

'If you mean Evalina then she's away on a shoot – I think she's in Brazil.'

Marishta pressed the barrel of the gun against Steve's temple even harder.

'Not that little whore – I'm talking about Irena... *my wife.*'

Steve's heart raced as the words *'my wife'* registered in his brain.

'What – you didn't know? Why does that not surprise me? So you thought you would spend the rest of your life in this...'

Marishta briefly scanned the room.

'In this beautiful cottage with its roses and its expensive kitchen. What she want nice kitchen for anyway?... she terrible cook,' said Marishta in broken English.

He moved the gun away from Steve's head but kept it pointed at him as he walked around to the front of the La-Z-Boy. He faced Steve who still had his mug of tea in his hand.

'Ah, a nice cup of tea – how very English, now put it down and stand the fuck up.'

Steve did as he was told.

He stood and faced the imposing Albanian. Steve had seen him in Eva's video but he'd only seen him once before in the flesh – on the night of the *ustawka* in the woods when Marishta and his cronies came off second best to the joint City and Rovers mob. He had lost a lot of weight since then and looked fit, lean and more than a match for Steve.

Marishta continued.

'I saw you on TV a few weeks ago yes? That's all I do all day, watch repeats on daytime TV and work out in the gym. You and *my* wife were on that Dragons programme – you not only stole her but you stole my tattoo machine you bastard!'

Steve braced himself for a strike from the Albanian that he thought was sure to come. Marishta studied Steve and screwed up his eyes in recognition.

'I saw that programme and nearly fell out of bed when I saw her and then I spotted you! I have good memory... I thought, I know him – we have met before, yes? Can you remember where Englishman?'

Steve shook his head. 'Uh no, I can't say I do.'

'You're a bad liar...' Marishta hesitated.

Steve thought the Albanian was hiding something. He knew more than he was letting on.

'So, where is she, my beautiful wife?'

'I uh, don't know what you're on about... I live here on my own.'

'Really? Then who is that in the photo over there?'

He nodded towards a cabinet in the corner of the room, pride of place in the centre of a clutch of framed photographs was a photo of Steve and Irena both smiling while looking lovingly into each other's eyes.

'OK, OK – yes she lives here with me but she's away at the moment. She's…'

Marishta swung his arm and smashed the gun across Steve's face. Steve staggered backwards and put his hand to his mouth, a smear of blood trailed across the back of his hand. He looked at it intently then spat out a mouthful of blood and spittle.

'Don't fucking lie Englishman! Where is she?' screamed the Albanian, his eyes wild with anger.

Steve stood upright and faced him once more. He nodded his head towards the ceiling.

'She's in bed – sleeping. But what do you want with her? She never mentioned she was married, not to you anyway.'

All sorts of thoughts went through Steve's head – and not good ones. He'd always felt uneasy and unsure about the story Irena had spun regarding her husband's untimely death, but this involvement with Marishta was something else.

What if he was telling the truth? Was Dragan made up? Did this make Eva, Marishta's daughter? It had never been discussed in front of Eva and he'd never heard her side of the story. He'd known all along that there were secrets the two of them had kept from him – something didn't add up and he felt sick to his stomach.

'I don't give a fuck what she's told you!' Marishta thrust the gun in Steve's face once more, 'just take me to her – and don't try anything or I shoot your fucking English head off – understand?'

Steve nodded, turned and walked towards the staircase. He slowly ascended the stairs wondering if Irena had heard the commotion and made her escape. He cursed the fact that she'd drunk so much the night before, knowing that she was now probably sleeping soundly.

He slowed down and tried to delay the inevitable, much to the annoyance of Marishta who jabbed the gun into his back.

'So, are you going to tell me where we met?' asked Steve, desperately trying to delay matters.

'Think back Englishman. You football hooligan, yes?'

Steve remained silent.

'You and your friends – we had big fight in woods the other year – ha! We lost but it was good fun, yes?'

Steve remembered the night well, but fun wasn't the word he would use. He stalled once more on the stairs and spoke to Marishta over his shoulder.

'Uh no, I think you must be mistaken.'

'You're fucking lying again Englishman. I know you were there, but you're a bit old to be an ultra, aren't you?'

'I don't know what you're on about. I'm no ultra and I don't know what you want with...'

'Stop your fucking lies. I know we met before. How do you think I tracked you down?'

Steve shook his head. He'd wondered how he'd found him since the moment he'd felt the pistol against his temple.

Marishta continued. 'Your friend – Preston, the prick who arranged the *ustawka* with me, I got hold of him through... mutual friends. He has a very loose tongue.'

Steve's eyes widened in anger. He remembered bumping into Tony Preston a couple of months back in a pub in town and telling him he'd moved to Frenchay but he certainly hadn't let him know his address.

'Preston doesn't know I live here though, how did you find out?'

'Too many questions but I'm not stupid Allen. I see all these adverts on TV for Rightmove,' he grinned, 'I check out website and found out last house sold in village... and there was something else.'

His grin turned into a chuckle.

'The Serbian flag flying outside. Bit of a giveaway you dumb English shit.'

Steve recalled Irena spotting the flagpole as soon as they'd moved in. She insisted on flying the distinct flag of her spiritual home, much to his and their stony-faced neighbours' dismay.

'So Preston grassed me up?'

'*Grass* – is that what you call it? Yes, your friend grassed you up. But that loose tongue, it very loose now – I cut it out. He won't be grassing anyone up from now on!'

Steve wouldn't exactly call Preston a friend but he certainly didn't wish him any harm.

'Tell me he's still alive?' he pleaded.

'Alive, yes but not very talkative,' laughed Marishta but his laugh quickly turned into a scream that chilled Steve to the bone.

He turned to see the Albanian clutching his face and the gun dropping to the staircase floor. Steve turned, bent down, picked up the pistol and looked back at Marishta who had now lost his footing and fallen back down the stairs.

Marishta was holding his face and Steve could see crimson blood seeping through his hands and what at first sight looked like a furry black hat sat atop his head.

The sounds of Marishta screaming mixed in with another higher pitched screeching and wailing – it was then that Steve realised it was not a black hat on his head but a cat.

Derrick was merciless in his attack on the intruder. His vicious, razor-like claws and teeth slashed and gouged at the eyes, nose and mouth of the screaming Albanian but finally Marishta managed to get a hold of the feline and he threw Derrick across the room where he thudded against the adjacent wall in a ball of fur and blood.

Marishta writhed on the floor in agony cursing and swearing in indecipherable words and sounds.

Steve became aware of someone stood behind him. He turned to see a motionless Irena at the top of the stairs, she was wearing her bathrobe and her hands were clasped over her mouth. He turned and looked back at Marishta.

The Albanian was sat up and wedged between the alcove wall and the jukebox. He was bloodied and dazed and his stare darted between Steve and Irena. Steve pointed the gun at his head.

'Steve! What is happening?' shouted Irena from behind him.

'What's happening? What does it look like? Your fucking husband has come for you!'

'Husband? Is that what he told you?' said Irena as she descended the stairs.

'Yes. Well is he, or isn't he?'

Irena came up behind Steve and put her hands on his shoulders.

'Uh… sort of. But it's not what you think.'

'Not what I think? He either is or he isn't. Perhaps you'd like to explain.'

Besin Marishta smiled wryly. 'Ha! The Serbian whore has not been truthful with her English lover. I wonder what other secrets she has kept from you, huh? You know she worked for us, Englishman?'

'Shut your fucking mouth! Don't listen to him Steve. He's talking shit. Yes, we were married but that was just so he could get out of Kosovo and come to England. He insisted on it, otherwise he would…'

Irena realised she was talking too much. She stopped abruptly.

'Otherwise he would what?' asked Steve.

'Otherwise I would tell everyone what really happened to your husband back in Pristina, eh Irena?' sneered Marishta.

'Don't listen to him Steve… shoot him. Shoot the animal now!' screamed Irena.

'Why?' answered Steve, 'he's not going anywhere. Just call the police and get him arrested for breaking and entering and attempted murder… and anyway I'm sure the NCA still have him on their radar for Chicken City. He'll get banged up for years.'

'No, you don't understand – he's evil, just fucking shoot him. Shoot him for what he's done to Eva!'

Steve tightened his grip on the gun and fingered the trigger as Marishta stared at him impassively.

'No Irena… phone the police. *Go on, get the phone!'* shouted Steve impatiently.

Irena remained rooted to the stairs.

'Phone the fucking police will you!'

Steve took his eye off of Marishta and glared at Irena, her face was contorted with fury and rage.

'No!' she screamed as she lunged at Steve from behind in an attempt to grab the gun.

A shot rang out and a bullet smashed into the Perspex screen of the Rock-Ola.

The two of them tumbled down the stairs, landing in a stunned pile in front of Marishta who seized the opportunity and tried in vain to grasp the gun as it spiralled across the polished oak flooring before disappearing underneath the jukebox.

Steve lay dazed on his back. Marishta made a grab for Steve's leg but Steve managed to kick out and land a blow to Marishta's face with his bare foot. The Albanian quickly changed position and lunged once again at Steve.

Marishta seized Steve's legs and pinned him to the floor. Steve grunted in shock as the Albanian then moved up his body and straddled his torso with his powerful thighs. He punched rapidly at Steve's face – one, two, three punches hit home causing Steve's head to rhythmically loll from side to side.

Steve tried desperately to shield the blows raining down on him. He made a grab for Marishta's face with both hands and forced the thumb of his right hand into Marishta's left eye. Marishta screamed in pain and momentarily stopped punching, Steve took advantage of the lull in the attack and landed a blow with his left fist, simultaneously heaving his body off of him. It stunned Marishta but not as much as the follow up blow from Steve's right fist that hammered into his already damaged left eye socket.

The two of them scrambled to their feet then grappled with each other once more before crashing through the doors into the kitchen area. The resistance and counter attack from Steve only served to enrage the Albanian more. He stepped up a gear and first punched Steve then grabbed his throat with both hands. The two of them stumbled backwards and Steve's back crashed against the solid cast-iron AGA.

Steve reacted quickly and twisted the Albanian around and made a grab for his hands, he forced them away from his throat and down onto the open roasting hob. Steve felt the heat on his own hands but it was nothing compared to the excruciating pain and burns inflicted on his adversary.

Marishta screamed in agony and stared at his already blistering hands. Steve took a step back almost in shock at what he'd done and not for the first time the acrid smell of burnt meat filled the kitchen.

The incensed Albanian lunged at Steve once more and the two of them tumbled to the floor and yet again Steve found himself on his back with Marishta sat astride him.

Steve's legs kicked out wildly as Marishta's burnt hands compressed like a vice around his windpipe. Steve choked and his bloodshot eyes bulged out of their sockets. The Albanian's crazed crimson-red face was inches away from Steve's and he could feel himself gagging for air. Marishta's grip was suddenly released as he reeled off of Steve and screamed in pain as a ball-peen hammer wielded by Irena smashed into the left side of his skull.

Steve gasped and gulped as he tried desperately to take in air. His throat felt raw. He gagged, rolled over on to his knees and violently threw up. Beside him lay a twitching and juddering Marishta who groaned in agony.

Irena stood motionless with the hammer hanging limply in her hand, its head dripping with blood. Steve studied it impassively. He looked back at Irena who returned his stare with cold, dead eyes. Marishta let out a low groan and much to Steve's amazement began to raise himself up.

Steve's mouth formed an 'O' but no sound came out as the huge Albanian struggled to his feet beside him. He thrust out his powerful right arm and steadied himself against the kitchen wall. Steve remained speechless as Irena took a step towards Marishta. This time she was armed with an even more ferocious and deadly weapon.

Steve's eyes widened in horror as Irena raised the Makita pneumatic nail gun and placed it against Marishta's forehead.

A three-inch sharpened stainless-steel nail smashed through Marishta's skull and into his frontal lobe with a sickening thud releasing a shower of blood, bone tissue and brain matter that splattered against Irena, Steve and a new oak wall cabinet.

Steve turned towards Irena and grabbed the nail gun but the damage had already been done. Marishta fell backwards to the floor in slow motion and the back of his head smashed onto the oak flooring with a thud that reverberated around the house.

Irena slowly walked towards the prostrate body of the dying Albanian.

He remained motionless as gurgles and blubbing sounds emanated from both his mouth and the holes in his head.

Steve stood frozen to the spot as Irena leant down over Marishta's body. She momentarily studied it before slowly and deliberately plunging a chisel into his exposed heaving throat. Hot blood spurted out like a crimson fountain and a huge red stain formed on her pristine, white bathrobe.

Steve stared blankly at Irena. His stare transformed into a look of fear and horror as she spat at the lifeless body of the Albanian.

Steve was scared. He didn't know whether to thank or curse her. She made up his mind for him as she stepped forward and put her arms around his convulsing body. The two of them embraced in a bloodstained mess.

'What the fuck just happened?' Steve finally asked through bruised and battered lips.

'What do you mean?' queried Irena.

Steve pushed Irena away from him, grabbed her arms and looked into her flat, emotionless eyes.

'Don't fuck with me Irena – I want the truth... all of it. Then after you've told me I'm calling the police.'

Chapter Forty-Six

The two of them sat at opposite ends of the room. Steve on his La-Z-Boy and Irena on the leather sofa. Neither of them had changed and their bloodied bathrobes looked at odds with the rest of the tastefully furnished room.

They both nursed large glasses of Glenmorangie while Derrick lay curled up on the windowsill nursing his wounds.

On the kitchen floor lay the motionless body of the Albanian gangster. There was a hole the size of a golf ball in the side of his skull, a three-inch nail embedded in his forehead and a deep incision in his throat that leeched blood onto the oak flooring.

'My husband – my real husband – Dragan. He and Neil Etchington became friends. I told you yes?'

Steve nodded his head slowly. He was still in a state of shock.

'They became friends due to... uh, mutual interests.'

Steve screwed up his eyes.

'Mutual interests?' he asked hesitantly.

'How do I put it? They both liked the company of… young girls.'

'*Both?* You mentioned Etchington was… abusing Eva, but you didn't mention your husband?'

Steve felt the blood drain from his face.

'Steve – my husband abused Evalina from an early age, unknown to me of course. Oh, I had, um…' she hesitated as she searched for the word in her mind, '…*suspicions* – but to my eternal shame I didn't act on them, until of course it was too late. The two of them, my husband and Etchington had been abusing Eva for a number of years.'

She hesitated once more before continuing.

'I told you I found Etchington coming down the stairs from Eva's bedroom... but he wasn't alone. He was with my husband, they had both been in Eva's bedroom.'

She took a sip of whisky and gathered her thoughts. The horrific memory clearly still etched in her mind.

'I attacked the two of them and my husband hit me... My husband's gun was in the room, it was then that my husband was killed.'

'You, you shot him?' asked Steve incredulously, his mouth agape.

She shook her head as she wiped a tear from her eye.

'No I did not... Evalina did.'

Steve stared at Irena. His mouth opened even wider.

'Fuck... what about Etchington? What happened to him?'

'Eva tried to shoot him as well, but she missed. He managed to escape but he returned later with Marishta and his thugs. But by then Eva was so uh.... traumatised, she just hid in the corner of her room shaking. Etchington arranged for the Albanians to take my husband's body and get rid of it. Like I said previously they burnt and buried it in a forest on the outskirts of Pristina.'

Steve shook his head and took a deep breath.

'I, I can't believe it. Eva told me her father was a good man, she said she loved him...' He felt sick as he recalled that Eva had told him he reminded her of her father.

'What did you do next? Is that when you left and came to England?'

Irena nodded.

'Yes. The two of them sorted out passports and visas and got us out. I transferred some money to the UK and they said they would arrange for us to be met in England when we arrived. They said they would look after us, get us jobs and somewhere to live.'

'And did they?'

'What do you think? Of course they did, but you can guess doing what. First, we moved from shithouse to shithouse in London and then they sent us to work. Me, in their laboratory in Birmingham to develop their fucking microchips and Eva... well, Etchington still had his eye on her. We thought coming here we might see the last of him but she was, how you say, the pay off. He got us out of the country, greased a few... palms yes? And his reward was Eva.'

Steve exhaled loudly once more. 'So how did this so-say marriage to Marishta come about?'

'That was no marriage,' answered Irena angrily, 'it was just to allow him to stay in England. He had been visiting the UK on and off for years courtesy of Etchington and using his import and export business as cover, so not only did he arrange for fake passports for me and Eva, he also arranged a fake marriage certificate which enabled him to stay here and...'

'And what?' asked Steve.

'And what do you think? He used to visit me in Birmingham and fuck me... so do you feel better now, knowing that that fat bastard raped me as well as Eva?'

Irena bowed her head, not wanting to look Steve in the eye.

'Uh, sorry, I, I, uh...' Steve stammered.

He began to understand the hatred that Irena had for Marishta and the reasons why she wanted him dead. Up until then he didn't know if Irena was aware that Marishta as well as Etchington had abused Eva. Steve knew he had – he'd witnessed it in Eva's odious video.

There was still one thing that puzzled Steve.

'So how come he knew you were a bad cook?'

He instantly regretted asking the trivial question. Irena's anger returned once more.

'He used to stay and make me fucking cook for him as well as suck his fucking cock – *you happy now?'* she screamed.

The silence returned.

* * *

'So now you know why we couldn't call the police back in Kosovo. They would've arrested Eva and me.' Irena said once her anger had subsided.

'Arrested? Really? After what the two of you had been through? Surely with Eva being a child the police would have seen it as justifiable homicide?'

'You don't understand Steve. Marishta and Etchington had many, many friends in the uh… *vlasti* … authorities… over there, and all of them Albanians. We would've been arrested and charged if we stayed, they would've locked us up. We had to leave the country and quickly.'

She downed the remainder of her whisky in one. The two of them fell silent once more.

'So what now?' she eventually asked.

'We call the police,' answered Steve bluntly.

'I don't think that would be wise. I think we should phone the cleaner.'

'A cleaner! A cleaner isn't going to be able to help with this fucking mess… and what about Marishta's body, what are we going to do about that?'

Steve stood up, paced around the room and rubbed his bloodied scalp.

'And anyway, we don't know any cleaners.' There was exasperation in Steve's voice.

'I didn't say *a* cleaner, I said *the* cleaner.'

Steve's brow knotted as Irena rose from the sofa, picked up her mobile, flicked through the numbers then made a call. She spoke in hushed tones for less than a minute then turned back to Steve.

'They'll be here in less than an hour so I suggest we get dressed,' she said matter-of-factly.

Chapter Forty-Seven

Steve watched through the kitchen window as a Jaguar XK and a Ford Transit drove along the driveway and pulled up outside the cottage.

Both vehicles were anthracite black, had tinted windows and Steve just knew the occupants would be wearing sunglasses – he was not to be disappointed. He hoped to God that none of the Neighbourhood Watch members were nosily peering through their windows.

There were six of them in total. The two who exited the XK wore black, sombre suits that matched their attitude while the four from the Transit wore hazmat suits that were as white as snow on a midwinter's day. Between them they carried Samsonite cases, a black body bag and a vacuum cleaner that looked as if it had been built by NASA.

Steve kept a low profile as Irena spoke to the taller of the two men in black. He'd taken off his Brunella Cucinelli sunglasses and glanced alternately at Steve and the body of Besin Marishta as Irena gesticulated wildly.

She pointed at the jukebox where underneath it the gun was lodged, the bloodied tools and eventually Derrick who was now displaying his customary indifference by sleeping soundly on top of the AGA.

They took just over three hours and by the time they'd finished, the house was not only spotless but also devoid of the dead Albanian.

Steve had hovered over the technicians as if he was observing his first child being born as they worked to retrieve the bullet from the inside of the jukebox. He breathed a palpable sigh of relief when eventually the silver-coloured slug was removed from the outer casing with the help of a pair of tweezers and deposited into a clear polybag.

They'd repaired the hole in the perspex of the jukebox with resin and replaced the pane of broken glass in the back door, the back door that Marishta had used to gain entry to the cottage.

As the two men in black exited, they paused and turned. The taller of the two stared at Steve intently.

'*Not. A. Fucking. Word.*' He said precisely.

'Now what?' asked Steve, when eventually the door shut behind the visitors.

Irena shrugged.

'Well I don't know about you but I'm starving.'

She headed towards the nearly finished and now pristine kitchen.

'Is that it, is that all you've got to say?'

Irena spun round to face Steve. She had showered and changed into tight blue jeans and a crisp white blouse. She looked as stunning as ever but there was a hard look in her eyes that Steve hadn't seen before.

'What do you expect me to say?' she asked angrily.

'I dunno, but you've just murdered – no fucking butchered – a man. OK a beast of a man who's raped you and Eva, but you've still killed him and you don't seem to be bothered about it at all. It just all seems so fucking normal to you!'

'I don't fucking believe you Steve… I thought you were a real man. From what you've said about your past, you believed in an eye for an eye – what's changed? We ought to be celebrating – that, that fucker had his claws into me and Eva for so long and now he's gone, gone forever. So what the fuck? Do you want me to apologise for smashing his brains in?'

'No, it's just that…'

'Just what? I've killed someone who's raped me and my daughter and you've learnt that Eva killed her father after years of abuse? You must understand Steve we lived in a fucking war zone. Terrible things were done by terrible people. Even after the war it was still a frightening place to live, the hatred between Albanians and Serbians ran deep – it still does. You don't know what we went through, it has scarred us for life… you knew we had fucking luggage Steve, get over it!'

Irena huffed and turned back towards the kitchen. It was as if they were having a petty disagreement over what colour Farrow & Ball paint they should be putting on the walls, rather than discussing the fact a man, even a man as odious as Besin Marishta had just been killed at the very spot Steve now stood on.

He could hear the sound of a frying pan crashing onto the AGA as he headed for the comfort of a hot, steaming bath.

'Baggage,' he muttered under his breath.

* * *

They sat in silence as Steve pushed the dried-up scrambled eggs and the burnt pogacha toast and sujuk sausage around his plate.

'What's up Steve, you not hungry?' asked Irena as she devoured the last remnants of the meal with relish.

'Uh, no not really – lost my appetite to be honest.'

Irena took his plate from the table and let her hand rest on his shoulder just long enough for Steve to realise it was a small act of contrition. He looked up at her and smiled weakly but something had changed between them – they both knew it.

'So how come you know those people – and who the fuck was that ray of sunshine you called the cleaner?' he eventually asked.

'They were people that Solutio used from time to time,' she shrugged. 'You know they work for your British Government, yes?'

He didn't, but he'd guessed as much.

'Marishta knew them. The two in suits used to accompany Echington on his visits. He gave me their number, told me they might come in handy one day.'

She laughed. 'Little did he know eh?'

Steve nodded and a false smile crossed his face.

'Where has Marishta been? Since he escaped from Chicken City? Did they say anything?' asked Steve.

'They said he'd been in a safe house – operated by them of course. Can you believe it? *Your* government have been looking after him! They raid Chicken City then he fucking escapes and some other shits in your government keep him safe! You couldn't make it up... they said he escaped last week.'

Steve was as pissed off as she was but he didn't like Eva's emphasis of the word '*your*'. He nodded.

'Yeah, he told me he'd seen us on Dragons' Den, guess up till then he didn't know we were an item.'

Irena smirked. She liked Steve referring to the two of them as '*an item*'.

'Somehow he managed to track us down – couldn't have been too hard. Can't be many Steve Allens who have invented a tattoo machine with the help of their beautiful Serbian girlfriend.'

Irena's smirk grew to a full beaming smile on hearing the words '*beautiful*' and '*girlfriend*'.

Steve thought it best left unsaid that he knew exactly how Besin Marishta had really tracked them down. He momentarily thought of his ex-boss Tony Preston and wondered if Marishta really had cut his tongue out.

Irena turned and wandered around the kitchen searching for the dishwasher, after opening several drawers and cupboards she eventually found it.

She turned to Steve and smiled.

'You know the cleaner told me we've actually done them a favour?'

Steve screwed up his eyes.

'What do you mean?'

'Getting rid of Marishta. They didn't know what to do with him. He was really under house arrest, but they feared one day he might escape and spill the – what is it... peas... *beans*?'

Steve nodded.

'How come they arrived so quickly?' he asked, puzzled at the prompt arrival of the cleaner and his team. It had only taken them thirty-odd minutes since Irena had phoned them. He'd presumed, correctly, that they were based somewhere in London.

Irena shrugged.

'They said they were already heading this way – said they had some business to attend to nearby.'

Steve's heart skipped a beat.

'Where? Did they say?'

'I don't know – over a bridge somewhere.'

Steve grabbed his mobile and quickly pressed redial.

'Come on, come on...' he said to himself as he waited for Simon Edwards to answer.

'What?' answered an irate Edwards.

'Get out now... get out of your place and just go!' Steve shouted down the phone.

'I can't,' replied Edwards. 'I'm waiting for a reporter to arrive from the BBC. I thought bollocks squire, if you're not going to help me, I'll do it myself... I Googled Alpaca farmers in the Cotswolds, you wouldn't believe how fucking many there are but after a few calls I found your mate Barry Mason. Anyway, I gave him a call and he gave me a contact in the Corporation. I told them everything, so they're on their way. Should be here within the hour and pretty soon the whole country will know what's going on – no thanks to you.'

'Barry Mason gave you a contact at the BBC – are you sure?'

'Definitely. They were really interested in what I had to say, especially the bit about the death of Fraser Winston. Not like you... like I said they'll be here soon.'

Steve shook his head. He knew all too well his old mate Barry Mason wouldn't act in such a way, not without contacting him first.

'Simon, listen and listen carefully. Your phone's bugged. Mine too probably. I expect they're listening to this call for fuck's sake! They would have diverted your call and you've spoken to someone else. There's no way that would've been Barry Mason... Look, I'm going to phone him up now and get him to confirm what I'm saying, but I'm ninety-nine per cent certain that you didn't speak to him so get out now! ... *Are you listening you arseholes?* We're on to you, so go fuck yourselves!'

Steve sighed in relief as he recalled the conversation he'd had with Edwards earlier, when he'd told him that he didn't believe a word he was saying and that he wasn't going to help. It had probably saved his, and Irena's, life.

Steve hung up and quickly searched for his ex-Fleet Street journalist friend in his contacts.

He stopped abruptly and thought about going to the phone box at the end of the lane but then thought of it as futile – if his and Edwards' phones were bugged, and he was certain they were, it would have been pointless.

'Alright you old wurzel, haven't spoken to you in ages...' answered Barry Mason.

He was curious to know what his old sparring partner wanted.

They hadn't spoken much in the last few years, not since the two of them had colluded to bring down the

Premier League. The thought of it still caused Barry to smirk and glow with pride.

'How's that tattoo machine business going, saw you on the tell…'

Steve interrupted – he had no time for niceties.

'Sorry mate, some other time. Look, have you spoken to that ex-copper Simon Edwards in the last hour or so?'

'You what? What's going on Steve?'

'Barry just answer me, yes or no?'

'Are you on about that sheep shagger who tried to bang you up a few years back – what about him?'

'Just fucking answer me will you? Have you spoken to him recently?' replied Steve angrily.

'No, I've never spoken to him… what's this all about?'

'I can't say just now, I'll phone you again sometime.' He hung up leaving Barry Mason staring at his phone in bewilderment. Steve called Edwards once more.

'Get out of your house now!' he yelled as soon as Edwards answered.

'But I…'

'Simon for fuck's sake! I've just spoken to Barry Mason and he confirmed he hasn't spoken to you. Now do as you're told and get the fuck out!'

The phone went dead. Steve hoped it was because Edwards had hung up and taken his advice and not for any other reason. He turned to Irena who had been listening and watching intently.

'What is it Steve? What is happening?'

'Looks like your cleaner mates have been monitoring Edwards.'

'Who?' she queried.

Steve had never spoken about the ex-cop to Irena – he had no reason to. He certainly wasn't going to go into any details about their relationship and how he too had once been a lover of Kirsty's.

'Simon Edwards – he's uh, an old mate. He phoned me earlier when you were asleep. He's a bit strange – into conspiracy theories, politics of fear and all that…' He trailed off – wary of telling Irena too much, a ghost of a doubt about her once again entered his mind.

'So? Why would they be bugging him? If they monitored everyone who was a "bit strange" in this country they would be watching the whole population!' she said with a giggle. Steve conceded she had a point but he wasn't going to discuss it any further with her.

Just how much she knew about shadowy government departments and their involvement in Chicken City, microchips and the untimely death of Fraser Winston was open to debate and not something he wished to delve into right now.

She'd told him about how she was part of the team who had developed the microchip and how she'd been forced to involve Eva in its trials but it had all been under duress – or had it? Steve returned a weak smile.

'You're right,' he answered bluntly.

* * *

'So what do you want to do for the rest of the day?' she asked, eager to take Steve's mind off of the earlier gruesome events.

Steve shrugged.

'I dunno, go out for a walk? I hear the White Lion's had a refit.' He said it without conviction and Irena saw right through it.

'Oh that's a shame, I thought you might want to go back to bed,' she said with a devilish grin.

'Sorry, not in the mood,' he answered, causing Irena to pout dejectedly in exactly the same manner as her daughter. Steve grimmaced.

Normally he would've jumped at the chance. There weren't many better things in life than spending a long

Sunday afternoon in bed with a beautiful woman but somehow Steve didn't think it appropriate.

Someone – albeit a people-trafficker and a rapist – had been murdered in his house a couple of hours earlier and a friend, of sorts, was being hunted down by God knows who. The events troubled him, he didn't need to elaborate – Irena got the message.

He wasn't sure what was bothering him the most, or even why it was bothering him at all.

He knew both Irena and Eva had troubled pasts so why should he be so shocked by the revelations from earlier on in the day and why was the death of Marishta causing him so much unease? *The bastard had been trying to kill me for Christ's sakes.*

Maybe the tragic death of Kirsty and that of Cherry, the girl who he'd thought was his own, still troubled him. Why was it that every female that had come into his life caused him so much grief, so much pain – even his wife of nearly thirty years had found succour in the arms of someone else, and to rub salt in the wounds, a woman.

How fucking useless am I?

'To be honest Irena, I wouldn't mind a bit of time on my own. I'm just going to have a couple of beers up the Lion if that's OK?'

He didn't wait for her to answer.

He rummaged through his wardrobe and found his Harrington. Even after all these years the jacket still retained the faint smell of Kirsty's perfume – it wafted through his nostrils once more.

Irena unbuttoned the top of her blouse and seductively run her fingers through her hair as he came down the stairs, but he was oblivious to her flirting.

'You look nice in that jacket…' she said as he pushed past, 'you ought to wear it more often.'

But he wouldn't. He'd always thought of it as Kirsty's jacket and it was going to stay that way.

He ignored her flirting and slammed the door behind him before heading for the solace of a beer glass.

* * *

After three pints of Timothy Taylor Landlord and two Appleton rums, on top of the earlier whisky, he was nearing his tipping point. He could drink more, a lot more as a youngster but those days had long gone.

'Go on love, just another rum please,' pleaded Steve in vain.

'I think you've had one too many already – especially for a Sunday afternoon,' answered the young barmaid who, even at a tender age, could judge when a customer had had enough and Steve had had more than enough.

'And anyway, your face is ruining the punters' appetites,' she continued.

He looked around the pub. Customers averted their gaze, not wanting to be put off their Sunday roasts by the state of Steve's battered face.

He wasn't going to argue. Truth be told he didn't want another drink, he wanted something different. In the parlance of old, he needed a livener.

He trawled through the numbers on his mobile and found who he was looking for, an old business associate of the late Gary 'Bulldog' Rattigan, who run an efficient, if slightly more expensive, delivery service.

He paced up and down in the pub car park in anticipation of the delivery. A youth, clad all in black, approached on an e-Bike, his face hidden behind a tight-fitting balaclava.

Steve adeptly passed the youth the folded-up notes and the exchange was done – it had taken less than twenty minutes since he first made the call. *I've waited longer for a pizza delivery on a Saturday night,* he thought.

Another three minutes later and Steve was in the toilet of the White Lion reintroducing himself to his old friend Charlie.

His eyes widened and he licked his lips in anticipation.

It had been several years but he hadn't forgotten the ritual – he tapped the polybag then emptied just the right amount on to the cistern, first checking that Vaseline or WD40 had not been smeared across it by the diligent publican.

He removed his credit card from his wallet then used it to press down on the cocaine several times to flatten it out. He chopped and divided the powder up into two fat lines – *cut your lines nice and fine*, he recited. He took a crisp new £20 note out of his wallet, deftly rolled it up into a tight tube and inserted it into his right nostril... the expectation sent his pulse rocketing.

He stopped abruptly.

The mirror above the cistern beckoned him. His beaten and bloodied face stared back at him accusingly. His bloodshot eyes first appeared blank but then began to bore into him. They delved deep down into his soul, into his very being, his eyes questioned him. He'd always had a dark side, a dark side that at times he rather liked. Visions entered his head, some good but mostly bad.

He pictured Eva naked on a bed in Chicken City. The pistol in her hand pointed directly at his head.

The nightmare image of Irena swinging the hammer and smashing it into Marishta's skull entered his mind.

He then saw the nailgun.

He heard the terrifying sound once more and saw the bone tissue slowly spinning through the air, the brain matter splatting against the wall.

Then the blood. *Drip, drip, dripping.*

He looked back down at the cocaine, the cocaine that could have been processed and packed in Chicken City by young girls just like Eva.

He wondered whose lives those two inches of white powder had touched and affected on their journey into a toilet in a public house on the outskirts of Bristol.

He wondered about the pain, misery and perhaps even death those two little lines had caused on their journey. The pain and misery that he had actually contributed to. He wondered about the blood he, and millions of other middle-class drug users, like him, had on their hands. *Working class,* he corrected himself.

He shook his head, licked his lips once more and lowered his head. He slowly but forcefully pushed his lips together… and blew.

The powder dissipated and disappeared in a white cloud and he emptied the rest of the bag down the pan. He smiled and flushed it away triumphantly.

* * *

'Irena, Irena – sorry, I don't know what came over… Irena?'

Steve looked around the uncharacteristically quiet, empty room. If the TV wasn't on showing some programme featuring Jamie Oliver or James Martin then the jukebox was usually blaring out a dance floor filler as Irena practised her moves whilst humming along to some Detroit masterpiece. But not this time.

He didn't need to read all of the note, the first sentence was enough…

'Darling Steve, I don't know what I've done wrong but I think it's best that I leave…' He skipped to the end.

'P.S. Please play J7 for me - Irena xxx'

He did as she requested.

The sound of Jimmy Ruffin singing *'What becomes of the broken hearted'* filled the room.

He slumped against the wall then slowly slid down it. Derrick looked at him with one disinterested eye and yawned.

Chapter Forty-Eight

Six weeks later

Steve wasn't entirely surprised by the events unfolding on his TV screen. But no-one, especially not those in their Westminster ivory towers and those in Thames House, could have predicted the sheer magnitude of the uprising against the plans to implant the entire population with microchipped ID cards.

The biased right-wing press had tried their hardest but no matter what spin they put on the story, the people of Britain weren't to be fooled. They knew what was happening – this was Big Brother on steroids and they weren't falling for it.

There at the front of the phalanx of demonstrators was the reinvented, and recovered, Simon Edwards. His hair was long, in a ponytail and flecked with grey, as was the untrimmed and untidy beard that sprouted out of his square jaw. His broad frame made the bright yellow T-shirt emblazoned with the red *All Seeing Eye* logo stretch uncomfortably across his rotund stomach, making it look as if it had been ironed over a wok.

The Eye of Providence logo had been an inspired choice for the ASL – the Anti Surveillance League – the group that had been formed rapidly in the wake of the Government's plans to introduce microchipped ID cards.

It featured the same flame-red six-feathered arrow that the Anti Nazi League had used in the hate-filled Seventies, but this time, the arrow was piercing the eye that sat atop of a light-emitting pyramid.

The Government had tried to promote the idea of a compulsory chip insertion scheme under new wide-ranging anti-terrorism legislation. It quickly became known as ISDS – Identity System for Detection of Subversives, describing it as a future-proof, multi-faceted platform that would enhance homeland security.

Its detractors – of which there were many, called it an abhorrent attack on civil liberties with echoes of Nazi concentration camps.

The link to Solutio and the migrant cities had also been quickly seized upon as billboards around the country, which previously had promoted the merits of the organisation, had been defaced and daubed with swastikas and the words changed from *'SOLUTIO'* to *'FINAL SOLUTION'* once more – it turned out the illiterate and budding graffiti artist in Barton Hill was right after all.

Steve knew exactly who was behind the expose of the once all-powerful conglomerate – he was now watching the perpetrator on his TV screen and he could clearly see him mouthing *'One, two, three, four, five, we don't want your fucking spies!'*

Steve knew Simon Edwards would be at the heart of the demonstration, he had received a handwritten letter in the post from him the week before telling him so.

Edwards had thanked Steve for warning him and on his advice, he'd fled the house. He persuaded the neighbour opposite – a sympathetic young lady friend as it happened – to let him stay for the rest of the day. He'd watched through the net curtains as a black Jaguar pulled up and two men dressed in black entered his house.

'I got a fucking photo of real-life Men in Black!' he wrote, causing Steve to laugh out loud as he read it.

Simon had observed them exit after about an hour with a box full of papers and discs, but it couldn't have been anything of any significance as he had everything he needed on his laptop which he'd taken with him.

He'd returned to his house to pick up some personal possessions and was pleased to find out that they'd actually tidied the place up. Edwards had even inserted a smiley face ☺ on the letter which made Steve chuckle to himself once more. The brusque, no-nonsense ex-cop was now living the life of Riley in a shepherd's hut on a hippy community somewhere on the Brecon Beacons. Steve shook his head in bewilderment.

The good news was that Edwards had given up drink and found a soul mate in the sympathetic neighbour who went by the name of Earthchild; it had been she who had introduced him to the eco-warriors of the commune.

The bad news was that she had also introduced him to the joy of magic mushrooms – this time it was followed by two smiling faces ☺ ☺.

The battle against the system, the system that Edwards was once proud to be part of, was continuing, he'd said. He was raging against the machine and fighting the dystopian nightmare of the implanted microchips...

'I'll show those fuckers in Westminster what a Brave New World is! Anyway, best go squire,' he continued, *'I've got a goat to milk, a demonstration to organise and there's a shit load of tantric sex to be had!'*

Steve raised his eyebrows and a wry smile crossed his face as he remembered the tough-talking, belligerent cop that had not only arrested him but who he'd brawled with several years earlier.

He begrudgingly admired the Welshman and he was thankful that it looked like he'd finally got his drinking under control, even if it had been replaced with a hallucinogenic drug habit.

At one time Steve had feared for Edwards' sanity and even his life, but it looked as though his anger and concern for the state of the country had been channelled in the right direction and he was at last finding his feet... and his voice.

He was not only engaging with the British people he was actually leading them. Unlike the Government.

Downing Street had badly misjudged the situation and although many of the indigenous population were still concerned with the flood of MIRAS into the country, the call for the introduction of ISDS had fallen on deaf ears.

Deep down in the soul of the British people there was a strong beating heart, there were enough good people like Simon Edwards in the country to make a difference – maybe it was the guilt over the death of Fraser Winston that haunted him and drove him on but whatever it was, Edwards had been vindicated. Steve couldn't have been more happier for him.

Marches and demonstrations, the like that hadn't been seen since the poll tax riots of 1990, had gathered pace like a runaway train in the last few weeks. The Government was not only looking at defeat in the Commons on the Bill but also at defeat in the next general election that had been called following a motion of no-confidence in the beleaguered Cabinet.

Just when Downing Street thought it couldn't get any worse, the United Nations added fuel to the fire and announced that they would be visiting the UK on a fact-finding mission to investigate the Government's link to the now defunct Solutio and the migrant cities. The Government, like a punch-drunk boxer, was up against the ropes and on its last legs.

'We interrupt the footage of this demonstration for some breaking news,' said a disembodied female voice.

'Reports are coming in of the arrest of ex MP and leader of the England Unite Party, Neil Etchington...'

The TV screen cut from the march to a care home in East Sussex.

The unedifying sight of the ex-golden boy of the right being pushed in a wheelchair, paralysed and dribbling, into a waiting police van filled the screen as the newsreader continued.

'Officers who have been involved in the long-running investigation known as Operation Waffle say further arrests are to follow.'

The face of the newly promoted, G3 Daniel Britton came into view. He was tight-lipped, stern-faced and Steve instantly recognised Fraser Winston's ex-second in command.

As the TV camera focused on the detective he mouthed *'we're coming for you'* grimly into the lens, sending an Arctic blast down the spine of a multitude of watching miscreant politicians, clergymen, high court judges and two men in Whitehall who possessed identical haircuts and regimental ties.

'This is for you Fraser,' said Steve with a self-satisfied smirk as he raised his eyes upwards.

'Sorry?' came a young voice from behind him.

Eva stood in the doorway holding two mugs of tea.

'Did you say something?'

'It looks like retribution day has finally come,' said Steve with an air of satisfaction as he nodded towards the TV.

Eva handed Steve a steaming mug then sat down on the sofa opposite him. She crossed her long legs then stared in silence at the screen as Sky news re-ran the footage of Etchington being wheeled into the police van.

Steve took in Eva's features once more.

She had a glow about her that he hadn't seen in the past, and it wasn't just down to the photo shoots in warmer climes. She had grown, and not just physically – she was now a woman, a stunning, beautiful, confident woman who had the world at her feet – and he was partly responsible for the transformation, for that he felt justifiably proud.

'Do you want me to turn this off?' asked Steve, concerned that the events and the sight of Etchington, albeit paralysed and in a wheelchair, could be too much for Eva to bear.

She didn't reply. She just shook her head slowly from side to side.

'*Jebeni perverznjak,*' she muttered.

Steve could only guess as to what it meant. He noticed her eyes begin to fill with tears.

'It's OK Eva, it's all over now. He's going to go to jail for a long time – and so will the others, many others.'

Steve got up and sat beside Eva. He clumsily put his arm around her and not for the first time she wept as she nuzzled into his shoulder.

'Why Steve?'

Steve couldn't answer. He had no idea why men behaved in the way that they did. He felt ashamed, even responsible once more for the evil that men did.

'I don't know Eva, I can't answer that.'

She wiped her eyes and looked up at Steve.

'Why can't all men be like you Steve? Tell me?'

'Like me? Uh, Eva I'm not perfect… not by a long way. Believe me, I've got quite a few skeletons in my closet.'

'Really? Care to tell me about them?' asked a voice from behind the two of them.

Irena entered the room holding a tray. Steve shook his head and smiled as her presence instantly filled him with joy.

Irena had returned the previous month with her daughter – much to Steve's relief – after a stay, first in a cheap hotel in Bayswater and then with Eva at her apartment in Chelsea Harbour, once she had returned from her prolonged photo shoot in Brazil.

Eva was shocked when her mother arrived on her doorstep with her belongings and distraught to hear that she and Steve had split up, even more so when she heard her mother crying herself to sleep every night.

Irena had not explained the reasons behind their split, leaving Eva oblivious to the fact that her long-time tormentor Marishta had been killed and that it was her own mother who had been responsible for his grizzly death.

The intense therapy that Eva had received the previous year had worked wonders, she was now rationale, empathetic and totally forgiving – especially when it came to her mother and her relationship with Steve.

The phone call from Eva to her proxy father had worked and Steve took little convincing to hot foot it east along the M4 to reunite himself with the two of them and bring them both back west to the place they now called home.

'I have made you some Balkan kifle,' beamed Irena as she presented Steve with a plateful of unappetizing and overcooked crescent-shaped cakes.

Eva studied the cakes then gave Steve a knowing smile. He returned it with a wink.

'Lovely… I'll have one later,' winced Steve as he thought of the inevitable heartburn that would be sure to follow.

'So,' said Irena, 'what were you saying – about what's happening, yes? It's good, no?'

'No… I mean yes,' replied Steve, 'it's very good.'

Irena and Eva exchanged glances and smiled. Irena stroked her daughter's face, before doing the same to Steve. Steve squirmed then spotted something else on the tray, a battered manila envelope with his name and address on it.

'What have you got there?' he asked.

'Oh this?' she glanced at the puncture-riddled envelope.

'It came in the post this morning. Sorry, but Otis got to it first.'

Steve stared at the Jack Russell admonishingly.

The puppy responded by wagging his tail furiously and yapping loudly, which in turn caused Derrick to grumpily stir from his slumber. Steve furrowed his brow, took the envelope and gingerly opened it.

'What is it?' asked Irena as Steve studied the contents of the envelope. Eva remained silent, knowing exactly what it was.

'It's uh, it's a folder of mine – the police had it, but for whatever reason they've returned it,' answered Steve.

His eyes then fell upon a white comp slip with a memory stick taped to it. Printed on the slip was the stark, black logo of the National Crime Agency.

There was a handwritten message in blue ink on the slip. Steve studied it then read it out loud:

'These belong to you I believe. I thought you might want them back. Thanks for your help but we've got enough evidence as it is and as for Besin Marishta's death, you know what they say, things like this are NITPI – cheers, Dan Britton.'

Steve passed the comp slip and the stick to Eva. She took it, read the message and smiled weakly.

Flicking through the folder, Steve momentarily stopped at random pages like he had done many times in the past. He read an arbitrary line or two... *murder... kidnapping... people-trafficking... drug distribution... child exploitation.*

Once again, he found himself examining and reading about the evil that men do. Men like Vernon Lewis, Earl Samson, Ronald McGuire, Paul Godden and Besin Marishta – the list was endless.

He looked at the names and the faces, some he had encountered, others he had not and prayed to God that he never would. He looked up at Irena and Eva, they were both watching him intently – and lovingly. They waited for his response.

Steve returned their gaze and gently touched Irena's cheek before opening the door of the log burner that blazed heartily in front of them. He threw the folder in and for a moment it sat defiantly on top of the blazing logs causing Steve to wonder if it was ever going to ignite.

He hesitated and thought about retrieving it from its fiery abode for him to once again ponder its evil contents, but it suddenly burst into flames and the charred pages accelerated and sped up the chimney with a ferocious roar.

'Did you not want to keep it?' said Eva with wide-open querying eyes.

'Keep it? What for?'

'Oh I dunno, as a reminder of someone from your past?' replied Eva mischievously. Her mother stared at her with raised eyebrows, having no idea what mind games her daughter was playing with Steve.

Steve shook his head in mild annoyance then nodded at Eva. She responded by screwing up the slip and tossing both it and the memory stick into the burner.

The two of them stared intently at the roaring fire as the flames consumed both the folder and the stick with vengeance.

Irena eventually broke the silence.

'What does NITPI mean Steve?'

Steve took his eye off of the fire and looked first at Irena then Eva, he once again admired the sheer beauty of both mother and daughter.

'Not in the public interest,' he replied flatly as he bit into his kifle with a grimace. He looked back at the TV. On the screen was an all too familiar image of desperate people in desperate situations…

'And in other news, yesterday saw the highest number of people ever crossing the English Channel in small boats.'

Chapter Forty-Nine

It had been playing on his mind ever since Besin Marishta had mentioned it on that fateful day in the cottage. He finally plucked up courage and made the call.

'Tony, is that you?' he asked as his call was eventually answered.

There was no response, only total silence.

'Tony… *Tony?*'

'Mwat yo 'kin mwant Allen?' came the garbled reply.

He did it, he really fucking did it – Marishta cut out Preston's tongue!

'For fuck's sake! I can't believe that bastard did it!'

More silence, then…

'What the fuck you on about?'

Steve raised a quizzical eyebrow.

'You can talk?'

'You what? Course I can fucking talk.'

'But that Marishta told me he tracked you down and cut your tongue out.'

'Oh that wanker… yeah he still had my number, he phoned me up asking me where you lived. I told him to fuck off but he said he saw you on the telly and that he wanted to give you something. I uh… might have mentioned that you lived somewhere in Frenchay. But no, did fuck all about cutting my tongue out.' He snorted out a laugh before continuing.

'Uh sorry, did I drop you in it?'

It was the first time Steve had ever heard Preston say sorry. *Very fucking nearly,* he thought.

'But… when you answered. I couldn't understand you, thought he must have done it.'

'What the fuck are you on about you Gashead twat? I was eating a red hot Madras, now what the fuck do you want?'

'Nothing you Shithead wanker, absolutely nothing,' Steve answered with a playful insult.

'Uh, that's a shame. I thought you might be after a job for old times' sake?'

'Old times sake? Are you fucking kidding?' asked Steve incredulously.

'No… It's just that I got a motor I need picking up from a dealership in Brum. It's a stunning foreign beauty. You interested?'

Thoughts of the last few years tumbled through Steve's mind. He recalled the last time he picked up a stunning foreign beauty in Birmingham.

'Think I'll give it a miss,' he answered with a rueful smile.

Discography

Something in the air – Thunderclap Newman. Label: Track. Number one for three weeks in 1969, from the album *Hollywood Dream*.

Israelites – Desmond Dekker and the Aces. Label: Pyramid Records. Number one for one week in 1969, from the album *The Israelites*.

Pressure Drop – Toots and the Maytals. Label: Beverley's/Trojan. Released in 1970, from the albums *Monkey Man* on Trojan and *Harder they come* on Island.

The Champion – Willie Mitchell. Label: London. Released in 1967.

Guilty – Tiger (Laurel Aitken). Label: Camel/Pama. Released in 1971.

Open the door to your heart – Darrell Banks. Label: London/Stateside. Released 1966, from the album *Darrell Banks is here!*

Dance crasher – Alton Ellis. Label: Treasure Isle. Released in 1967.

Seven letters – Derrick Morgan. Label: Crab/Pama. Released in 1969, from the album *Seven letters* on Trojan.

Johnny Pram Pram – Derrick Morgan. Label: Doctor Bird. Released 1968, from the album *Best of Derrick Morgan*.

Can't get used to losing you – Andy Williams. Label: Columbia. Number two for one week in 1963, from the album *Days of wine and roses*.

Goodnight Irene – The Weavers. Label: Melodisc. Released 1950. Number 1 in US Billboard charts for 13 weeks.

Ghost Town – The Specials. Label: 2-Tone. Released 1981. Number one for three weeks. Also released on *Ghost Town* limited edition LP 2022.

My Girl – Otis Redding. Label: Atlantic. Released 1965. Reached number 11, from the album *Otis Blue*. The original Temptations version on Motown only reached number 43 in 1965 but reached number 2 in 1992 following its re-release.

Wherever I lay my hat – Marvin Gaye. Label: Motown. Released 1969. 'B' side to *Too busy thinking about my baby* which reached number 5 in the UK charts.

First I look at the purse – The Contours. Label: Gordy / Motown. Released 1965.

Move on up – Curtis Mayfield. Label: Buddah. Spent ten weeks in the UK charts in 1970 peaking at number 12. From the album *Curtis* on the Curtom label.

Fix you – Coldplay. Label: Capitol. Released 2005, reached number 4 in the UK charts. From the album *X&Y*.

Change (Makes you wanna hustle) – Donald Byrd. Label: Blue Note. Released 1975 as a single from the album *Places and Spaces*.

Wipe your feet and dance – Wee Willie and the Winners. Label: Mercury. Released 1975. Massive in the clubs but not a dent on the UK charts.

What becomes of the broken hearted? – Jimmy Ruffin. Label: Motown / Soul. Released 1966, reached number 8 in the UK charts, rereleased 1974 reaching number 4.

Acknowledgements

I first pen to paper or rather fingers to keyboard to write *Chicken City* shortly before the EU referendum in 2016. I was convinced the people of Britain were *not* going to vote for Brexit and therefore the first iteration of the book reflected that. So, when the result came in that in fact the electorate of the UK had voted to leave, I was both surprised and mildly annoyed as I had to revisit and rewrite large swathes of it.

But was I disappointed we left the EU? Well, this is a novel and not a dry, political scholarly tome so let's leave it at that.

The idea of the migrant cities came about through watching one of Simon Reeve's excellent documentaries – 'The Mediterranean', where the intrepid journalist visits the polytunnels of Almeria... in true Simon Reeve's style all I can say is *'bloody hell'*.

Not only are these monstrous places a huge blot on the landscape, they also pollute the land and the Med and perhaps worst of all, employ masses of slave labour, mostly from Africa, who are housed in the most appalling conditions and all with the tacit approval of the European Union – disgraceful.

Of course, we all appreciate cheap food but next time you buy tomatoes and strawberries in the depths of winter just stop a moment to think where they've come from and who's been used and abused to grow and pick them. Just search on iPlayer for Simon Reeve's Mediterranean, Series 1, episode 4 – it really is an eye-opener and not in a good way.

As mentioned in the prelims all the characters in *Chicken City* are fictitious and any resemblance to actual persons, living or dead is purely coincidental...

well that's not strictly true. Jay Freestyle is a real life, self-taught freestyle tattoo artist who resides in Amsterdam. Check out his work, it's amazing and I thank him for granting me permission to reference him and his stunning skills.

There's also Danny Dyer and Amanda Holden, she's real – well, most of her I think and of course there's Bristol's finest funk and soul band, The Soul Strutters – James, Jack, Barney and Eric are the real deal and well worth checking out.

I would also like to give thanks to my wife, Carole for putting up with the endless tap, tap, tapping and writing and rewriting that she has endured over the years – it will be worth it, this time next year we'll be millionaires.

Other thanks and acknowledgements go to Peter Stillman for proofreading the first version of *Chicken City* – nine years on if there are any errors or typos in this final proof, then it's down to me and not Peter. I must also thank my two long-time friends David Ward and John Taylor for their help in the writing and production of *Chicken City*, I have known the two of them for a combined total of over one hundred years, now that is scary.

Two other mates of mine who I need to mention are both in the throes of writing books: stick with it Maf Derrick and Miles Davis – if it was easy, everyone would write a book. There are many who say they can, but there aren't so many who actually do. Believe me, it will be worth it, not financially, but it will be worth it.

I must also acknowledge my fellow Bristol Rovers fans, you have my deepest sympathy. In the words of Delroy Wilson, '*Better must come*'... and finally a word to my old boss from my trade plating days – Rich Gurney who gave me a job when no-one else would. Thanks Rich.

Finally spare a thought for all the world-weary tradeplaters out there. If you see any sad old boys by the side of a road with a pair of red and white trade plates under their arm and their thumbs pointing skyward, please stop and give them a lift.

About the author

Chris Brown was born in Bristol in 1955 and has lived in the city that he loves/hates in equal measures, his whole life. He has been married to his wife Carole for over 40 years and they have two children, Daniel and Chloe and two grandchildren Max and Lily.

He is as passionate about ska, reggae, soul, funk and punk as he is about his football club, Bristol Rovers.

* * *

Chicken City is Chris's second novel and is a follow-up to *Guilty Tiger* (see back cover). It's available on Amazon and also direct from the publishers, FeedaRead.com

He has had two books published previously, his highly acclaimed autobiography *Bovver* and its subsequent rerelease *Booted and Suited* which included new copy and photographs from his life growing up in Bristol in the 1970s. It is available on Amazon, all good book shops as well as some dodgy ones and direct from the publisher, John Blake.

Booted and Suited gained the following reviews:

'Social history with steel toe caps' – John King, *Football factory*.

'A jaw-dropping account of the 70s' – *Bristol Evening Post*.

'An absolute must for anyone remotely interested in football, fashion or music. Brilliant!' – *Sunday People*.

Printed in Great Britain
by Amazon

47426540R10215

THE ASCENT

A JOURNEY ABOVE CANCER

BY ALEXANDRIA QUINN

"This book is dedicated to those who need to read it; to those who are facing their own internal mountains; to those who find themselves in need of a helpful guide."

Alexandria Quinn

Prologue

It takes a particular disposition to climb a mountain; such challenges require more than just physical strength and endurance. They require a strong mind and endless determination that only a select few possess. Mountains are not made for the faint-hearted. They were formed only for the brave; for those willing to scale their enormous heights, readily placing their lives in the mountain's grasp and not knowing if they'll return, dead or alive.

My fascination with mountains began long before cancer. It began when my husband and I spontaneously booked a trip to Everest base camp. Everest had been a lifelong dream of his despite having no previous mountaineering experience. I, however, took a little more convincing before I would agree to such an enormous challenge – let's face it, it isn't your average holiday goals! But the trip was eventually sold to me. When I heard of the spiritual enlightenment that awaits in the presence of the highest point on earth, such an experience enticed me. I had spent a lifetime waiting for my big awakening. Maybe on Everest I would find the answers I was seeking.

In the end I became more obsessed with Everest than my husband. I threw myself into base camp training, whether it was timed hikes up my nearest mountains or gruelling workouts in the gym. I dedicated my time to becoming the best and fittest version of myself. Determined to complete the trip without issue, Everest soon became the centre of my life's focus. It bewitched my soul, and I put everything I had into reaching its alluring heights.

I was in the best shape of my life: strong, fit, and healthy – except that I wasn't. Just months before we were due to embark on the biggest venture of our lives I heard those dreaded words: *'I'm sorry, it's cancer.'* Surely it was a mistake?

I couldn't have cancer – I was about to climb Everest! Well, to base camp, at least. My denial was understandable. I had forced my body beyond its limits and it had prevailed. Now, all of a sudden, it failed me. I felt cheated, let down and betrayed, with no choice but to stand before a new mountain – one I had never expected to climb. A mountain more deadly than Everest herself.

I stood paralysed at its cancerous base gazing up at its monstrous heights wondering if I was brave enough to make my ascent and strong enough to make it down alive.

Part 1

Fortune really does favour the brave.
Be brave.
Take risks.
Live your life.
Smile.
And don't forget to look UP.

Ben Fogle, UP

Chapter 1

-First Steps-

I've been climbing mountains my whole life, long before I ever laid eyes on them.

My journey to the top begins and ends in Belfast. It was summer 1991, and it was raining (it always rains here). But raining or not, nothing could dampen this day. This day was special. It was the day my parents were expecting their first child together – me.

My mum had been rushed into the old maternity ward at the City Hospital with my dad accompanying her in the ambulance. Mum, aged twenty-three, was in her prime, and excited to be adding a baby girl to her small family unit. Dad, much older at forty-six, delighted in being a first-time parent; still unable to comprehend that he was finally going to be a father. My older brother, Matthew, was waiting at home with our granny and had already decided he didn't want a baby sister. But that didn't last too long.

Although we were a small family, we were a close one. Better still, we were unique. My brother and I were blessed to have parents from opposite ends of the world, which was reflected in our very different upbringing, cultural and otherwise. Dad was born and raised in Egypt and Mum grew up in Northern Ireland. Worlds apart, yet each with their own difficulties.

My dad's life began in the Mediterranean port city of Alexandria (الإسكندرية), the city from which I inherited my name and had a chance to visit in my early twenties. Alexandria is a quiet coastal refuge and popular holiday spot for many Egyptian families, but unfortunately when Dad was young house prices were high in this upmarket area and when his parents fell into financial difficulty they were forced to sell their beautiful villa by the sea and move to Egypt's busy and chaotic capital, Cairo.

Cairo is a fascinating city. No matter how many times I visit, it still continues to blow my mind. It's the largest city in the Arab world with a population of over twenty million, and is a city where the rich are rich and the poor are poor. There is no in between; it's a city split in two. Not because of religion or political beliefs, but divided by poverty. The poorer areas remain hugely overpopulated with families living on top of each other in a labyrinth of dingy alleyways and mountainous waste piles, while the richer half of society live in newly built luxury accommodation in safe, gated communities.

Regrettably my dad and his family lived among the poor in a two-bedroom apartment in the heart of the city centre. My grandparents, my three aunties and my dad (the only boy) were crammed together under one tiny roof. Yet, despite their cramped living conditions, they were happy. The family's financial strain, however, was eventually passed onto the children, forcing my dad's older sister, Samia, to give up her dream of attending university and becoming a journalist, and instead head straight to work when she finished school at 16. Unlike the UK, education is a privilege in Egypt; its doors only open for the wealthy.

Conscription in Egypt is another reason why many young Egyptians are deprived of further education. Men aged eighteen to thirty must enlist in military service and they can choose to do it before or after third-level education – if they want to continue their education, of course. If they choose to attend university first, they must complete their service after achieving their degree, which isn't overly enticing, not by that stage anyway. Exemptions from the military are only granted on medical grounds, and, luckily for my dad, he was exempt because of his flat feet (a feature I inherited), which deemed him a useless runner. But Dad wasn't disappointed.

He knew that education, not the army, was his pathway out of poverty, so, against his father's wishes, he enrolled in law school. Determined to secure a career that allowed him to leave Egypt and its poverty-stricken land behind for good.

I know very little about my dad's early years because sadly his childhood was something he never got the chance to share with me. My version of his history was actually gathered from my older cousin, Amir. He and my dad were exceptionally close, so I naturally turned to him to fill in the blanks for me. A lot of what Amir shared came as a huge surprise, especially when I learnt that my dad left law school, quitting after his first year. I had always believed my father was a decisive man, that he had his entire life figured out from the get-go – unlike myself who had no clue what to do when I left school. Turns out we're more alike than I thought.

After quitting law school my father found employment as a waiter in the Cairo Tower, a revolving restaurant offering panoramic views of the wonderous city. Dad enjoyed the work and quickly recognised the opportunities for progression, so he enrolled in catering college. A smart move. Over the next four years he excelled in his studies and earned himself an international work permit to London, succeeding in finding his one-way ticket out of Egypt.

My dad's tenacity, determination and success are traits I value immensely; traits I would one day realise I possess myself – after I found out I had cancer. My dad was living proof that anything is possible. If you set your mind to it and work hard for it, you can achieve your dreams. He was a man admired by many, a man highly respected, and a man I adored. There is no greater hero in my eyes than my beloved father.

My mum's childhood was equally as challenging but under much different circumstances. She was born into a period of violence and fear during the height of the Troubles. Northern Ireland, just like Egypt, was a divided nation ruled by politics and paramilitaries.

Belfast, like many Northern Irish cities, was a battleground between Catholics and Protestants and state forces. My mum was raised in the heart of the conflict – the Shankill Road. A proud Protestant area that borders a proud Catholic one – the Falls. Both areas suffered tragic losses at a time when bomb explosions, open gunfire, protests and murder were part of everyday life.

When I later asked my mum if she afraid growing up in the Troubles, she answered, *'No, it was just part of everyday life.'* To her, the brutality and violence was normal, which saddens me greatly. As an outsider looking in, I can see the damage such an upbringing has had on my mother and the whole population of Northern Ireland; especially the negative impact it has had on the nation's mental well-being, which I have witnessed first-hand working as a mental health nurse in Belfast. Is it any wonder Northern Ireland has the highest suicide rate in the UK, or that alcohol and drug abuse is at an all-time high?

It certainly wasn't normal when Mum's grandad was tragically blown to pieces in a bomb explosion meant for someone else while taking his evening bath, or for her brother's stepdaughter to lose her life at the age of thirteen after a bomb went off in the local fish shop. Just another child who lost her life in a conflict she was barely old enough to understand. Nor was it normal for my dear uncle to pull her lifeless body out of the rubble, a memory that haunted him for the rest of his life and that drove him to excessive drinking and an early grave. The horrors of the Troubles were certainly far from normal, but for those who lived and breathed them they were sadly *'just part of everyday life.'*

After finishing secondary school, my mum decided to try out a career in modelling. She was a slim and attractive young woman who fitted the job description perfectly, but she was unimpressed with the falseness of the industry and decided to seek out a different line of work instead. After a few temping jobs, she took on waitressing in the Europa Hotel – the hotel where my dad just so happened to be general manager. And so their love story began. A few whirlwind years later and here they were in the City Hospital awaiting the arrival of their baby girl, me.

* * *

Our family didn't remain in Belfast for long because in 1993 my dad was offered an exciting business opportunity overseas managing a new corporate hotel. Situated in the north-west of England, on Blackpool's famous promenade, was the Imperial Hotel. It didn't take my parents much convincing to leave Belfast behind and start afresh. I was two and my brother was five when we moved. I know my brother missed Belfast terribly but I never gave it a second thought, not until I reached my late teens, that is. As a child, Blackpool was a playground in a whole other league. With its amusements, theme parks, donkey rides on the beach, sticks of rock, Blackpool Tower and the dazzling Blackpool Illuminations, what wasn't there to like?

My parents bought our home just outside the busy town centre, in a quieter area, a village close to the sea. Mum chose the house and everything in it, and although it was beautiful, to me it never really felt like home. It was a show house when we bought it and my mum kept it that way. The floors were cold and tiled in Mum's favourite colour, black; the glass cabinets were jam-packed with expensive ornaments that forever needed dusting and I was terrified of breaking. The house had two sitting rooms – the fancy one my parents used with a dining room attached, and a slightly less fancy one that my brother and I used. As well as those rooms, we had a breakfast room (that I don't ever recall eating breakfast in) and a study for my dad. It was the biggest house on our block; a corner house with a stunning exotic back garden filled with monkey puzzle trees and sweet-smelling jasmine. It was my mum's dream house, her pride and joy. For a long time it was a happy home, until the atmosphere inside turned as black as the cold floor tiles.

My memories of my early years are few and far between – the result of a trauma response, according to my counsellor, but what I can remember is mostly happy times: days spent at the beach with my mum; walking the illuminations with my big brother, light-up yo-yos in hand; bedtime fairy tales read to me by my sweet father;

Sunday carvery at the hotel where the staff made a fuss of the boss's children; family outings to local hotspots; regular trips to the Lake District; and weekends up in Scotland. Yes, my childhood was certainly a happy one, albeit a lonely one.

I remember being an exceptionally quiet child. I had no friends before primary school because my parents took me out of nursery before I had the chance to make any. I accidentally burned myself on a hot radiator, and although the injury was minor my parents were maybe a tad overprotective, especially my dad, and were convinced I was safer at home. The knock-on was that I was rarely around children my own age and so I failed to develop those all-important social skills that would benefit me when I was older, which probably triggered my social anxiety in later life (also according to my counsellor).

However, despite being a loner through most of primary school, my early years were certainly never dull and I never felt like I was missing out. Thanks to my dad's hefty pay cheque, I'd say my brother and I enjoyed a very privileged upbringing. We wanted for nothing – the latest toys, the best of clothes, another pet bunny rabbit (I had six in total). Anything we asked for, we got. Although we weren't spoilt children, just lucky, I guess.

We holidayed several times a year. When we weren't exploring old monasteries in France or visiting the pyramids and my grandparents in Egypt or catching up with our family in Northern Ireland, we were enjoying holidays at our timeshare in America, which my dad bought shortly after I was born. I was still in my pram on my first trip to Disney, and I was hooked from the very beginning – from the first time I laid eyes on Sleeping Beauty's castle and witnessed the Princess Parade.

During that first trip my parents bought me a Minnie Mouse teddy bear – the traditional one with the red-and-white polka-dot dress and bright yellow shoes. I named her Minnie Ha Ha, for reasons unbeknown to my adult self, and she has never left my side since.

She was a patient in hospital with me when I had my tonsils and adenoids removed. The nurses even ensured she had the correct name band on her wrist to match mine. She travelled with me on every adventure across the globe – my poor dad having to drive all the way home from the airport to retrieve her before one of our long-haul flights. She lay beside me when I cried myself to sleep, distraught with grief. She stayed hidden in my handbag as a stowaway when I slept at my first boyfriend's house. She sailed the ocean with me when I moved back across the water. She slept in between my husband and me after we were married. She remained in my arms when I had my first bout of chemotherapy. She soaked up my tears after I had my single mastectomy. Her white hands are now stained red with my blood. She knew my story long before I wrote it; seeing each chapter unfold as I lived it. A little piece of my childhood remaining with me always.

* * *

I was ten when my parents decided to buy a local shop named The Tap House. My dad wasn't keen on the new business venture, but his hotel career had unfortunately been cut short and there weren't many other options that allowed him to work so close to home. The shop was a small convenience store selling the basic essentials as well as cigarettes and alcohol. With a decent tidy flat above to rent out, the business had potential but, alas, its potential never manifested. Not for my parents anyway.

The shop made very little profit no matter how much money my parents pumped into it, no matter what new ideas they came up with to try and increase business. It just wasn't successful. Not only did it cause our family financial strain, it also meant my dad ended up working around the clock because we couldn't afford to pay more than one member of staff – Pam, who became my lifelong friend. My mum could only help out here and there after taking on full-time employment in a local restaurant to try and keep us afloat, meaning the bulk of the hours were left to my dad. The lonely fourteen-hour shifts deflated him and his spark for life and adventure soon diminished.

Our family went from a life of luxury to watching every penny, a difficult adjustment for my parents to make. My dad tried his best to keep the mounting debts hidden from me and my brother, but the growing tension and heated discussions between my parents after bedtime were hard to miss. It broke my heart to watch my dad go from a respectable businessman to what he perceived as a failure. Even at such a young age I saw how much the demotion cost him. A man without pride is a broken man, and my dad was now unfixable. Worse still, I had no idea how to help him.

I knew I was failing him. I called in with him as often as I could to try and keep him company and break up his monotonous working day. I found him asleep in a tiny armchair in the back room on more than one occasion, his head bowed in exhaustion – a sight that still haunts me to this day. I knew my father was miserable but I didn't know how to make him better. Over time I called in less and less. Now preoccupied with high school and its petty teenage dramas, I was too young and naive to fully understand my father wasn't well.

Chapter 2

-A Black Christmas-

It was a Saturday evening in early December and our street already looked like a Christmas movie set except for our house, which was currently the only broken bulb in the Wolsey Close light chain. But Mum finally gave in to neighbourhood peer pressure and carted the decorations down from the attic. I was delighted. After all, it wasn't officially Christmas until your tree was up, and decorating the tree was my favourite part of the holidays. Well, besides the presents, of course.

Putting the tree up was a full-day family ritual starting off with cleaning. My mum and I spent the entire morning gutting out the front room. Every surface was meticulously cleared and polished; the floors swept and mopped, at least twice; the windows gleamed from an entire bottle of white vinegar and countless newspapers. The room was finally ready. An empty shell all set to be transformed into a winter wonderland.

The afternoon was spent preparing the Christmas banquet – a selection of finger food to nibble on while decorating the tree. I was in charge of cocktail sticks that were to be threaded with a combination of tinned ham (which you would never entertain any other time of the year), cubed cheese and pickles. I popped another piece of cheese in my mouth and hummed along to the old Christmas album playing in the corner, not lifting my head until my silver tray was full. Once satisfied that I had made enough to feed the five thousand, I took a breather and glanced up at the golden swinging clock in front of me. It was almost time: my dad would be home any minute now and we could finally get started.

Just then the phone rang as if he had read my mind. I smiled knowing Dad's persistent ring, but my smile quickly fled as I watched the phone slide from my mum's shaking hands and the colour drain from her face. She let out a muffled cry that I couldn't quite understand, but my brother had. I heard him bound down the stairs looking frightened, which in turn frightened me. He threw me my coat and ushered me out the door, the three of us heading up the street to The Tap House.

I arrived at the shop first but the uniformed men wouldn't let me in. My brother got there moments later and barged his way through with force. Mum stood beside me catching her breath, her pale face now glowing red in the cold, frosty air. The men in uniform moved from the doorway to let paramedics carry out a man on a stretcher. His chest was bare and had two white pads attached to it, and an oxygen mask covered his face. I could see no sign of movement on the stretcher. My brother walked slowly behind, his head bowed low to hide his tears. The ambulance doors slammed shut, the blue lights flickered on, the sirens started wailing, and that was the last time I ever saw my father alive. He died in the back of the ambulance that cold December night at the young age of fifty-eight. The coroner's report concluded it was a heart attack. Mum blamed her husband's early death on his unhealthy smoking habit, and I blamed his death on her and that damn shop.

I said my goodbyes to my father in the funeral home three days later; a goodbye that has stayed with me. Even now when I close my eyes I can still see the ice glistening on the footpath below my tiny feet; I can feel the cold bursts of wind cutting through my much younger face; I can replay the morbid glow of the Christmas lights in the funeral parlour windows, dancing away to their sorry tune; I can smell the distinct smell of death that lingers throughout the building – a smell that still makes my stomach retch.

My brother was the first to enter the room where my father lay, closing the door behind him; not wanting us to see him raise my father's lifeless body into his arms to cradle him one last time. Mum and I went in together for moral support. I approached the coffin with caution, afraid of what I'd find inside. I cast my eyes over my father. He was dressed in his finest navy pinstriped suit, carefully chosen by my mother. In death a proud boss again. I placed his stony slender hands in mine and kissed them ever so softly, afraid they would crack beneath my lips, and whispered my final goodbye.

A week after my father's funeral I was found lying in an deserted field covered in my own vomit, an empty vodka bottle beside me. I could hear the distant panicked voices of my friends phoning for an ambulance before the sky went blurry and I blacked out. I woke in a moving vehicle with a strange man standing over me. I recognised the uniform – I had seen it before, quite recently. I felt something sticking to my chest and peered down at the familiar white pads attached to my chest, the same ones I'd seen on my father. I heard the sirens squealing, the same sirens I'd heard the night my entire world ended. I closed my eyes willing it all to be over, to be reunited with my beloved father and escape my inconsolable grief.

Instead, I woke in a hospital bed a few hours later, bursting into tears knowing I'd been so close; so close to seeing him again and then had the opportunity snatched away. Instead of my beautiful father's angelic face I saw my mother's angry one coming towards me. I quickly closed my eyes, pretending to be asleep a little longer. Alas, feigning sleep could only delay the inevitable reprimand a short while. After my scolding a doctor came to assess my mental state. He barely gave me five minutes before determining I was only another self-destructive naughty teenager and sent me on my merry way, just in time for my morning paper round that my mum still made me do – even with twigs and vomit matted in my hair.

From the day we lost my father my relationship with my mother became a turbulent one. I wasn't the only one to turn to alcohol for consolation. Mum drank heavily too and wasn't the nicest person with drink on board.

Of course, I didn't know it then but my mum was using alcohol to escape her grief too. I never put myself in her shoes. I never acknowledged that she was now a young widow with two teenage kids to raise alone. My father's death wasn't spoken of in our house; it was a forbidden topic that was only ever mentioned during alcohol-fuelled rows. Neither of us sought grief counsellors or outside help. Instead, we developed our own unhealthy coping mechanisms; unhealthy habits that only pushed our family further apart.

For years after my father's death my mother refused to put up a Christmas tree. Once she remarried, she took herself off for the holidays; never wanting to spend them at home. I spent my Christmases either at friends' houses or with my brother and his partner Sophie. When I moved into my own house I bought a black Christmas tree that I put up every 3 December, on the anniversary of my father's death. A morbid ritual that I carried on in his honour. Until I got cancer, that is.

* * *

I've always found myself drawn to confident women. Brave women who aren't afraid to speak their minds; women who are assertive, respected and desired; women who own the room without breaking a sweat; women who own themselves. Women who are the total opposite of me.

After my father's death I was more lost than ever when, by some miracle, I fell in with one of these confident females who offered me a helping hand. Her name was Kelly. Kelly lived a few doors from our dreaded shop and just so happened to stop me one morning to pass on her family's condolences. I was surprised by the kind gesture. Kelly was one of the popular kids at school and I was unaware she knew I existed, but for some unbeknown reason, on that particular day, she decided to befriend me, and my life drastically changed. Again.

Suddenly I was popular. People actually liked me, which was so alien I couldn't accept it at first – after all, I'd spent most of my life invisible. How come people could see me now? Desperate to fit in with my new friends, I moulded myself into someone I wasn't. I wore heavy make-up, rolled my skirt up way above the knee, started smoking, acted the maggot in class, disrupted lessons, was rude to my teachers, made fun of girls who were invisible, like I used to be. It wasn't that I fell in with a bad crowd, because they weren't – they were good kids. I was the bad one.

My grades started slipping. I was no longer the A* student my dad had been so proud of. I was downgraded classes, no longer smart enough to keep up with the top set in maths, English and science. In fact, I was predicted to fail every one of my GCSEs. Not that I cared at the time.

I started drinking heavily at the weekends, often making a fool of myself or accidentally hurting myself under the influence of alcohol. I got so drunk one night that I fell and smashed my face off a kerb, knocking my front tooth out and busting my lip clean open. Worse still, I was that intoxicated I didn't even know I'd done it until I saw my bloody reflection in the mirror. I was out of control. I lost my dignity and my virginity all in one go and I was ashamed. And the more ashamed I was, the more I drank to forget the shame, and so the cycle continued.

Mum tried putting me under house arrest, permanently grounding me, but I always talked my way to freedom eventually. My teachers pleaded with me to end my reckless behaviour, so I stopped going to school. My brother slapped me out of utter frustration after I was suspended for the second time that year, so I retaliated by yelling *'You're not my real brother',* succeeding in hurting him the only way I knew how. I went from grade A student to grade A idiot, and that's putting it politely. What can I say other than I was a messed-up kid who missed her father and was pissed off at everything and everyone for taking him from her?

After another heated row with my mum I decided to live with my brother for a while to give us both some space. He had moved into the flat above our hateful shop and allowed me to crash there for a while. His living room was now my bedroom; his sofa now my bed. I was mistaken in thinking he would give me an easy ride. Instead, he laid down the ground rules immediately. Rules I now had no choice but to obey if I wanted to keep a roof over my head. My brother and I made a deal: I attended school every day, did my homework every evening, only drank when I was in his company (where my behaviour could be monitored) and was only allowed to sleep over at Kelly's house, a few doors down from him.

It meant no more bunking off school or falling behind with my schoolwork. No staying out at random house parties or drinking in the streets. As unfair as it sounds to any ASBO teenager, this strict set of rules was the kindest thing my brother could have done for me. I didn't mind my new restrictions and enjoyed my brother's and Sophie's company. They treated me like a daughter and I had a place to call home. However, the move didn't come without sacrifice.

After I moved into the flat my relationship with Kelly simmered, mainly because I wasn't able to attend the same social gatherings as she was any more. She soon chummed up with another girlfriend and I was naturally left behind, which hurt at the time – quite a lot actually. I felt betrayed by my best friend, especially when I lost more than just Kelly. I also lost her family, who I had been incredibly close with too. But such is life. Not all friendships are meant to go the distance, as I have learnt the hard way. Kelly continued to filter in and out of my life over the years. She visited me in Belfast, she came to my wedding reception, she got in touch after cancer, but then disappeared by the end of chemo. I'm not angry with her, though. Like I said, not all friendships are meant to go the distance.

Miraculously I managed to pass all my GCSEs, thanks to my brother, I suppose. I even managed to get an A* in art. After school ended and it was time to apply for colleges, I made sure I chose a different one from my old school friends. I was ashamed of my behaviour in high school and I desperately wanted to get rid of that version of myself.
College offered me that – the chance to start afresh, away from anyone who knew me before. A chance to recreate myself.

I chose to study business studies and travel and tourism at A level. Not because I wanted to, but because I thought my dad would have wanted me to. I had no idea what I wanted to do with my life other than wanting to travel, but I felt my life and career needed to live up to the same high standards as his. Going travelling certainly wouldn't suffice. I wasn't aware back then that my life didn't need to replicate my father's for it to be meaningful.

Unfortunately the subjects I chose were harder than I anticipated and left me doubting my academic capabilities. No matter how hard I tried I just couldn't keep up, especially in business studies. It went straight over my head and I knew I would never pass my exams. As usual, I struggled to make new friends. Without a confident female by my side I had no voice. I was invisible again and I was embarrassed by it. Eventually I convinced myself I wasn't smart enough to study A levels and wasn't going to put myself through another year of social awkwardness, so I quit. I finished my first-year exams, dropped my pen on the paper, walked out of the exam hall and never looked back.

Quitting college was the first decision I ever made for myself. It was impulsive and scary but I chose to do it. No one influenced my decision, just me. It felt right for me at the time, even if it did make me feel like a failure. I had no plan, no idea of what to do next, but I quit anyway. Maybe some journeys aren't meant to be straightforward. Mine certainly wasn't.

* * *

I was working in an upholstery business when I came across an ad for an apprenticeship at a local nursery. At the time I was employed by my mum's new husband, John, and as much as I was grateful for the work and the more than decent pay cheque, I was totally useless at the job. I oversaw front of house, answering the phone and helping customers who called into the store. Most orders were placed over the phone or computer, thankfully sparing me the embarrassment of pretending I knew about fabrics and furniture. The work was lonely and, to put it kindly, boring.

The furniture was made in the factory behind the reception and I preferred to keep the door between the two firmly closed. The factory lads all knew I was useless and that I'd only been hired because the boss had a new missus. The less interaction with them the better. It was not a job for an eighteen-year-old. There were no opportunities to make new friends or progress in a career, and there was certainly no craic at the office. Well, not on my side of the door anyway.

Although I was thankful for the favour from John, I was understandably bored stiff, so I applied for the apprenticeship. Not because I was overly passionate about working with young children, but because it offered something better than my current situation. As well as a recognised qualification in childcare, there was the chance to mingle with girls my own age and a chance to build a new life again.

The nursery was segregated into three parts: a baby unit, two and three year olds, and preschool. I was luckily allocated the two and three year olds because babies weren't really my forte, to be honest – not then anyway. Toddlers are much more entertaining

– so mischievous at that age it was comical. Of course I'd have probably found it much less amusing if they were my children, but they weren't, which was the beauty of the job. Nursery routine was simple and easy to follow, meaning that for once I didn't feel stupid or out of my depth. I felt relaxed there and made a few lifelong friends, one being Chloe.

Surprisingly, I had known Chloe most of my life. Our brothers had grown up together and were very close, but Chloe and I had remained strangers until now. We had never exchanged more than a polite hello prior to working together.
We were polar opposites, yet the perfect match. She was loud and bubbly – a girl who oozed confidence; whereas I was quiet, withdrawn and massively uncomfortable in my own skin. She was a girly girl and I was a tomboy. Even our favourite colours clashed: hers pink and mine a morbid black. She was open and wore her heart on her sleeve; I was a closed book, allowing only a select few to read past my first chapter. I suppose I was the dark and she was the light, and somehow we just clicked somewhere in the middle.

When I was with Chloe I felt confident, just like I had with Kelly, and just as before I fed and thrived on that false confidence knowing I couldn't survive without it. For a while we were inseparable and did everything together, rarely going a day without seeing each other. During one of our standard movie nights, that usually occurred when we were too hungover to do anything else, Chloe and I decided to watch Eat Pray Love. Julia Roberts plays Liz, a journalist, who shares my passion for travel, and luckily for her makes a living out of it. Outside of her jet-set lifestyle, though, the rest of her world is crumbling. She is married to a man she no longer loves, lives in a beautiful home she designed herself but no longer feels part of and has become a woman without purpose, without faith, without an appetite for life. A woman *'without a pulse.'*

The film follows Liz as she falls apart after filing for divorce and losing everything she owns. Hoping to remember how to eat, pray and love, she embarks on a journey of self-discovery starting in Italy, travels on to a guru meditation camp in India and finally finishes in Bali. During her travels Liz learns to eat again, and by replenishing her appetite for food she rediscovers her appetite for life. She learns to pray through the art of meditation, allowing her to successfully restore her balance and feel content with life once more. Finally Liz learns to love again when she meets a hot Australian man in Bali, and quite literally sails off into the sunset with him!

By the end of the film Chloe and I were both in tears and thinking the exact same thing: OMG, Alex, you are Liz! Not because I'm a Julia Roberts lookalike (I wish) or that I wanted to leave my non-existent husband, but because I was lost and needed to find myself again, just as Liz had. From that day forth I became obsessed with my own journey of self-discovery. I wanted to travel to Italy, India and Bali and recreate my own version of the film and get my happily ever after. Chloe, of course, agreed to come with me, and we spent hours locked away in my bedroom hypothetically planning our big escape.

Although we talked about it like it was our dream I always knew it was mine, not hers. Chloe, like most young women, wanted to get married, have a big family and settle down in her home town close to her family and friends. Whereas I had no desire to remain in Blackpool, nor did I desire the conventional lifestyle. I wanted more. Realistically I'd been craving an escape from Blackpool ever since my dad died, and after watching my now favourite movie my mind was made up. Eat Pray Love only confirmed what I already knew: that I didn't belong here, that I was destined for something else; something bigger than Blackpool, something bigger than me.

But several years passed without change. I was still stuck in the same miserable seaside town no closer to catching that dream flight as I was when the idea first came to mind. Chloe, however, had found her movie ending. She had settled down and was in a serious relationship, like all my friends were now. Although I was delighted she had found her special someone, I missed the good old days when it was just the two of us against the world - usually drunk in our local pub!

Even though Chloe tried her best to include me in her new life, I knew I had to take a back seat and let her live hers while I tried to figure out mine. I had to accept that my closest friend and I had reached a crossroads. With a heavy heart, she went her way and I went mine.

Chapter 3

-Appearances Can Be Deceiving-

A mountain's appearance can often be deceiving. You can start your ascent in the brilliant sunshine without a single cloud in the sky, yet when you reach the summit you can be greeted with turbulent winds, pelting rain or thick dense fog. Mountaineers must, therefore, be prepared to encounter all climbing conditions when they make their ascent. Just as a mountain's appearance can play tricks on you, so did mine. On the outside I was a relatively *'normal'* young women entering her twenties, but on the inside I was screaming.

Like many young women I found my insecurities overbearing. Being single was just one of them – as if being single was the worst thing in the world. I felt this desperate need to be in a relationship, like all my friends were, so that I could be *'normal.'* To me, being single automatically made me an outcast because I was completely alone. Like so many, I believed we humans are destined to partner up with someone – as if our sole purpose in life is to pair with another. But what if that's not the case?

It's a shame that so many of us feel forced into relationships we often don't want to be in just to be accepted among our peers. Even worse, society has now added a timescale in which we must find this significant other. Nowadays if you're not married by thirty or at least have a ring on your finger, you're classed as some sort of reject, which is ludicrous. Surely there's no timeframe for love? Or what if you don't feel the need to conform to society's unrealistic expectations? What if you're perfectly happy going alone at this thing called life? If I'd have been braver, I'd have done just that. I'd have given relationships a miss for a while and chose adventure over love – because adventure was my love, back then, at least.

But I wasn't brave enough to just be me, to just go for it and live my life exactly the way I wanted. Instead, I chose to be like everyone else, and, in turn, I rejected my true self.

I went through numerous pointless relationships, one after the other, believing I was in love every time. But my relationships never lasted longer than six months and I was always the one getting binned, not the other way round. I dated your stereotypical potheads – guys who love cannabis more than they can ever love a woman. Men – or should I say boys, whom I had absolutely nothing in common with; men who lacked ambition, passion or any kind of drive. Those who did possess such qualities, soon realised they didn't want me in the picture. I was hardly an attractive person myself, either in looks or personality.

I came close to love only once before meeting my husband. He was older than me, one of my brother's close friends. He was my schoolgirl crush – the type of crush you're always awkward and embarrassing around. I'd get my words muddled up whenever he tried to speak to me, or clumsily spill drinks everywhere when he was about, or drink too much and make an idiot of myself as usual. He always seemed to catch me at my worst. There was no way he could ever fancy a girl like me, although we did share a few common interests. The main one being we both wanted to leave Blackpool. He wanted to emigrate to Thailand, and he filled my head with visions of living a free life in South East Asia. I dreamt he would take me with him and we would live happily ever after in a bamboo house with no electricity in the middle of the rainforest, like Tarzan and Jane. Yes, I was a hopeless romantic back then and a hopeless fool.

Years went by and we both dated other people but I always had a soft spot in my heart for him until one night I drunkenly confessed my feelings. Relying on alcohol to give me false courage and waiting for his instant rejection, I was pleasantly surprised when he didn't laugh in my face and promptly knock me down.

Instead, he agreed to give us a go. Sadly Tarzan and Jane just weren't meant to be, though. We had only been dating a few short weeks when he suddenly decided to end it. I never really understood his reasons why. His rejection without a valid reason left me understandably hurt, and I never really forgave him for that.

As I hit my early twenties I started to believe that my bad luck with men was all down to two things: my weight and my unnatural body hair. I was a curvy girl, a typical pear shape – small boobs, big hips and a large round bum. I wasn't overweight – in actual fact I was one of the smaller girls in my group of friends, yet I genuinely believed I was the heaviest. I was obsessed with how my body looked. I hated my chunky thighs, childbearing hips and oversized ass. I followed all the latest fad diets: the juice diet, the Atkins diet, SlimFast. I'd substitute juices for meals, or milkshakes for meals, or tasteless cardboard chewy bars that were meant to be a treat for snacks. I'd starve myself all week only to binge at the weekends, consequently ruining my weekday efforts. I didn't know how to lose weight healthily or how to exercise properly. I hated gyms and avoided them like the plague, always too conscious that people would be looking at me (like most gym phobics believe). I watched exercise DVDs at home instead, usually from the latest celebrity in the spotlight who had achieved a remarkable body transformation. I didn't take into consideration that these celebrities most likely had their own nutritionist, personal chef and personal trainers, or that most of them ended up piling the weight back on shortly after because their weight loss was unsustainable. I just saw a skinny celebrity on a DVD cover and thought I'd magically look like them too.

Unlike my friends who were all super confident, I was super self-critical and preoccupied with my outward appearance, especially my abnormal body hair, which was possibly a result of my Egyptian heritage. It started when I hit puberty, and naturally I was teased in school because of the unfeminine body hair that covered my legs and arms, and my hairy top lip and monobrow. The boys would made monkey noises behind my back, until one day I stole my mum's razor and shaved everything – including my forearms and top lip, which aren't supposed to be shaved and tend to grow back worse! It worked, though. Once I was hair free the boys soon stopped referring to me as a zoo animal. But the damage, of course, was already done. From that moment on I was tormented with an unhealthy hair-removal obsession. Well, until I had my breast cut off and realised there are worse things than hairy legs and a subtle moustache.

Years passed before I heard that my unnatural hair growth could have been down to medical issues, not my Egyptian blood. A treatable hormone imbalance, for example, could be the cause. Up to ten per cent of women are affected with this imbalance, known as hirsutism – hair growth in a typical male pattern meaning you get hair where most women don't because of high levels of male sex hormones. Successful treatments include oral contraception used to regulate the function of the ovaries and reduce the number of androgens they secrete, as well as laser hair removal provided on the NHS. Damn it! I was never offered either treatment because I never confided in a doctor. Instead, I let my body hair rule my life. It controlled what I wore, when I went out, when I went on holiday, when I had sex. For a long time it controlled my entire existence.

If only I had known that in less than ten years' time I would be diagnosed with cancer, oh, how I would have done things differently – treated myself differently, lived my life differently. If I had been able to predict the future and understood that I was living on borrowed time, I wouldn't have wasted so many years hating myself and often wishing my life was over already. I took the promise of tomorrow for granted. I didn't understand how precious my years were. Consumed with insecurity and self-hate, I wasted years merely existing without actually living.

So when death arrived at my door, to take me far too young, I couldn't help thinking – had I brought death upon myself?

* * *

If I could choose one word to describe my early twenties, it would be *'lonely.'* Everyone I cared about had successfully entered adulthood, bought their first homes, had children, got married. But I was still single, childless and living at my mum's house. I spent most of my time either working or drinking myself into oblivion. My life was going nowhere fast and I felt powerless to change it. My drinking increased and my self-loathing grew intolerable.

I soon found I was only able to socialise with alcohol on board. I was so anxious without it I couldn't walk into a room by myself. I couldn't attend birthday parties or other social gatherings without already being inebriated. I could barely even make it to Asda without having a panic attack and feeling like everyone was looking at me. My anxiety ate away at me and eventually I started avoiding situations that provoked it, which was pretty much everything other than work. I spent most of my time alone. I withdrew from my friends and family, feeling like a burden to them all. I didn't want to ruin their happiness.

Both my mum and brother had moved on with their lives and left the family home. Mum had remarried and was living in the Lake District. My brother had his own place too and was now a father, and I was left to roam our once happy home alone. It was nobody's fault. I couldn't be angry or upset with anyone. Everyone had the right to enjoy their lives. No one could have helped the fact that I hated mine.

It was the saddest and unhappiest time of my life. I felt like I had no one to turn to, no way out. I found that the more time I spent alone the less I wanted to see people. I couldn't bear to admit that I was depressed and refused to seek professional help. Intrusive thoughts tortured my mind constantly. I began imagining myself crashing my car into a tree or taking tablets and drifting off to sleep forever, which I tried once but messed that up too. As soon as I'd swallowed the last paracetamol and realised what I'd done, I phoned my brother crying hysterically. He brought me straight to hospital to have my stomach pumped, and I got to listen to insensitive nurses repeating to one another that *'I was a waste of a bed',* which I probably was. Truth was, I didn't want to die; I just didn't want to live. Not my life anyway. If I could have hopped into someone else's, I'd have been more than happy, but of course that wasn't an option.

During that overnight hospital stint, in my hospital gown and hospital bed, I knew I needed to make some drastic changes if I ever wanted to see a future. Only a few months later I mustered the courage, took a huge leap of faith and set myself free.

After a long and very emotional phone call with my granny in Northern Ireland, I booked a one-way ferry ticket and moved home.

Back to Belfast. Back to where I belonged.

* * *

Before I could leave my old home for good, however, I wanted to ensure I was on good terms with everyone I was leaving behind, including my mother. Our relationship was still very turbulent and I wanted to try and resolve that before I left, for both our sakes. We talked and agreed to book a trip to Egypt together, departing the month before I planned to leave England. It would seem both my motherlands were calling me home: Egypt and Northern Ireland. I had to visit them both to start afresh. Although we had visited Egypt regularly when I was child, none of my family had ventured back there since the death of my father.

Just like us, the country had evolved and changed, for the better and for the worse.

Tourism had taken over the Third World country, which was a good thing for many as it brought in revenue and provided jobs for Egypt's ever-growing population. But for me tourism had stolen a little piece of Egypt's heart. When we landed in Cairo I saw how the opportunity to make money had sliced into the once vast desert to make room for expensive hotel resorts directly facing the pyramids. Now these enormous shrines and temples faced the latest five-star hotel and spa; their authenticity stolen by tourism, their magic minimised by commercialism.

We travelled further south, making our way to Luxor and the Valley of the Kings. During the journey I found myself thinking of my beloved father more than ever. Wondering what his life had been like when he lived here, before I knew him. I felt close to him there, in Egypt. I felt that connection I'd been chasing ever since his death. I felt his presence from the moment I stepped off the plane and it comforted me. I was in a state of limbo soon to embark on the biggest adventure of my life, and I needed his guidance now more than ever.

Mum and I had chosen to take a Nile cruise, a lifelong dream for both of us. Sailing from Luxor to Aswan, the cruise would take us through some of Egypt's greatest wonders. I'd never cruised before and found it surprisingly enjoyable. The stillness of the river gave me a chance to quiet my mind. Time seemed to stand still along this river of secrets, allowing Mum and me to take the time to finally talk. We bonded along that journey, opening up to one another after years of silence. The trip was a success and I was relieved. I knew I could now leave Blackpool and my family behind with no regrets.

I found a piece of me in Egypt; a part of me that I had buried long ago. I allowed myself to get lost among the rows upon rows of sandstone pillars in the 250 acres of Karnak; a city of temples and Egypt's most remarkable religious complex dedicated to Amun, Mut and Khonsu. I listened to our tour guide's explanation of the temple with high-tuned ears.

Egypt had always fascinated me, but now, as an adult, I finally understood why: it was breathtaking. It was steeped in ancient history, my own history, my heritage.

When we visited the Temple of Hatshepsut I was spellbound. Here before me was a temple dedicated to the third female pharaoh in three thousand years of ancient Egyptian history. This pharaoh and woman of great power was part of my ancestry and therefore part of me. As I wandered through her glorious temple I was ashamed to admit I had turned my back on my lineage for so long. I decided I would no longer hide who I was. I would be proud to descend from such greatness and I would be proud to be an Egyptian woman.

One of the trip's highlights, and my personal favourite, was the Temple of Philae. A temple that had been completely relocated and restored after its original location flooded. The idea that the ancient Egyptians were able to move an entire temple simply blew my mind. The ruin was successfully moved to an island only accessible by tiny boats. Dedicated to the goddess Isis, it is perhaps the most beautiful of all the Egyptian temples and one that took my breath away.

But, as fascinating as these ancient ruins were, the most significant part of the holiday for me was the Nile itself. The world's longest river and the source of Egypt's vast history. During that week-long cruise I found myself gazing out at the children playing at the water's edge waving eagerly at the boats passing by. These children had very little, and yet here they were smiling at strangers who soaked up their lands – lands that they couldn't afford to enjoy themselves. I searched the schoolboys' faces and saw my dad in each and every one of them. I watched elderly ladies rowing up beside the cruise liners on their tiny wooden row boats hoping to sell handmade goods to those on board. Giving their customers a toothless smile, they tossed silk fashion accessories to tourists on board and held their hands out for coins.

The simplicity of life along the Nile made me assess my own life and how much I now valued it. As I watched those dreamy burnt-orange sunrises and sunsets reflecting off the water's edge I reflected on my own life, wondering if I'd made the right decision to move home and questioning whether my leap of faith would actually pay off. Like the wonders of the Nile, only time would tell.

I left Egypt in a river of tears, not wanting to leave the country where I had felt such a strong connection and afraid to face the changes waiting for me when I returned home. But I had made my decision and I had to stick by it. I had to be true to myself just this once and not cave into fear.

Chapter 4

-The Adventure Begins-

It wasn't Italy or India or Bali but rainy Northern Ireland where my adventure finally began. Situated by the sea, just outside Belfast, Bangor is a small commuter town slightly bigger than the one I left behind. Although the town isn't overly exciting, there's still a steady hustle and bustle about the place. The people are friendly and welcoming, unlike the stand-offish community I had left behind, and it seemed like the perfect starting point to build my new life. I spent most of my days down at the beach walking along the coast, exploring and soaking up the last of the summer sun. The seaside was a comfort to me, especially on the days when I was missing home, which I often did.

I had moved to Northern Ireland with nothing to my name and only my little car and limited possessions. I had no savings, no employment and no financial security. I knew no one other than my grandparents, aunties, uncle and a few cousins whom I had never really spent any quality time with. I had taken a huge gamble with my decision to move but I had a solid plan: I intended to go back to college to finish my A levels and go to university and study for a nursing degree. I figured nursing would open up new career opportunities, including working abroad. I had my eyes set on Australia as my final destination. Belfast was only a stepping stone on to a bigger journey ahead. Except I never left in the end.

The first few months were tough and I often wondered had I made a huge mistake, but my granny kept my spirits high. She welcomed me into her home, treating me like one of her own. Now that I was blessed with the company of my grandparents, I was never really alone. My granny and I would sit for hours at her kitchen table smoking and drinking endless cups of tea and coffee, setting the world to rights.

I was able to talk openly with her about why I had moved, and how desperate I was to change my life. She motivated me on my bad days, ensuring I never gave up. Miraculously I didn't, and that I owe to her.

I must have applied for fifty plus jobs in my first few weeks in Bangor. I answered every vacancy no matter what the vocation and was rejected by every single one. I never even made it to the interview stage. I was, believe it or not, rejected for charity work at the local dog shelter – people didn't even want me to work for them for free. I naturally became downhearted and constantly worried about my finances but I kept on applying, hoping something would turn up soon. In the meantime, I enrolled in college and threw myself into my studies in preparation for university.

Thankfully I only remained unemployed for two months. I found a job in a local nursing home (both my granny and aunty had worked there, which probably swayed the interview in my favour, but I wasn't about to complain. I was just happy to be earning again). Six months later I was offered my first trust post with the NHS. My new job involved working with children and young people with learning disabilities and challenging behaviour. The job was massively out of my comfort zone, especially with having no previous experience in this area, and I spent the first three months crying on my way in to work and crying on my way out. The children often became aggressive and were exceptionally difficult to manage. My colleagues and I were injured on a regular basis and the tension and stress of the environment had a huge impact on our physical and mental health. Although the job was frightening at times it was also rewarding and swayed me towards a career in mental health nursing rather than general.

Despite the unit being highly stressful, it was here I met my closest friends. There was Gillian – an angel in disguise, Jenna – my feisty feminist, Karen – my adventure buddy and Barbara – my intellectual go-to girl. Our friendships came naturally, forged in difficult situations and maintained long after we all left the job. I found myself connected to them in a different way to my girlfriends back home. I suppose we had more common ground given our chosen careers, and after finding them my transition to life in Northern Ireland was almost complete. Within a year everything had fallen into place. It's amazing what you can do when you put your mind to it. Excuse the cliché, but it's true. I finally felt like I was on the right track. Once I had removed the negativity from my life, everything seemed to run smoothly. There was only one thing I was missing: a significant other.

I joined an online dating agency – something I'd never done before but apparently it's the only way to meet guys these days. I wasn't expecting love but was hopeful for a date or two, at least. I liked the idea of hiding behind a computer screen and not having to worry about what I looked like or if the men behind the screen found me attractive or not. I could just be me. Turns out online dating never really was for me. I only went on two dates. The first one was a complete disaster. The second date was with my future husband.

* * *

Graeme and I had been chatting for a few weeks before we decided to meet. I chose the location – The Jamaica Inn, a cute restaurant situated along the seafront in Bangor, and close to home just in case Graeme turned out to be a crazy axe murderer. I had chosen to sit outside to make the most of the gorgeous sea view. Under the heaters and twinkling fairy lights, it was more romantic than I had anticipated and that made me uncomfortable. I didn't really do romance – not any more, but as far as first dates go this one couldn't have been more perfect!

I found myself attracted to Graeme instantly, drawn to his bright blue eyes and easy-going smile. He talked so confidently and seemed so relaxed, while I was a nervous wreck hiding my shaky, sweaty hands under the table. His life sounded so fresh and exciting, I let him talk, interested to hear more. He had a lot of hobbies and interests, unlike me. He was into sports, but not your usual type. He shot clay pigeons – a sport I'd never heard of until then, and had shot professionally for Northern Ireland, travelling to South Africa in his teenage years to compete. The complete opposite to my teenage years of underage drinking and reckless behaviour. Let's not mention that yet, Alex! He was a keen fisherman and had spent three weeks out in Canada on a fishing trip. All his adventures sounded fascinating. Here was a man who actually had hobbies and interests that didn't revolve around drink, drugs and partying; setting him miles apart from the boys I had dated back home. I found his uniqueness intriguing. Yes, he was a little odd and spoke with a country accent, which I struggled to understand, but I decided I liked him.

Over the next few months Graeme introduced me to his world and I fell in love with it. Every date was an adventure. I acknowledged the thought he put into each experience – it was sweet. I assumed he was trying to show off Northern Ireland in the hope that I'd want to stay, but I had no intention of going anywhere, not for a while anyway. I had made Graeme aware from the start that I still hoped to move to Australia but he was determined to convince me otherwise.

He taught me how to fish, how to shoot, how to golf, how to sail and how to make love, not just have sex. He showed me how to have fun in ways I never could have imagined. We dedicated our time to getting to know one another, taking it slow and steady. I knew his secrets and eventually he knew mine, and surprisingly he accepted them. We cared for one another deeply, and I knew this was different to any past relationship. This was something more.

But what I liked about Graeme more than anything was his determination to make me happy, his awareness of my internal sadness and how much he tried to rectify it.

I fell in love with Ireland, both north and south, and I fell in love with Graeme, the man who finally brought me back to life.

Our first holiday abroad was naturally going to be Egypt – although it had been Graeme's choice not mine, to my surprise. We had booked the trip for my twenty-fifth birthday in June and I was super excited, as I always am before a holiday. Graeme, however, was uptight and slightly off. I didn't know what his problem was but I was already getting irritated by it. He barely said a word in the airport or on the five and a half hour flight. I couldn't understand his behaviour and quite frankly it was ruining our holiday before it even began.

We arrived in Egypt after dark. The restaurant was closed but the bar was still open. We had just finished our second drink when Graeme decided he wanted to go to bed. Already? Maybe he wanted to have hot, steamy sex? Or maybe not. He got straight into bed, gave me a quick peck on the lips and rolled over. So much for a romantic holiday, hey?

The following morning we attended the standard hotel welcome meeting. Browsing through the optional activities and excursions provided by the hotel, Graeme was only interested in one activity: diving. Of course he had no interest in seeing the pyramids or any other cultural excursions. Luckily I was keen to try diving as well. It was something I'd always wanted to do, and we'd spoken about it a few times. In the end we chose a couple of trips. I wanted to make our first holiday as memorable as possible, so we booked a trip to the pyramids, a diving experience, swimming with dolphins and a day out at sea. Graeme was so keen to dive he booked it for the following day.

There were six of us in total on the dive, with two instructors there to keep us right. We were taught the techniques on the beach first and then given the opportunity to practise them in the sea. Before I knew it we were ready to dive – apparently. The oxygen tank was so heavy I could barely wade through the water. My legs were trembling and my anxiety was kicking in as always.

I started panicking and could barely remember a word the instructors said other than thumbs up meant you wanted to resurface.

Graeme was a natural, of course, as he is with all outdoor activities, and I was a disaster. I struggled to equalise under the water. My ears screamed with the pressure and I couldn't get my buoyancy under control. I was either crawling along the seabed or floating off into sea space with the instructor frantically swimming after me, grabbing my ankles and yanking me back down to safety. It was embarrassing. The other holidaymakers were managing fine, but not me. I never saw the swarms of bright orange fish circling us, or the rainbow coral dancing along the seabed. I think there may have been a shipwreck too, but I never caught sight of it either. I was completely blinded in my panic and distracted with the pain in my ears. I was not enjoying the experience. Never again! I thought.

Just when I was about to stick my thumb up and abort, the instructor spun me round. Bobbing in front of me was Graeme, and he was holding a wooden sign in his hands – why did he have a sign? What did it say? I could just about make out the writing through my steamy goggles: Will you marry me, Alexandria? I inhaled one massive gulp of air and my ears suddenly popped – thank God for that!

I was delighted and shocked with his unexpected proposal. We hadn't even mentioned the word *'marriage',* and yet here I was now engaged. I was ecstatic and terrified at the same time. We spent the next few days scouring Egyptian jewellers to pick a ring. The sentimental value of picking my ring in Egypt wasn't lost on me. My ring would come from my dad's birthplace, making it the greatest treasure of all, and was part of Graeme's decision to come to Egypt in the first place. In the end I chose a beautiful 24-carat white gold ring with a generous diamond and unusual surrounding stones. I couldn't take my eyes off it as it twinkled in the sunlight.

Now that Graeme was back to his normal self we could celebrate and enjoy Egypt. He had obviously been worried about the proposal – even though my answer was always going to be yes, but he could relax and take in Egypt for all its beauty now. He actually enjoyed the pyramids more than I did in the end. He embraced the Egyptian culture full-heartedly, which warmed my own heart even more. Sharm El Sheik will forever be our most memorable holiday for so many reasons. By the time we arrived home I still couldn't comprehend that someone loved me enough to marry me. It was the most peculiar feeling and one that I never wanted to end.

* * *

'Why do you want to be a nurse?' a lady in the panel of four asked me at my nursing interview at Queen's University. The most common answers I knew went along the lines of: *'I've wanted to be a nurse my whole life'* or *'I looked after my granny and grandad when I was a teenager'* or *'I'm just a caring person by nature.'* All of which may be true, but more often than not were for the benefit of the interviewer.

Obviously there is something that draws people to the field of nursing – maybe a trauma that occurred within their family, a trauma that happened to the person themselves, the nursing gene runs in their blood or they just like the security of having a job that's promised for life with a decent pension. But more often than not people choose to be a nurse because they are damaged in some way and are seeking to fix themselves.

Truth was, my decision to study mental health nursing wasn't made overnight. It was an idea that developed over several years. It began when I took on a home care job in Blackpool working with the elderly and discovered I was surprisingly good at looking after other people. Caring for others is something that comes naturally to me, more so than caring for myself.

Better still, I enjoyed the work, which was also surprising as I didn't enjoy very much back then other than drinking myself into oblivion.

Naturally I was swayed towards the field of mental health after battling my own mental demons for the majority of my life. I figured, in learning how to help others I may at long last figure out how to help myself. That was the real reason I wanted to be a nurse – because I was damaged goods and I needed to learn how to heal myself.

Of course I passed the interview with flying colours. My rehearsed response that didn't include any of the above went down a treat. Revealing my truth at that stage may have led to failure and failure was not an option. Not this time. So a few weeks later there I was standing in the queue for my first lecture at Queen's University feeling as miniscule as a mouse among an angry herd. My instinct screamed at me to turn tail and run. My palms were clammy, my heart racing, my anxiety stifling.

I was in way over my head. You can't do this, you can't do this, my inner mean girl repeated. Just as I was about to agree and make a swift exit, a young blonde turned and gave me an awkward smile, calming my nerves instantly and convincing me to stay put. The young, pretty blonde was Katie, and we clicked from day one – even more so when we discovered we both shared a passion for travel. By the end of our first lecture our hypothetical trip to Thailand was born, and over the next three years we made that trip a reality.

My friendship circle in uni was small. There was just the three of us: Katie, Georgia and me. I was six years older than them both but the age gap never really bothered me. I liked listening to their relationship dramas and scandal. It made me chuckle. After all, I had been there, done that and worn the bloody T-shirt! I liked being the older, wiser friend for a change. Being responsible was refreshing – well, at least when I was sober, anyway. Some things will never change, hey?

University wasn't quite what any of us were expecting. Our chosen career turned out to be a full-time job long before we qualified. Freshers' parties and summer holidays in Ibiza were totally out of the question. A nursing degree is a seven-day week commitment, unlike most degrees. It was the most stressful three years of our lives, and each of us had a breakdown at one point or another – sometimes on multiple occasions. The pressure was immense. As a matter of fact, it was more than immense – it was completely exhausting.

Unfortunately I had to work and study, like the majority of mature students do. I didn't have the advantage of still living with my parents. I struggled to juggle my job around placements and eventually had to give up my permanent post and work as bank staff instead. Now, bank work is great because it's flexible but it's also temporary, which means there is either loads of work available or none. To get round this, I worked like a horse when the shifts were going to finance myself through the dry spells. University very quickly became all work and no play. Between placements, lectures, exams, assignments, work and bills to worry about, it was a real struggle.

I ended up working night shift instead of days because it meant I could work and go to uni – even though this was probably illegal because there weren't enough rest hours between the two. In fact, there were no rest hours between the two. I'd go from night shift straight to lectures surviving on copious amounts of coffee and energy drinks to get me through the day. In the evening I'd crawl through my front door and collapse on the sofa in an exhausted, shaky mess. It was unhealthy but it was necessary.

I barely saw Graeme or my friends or family during uni – I just didn't have the time. And any free time was dedicated to assignments and revision, and that was my life for three long, tiresome years. The only break I got was my holidays and I lived for them.

Chapter 5

-Some Things Are Meant To Be-

At the end of first year I took a trip with my soon-to-be in-laws. The six of us – Graeme's parents, Andrew and Lynda, and his sister Laura and her husband Willi, jetted off for a two-week break to my parents' old timeshare in Orlando, Florida. We had a jam-packed schedule, ensuring we squeezed in everything Orlando had to offer; purposely saving my favourite park, Disney, to last. We were visiting during my favourite time of year, Halloween, and Disney were throwing their unmissable Mickey's Not-So-Scary Halloween Party.

We arrived at Disney's Magic Kingdom at 7 p.m. sharp, just after sundown. Those with day passes were just leaving as the night owls were entering. There were pumpkin displays everywhere, with over three hundred pumpkins used in Disney's Main Street windows and shopfronts alone! Even more impressive, I later read that no two pumpkins are alike as they are each carved individually by select members of the Resort Enhancement Team. The place looked incredible. Everyone was in fancy dress – entire families had come dressed in costume. I didn't know which way to look.

Andrew and Lynda had decided to sit this one out and have an evening to themselves, so it was just the four of us. We entered the park, were handed trick-or-treat bags and a map of the Halloween trail, and off we went to trick or treat around Disneyland. A dream come true. The weather was horrendous that evening, which only made the night more memorable. The rain forcefully lashed from the heavens but we didn't let it spoil the party. We bought matching Mickey Mouse raincoats and continued along the haunted trail, filling our bags with candy as we went; Laura and I in our element with the two boys traipsing along behind.

When the skies finally cleared the Sanderson Sisters took to the stage performing a tribute act to Disney's Hocus Pocus. Laura and I squeezed our way to the front of the crowd hoping for a better view of the sisters, Winnie, Sarah and Mary, and leaving the boys sitting against a gravestone looking bored already. We managed to secure the perfect spot directly in front of the stage and squealed our way through *'I Put A Spell On You.'* After the witches had finished, Mickey's Boo-To-You Parade started accompanied by Halloween music, spooky costumes, Disney villains and spooktacular dancers. Every character was dressed in costume, including Minnie Mouse. I spotted her standing on her float wearing a dark plum witch outfit waving her broomstick at the crowd, which was more than enough to make me cry – for the umpteenth time that holiday. Disneyland has a funny way of doing that to you – evoking powerful emotions intense enough to make grown adults cry. There's an innocence about the place that naturally brings people back to their childhoods; back to when make-believe was real and happily ever after really did exist. That's how I felt that evening as I stood dripping from head to toe watching the epic show dazzling before me; weeping silently to myself while reminiscing about happy memories from my childhood, back when my family was whole.

Any trip to Disneyland is a special one but this one in particular was special for me. Firstly because I was visiting Orlando as an adult this time round, meaning I could fully understand the magnitude of the theme parks, shows and events and appreciate their creativity, technology and general awesomeness. Secondly, it gave me the opportunity to bond with my in-laws, especially Laura. Although Laura and I had always been friendly, I had never considered us to be close, but after spending two weeks in the most magical place on earth I had gained far more than a friend – I had gained a sister.

It was comforting to feel valued and accepted into a family again. My own family was still a broken one, unfortunately – maybe more so now than ever. Since moving away I'd become even more alienated from both my brother and my mother. Sadly, as new family relationships blossomed, old relationships continued to wither.

I admit I had made less time for my family back home in Blackpool. I was busy creating a new life for myself, which meant I didn't prioritise my old one. Yes, that may have been selfish, but my life had taken a new direction and for once I had to put myself first. I had my own family now, a fiancé, friends, a home to run and a degree to complete. Not to mention that I didn't live just round the corner any more.

I did my best to visit when I could but there was no denying my brother and I had grown apart. I felt that he resented my new-found happiness and lifestyle that I had worked so hard to achieve. He had visited me only once in the three years since I had left home, which Graeme had arranged as a surprise for Christmas. I was delighted to spend time with him and my nephew, Ethan, over the holidays but my brother spent the entire week behaving like he didn't want to be there. He seldom contacted me after that awkward visit and never gave any reason for his strange behaviour. When I FaceTimed my nephew, my brother left the room, which made me upset and uncomfortable, so after a while I stopped communicating too – both with him and Ethan, which I knew was wrong. Ethan was just an innocent victim in our stupid sibling feud. When my brother had his second son Conor, our feud escalated beyond repair.

I delayed meeting newborn Conor until I visited for Ethan's birthday just a few months later. I felt this was justified because it meant I wouldn't have to travel over twice in such a short space of time, but my brother didn't agree – especially as I managed to squeeze in my trip to America before meeting my youngest nephew (which had been booked prior to Conor even being conceived – but that wasn't valid, apparently).

A week before Ethan's birthday a horrible argument blew up between my brother and me – one that had been brewing for months, I guess. After almost a year of silence neither of us had a nice word to say to the other, and by the time the phone call was terminated the damage had been done.

Weeks passed without contact. Weeks that turned into months. Months that turned into years. Not a day went by when I didn't think of my brother and his children. Not a day went by that I didn't regret that awful argument. But I was too proud and too stubborn to be the one to apologise, believing he was just as much in the wrong as I was. I didn't meet Conor until he was three years old and by that time Ethan was six, a fully-grown boy. I was then twenty-eight and in the midst of a chemotherapy battle, unsure how long cancer would grant me with the boys to make up for all that lost time.

* * *

When Graeme and I tied the knot only his parents, my mum and her new husband Oscar were present. We had agreed on a non-religious ceremony, after much dispute. I had wanted a simple celebration, whereas Graeme wanted the traditional white wedding. But I wasn't a woman of faith, so a religious ceremony was completely out of the question for me. Not to mention that a wedding without the bride's family would have been an embarrassment. We compromised on a low-key wedding abroad followed by a big reception at home on our return from Italy.

We invited a hundred guests to our reception at our local golf club – mostly Graeme's family and friends as I wasn't speaking to any of my family except my mother. Unfortunately after the fall out with my brother, my relationship with my granny had also soured.

She had always been exceptionally close to Matthew and naturally sided with him after our argument. We spoke for a while after but our conversations soon become forced. My weekly visits to Bangor turned to fortnightly and then monthly, until my granny and I stopped speaking altogether. Neither one of us really knew why and both of us blamed the other.

I thought about contacting my granny often, but as time went on I lost the courage to pick up the phone. I tried to reconcile by inviting her to the wedding reception but both my granny and my auntie ignored the invitation. After much contemplation I decided not to send my brother and his family an invite at all; unable to deal with the hurt if they rejected me too. What should have been a happy and exciting time for me was unfortunately tainted with sadness. Part of me blamed myself for that sadness and part of me blamed them. I felt a mixture of hurt and resentment; a combination of love and hate.

Graeme and I were married on 29 August 2017. We had chosen the beautiful coastal town of Sorrento as our wedding destination and the ceremony took place on a clifftop facing the stunning Italian Riviera. I was dressed in a fully beaded gown designed by Justin Alexander and the jewels glistened and sparkled under the forty-degree sun. I wore my hair in a curly updo – with a jewelled headpiece picked by my dear friend Gillian, to show off the intricate back design of my dress. My skin glowed with a natural sun-kissed tan and I continued the theme of the natural look – minimal make-up and simple jewellery, not wanting to take any attention away from my dress.

I approached the aisle. My dad's photo smiled up at me from a table filled with stunning yellow roses, my favourite flower. I closed my eyes for a second, feeling the warmth of the sun on my face, and imagined his presence. But it was my mum who gave me away that day – the last person I ever imagined walking me down the aisle. She was dressed all in pink, blending in with the pink rose gardens behind us. I clung to her nervously, terrified I would fall, but I made it up the aisle in one piece.

My mum kissed my cheek and let me go as Graeme turned to me looking as nervous as I was. He smiled sheepishly and whispered, *'You look beautiful.'* I squeezed his hand tightly and didn't let go.

We had written our own vows. Graeme went first with a few short and sweet lines followed by my own lengthy poetry: *'From sunrise to sunset, till death do us part, I promise to love you with all my heart.'* Never once had I considered how quickly those vows could apply to our marriage. We sealed our promise with a kiss, a display of a lifetime commitment to one another. Unbeknown to us, cancer had very different plans.

A guitarist played an acoustic version of our wedding song, Van Morrison's *'These Are The Days'* while we signed our marriage certificate. We had been stuck between Van Morrison and Elvis Presley's *'Can't Help Falling In Love',* but after much debate we went with Graeme's choice of Van Morrison. The guitarist played the song ever so sweetly behind us and I sang along to the lyrics in my head.

A few photos were taken by the cliff edge and in the surrounding gardens, and that was it – the ceremony really was short and sweet. We travelled back into town in an old Fiat 500 – a traditional Italian car, and my heart rate returned to normal as we followed the winding cliff edge back into town. My body began to relax. That was it, the hard part was over. I still clung onto Graeme's hand, though, not quite ready to let it go.

We had asked the photographer to follow us into the town square so he could get some natural shots of us walking through the old cobbled streets. Passers-by clapped and cheered as we walked through the narrow alleyways of Sorrento. *'Bella, Bella,'* they shouted. It was so surreal. Everyone's eyes were on me, and in that moment I really did feel like a princess in my beautiful sparkling gown.

We had chosen a quaint outdoor restaurant for our wedding meal; a garden lit with a soft fairy-like glow that reminded me of a scene from Shakespeare's A Midsummer Night's Dream.

I ordered steak and Graeme ordered pizza. My mum read a short speech and we toasted with champagne followed by a slice of traditional Sorrento lemon sponge. We ended our perfect day with a champagne bellini on the hotel terrace watching the sun go down behind Mount Vesuvius. Incidentally, most of my wedding photos had that mountain situated perfectly in the background. It seemed the mountains had always called out to my soul.

After sunset I changed into a lighter dress and removed my wedding shoes. The six of us chose a table close to the hotel band and relaxed to the music. The last song of the evening began with that all too familiar musical intro. I looked at my husband and smiled as he took my hand and we had our first dance to Elvis Presley's *'Can't Help Falling In Love.'* It had been chosen at random – no one in the audience had requested it, which was our proof that some things really are meant to be. It would seem I got my happily ever after after all.

Chapter 6

-A Black Dog-

I have two black dogs in my life: one that is depression and one that I named Bear.

Many of you will have heard of the Black Dog Campaign, but for those who haven't, let me fill you in. The campaign is about a metaphoric black dog that follows its master - aka a person suffering with low mood or depression, everywhere they go; holding their owner back and preventing them from living a full and happy life. Eventually the master learns to embrace their black dog, tame it, love it and ultimately teach it to heel.

I had been tormented by my very own black dog ever since the death of my father. That unwanted shadow cornered me in my parents' hateful shop on the night I lost my father, and just never left. No matter how hard I tried to shake him, he remained a constant in my life - untameable, unmanageable and unbearable.

My second black dog came into my life as I finished my degree. Graeme had promised me a puppy for my graduation present and I held him to his promise. I had been looking at Springadors - half Labrador, half springer spaniel, but they seemed a little hard to come by, especially in Northern Ireland. Graeme had hinted that he would source my specific pup while I was in Thailand, so I assumed he would surprise me with one when I got home. But a week before I was due to leave we came across an online advertisement for a black Labrador puppy that needed rehomed urgently.

The address was only a ten-minute drive from our house. Surely there was no harm in looking, right?

When we arrived at the owner's house I instantly felt bad vibes. Their home was severely neglected – rubbish and dog waste covered the front garden. It didn't look like a place humans would want to live never mind a dog. I navigated my way through the maze of waste and knocked on the front door. A young teenage girl answered and told me her mother wasn't home but we could see the puppy anyway. We weren't invited inside, which I was thankful for. I could hear other children inside and wondered who was taking care of them and the puppy. I hoped there was some parental guardian on the premises at least.

The pup was just raring to go, wiggling and squirming in the young girl's arms. She dropped him gently and he bounded straight towards me, jumping up at my legs and nibbling at my hands. I could tell he was going to be a handful already but his energy was infectious. He darted about the driveway with his tongue hanging out of his mouth, panting like someone had just administered him adrenaline. I couldn't help but giggle at the sight of this goofy black furball.

Not only did he have a vibrant personality, but he was a handsome fellow too. His coat was completely black – not a spot of white on him, and he was super shiny like a baby seal. He looked healthy despite his unhealthy surroundings. But what captivated me the most about this black dog were his beautiful black eyes. I looked into those eyes and I was sold.

We drove out of the housing estate half an hour later with our gorgeous puppy curled up in my lap. We sealed the deal with a teenager, which I wasn't sure was even legal, but we had paid the full asking price at least. As we were exiting the estate, a neighbour waved us to pull over. My heart instantly sank; I didn't want to hear what they had to say. Turns out my pup had been mistreated

– I knew it! His owners had left him chained up outside at night with no shelter or light. The neighbours had heard him howling, obviously frightened. He was only ten weeks old, just a baby, and he needed nurtured and cared for, not dumped outside along with the rubbish. I cradled my little fur baby even tighter and made a promise to him that I would keep him safe forever. He would be treated as a king from that day forth, and he has been.

I fell in love with my new black dog instantly. He was part of our family from the minute I had laid eyes on him. Graeme and I joke about the intensity of my love for our dog, who I later named Bear. My whole life revolves around him and I wouldn't have it any other way. I honestly believe we were supposed to buy a dog that day, Bear specifically. Call it coincidence or call it fate but Bear needed rescued and we saved him. When I got sick Bear was the only one that never left my side. His loyalty and love stretched beyond the limits of mankind. A dog's love is unconditional and knows no bounds. Me and my black dog rescued each other in the end.

Unfortunately the uninvited black dog inside my head was becoming more of a problem. I was in such a rush to live my life I had stopped enjoying living it. I was so preoccupied with the future I no longer had time for the present. When I finally finished university, after three years of hard work, dedication and exhaustion, I graduated with a first-class honours degree (the highest grade possible). I should have been immensely proud, yet I felt no pride in receiving it. Before I'd even worn my blues – my nursing uniform, I was already pondering what career I could pursue next; how I could climb the professional ladder quicker; how I could earn more money sooner, despite sacrificing my marriage and relationships with my family to become nurse in the first place.

I had given so much of myself and my time to my career, I had saved very little for anyone else. Although Graeme and I loved each other dearly, our marriage was far from perfect – is there even such a thing as a perfect marriage? The honeymoon stage was long gone, and the fairy-tale romance now a forgotten whisper. We argued a lot – like many couples do, especially in that first year of marriage.

But the arguments increased to the point that we couldn't agree on anything any more. Our main problem being that we were, and still are, total opposites. Even though opposites are meant to attract, attraction isn't necessarily the be-all and end-all of a relationship. It takes far more than lust to sustain a healthy marriage. Moving in together was harder than I ever anticipated – especially out in the sticks where we had purchased our first home.

The house was close to Graeme's family, friends, work and beloved golf course but wasn't close to anything that interested me. I wanted to live halfway between the country and the city where there was plenty going on; in a location that would have been suitable and fair for both of us. But Graeme refused to compromise, which meant I was forced to uproot my life yet again. It took years for me to adjust to country living – the sudden isolation, the loneliness, the boredom that all came with living in the middle of nowhere.

We began our married life in a tiny country village where the only source of conversation came from fellow dog walkers in the small park at the end of our road. There was one corner shop (that reminded me of our cursed shop in Blackpool) and one local pub that was rarely open and barely bigger than my front living room. And that was it. There were no local restaurants, no quirky lively bars, no entertainment and no opportunities to socialise and make friends. Just me and my two black dogs for company.

To make things worse Graeme was rarely home. We had got so used to living our lives apart while I was at university, we rarely spent time together now. Once again, those familiar feelings of loneliness crept back in and my depression with it. Graeme knew

I was unhappy. He knew of my desire for a different life and my dreams of moving to Australia but his heart would always remain firmly in Northern Ireland and I had known that when I married him.

I thought about trying for a baby but I knew a baby wouldn't fix us either. I thought about leaving but we were only just beginning. How could I give up on us already?

Realistically, I don't think it would have mattered if we had emigrated to Oz – I doubt I'd have been happy there either. The problem wasn't where we lived, or that my husband was preoccupied with his hobbies, or that I was dissatisfied with my career. The problem lay with me and my relentless mind. Even though I had all I ever wanted, I still felt a deep emptiness that I just couldn't explain. I still didn't feel I was living the life I was destined for. I was still unsure and indecisive of what my future held. I was still lost.

Despite studying mental health nursing for three years and learning all the necessary tools I needed to break free of my depressive black dog, I still refused to access any of the supports available to me – supports that were proven to be successful, supports I encouraged my patients to engage with. I remained ambivalent towards mood-stabilising medication or antidepressants, though I encouraged my patients to remain compliant with theirs. Psychological interventions and talk therapies terrified me and I wasn't mentally prepared for what they would unearth, so I avoided them like the plague while continuing to advise my patients to talk openly and communicate with me. I found therapeutic activities such as relaxation and developing creative skills pointless but pushed my patients towards occupational therapy. I was a hypocrite hiding behind my blue nurse uniform, unable to follow any of my own advice and refusing to admit to myself that I was just as messed-up as my patients.

Stupidly I pinned solving all my problems on my big trip to Thailand. I believed it would provide me with some much-needed time out; time to recharge my batteries, reboot my marriage, restore my balance and finally find myself at long last. Yes, I was back to Eat Pray Love. Again!

I imagined I would go to Thailand and immerse myself in Thai culture: visit Buddhist temples, have relaxing Thai massages on the beach, eat healthy and exotic food, go on jungle treks with elephants, bathe in cleansing waterfalls, learn yoga and the art of meditation, and in the midst of this tranquillity I would miraculously discover my life purpose and my true self. I didn't know then that my purpose was never going to be found on some epic holiday. My purpose could only be found within.

* * *

Thailand turned out to be everything I imagined it would be, and at the same time everything I hadn't. The country was indeed beautiful – there was no denying that, with photo-shoot beaches, jungle terrain and stunning Buddhist temples. It had the scenery, the wildlife, the culture, the beauty – it had it all. But unfortunately it wasn't the Eat Pray Love experience I had been hoping for. Mainly because I was too busy drinking and running away from myself and my unsolvable problems.

Katie and I spent the first week of our trip exploring temples, feeding and bathing elephants, soaring through jungle tops on zip wires and visiting traditional Thai street markets. We ticked off all the standard bucket-list activities. I even got a traditional Thai bamboo tattoo of an elephant on my ribcage. We were definitely living the dream.

On week two we joined a group of thirty people from different nationalities and walks of life. Led by our tour guide – a ladyboy from Bangkok, who was completely wild – the group itinerary took us from one party scene to the next with a few opportunities for activities along the way, which we were usually too hungover to engage in. The days rolled into one big drunken blur, and despite staying in some of the most beautiful surroundings I had ever laid eyes on, I was too drunk to fully appreciate any of it.

The tour came to an end with the infamous Thai Full Moon Party – an all-night beach party on the evening of the full moon. Katie and I were in our element drinking buckets of vodka and dancing among hundreds of tourists without a care in the world. Dressed in our fluorescent T-shirts and multicoloured face paints, we were having the time of our lives.

But while I was chasing my youth and trying to figure out who the feck I was in Thailand, my husband was home alone looking after our new puppy, paying our bills and missing his wife. I had selfishly given little thought to how my trip, and reckless behaviour, would affect my husband. We barely contacted each other during my month away –something we both blamed on the time difference but really it was because I was enjoying myself a little too much. Graeme would ring when I was getting ready for another big night out. I always told him I'd ring him back when I got home, but I never did. I was usually too drunk and passed out by that point. I knew my behaviour was selfish. I was a married woman approaching my thirties, not some carefree lassie with no responsibilities on a college gap year. I had hoped Thailand would bring us closer together, but all it did was drive us further apart.

Naturally, when I returned home I wasn't greeted with the warm reception I'd hoped for. There was a horrible tension in our marital home – a tension that had been caused by me. Graeme and I accepted we were unhappy and spoke seriously about separating, but we chose to stay together and try and make it work out of love and out of fear – fear of losing the other. It was a tense time in our marriage with one nagging question looming over us: was love really enough any more?

Chapter 7

-Everest-

My solution to my marital problems were simple: avoid, avoid, avoid. I took on extra shifts at work, preferring to be on the ward than at home. Rarely taking a day off, even though I was exhausted and stressed out of my mind, I found it easier to handle the challenging ward dynamics and sometimes difficult psychiatric patients than face the confrontations between my husband and me. When I wasn't working I was in the gym.

I started with a personal trainer and found a new love for weight training. At first my goals were healthy and achievable ... until I started obsessively counting calories. Then everything revolved around numbers. Between calorie counting and weighing myself every morning, I was like a woman possessed; determined to keep losing weight even though I was already very slim. My training intensified after Graeme and I booked our trip to Everest base camp. Both of us knew the trip would either make us or break us. Our marriage was now in the unpredictable hands of the mountain.

Everest is a goal for many fitness fanatics, keen hikers and people who genuinely enjoy living on the edge – of which Graeme is none, by the way, so I was surprised when he first mentioned the trip to me. I turned it down immediately – trekking for fourteen days through barren lands, winding paths, ice and freezing snow just did not appeal; never mind the altitude and level of fitness required to tolerate such heights. I pleaded, could we not try and resolve our differences on a Caribbean cruise or an exotic trip to Bali? But Graeme was relentless.

Thailand had been my dream and Everest was his. I'd had my fun, and now it was time for him to have his, and I could hardly argue with that.

In an attempt to interest me, Graeme played me a YouTube clip of a couple who had videoed their experience on the mountain. I feigned interest at first but as the video continued I became more intrigued. I couldn't deny that the scenery was breathtakingly beautiful. We watched the pair trek through wide open valleys and dense forest lands, over tiny wooden rope bridges and across glacial rivers, and through Sherpa mountain villages. It looked magnificent and certainly a once in a lifetime experience.

It wasn't the physical aspect of the trek that drew me in – or even the views, it was the spirit of the journey; the chance to visit authentic Nepalese communities: Kathmandu, Lukla, Namche Bazaar, Tengboche, Dingboche and finally base camp, and the opportunity to taste the sensual flavours of Himalayan cuisine. As a foodie I was keen to try traditional Nepalese dal – a soup made of lentils and spices served over boiled grain; tarkari – spicy vegetable curry; delicious momos – steamed dumplings filled with mincemeat; traditional Himalayan teas, such as butter tea, made from butter, ghee and salt; and strong alcohol intended to warm hikers in the freezing temperatures.

I wanted to experience the religious traditions of the Sherpa people, who practice the ancient school of Buddhism; to observe the simplicity of the Tibetan way of life; to watch elite mountaineers who live and breathe the mountains – to even get the chance to speak to such unique individuals, who make a living from guiding tourists through one of the most dangerous terrains on earth, often losing their lives in the process.

It only took one video for me to see that Everest was more than just a mountain and the trek was more than just a difficult hike. The journey to base camp has been referred to by many as the *'steps to heaven'* and after watching that video I agreed with them. I was hooked. I started conducting my own research into the mountain.

I watched the 2015 film Everest. Based on a true story, almost every character died during the expedition. But that didn't put me off. I read Ben Fogle's account of his journey to the summit in his book UP and similar accounts of those who had made it to the top. Fascinated by their experiences, I soon recognised a common occurrence between the mountaineers' memoirs: those who had been brave enough – or perhaps crazy enough, to find themselves in the presence of Everest had changed significantly on the journey.

The fitness fanatics had connected to the mountain on a spiritual level as well as connecting with themselves; becoming aware of what was important in life, what mattered and how valuable life truly is. Such enlightenment often occurs when faced with our own mortality. When we are pushed beyond the limitations of normal daily living we become more in tune with our divine selves. Everest offered such rare liberties. If you were lucky enough to make it down alive, that is.

My training schedule for Everest was relentless. I trained before and after work – whether that was at five thirty in the morning before a long day or straight after night shift with zero hours' sleep. I incorporated a mixture of cardio, strength training and endurance into my fitness regime, which included walking on the step machine with a 30 kg weighted jacket slung over my shoulders and regular hikes up the Mourne Mountains – the only mountains close to our home. I timed myself up and down those mountain hills, ensuring I beat my time on each occasion. Never really seeing how spectacular they were, my eyes glued to my watch instead of my beautiful surroundings. The regime was enslaving, and I took great pleasure in the progress I was making. Every achievement was one step closer to that mighty mountain – and that mighty new me. Or so I believed.

Initially Everest had been my sole goal – the reason behind such demanding gym workouts and the ridiculous diet plan I had set myself, but before I knew it my weight had become my only focus. As I mentioned earlier, I've always been curvy, but all of a sudden I was a slim size eight. My legs were solid – I had quads, actual visible quad muscles! My back was defined, my arms toned, my butt firm and pert. I couldn't help but be impressed with this new hot bod staring back at me in the mirror. But my new self-love was also self-hate.

I couldn't go a single day without training in the gym or without weighing myself. Every time I reached my target weight I lowered the target. The lower my weight the more my confidence soared. For the first time in my life I felt attractive and, dare I say it, sexy. I bought skimpy new outfits that I would previously have avoided; delighting in showing off my brand-new body. I plastered my Instagram with progress pictures of me in my gym gear wearing only a sports bra and thong (against my husband's wishes), delighting in the compliments I received under each picture. But what I didn't share was the anxiety I felt every time I went over my calorie deficit, or the shame when I frequently used laxatives after eating a takeaway, or that I starved myself all week for one night out at the weekend, or that I often woke in the middle of the night to add a forgotten food item to the count. I didn't share the heated rows between my husband and me when he told me I'd gone too far, or that my friends were bored listening to me talk about food and calories, or how I cried if I put on a single pound. No, I kept that part of my weight loss well hidden.

* * *

I was sitting in the passenger seat of my friend Jenna's car with a tin of strawberry cider in one hand and my phone in the other, posing for another ridiculous selfie. My two girlfriends were laughing and joking behind me. We were on a girls' trip – Dublin bound. I was dolled up to the nines, my hair curled, with two buns on top of my head that were meant to look like horns.

My eyes were painted bright pink with layers of glitter, done professionally that morning. My eyelashes were over the top and heavy; my lips overdrawn to stand out.

Jenna sat beside me donned in her Scary Spice outfit – leopard-print clothing and bright green eyeshadow. Karen was dressed as Baby, all in pink with pigtails in her hair, and Barbara, well, Barbara's just Barbara – she doesn't conform to dress codes, and I was Sporty Spice, of course, dressed in a white cropped T-shirt, black shorts and chunky platform trainers. In case you haven't guessed yet, we were on our way to see our favourite nineties girl band – The Spice Girls.

We listened to the girls' album on repeat the whole way down. I'd been listening to it for weeks now to ensure I remembered every lyric. The energy in the car was pumping – every one of us singing even though only one of us could actually sing, and it certainly wasn't me. But I sang along anyway as if I hadn't a care in the world.

Barbara requested a toilet stop for the third time – I swear that girl's bladder must be the size of a pea. We stopped at another Applegreen petrol station and I went in with her this time, even though I didn't need the toilet. I wanted to check my bra. Strange,

I know, but I was wearing a white *'Spice it Up'* T-shirt and was scared it would give away my dirty secret. I closed the toilet door and took a quick peek. Phew, there was only a small blob of blood. I wiped my nipple clean and hoped it would behave itself, just for today. I headed back to the car, mentioning nothing to my friends. Now was not the time. We were meant to be having fun, remember?

I'd first noticed the bleeding two weeks prior to the concert. I'd been at a physio session working on some pain in my right ankle – torn ligaments, the physio thought, probably from overdoing it in the gym training for my big Everest trip, and now the New York Marathon that I had somehow been roped into completing. After seeing the physio I had come home to change and noticed an orangey-red bloodstain in my white sports bra and instantly felt afraid – more than afraid, actually, more like terrified. I knew from the moment I saw that stain it was a sign of something sinister, but I was too afraid to believe what I already knew in my heart, so I convinced myself it was just fake tan, even though I hadn't worn fake tan in months.

The following morning I took a hot shower and decided to have a poke around my left breast, obviously hoping to find nothing and just bin the dirty sports bra – never give it a second thought. Oh, how I wish that had been the case. Instead, I stared down in horror and watched the dark thick blood ooze from my nipple, and I knew. I knew from that moment on. I had cancer.

I contacted the doctor the following morning. My doctors are notoriously difficult to get an appointment with, so I was surprised when the receptionist asked me to come in that afternoon. I was glad to be seen by a female doctor – I didn't fancy a male copping a feel at my breasts. The doctor was young and pleasant enough. I decided I liked her. I have an awful habit of judging whether I like someone or not within moments of meeting them. In most cases my first impressions aren't right but on this occasion they were. I held my breath as the good doctor examined me and waited for the bleeding to start. But none came. Of course, my boob was going to make a liar out of me. Or maybe I had imagined it all, please, God.

Even without the mystical bleeding, the doctor could feel a large, hardened mass of breast tissue down the side of my left breast. It seemed to be deep, near the chest bone, which was probably why I had never felt it. She referred me to the breast clinic and red-flagged my appointment but reassured me it was only a precaution because of my apparent nipple bleeding, which she believed was more than likely caused by an infection. After all, I was only twenty-seven. It was highly unlikely to be the dreaded C-word. I exited the surgery, sat in my car outside and sobbed. I already knew she was wrong.

An urgent referral usually takes two to three weeks. My appointment came ten days later and was scheduled on the day of the Spice World Tour. What were the chances?
I had been a Spice Girls superfan ever since I could remember. As a child I had been guilty of wearing the platform shoes and Union Jack crop tops. My favourite Spice was Ginger back then and I loved dressing up as her. I watched the girls' movie on repeat even if the plot was a little weird and silly. I knew the likelihood of the Spice Girls ever doing another concert was slim. This was my one and only chance to see my childhood idols, so I decided to reschedule the breast appointment. The cancer would still be there in a few days' time regardless, I thought.

So here I was on my way to Dublin singing my heart out to *'Spice Up Your Life'* and ignoring the wet moisture oozing into my bra. I never mentioned the C-word on the two-hour car journey or throughout the concert. I kept my disease to myself, already ashamed of it. Despite my fears I felt like a million dollars that night. I was the slimmest I had ever been – down to a tiny size six now. I showed off my new body that I had murdered myself for, quite literally it would seem, and posed for pictures with my friends.

I drank way too much, smoked way too much and waved my light-up wristband in the air in that illuminated arena, squealing away to my favourite songs like I just didn't care. All the while knowing I had cancer.

I spoke of the bleeding only with Barbara, much later in the evening, when I had drank enough alcohol to reveal my secrets and was seeking her sound advice. Barbara agreed with my GP and was adamant it was only an infection. After all, I was way too young, too fit, too healthy. There was no way it could be the C-word. *'It will all be fine,'* she reassured me, but I knew she was wrong too.

Four days later I was sitting in those horrible blue plastic hospital chairs staring Dr Death in the face, wishing I was back in that arena again, happy and carefree, showing off the body that had completely failed me, singing '*Spice Up Your Life*'.

Part Two

we're the mountains
we need to climb;
we're our own impossible peak.
everything that we seek
is dissolved by success;
only the trackless path
is worth travelling on.

Ben Okri, Everest

Chapter 8

-Why me?-

'I'm sorry, it's cancer.'

I wasn't shocked when I heard the dreaded C-word finally said aloud for the first time. I just stared blankly at the middle-aged doctor with the serious expression on his face and replied, *'That's fine.'*

It was only when the doctor, who I later nicknamed Dr Death, mentioned the word *'mastectomy'* that I finally broke down – alongside my friend. I sobbed not because I had cancer, but because I had to undergo major surgery and lose my breast. I sobbed not because my life was now threatened by a deadly disease, but because of my body. The body that I had just worked my ass off to achieve was now going to be ruined forever.

'The main thing is it's treatable', he said with half a smile. I pondered the word *'treatable'* – what did that even mean? I had no idea what cancer treatment entailed back then. In fact, I shamefully knew very little about the disease other than it kills millions of people and can be incurable.

I was moved to another room, offered more tissues and was greeted by a red-headed nurse who explained that she was now my Breast Care Nurse, or BCN. She attempted to comfort me as best she could, but as a stranger she didn't know me, not yet anyway. She guided me through a rather lengthy pink information book. (Yes, everything to do with breast cancer is pink even though there is nothing pretty and pink about it.) I watched my BCN run through this pink mumbo jumbo. Her mouth was moving but there was no sound coming out.

I stared down at the pink folder instead, in an attempt to make head or tail of what she was saying. But the only word I could see on every page was CANCER.

Eventually I was allowed to leave, with all my information and contact numbers in hand. I was armed with the relevant information to take on cancer. Apparently. I phoned Graeme at work and sobbed down the phone. I can't recall exactly what I said or his initial response, I just knew he was on his way to me. As I left the hospital I was aware of how incredibly tired I suddenly felt. My body felt lifeless; as if it had immediately started shutting down when it heard the C-word, just like my brain had.

My black dog smiled his toothy grin at me, and his big black tail wagged with evil excitement. My overwhelming fear was sending him into a frenzy. It's difficult to put into words, but it's a fear I imagine to be similar to that of a murder victim; the fear they experience before they take their last breaths while staring into the evil eyes of their killer. That's how I felt at that moment – like I was staring death in the face with nowhere to run, nowhere to escape. I didn't know what to do or where to go, so my friend carefully directed me back to her car and, somehow, I ended up on my in-laws' doorstep like a little lost sheep, hoping someone would be home.

I rang the bell and waited. My mother-in-law later confessed that she had been too afraid to answer the door that day. She knew I had been at the clinic and sensed the news wasn't good, so she hid in her back room and willed me to go away. When I didn't go, she had no choice but to answer the door. I hadn't noticed her delay – I was too distracted by my annoyingly chipper black dog beside me.

Again, I can't remember what I said to her when she eventually opened the front door. I just recall her throwing her arms around me and crying hysterically. My father-in-law Andrew had no words.

He just sat speechless and sobbed quietly at the kitchen table. When Graeme arrived I managed to walk over to him on unsteady feet, with my black dog nudging me along. My head was dizzy and my eyes were puffy. I felt Graeme's body trembling as he held me close. I sensed his fear matched my own. *'We will get through this together,'* he whispered, and my black dog stared from one cancer victim to the other, continuing to beat his tail off the ground.

I only told a select few about my diagnosis. I cowardly sent out a generic text message to a handful of my closest friends in the middle of the night, sobbing on my sofa and clinging onto my actual black dog, Bear, while trying to process what the hell had just happened to me. To make things even worse, the day I was diagnosed I still wasn't speaking to any of my family – my mum now included. I wasn't going to contact them now, just because I was dying. I didn't want their pity. Instead, I decided I would face this battle alone. The less people who knew the better.

However, Chloe disagreed and told my brother the following morning. Only minutes after their conversation, my brother picked up the phone and rang me for the first time in three years. *'It's me,'* was all he could muster through his tears. My mum rang shortly after, annoyed that I hadn't called her when I had first discovered the bleeding. Maybe they did care about me after all?

The next morning I was left alone. Graeme had to speak with his managers and explain our devastating situation. I said I'd be fine by myself for an hour or two, but I wasn't. Suddenly I was afraid, afraid to be alone, as if I would just snuff it at any given moment now that I had cancer, so I arranged to meet Jenna. She had received my death message through the night and knew my situation. I chose to meet at my favourite coffee house, Time – how ironic, I thought, as I glanced at the signpost outside: TIME – the very thing I was seemingly running out of.

Jenna asked the questions and I answered them as best as I could, but it felt like we were talking about someone else's cancer, not mine.

I struggled to make eye contact with Jenna, and when I did I started to tear up. Then Jenna mentioned Everest and my composure melted entirely, and I cried into my coffee cup. I knew the trip would be cancelled now. I knew Graeme and I would never make it to the highest mountain in the world. Well, not with each other, anyway. Even if I somehow survived cancer, I doubted I would ever be fit for base camp. I doubted I'd even manage my regular home hikes in the Mourne Mountains never mind Everest. All those hours on that bloody step machine with that damn weighted jacket had been for absolutely nothing.

'You have your own Everest to climb now, Alex,' Jenna whispered, gently taking my hands and crying along with me. Except this mountain was even deadlier.

* * *

I experienced my second period of grief in my young life after being diagnosed with cancer – which is unfortunately common for anyone with the disease. It's difficult to avoid the overwhelming sense of loss after hearing the word *'cancer'* – and not just loss of hair or breasts or other limbs and organs, but loss of life.

After the initial shock of my diagnosis wore off, I grieved for the woman I was, and I mourned my old life – a life I had been robbed of and a life I knew I would never get back. Nothing would ever be the same again – I would never be the same again, and I couldn't help but ask why. Why had this happened to me? Why did I have cancer? Why me?

Naturally I started looking for answers and always came to the same conclusion whatever avenue I explored: this is my fault. I began an in-depth analysis of my life beginning with childhood. I retraced my tracks trying to put the clues together. I figured that the loss of my father was probably the initial trigger – that childhood trauma must have seriously impacted my physical and mental well-being, making my body more susceptible to disease.

Losing my dad the way I did also made me believe I would die young – a belief that only added further stress to my already stressful life. Maybe that belief had somehow manifested into reality. Maybe I had believed myself into having cancer.

Then there was the fact that I was a smoker and had been since the age of twelve. I mean, I had willingly poisoned my body with those cancer sticks for the last sixteen years and then had the cheek to ask, why me? Although there isn't a strong link between breast cancer and smoking and it was highly unlikely that smoking had been the root cause, according to my oncologist, of course I blamed my daily ten for giving me cancer.

Or maybe I had cancer because I was a bad person: because of all the drink and recreational drugs I had consumed when I was younger, or the family fall outs, or the arguments with my friends. I mean, good people don't get cancer, do they? As a child I believed God took my dad away because I was a bad child, and now he had given me cancer because I was bad grown-up. Even worse, I had refused to believe in God after he stole my dad from me, so maybe this was my punishment. Maybe I deserved this?

Or maybe I had cancer because I had been living in fight or flight mode for most of my adult life, riddled with anxiety and depression yet never seeking help for either. From working in overdrive for the last five years and never giving my body or mind a break, for putting myself under unnecessary stress during university, for punishing my body by living off caffeine and zero hours of sleep, for choosing to work in the most stressful and challenging environments, for worrying about my marriage constantly and doing everything I could to sabotage it, for falling out with my whole family and becoming even more isolated than before. I mean, is it any wonder I was now dying?

Or maybe I had cancer because I had spent the last year practically starving myself; not giving my body the right nutrition it needed to function and then slaughtering it in the gym every day and expecting it to remain healthy. I'd come home from most workouts and collapse on the sofa in an exhausted mess, sleeping for hours afterwards. Occasionally I had wondered if this was normal but I'd always put it down to overexertion and too many night shifts, not cancer. I hadn't realised there was a disease eating away at my body, or that my obsession with my weight had possibly initiated it.

The truth is, I will never know why I got cancer – but that didn't stop me torturing myself looking for the answer. I now believe it was probably a combination of all of the above that led to my diagnosis, but I'll never be given an evidence-based reason behind why me.

After the why came the guilt, and even worse the regret. I looked at my life and wished I'd lived it differently. I'd wasted so much time being an angry, stubborn, foolish woman and missing out on valuable time with my family; missing out on valuable time with my husband. I wished I had met Graeme earlier and started a family of my own when we had the chance. I doubted we would ever become parents now, or I wouldn't anyway. I looked into my husband's eyes and wondered if he would remarry.

Would he find love again? Would he have a family of his own? Would he replace me? I couldn't blame him if he did. He deserved to be happy. Cancer was my punishment not his.

My thoughts naturally turned dark. Consumed with self-loathing, self-pity and hate, I spent days hiding in the house, sitting on the floor crying hysterically. Sobbing so hard, I literally thought my heart was breaking in two. When I wasn't crying, I was screaming. I would scream at myself, at a God I refused to believe in, at my husband, at my mum, at my brother, at thin air. I was so angry at everyone and everything, and I hated myself for it. I hated how everyone else's life continued while mine stopped dead in its tracks.

I envied Graeme as he left for work every morning; his routine carrying on as normal while I was stuck at home watching mindless daytime TV and wallowing in my own despair. How could he function as normal? How could he go to work at all? How could he leave me here alone?

I resented my friends heading off on their summer vacations and girls' nights out. How dare they continue to live their carefree lives. How dare they have fun without me.

I was jealous of my work colleagues having craic in the staffroom and out at work parties. Did they not know their colleague and supposed friend was dying? Did they not care at all? I started to feel like no one really cared and that hurt and, even worse, made me bitter.

You see, when a person is diagnosed with cancer they immediately enter a club. The only club no one wants to join: The Cancer Club. From the day you hear that dreaded word, you automatically become an outcast. People perceive you differently than before. They approach you differently, look at you differently, speak to you differently, treat you differently; or they don't know how to be around you at all and hide away instead. Only those in The Cancer Club will truly understood how you are feeling. Unless a person has been directly affected by the disease themselves, they can never fully understand your suffering no matter how hard they try. An outsider can never fathom what it truly feels like to live with the assumption that you're dying. Whenever people tried to relate to me, it only made me angrier and more upset because it was a lie. They didn't know how I felt. They didn't know my crippling pain, my fears, my sorrow, my grief. How could they?

Now I'm not saying my illness didn't affect those around me. It undoubtedly did, and I'm sure I wasn't the only one who shed tears over my cancer or lost more than a night's sleep over it. But unlike me my family and friends could still plan for their futures – have babies and raise their children, plan big trips away, take a new job offer, go to work every day, enjoy themselves in general. Their lives hadn't really changed. Yes, I was probably in the back of their minds but I knew that as much as these people loved me, cancer didn't infiltrate their thoughts twenty-four hours a day, every day, like it did mine. They were still able to escape the disease because they weren't the ones living with it, whereas I had nowhere to run and nowhere to escape because my cancer was mine and mine alone to bear.

How could I not sit in bitter contemplation and ask, why me?

* * *

I was diagnosed two weeks before my twenty-eighth birthday – happy birthday to me! I always liked to celebrate my birthday away, so Graeme had booked us a trip to Cannes in the south of France before we knew about the dreaded C. I, naturally, didn't feel like celebrating this one – not now that my life was ruined, but the holiday was already booked and paid for, and I had already decided that this holiday, and birthday, would be my last. Surely I'd be dead before the next one.

Before I could make my final outbound flight, however, I had scans to attend to. Scans that would detect if the cancer had spread, which I was adamant it had. Call me pessimistic but I had already envisioned my body riddled with the vicious disease. It was only a matter of time before it would finish me off for good.

Chloe and Kelly flew over for scan day. I didn't ask them to but they came anyway. I sat with my two oldest friends – one of whom I hadn't spoken to in years, in the hospital waiting area; all three of us trying to make light of my situation, all three of us afraid to show fear in front of the others. After hours of being hoked and poked at with needles, blue dye, giant polo-mint machines that made me feel like I had pissed myself, I was free to go. I walked out of the last scan and lost the feeling in my legs. My false facade collapsed beneath me. The tears started to flow, and my old friends broke down with me.
We stood in our own private bubble of hell in the middle of the busy hospital corridor, no longer capable of ignoring the cancer in the room. All we could do now was wait.

I had been told the date I would get my results: 10th June, the day after my birthday, so I decided to make my last birthday a memorable one and celebrate it while I was still capable of celebrating anything. Graeme and I travelled to Monaco for the day – a millionaire's playground that instantly stole our hearts. We spent hours down at the harbour admiring the fancy ships and yachts. I imagined what a life at sea would feel like – how freeing it would be. Oh, how I wished to be free. A gift I had taken for granted until now. We walked along the Monaco Grand Prix track, which I have to admit was rather impressive – and that's coming from a non- Formula 1 fan. The views were spectacular at every twist and turn. I imagined the adrenaline coursing through the drivers' veins as they sped along the track and how alive they would feel as they raced. I wished I could feel that life in my veins again instead of decay.

We had lunch at the highly recommended Café de Paris where Graeme treated me to a fancy-pants birthday meal and a bottle of fancy French wine. My man doesn't like wine, so I necked the entire bottle myself. Sure, why not? I'd not be having a birthday drink next year. I watched the Ferraris and Lamborghinis pulling up outside the casino we were facing, in awe and slightly jealous of how the other half live. Graeme and I had dressed for the occasion, though, and we almost passed for rich kids. Him in his white shirt and trousers, silver Ray-Bans and shiny shoes, and me in an orange and cream pinstriped dress paired with white heeled sandals and matching handbag. We both looked the part. You would never have known we were members of the working class, let alone that I had cancer.

The casino oozed class from the moment you entered. I sat at the bar sipping on a glass of sparkling champagne whilst Graeme sat at the blackjack table, in his element, thrilled when he won a bob or two. I found myself relaxing in those luxurious surroundings, especially after an entire bottle of wine and a glass of bubbly. When we got back to the hotel I allowed Graeme to touch me for the first time since I'd been diagnosed. I hadn't wanted to look at my body after I had found out it had failed me, so naturally I hadn't wanted Graeme to see or touch it now that it no longer felt like mine. But that night I managed to own my own skin just one last time. When we finished having sex I cried myself to sleep wondering if that was to be our last night of passion together.

The following morning we hired a pair of sunloungers on a private beach away from the crowds. Today was another big day: it was the day I got my results. I wore a bright orange plunging swimsuit that I had bought specifically to show off my small, pert breasts for the last time. Graeme and I fooled about taking pictures of me at the water's edge, posing like a model. He usually hated taking my picture but that day he didn't seem to mind.

As the hours passed our nervousness intensified. At 2 p.m. on the dot I got the call. My hands shook as I answered. This is it, this is where they tell me I'm dying. But the news was quite the opposite. The cancer hadn't spread and was contained entirely to my left breast, or so they believed, but it was very close to my chest wall and I would still require a full mastectomy. I cried tears of joy while Graeme popped the champagne. For the first time since my diagnosis I allowed myself to feel a tiny glimmer of hope. Maybe, just maybe, I could survive this.

Chapter 9

-The Red Devil-

I returned home from the French Riviera to my first oncology appointment. My oncologist was the complete opposite to my breast care consultant. He had a happy, friendly demeanour as opposed to Dr Death's composed and serious nature. He was an older man – I would estimate late fifties, early sixties, and was dressed in a shirt and tie. He greeted Graeme and me with a dazzling debonair smile and a firm handshake, which made me feel a little more at ease. This man clearly meant business (although he had extremely dark eyebrows that reminded me of Jim Levenstein's dad from the American Pie movies – Eugene Levy, in real life, which made his appearance slightly comical. He will forever be known as *'Jim's dad',* Graeme and I decided).

Jim's dad explained my cancer in great detail. He was extremely knowledgeable and quite fascinating to listen to – or would have been if he wasn't talking about me. I learnt that my cancer was oestrogen driven, which apparently is the best breast cancer to have. I'm not sure there is any best cancer to have, but, hey, I went along with it. The reason it's better is because there are preventative measures available following treatment for oestrogen-driven cancer; treatments that could reduce my risk of a recurrence. Such measures were in the form of hormone therapy; a therapy that would prevent my ovaries producing oestrogen, hence ridding my body of the fire that had fuelled my cancer in the first place – or something like that. The downside, however, is that oestrogen-positive cancer also tends to be less receptive to chemotherapy, meaning chemo may not work.

Jim's dad didn't hide the magnitude of my problem. He was brutally honest when he explained my scan results and didn't cushion me from the outcomes. I was grateful for his honesty – as well as terrified by it, but I needed to know the truth and respected the man with the big, dark, funny eyebrows for giving it to me. I still respected him even after he asked me to make the hardest decision of my life: *'Do you wish to delay chemotherapy to undergo fertility treatment and preserve your eggs or proceed immediately with active treatment at the risk of becoming infertile?'*

Jim's dad told me he didn't want to influence my decision but made it clear that he advised me to proceed with chemo immediately. I'm not stupid. I had grasped that my cancer was severe. The breast cancer I had was Stage 3 oestrogen-positive invasive ductal carcinoma – a tongue-twister at its finest. My tumour was large (the size of a lime by the time it was removed) and my breast ducts were riddled with the disease. I knew that if I delayed treatment, I risked the tumour growing bigger and spreading into the nearby lymph nodes, meaning my chances of survival would be much less.

Graeme and I weighed up the pros and cons in a matter of minutes and decided that having a baby wasn't worth risking my life. I feared leaving a child without a mother more than I feared never becoming a mother at all. So, on that day and with a heavy heart, I signed the consent form to begin chemotherapy and gave up my dreams of motherhood, which was probably the most selfless act I have ever made.

Chemo is known to cause infertility in women who are premenopausal, like myself. The drugs can affect the functioning of the ovaries and the quality of a woman's eggs, hence making conception much more difficult. I was told that my periods would likely stop – maybe temporarily or maybe permanently, although my oncologist was hopeful they would return because of my young age. Still, it was a gamble I'd have preferred not to take. A gamble most women don't have to take because breast cancer treatment usually involves surgery first, giving women time to harvest their eggs. But

my treatment plan was back to front: I was to have chemo first and surgery later, as advised by my oncology team.
The logic behind this was to try and shrink the tumour before it was removed to lessen the extent of surgery.

Although I had the right to refuse their plan and seek a second opinion, I chose not to. I wasn't the expert here and I trusted my team, but, Sod's Law, it turned out their plan didn't work. Chemo failed and I lost more than just my hair because of it. But even experts cannot predict the outcome of cancer treatment. Every human body is different and complex. Each body will have a different response to chemo drugs. Jim's dad could never have known that my body wouldn't respond.

And as if being forced into making a decision about whether or not I had time to freeze my eggs wasn't enough, that day I was hit with a double whammy. Never mind how life-changing the previous conversation had been, now I had another upsetting scenario to contemplate: there was no possibility of having an implant immediately after my mastectomy. My cancer was just too extensive and they would have to remove everything – my nipple, breast muscle, breast skin and surrounding breast tissue. It left me no room to have an implant fitted underneath. My oncologist talked me through other reconstructive options, but warned me that a reconstruction would never completely replicate my breast. I would also never have feeling in a fake boob and would have to have a fake nipple reconstructed and tattooed on.

In Northern Ireland there are only three types of breast reconstruction available: the first type, as I mentioned above, uses an implant situated underneath the muscle of the breast wall, which my medical team had already ruled out for me. The second type uses a flap of muscle from the latissimus dorsi muscle in your back. The third and most drastic type of reconstructive surgery uses fat and tissue from the lower part of the belly. I, of course, didn't have enough fat in my lower belly after my stupid six-pack goals.

Therefore my only choice was the second one – my lats. But that wasn't a straightforward choice either (when is anything in this game?) because surgery can lead to a weakened back and shoulder muscles, and further complications in later life.
For me that would mean weight training would be difficult, and it would also involve cutting directly through the Arabic tattoo I have on my back – a tattoo I had chosen especially for my father, a special quote I had found when I was eighteen that symbolised my pain after losing the most important person in my life. I looked at my husband and he knew instantly what I was thinking: reconstructive surgery wasn't an option, at least not in the immediate future anyway. At twenty-eight I would be a *'freak'*, and could potentially have to live with only one boob for the rest of my life.

* * *

I was sitting in the dreaded chemo chair watching a nurse flood the red devil poison into my veins – the poison that could take away my fertility, my hair, my nails, my self-esteem, my confidence, my independence and my identity, and still I smiled watching it snake its way into my body. I chatted to the nurse as she pumped six large syringes of chemo into one tiny vein in my wrist. I made jokes with my husband, wanting him to feel at ease. Acting my way through the procedure with an Oscar-winning performance, hiding the terror I felt within.

Six hours later I left the hospital feeling relatively normal. I hadn't mutated into some kind of chemo monster, not yet at least. I came home, got into my new Princess Jasmine jammies that Gillian had bought me and drank the ginger tea my cousin had brought up to help with sickness. So far so good. I sat in my new massage chair that Graeme had purchased to keep Bear from jumping up at me during treatment. Even though I hated the thing from the moment

I saw it, I sat in it to appease him, but to me it was a sick chair. My sick chair.

I was on to my fourth episode of The Walking Dead series and still no sign of any sickness when I found myself surprisingly hungry – actually I was famished. I hadn't eaten a thing all day in fear of bringing it back up again but all seemed well on the sickness Western Front. Stupidly I thought it was a good idea to order Chinese – chicken curry and egg fried rice, my favourite dish. Surely I deserved a treat after what I'd been through that day, and I figured I had been lucky to somehow escape the sickness.

Less than an hour later I seriously regretted that chicken curry. After heaving up the last bloody grain of rice followed by my entire stomach contents, I made a mental note to myself: in future no more takeaways after chemo. I was shocked at how quickly the sickness kicked in. One minute I was sitting comfortably in my sick chair, belly full of Chinese, Bear curled up at my feet, watching zombies on the TV, and the next minute I felt a severe rush of heat coursing through my body and began vomiting uncontrollably. The anti-sickness meds hadn't even scratched the surface.

As the night progressed the sickness got worse, even though there was nothing left in my stomach to bring up. I genuinely believed this was the end – that I'd been obliviated by the first round of chemo. Ding, ding, knocked out in the first round. I moved into the spare room to avoid waking Graeme every ten minutes or so when another wave of sickness washed over me, and eventually gave up on a bed altogether, making the cold bathroom floor my permanent residence for the night.

If you imagine that first dose of chemo as worse than your worst hangover – the type where you can't move from bed for days and lose half a stone in vomit – well, yes, chemo hangover was a whole new level of hell. My head pounded as if my skull was caving in. My body went from boiling to freezing in a matter of seconds. My jammies were drenched in sweat. My pulse raced so hard and fast I could hear it pounding in my ears. My hands shook, my legs shook – everything shook. I felt dizzy and light-headed, and I just couldn't stop being sick. I spent the rest of the night curled round my toilet bowl, sobbing my broken heart out. I contemplated just ending it all – going straight to hell would surely be kinder than enduring eighteen weeks of this!

To make the whole situation even more upsetting, my dear husband slept through the entire thing. So much for *'We will get through this together',* huh! By 6 a.m. I felt so weak I started to worry that my heart would just give out. I crawled to the bedroom and woke Graeme, told him to ring the emergency chemo helpline and made my way back to the bathroom to vomit some more. Graeme was told to bring me to hospital immediately. My feet could barely carry me out of the car and up to the ward (which of course had to be on the top floor at the very back of the corridor). I clung to Graeme with all my might while secretly considering pushing him down the escalator.

The staff had a bed prepared for me already. A young nurse completed my admission as I lay with a cardboard kidney dish on my lap, vomiting between questions and answers. I saw the pity in her face as well as the fear in her eyes; the realisation that her patient was so young, and, holy shit, this could happen to her too. I was living proof that cancer didn't discriminate – it didn't care about age, race or gender. It could appear in anyone and I knew that scared people who met me.

The young nurse gave me anti-sickness injections and started running IV fluids. Eventually the sickness subsided and I finally got some rest. Graeme stayed with me, trying to make up for his sleeping beauty act during the night. I arranged for Georgia – my friend from uni, to take his place for an hour while he fetched me an overnight bag. She tried to keep my spirts up, bringing me new jammies and treats, but all I wanted to do was cry.

I spent the next two days in hospital staring at the empty ceiling and feeling utterly hopeless, trying to understand what the fuck was happening to me. How could my body – that had been so strong only days ago, now be such a fragile mess? Even worse, how was my body going to survive five months of this torture? Just one dose of chemo had completely annihilated me. I lay in my hospital bed wondering if it would be easier to refuse the next dose of chemo and allow cancer to take me sooner rather than later. I mean, it would kill me eventually, so why prolong the inevitable?

* * *

For those of you unfamiliar with the science behind chemotherapy, here's a quick lesson: chemotherapy is injected directly into your veins and then circulates through your body via the bloodstream. The drugs are to target and kill cancer cells.

When a person has cancer, the cell mutates and divides into two cells. Unlike healthy, normal cells, cancerous cells divide much more rapidly. They split into two, then four, then eight, until there's a mass of mutated cells. This mass of cells eventually becomes a lump known as a tumour. Chemo is used to kill off those crafty rapid-firing cancer cells, but unfortunately it can also kill off healthy cells in the process. The healthy, non-cancerous cells in the body that are constantly growing, dividing and continuously renewing themselves – your hair, nails, bone marrow, skin (the largest cell in the human body) and the cells lining your digestive system – are also fair game. Chemo targets cells with rapid growth, which unfortunately means it can also target those healthy cells, hence why people who are receiving chemotherapy often lose their hair and nails, can experience extreme bone pain and often have bowel issues during treatment. So, to wrap it all up: chemo kills the bad cells and the good cells, leaving little alive in the process. In the end, the body will eventually repair itself, but in the meantime I was stuck with one that had been completely ruined.

First there was the hair loss, which began exactly two weeks after my first dose of chemo. My hair was wet, having just washed it, and I was combing it through when it started falling out in large chunks into my lap. I had said from the very beginning that I would take my own hair – I wasn't going to give cancer the opportunity, but that didn't stop me crying for hours upon hours at the concept of having to brave the shave. Losing my hair was heartbreaking. It was never *'only hair',* as people would often say to me, it was my identity, my femininity, a part of me. If it were *'only hair',* why didn't everyone else shave their heads too?

In the end, I lost more than the hair on my head – I lost my eyelashes, my eyebrows and all my body hair, which was ironic considering I had tried to rid myself of said body hair since I was a teen. However I felt no joy when I asked the hairdresser to shave my head, or when my pubes came out in clumps, or when my eyebrows and eyelashes suddenly disappeared from my face. After years of wishing to be hair free I got my damn wish and I was miserable for it.

When people think of chemo they automatically think of the obvious side effects: the vomiting, dramatic weight loss, male and female baldness, but what about the other side effects – the ones that aren't talked about? We know very little about them, me included until I experienced them for myself. I didn't know about the night sweats – or for me night chills, the insane insomnia that drove me to tears, the oral thrush that turned my tongue green. I didn't know that my toenails would turn black and fall off one by one, or that I would gain weight – not lose it, because of the steroids used to control the vomiting. I didn't know about the nasty metallic taste left lingering in my mouth, or the constant pain in my battered body – in my joints, in my muscles, in my bones. I didn't know about the ongoing toilet problems I would have to endure –

either severe constipation or severe diarrhoea. I don't know which was worse: practically tearing myself open on the toilet or the very real possibility of pooing my pants in public. Most of us are uneducated in these delightful side effects of chemotherapy. Even when I glanced over them in the information booklets provided I still wasn't prepared for what was in store. I don't think anyone could be prepared for all that.

Chemo was monotonous as much as it was relentless. Every night I'd wake at 3 a.m. on the dot – not a minute before or a minute after. It was uncanny. I'd wake from my short slumber drenched from head to toe in cold sweat and my entire body trembling. I'd run a scolding hot shower to warm myself up again, and I'd stay there for a half hour, maybe an hour or maybe longer; I wasn't aware of time any more. I'd sit on the shower floor with the scalding water beating off my battered body, hugging my knees to my chest and crying silently to myself. Eventually I'd emerge, wrap myself up in my fluffy dressing gown and head downstairs where I'd curl up on the sofa and cry some more, burying myself in Bear's jet-black fur, contemplate my existence and wonder was it worth fighting for. Those nights were long and torturous. When the rest of the world was silent and the only sound was my despair.

One time I woke at my usual 3 a.m. and headed to the bathroom for my habitual hot shower. I caught a glimpse of myself in the shadows of the mirror and no longer recognised the woman staring back at me. My face was pale and sickly. My head shiny and bald. My eyes black and sunken. My cheeks bloated and puffy. I had aged in a matter of weeks. My entire appearance had completely changed. I was no longer Alex. I was just another girl with cancer.

I came downstairs, made a coffee and chose a depressing movie – just to make myself feel even worse. Tonight's choice, Pearl Harbor. A guaranteed tear-jerker where almost everyone dies. It suited my gloomy mood down to the ground. When the movie ended I sat in silence staring blankly into space, soaked in my own tears – tears over the movie and tears over cancer. I was done, completely and entirely done. Cancer had won. I didn't want to fight any more; I just wanted it all to be over, even if that meant dying. I scrolled through my playlists on my phone looking for sad songs that would make me feel even more suicidal. I came across a Beyoncé song, *'I Was Here'.*

I listened to the lyrics and in that moment everything changed. I realised I no longer wanted to waste what precious time I had left wallowing in self-pity. Instead, I wanted to live each day to the fullest and know that it counted for something, to touch the hearts of those who knew me, to be remembered for my strengths not my weaknesses, to show the world I wasn't ready to leave just yet, to prove to myself *'I was still here'.* I played the song on repeat, over and over for hours upon hours allowing her words to sink into my soul.

In the darkness of my despair, my perspective of my illness began to slowly shift. I was suddenly able to see the small positives in what had been an enormous negative in my life. I began to believe I could use the misfortune of my diagnosis to help others by raising awareness in the younger population. I could share my story and show young women like me that they aren't immune to this disease. I could make a difference to somebody's life even if it was too late to save my own.

I knew it was time for my pity party to end. I would no longer allow my vulnerability and depression to sink me. I wasn't raised to be a quitter; I was born to thrive. I started to wonder if my battle against cancer was truly lost. Could I reflect on my life and know that I had really lived it – had I really made the most of it? As I watched the sun begin to rise with Beyoncé's words ringing in my ears, I felt myself awakening from my cancerous slumber, soaked in my tears and trembling with excitement, knowing *'I was here'* at long last. I was finally alive!

The first thing I decided to do was come clean and stop hiding my cancer – stop hiding my truth of the situation I found myself in and, more importantly, stop feeling ashamed of it. So I wrote a social media post – the quickest way to alert the world of any situation nowadays, and shared it. After seven weeks of desperately trying to keep my cancer a secret I was finally ready to speak my truth: the good, the bad and the ugly truth; the reality of what it means to be diagnosed with cancer before the age of thirty. I wrote my lengthy post and with trembling hands pressed to post.

Eventually I went on to share my entire journey. For me it was a form of expression that allowed me to voice thoughts and emotions that I would otherwise have been incapable of releasing. I removed the mask I had been hiding behind and showed the world my naked vulnerability beneath. I didn't do it for sympathy or for likes or for followers.

I did it for me, and for everyone who felt like they were facing cancer alone. The response was phenomenal – hundreds of people commented and reached out to me. Their words of comfort empowered me and their responses fuelled me to do more, to share more, to help more, and so I came up with a plan of how I wanted to spend the next months of my life during chemotherapy; how I was going to show the world I was here.

I started thinking about productive ways to spend the free time that had been forced upon me. I researched beautiful places in Ireland that I hadn't yet visited – beaches, national parks and mountain regions, and wrote them down. I pondered things I'd enjoyed doing in the past and activities I wanted to get involved in in the future, and I wrote them down too. I considered the little things I could be doing at home instead of watching Come Dine with Me on repeat day in, day out, and I wrote those ideas down as well. I thought about small and simple accomplishments I could achieve during treatment and jotted them down. Before I knew it, I had created my very own bucket list – not the typical bucket list that commonly includes jumping out of planes or visiting every continent in the world. No, this list was different; slightly less exciting, but much more meaningful. This was my chemo bucket list.

The list became my new goal and focus – as well as my distraction, I suppose. I wrote down thirty goals in total, thirty things to complete before the end of chemo, and I shared them with the world. I showed those who were suffering that it was still possible to live while receiving cancer treatment, and I taught those who weren't to appreciate that life is precious and not to be taken for granted. Cancer can come knocking on anyone's door at any given time – I was living proof, but by sharing my new life, my life with cancer, I hoped others would learn to make the most of their own – to appreciate it, to live it, to love it.

I planned to finish the bucket list with a trip to Disneyland Paris at the start of November – what better reason to revisit Disney, hey? In the isolation of my chemo sick chair I created a Disney manifestation.

I imagined how the park would dazzle even brighter, with twinkling Christmas lights and decorations. I visualised snow on the ground, making the park even more magical, and the characters dressed in festive costumes in the Christmas Parade, a whirlwind of festive red and green. On the days I was bedbound and crippled in pain I planned my Disney outfit: a furry oversized coat with matching coloured booties, jeans and a cosy jumper. I scrolled through wigs online, torn between a long, curly pastel-purple wig or a short bobbed icy-blue one. At least I would look like a princess even if I didn't feel like one.

Every time I was hit with nausea and fatigue I pictured having my photo taken with Mickey and Minnie in their Santa suits and how I would smile. Every time I lay in bed unable to move as my muscles and bones burned in agony, I imagined jumping on one of the rides at Disneyland – the icy fresh air cooling my overheated body as I soared through the sky. Every time I felt like giving up on treatment altogether I thought of the stunning firework display at Sleeping Beauty's Castle, imagining the snow on the ground and the warm cup of hot chocolate in my hands. I pictured it that intensely I could almost taste the cocoa. I held onto that Disney dream like my life depended on it, and for a while it did.

My Chemo Bucket List

1. Live through all six cycles of chemo
2. Walk across Carrick-a-Rede Rope Bridge
3. Stand at the top of the Cliffs of Moher
4. Visit Killarney National Park
5. Climb Mount Errigal
6. Have a zoo day
7. Go for a picnic
8. See the Slieve League Cliffs
9. Go for a bike ride
10. Complete the 7 Peaks Challenge in the Mourne Mountains during chemo
11. Visit Glenveagh National park in Donegal
12. Have afternoon tea at Grand Central Hotel in Belfast
13. Eat breakfast at The National with my friends
14. Get dressed up and have a night out at Babel rooftop bar
15. Ride a horse
16. Stay in a bubble dome
17. Have Sunday dinner at The Barking Dog restaurant
18. Try a new dish from the Nu Delhi Indian
19. Bake chocolate brownies
20. Read my favourite book, Gangster, by Lorenzo Carcaterra (the book my dad was reading when he died)
21. Watch my favourite movie Eat Pray Love
22. Revisit the Guinness Factory in Dublin for a pint of the black stuff
23. Eat Italian cuisine at The Chubby Cherub restaurant
24. Keep the fucking orchid alive (I unfortunately went through four orchid plants during chemo – they all died)
25. Train at the gym at least two times a week to maintain some level of fitness
26. Have a beach day, building sandcastles and eating fish and chips
27. Host a dinner party for all my girlfriends at the end of chemo
28. Dress up as Wednesday Adams for my Halloween party
29. Throw Bear a big birthday party
30. Visit Disneyland Paris for Christmas when chemo is finally finished!

Chapter 10

-A Photograph-

For me cancer was as liberating as it was controlling. Before cancer I had felt a great emptiness in my life – as if I'd been wandering around half blind, deaf and numb; searching for something and always finding myself wanting. But cancer taught me to slow down and open my eyes, to finally seeing the world I had been missing out on. To hear, smell, taste and touch, and to live in the present moment rather than the pain of my past or the uncertainty of my future. Cancer taught me to appreciate life in all its glory, and I wanted to remember it all – every precious moment, so I photographed the entire journey and shared the truth of what cancer meant to me.

I had always had a love for photography, even though I'd never studied it. I had a natural flair for capturing the perfect image, so I used this to my advantage to capture life as I knew it. To portray not only what cancer looked like but also what it felt like, and how it changes our perception of the world around us. Nature became my muse and I found myself in awe of this free gift to mankind. A gift I hadn't had the time to acknowledge until now – the detail in a single flower, the grooves in an old oak tree, the simplicity of a ripple on a still, black lake. Images that had never caught my eye before now.

I had been blind to it all – too busy living, except that I wasn't really living. I was merely existing. I had never fully understood that my life was a gift and that was what I captured in my photos. I snapped this one beautiful life I had been gifted with and created an album for moments otherwise lost in time. I shot the entire cancer journey from start to finish, ensuring I had visual evidence of the good times and the bad so I'd never forget the very thing that tried to break me.

The endless tears, the belly laughs, the baldness, the heartache, the sick days, the achievements, the pain, the loss, the uncertainty and all the possibility. I wanted to remember it all. And I was praised for it, surprisingly, for showing the cruelty and the irony of living with a life-threatening illness and all it entails.

People found my photos and accompanying words inspiring – a word I never imagined to describe me. Apparently my social media posts and images were refreshing. Somehow I ended up changing more than just my own life – I changed other people's without ever even meeting them, all with a handful of photos and a few words of wisdom. And in the end this filled with me more pride than any degree or amount of success or travel experience could ever give me.

I must confess, though, that my favourite photos of my cancer journey weren't actually taken by me. They were taken by my friend, and fellow photographer, Gillian during a weekend trip to Letterkenny – a town in County Donegal. I had chosen this town specifically because its location is close to two of my bucket-list challenges: Mount Errigal and the Slieve League Cliffs.

We tackled the mountain on Day 1. Now Errigal is certainly no Everest, but it's still a challenge nonetheless. Interestingly, at the foot of Errigal stands a stone monument built in honor of the famous Irish athlete, Jason Black, after his successful summit of Everest. I took a photo of his words engraved into the stone: *'No mountain is too high or no problem too big to conquer.'* I was one of the few who could truly relate to his words. Cancer was my mountain and a problem I was determined to conquer.

It seemed Everest was still calling my name, or perhaps just mountains in general – I certainly climbed a lot of them during treatment. I had no previous love for hiking other than the physical challenge it provided. I had never really stopped to just breathe in the peace and tranquillity of the mountains before, but now that I was staring death in the face the mountains had become one of the few places I felt free from its vicious grip. Free from fear. Free from my cancerous nightmare. Each climb proved to be an emotional struggle as well as a physical battle – Errigal included. A test of me against me, or me versus cancer, or my mind versus my decaying body. I stared at Errigal's steep incline as if she were Everest herself. And I was determined to conquer her.

I was on to chemo number five and was suffering severe fatigue, breathlessness, joint and bone pain – just to make my challenge even more difficult. Although Errigal is only 751 metres above sea level, and one of the smaller mountains I climbed during chemotherapy, it was by far the toughest and my favourite mountain of them all. I spent quite some time on that mountaintop gazing out at a whole new world before my eyes. I watched the clouds float dreamily by, felt the wind cut across my face, smelt the crispness of the unpolluted air and experienced something changing inside me.

I knew I wasn't the same person I had been prior to this cancer journey. I was different somehow. Oddly enough I felt more myself with cancer than I had ever felt without it, and all this change was captured in a single photograph. A photograph of me standing tall and triumphant on a mountaintop with my bare face on show – not just make-up free but eyebrow and eyelash free too. My skin was as pale as a white A4 sheet of paper, my golden-brown wig was matted from my sweat and tussled and untamed in the wind. My face was puffy from the drugs that were keeping me alive. My hips and thighs had returned to their curvy, plump selves – wide, squidgy and pimpled with cellulite. This was me. This was my body. This was my face. Bare to the world. When I looked at that photo I no longer saw my ugly cancerous reflection or my chubby thighs or my messy wig. I saw a woman I was immensely proud of – with or without cancer.

After Gillian and I descended Errigal we headed out for a well-deserved drink in celebration of our achievement (after a shower, of course).

For once I didn't care what I was wearing – wig included, or that I had no eyelashes, or that I had to squeeze into my jeans and was barely able to do up the button. None of it mattered any more. I was no longer ashamed of my cancer. It was a part of me and a part I had learnt to accept. I let myself go that evening – drank way too much wine, danced till my feet blistered, chatted to random strangers with ease and confidence, laughed with my best friend and had fun. Yes, it's still possible to have fun even with cancer.

By the time we got back to the hotel I was exceptionally drunk and had somehow lost our room key – oops! Gillian took charge, found the porter and asked for a new key while I sat on the floor slumped against the wall giggling to myself at our situation. I then decided I'd had enough of my showstopper wig for the evening and tossed it across the corridor. When the porter returned with the new key he didn't know where to look, and all I could do was laugh. I literally rolled around the hotel corridor laughing hysterically, like some sort of maniac, with my bald head on full show. Even Gillian couldn't stop herself from giggling at me.

The following morning she sent me a photo I barely remembered being taken. I posted it – my first picture that I shared with no hair – along with the caption: *'When you're blocked, bald and don't give a fuck!'* and at the time I meant it.

When I finally put the chemo album together and looked at each photographic memory of my bucket list one photo at a time, I realised, at long last, that I had found where I belonged. The bucket list had given me the opportunity to visit some of the most beautiful places in Ireland – north and south; places I probably would never have chosen to visit had it not been for cancer. The more of Ireland I explored, the more my desire to emigrate dissolved. I came to appreciate the beauty in the country I lived in – even with the rainy weather, and appreciate the friendly, down-to-earth people who inhabited it. Australia was soon a forgotten dream; Northern Ireland was my home. It always has been. It was where my parents met and where I was born. It was where I chose to run to when my previous life became unbearable. It was where I built and established my adult life. Where I found love, decided on my career and met most of my closest friends. Northern Ireland is where I had been happiest – even if it is where I was diagnosed with cancer. It no longer made sense to me to leave my home behind and start again. I now accepted that Australia had been nothing more than a dream; a dream that I'm not sure ever meant anything to me other than it was what everyone else did. At long last I was satisfied that I had found my permanent home, and I had cancer to thank for that.

* * *

You'd be surprised to know how many marriages don't withstand the test of cancer. I was when I first came across an Instagram feed that had posted: *'Hands up how many of you got dumped during cancer treatment?'* Surely this was a joke? But it turns out it wasn't. I couldn't believe the comments below. Hundreds of relationships had ended because of the pressure the disease forced on a relationship. Apparently it was common for people to walk out on their partners with cancer – some leaving before their spouse had even left the hospital after diagnosis! Although I was disgusted by the thought, it made sense in some ways. People clearly couldn't handle that amount of baggage. Graeme never walked out on me but I still got to witness first-hand how cancer can shake a marriage to its core.

During treatment family dynamics naturally change. Roles can be reversed if those with the disease are incapable of their usual day-to-day lives. Patients often aren't able to work, and running a house can be exceptionally difficult, especially for those with children. In our house Graeme became the sole provider and I was, by default, the housekeeper because I was *'off work.'* It never seemed to register with my husband that I wasn't off by choice – it was forced upon me. Household chores were now strenuous for me: hoovering made me breathless, standing to cook exhausted me and walking Bear was painful. I expected Graeme to help. Unfortunately he didn't.

The deeper into chemo we went the more our emotions heightened. Communication between us broke down and intimacy was a struggle, especially after the hair loss, weight gain and surgeries. I can count on one hand the times Graeme and I had sex after I lost my hair, and I can recall how I cried out of shame and embarrassment after each of those times. Losing my breast only made intimacy more difficult, and then came menopause. Our marriage was doomed from diagnosis. Survival mode took over for me and soon I had no energy to waste on my failing marriage.

Graeme's approach to cancer was to remain strong, to keep going, to maintain some form of normality, to try and keep me positive. But I didn't need someone to be strong for me. I needed someone to break down beside me. I needed someone to feel my pain and sense my fear. I needed Graeme's compassion not his show of strength. Eventually I decided it was easier not to rely on my husband at all. That way I wouldn't be upset if he let me down, again. On more than one occasion I asked Graeme to leave, and at the time I really meant it. I wrote him a painful letter one evening and ended our marriage entirely. But despite my best efforts to push my husband out of my life, believing it would be easier to face cancer alone, he stayed for the long haul, which I am now incredibly thankful for.

Chemo was a testing time for both of us. It rocked our marriage so hard we were sure it would sink us entirely. But on the day I rang that chemo bell, in the proudest moment of my life, it was my husband I wanted by my side. I smashed that bell like my life depended on it as much as my marriage depended on it. Determined to make it heard throughout the Cancer Centre, I rang it for me and I rang it for us. Graeme and I had made it through our first hurdle with our marriage still intact. Just about.

I finished chemo on a Wednesday afternoon and planned my big celebrations for the Friday evening. Initially I wanted to host an Egyptian-themed dinner party for me and my girls in honour of my Arabic roots and in honour of my friends who had become as much a part of my bucket list as I was, ticking off most of the activities alongside me. But by the time the party came round I was completely exhausted from my treatment regime and ended up ordering ten boxes of Domino's Pizza and stocked my fridge full of Prosecco, hoping this would suffice.

The party was my way of thanking my friends for all they had done for me over the last eighteen weeks. They had been my rock through chemotherapy. Nothing was too much to ask of them. They had all sacrificed their time to help and care for me; never once asking for anything in return. I stood in my front living room surrounded by my girls and felt truly blessed to be part of such a special group of friends. I reflected on the days when I had struggled to communicate with people and the difficulty I had faced making friends when I was younger, yet here I was standing in a room filled with people who loved and cared for me with or without cancer.

These women (they know who they are) saw me on my knees at my absolute worst, and they saw me at my best flying high on mountaintops. They were there for me 24/7 no matter the time of day or night. They became so in sync with my pain that they knew exactly when my breakdowns would occur – even if said breakdowns were in the middle of the night. Someone would text at the exact moment I lost my shit, knowing I would need them.

It was uncanny how in tune we had all become. They knew I was having a bad day before I even knew I was having a bad day. It was like they could read my mind. Their friendship, love and loyalty humbled me deeply. I owed these girls so much more than just a party. I owed these girls my life.

I was on cloud nine, an end of chemo high – a buzz better than any drug. I felt as though I had conquered the world and the worst was over (so I thought), that I had totally smashed it.
My girls and I toasted to that. Onwards and upwards now! However the next day my high came crashing down to the surface when I woke with a sore chest. I brushed it off at first, blaming it on the alcohol and cigarettes (yes, I smoked through chemo). I decided to have a chill day and spent the afternoon browsing hotels in Paris, daydreaming of my romantic getaway with my husband to the city of love. I went to bed that evening feeling completely wiped. Maybe I had overdone it this time?

When I woke the next day my chest was so tight and raspy I was struggling to breathe. I rang the Cancer Centre immediately and drove myself to hospital. The doctor listened to my chest and diagnosed a severe chest infection. I was treated with IV antibiotics and a course of tablets to take over the next week. My surgery was only a fortnight away and I prayed my chest would clear by then. But still the nurse warned me that the operation would more than likely be postponed after my chest infection because my body had to be fighting fit for the mastectomy. I left the hospital in tears.

Paris had been planned around my surgery date. If it wasn't going ahead as scheduled, I would have to postpone the trip until after Christmas, when I had healed. Paris had been my obsession for months – the one thing I desperately clung to throughout chemo. The setback knocked me harder than chemo had itself because it meant I couldn't complete my bucket list. I had failed to complete my goal and in turn I had failed myself.

Chapter 11

-Let It Go-

The setback was only short-lived however. D-Day was upon me – my surgery date had come. Mum stayed with me the evening before for moral support but I had little to say to her or Graeme. My thoughts were naturally elsewhere. I tried to get some sleep but woke around four. I paced the kitchen for a while, unable to settle. I got dressed and took Bear out for his usual morning walk through the park and along the river. I watched his tail wagging happily in the bushes as he sniffed about him. I stood and wept, wondering if this was our last venture together. Graeme carted him off to the kennels shortly after we got home, and I cried some more as I hugged my baby boy goodbye.

I arrived at the hospital early, ready to face Dr Death who was carrying out my procedure. When I saw him walking up the corridor dressed in his scrubs, my stomach churned. The very sight of him gave me the chills. He gave me a quick nod as he passed, which I returned, nodding back to my own Grim Reaper. I waited in the busy corridor for my name to be called and walked through door number one where Dr Death was waiting.

I listened to my surgeon go through the procedure, once more, and I nodded along – unsure what I was really nodding to. I had to give my verbal consent that I, Alexandria Lindsy Quinn, consented to have a mastectomy of the left breast. My voice shook as I spoke, but what choice did I really have? I could either agree to surgery and possibly live a little longer or decide against surgery and most definitely die.

Neither option was appealing but I will always choose life over certain death – well, at least I think I will.

Just to make doubly sure I had agreed, I signed consent before my surgeon proceeded to mark an X in permanent marker above my diseased breast – in case they accidentally removed the wrong one, he joked. I laughed at his attempt at humour and gave him a grim smile.

Behind door number two was the anaesthetist – an exceptionally tall man, I noted, who babbled on about pain relief and morphine. His words made no sense to me because my anxiety had taken full grip. Nothing was comprehensible any more. I nodded and signed another consent form – for morphine, I think? – and then moved on to door number three.

A surgical gown and TED stockings were waiting behind this door. I fumbled with the stockings, unable to stop my hands shaking, and eventually called for help. The nurse who answered was young – around my age – and, again, I saw the horror on her face: the shit-this-could-happen-to-me look, before she quickly composed herself. A cheerful HCA (healthcare assistant) came next to take my blood. But my veins were that damaged from chemo, she was unsuccessful and a phlebotomist (a master bloodsucker) had to take over. Unfortunately she had to go into the same vein in my hand that had just collapsed, and it swelled up like a golf ball. She apologised as she hoked and poked at my hand, while I held my breath, gritted my teeth and smiled politely back at her not wanting to be rude.

Finally, door number four – the waiting room. Loose Women was playing on a small TV in one corner. Two older ladies sat in their gowns opposite me, and a young man was in the opposite corner. I wondered what he was there for. Nobody said a word. I gave them all a quick smile and then kept my eyes firmly glued to the TV strongly fighting the urge to either vomit or burst into tears. My surgery was scheduled as the last procedure of the day – typical! It was going to be a long afternoon. I knew the two ladies and the gent would both go down before me, so I told Mum to go and get herself lunch and Graeme could go after. But only minutes after she left, a nurse came to take me down to theatre.

From the minute she spoke, I decided I didn't like her. She called out my middle name repeatedly, and when I politely informed her it wasn't my name, she continued to call me by it, much to my annoyance. Her tone was brash and insensitive as she attempted to hurry me down to theatre. I protested that my surgery wasn't until 3 p.m. but she ignored that too. I resorted to pleading that I wanted to see my mum before I went down and begged her to give me five minutes to get my mum back, but she was oblivious to my request and ushered me on down anyway. Graeme walked with me so far before she turned and shouted, *'No family past this point.'* I gave my husband the briefest of hugs, unsure if it would be our last embrace, and followed the Hitlerian nurse into another waiting area where I waited, alone, for over two hours. For what seemed like an eternity. Like time itself stood still. Two hours is a long time to be left alone in a state of panic, and by the time the clock struck three and the medical team drew back my curtain and wheeled me into the torture chamber, I was beside myself.

My heart was racing that hard I thought it was going to rip clean out of my chest when they attached me to monitors and probes, and my eyes darted around the room like a rabbit caught in headlights. Again, I had to verbally consent. As I said the word *'mastectomy'* for the fifth time that day, I started to hyperventilate and completely broke down. All the fear I had been holding deep within rose to the surface with a poisonous vengeance. I couldn't breathe and started sobbing inconsolably, choking on my own tears.

I can't do this. I don't want a mastectomy. Please don't take my breast away. Please don't turn me into a *'freak'* forever, I screamed inside my head. But no one heard my silent plea. Then one kind nurse took my hand, as if she had heard my unspoken words, and whispered, *'You've done brilliant.'*

Her angelic face was the last thing I saw as the exceptionally tall man hurriedly inserted the anaesthetic and knocked me out.

I woke up in recovery, confused and disorientated, and immediately burst into tears. Again. The whole experience had been the most dreadful thing I'd ever endured. I can relive the trauma of my surgery just as vividly as I can relive the day I lost my beloved father. I can recall the entire experience – the beeps of the machines attached to my body; the whiff of my own dry blood and sweat beneath the blankets; the tightness of the blood pressure cuff around my right arm; the uncomfortableness of the drain hanging from my left ribcage; the site of the drain filling with pus and blood, that made my stomach heave; my feeble attempts to avoid looking at the flat area beneath the bandages, the place my breast used to be. I can remember it all. Unlike chemo, surgery is a memory I wish I couldn't recall. There are no proud moments on mountaintops or drunken antics in hotel corridors in those memories. There's only pain and sorrow.

Once my vitals stabilised I was transferred to the ward where Graeme was anxiously waiting. I was attached to oxygen, IV fluids and PCA (patient-controlled analgesia) containing the potent opioid morphine. A button in my hand meant I could self-administer my own pain relief as and when required, so each time I pressed the button a small amount of morphine was delivered via my cannula.

After visiting time was over and Graeme had kissed me goodbye, I relied heavily on that morphine to get through the night. I was crippled with pain. The surgery site was so tight and stiff that I couldn't lie down flat in fear I'd tear the entire wound open. I couldn't get comfortable whatever way I shuffled about the bed, and as the anaesthetic wore off the pain grew sharper and more intense as the night progressed. I kept clicking at the opioids on tap in the hope they'd eventually knock me out and I'd finally get some rest. I didn't worry that I might be using too much morphine – the machine locks out after each dose is administered and won't release any more drugs until safe to do so. I eventually got a few hours of drug-induced rest and that was all that mattered to me.

The following morning my nurse said that I'd most likely be discharged that afternoon. The majority of patients who have breast surgery are only kept in for one night as long as they don't live alone and have family members who can help them. The aftercare following a mastectomy is very similar to that of caesarean: no lifting, no cleaning, no driving, etc., which suited because I had very little movement in my left arm where they had carried out the sentinel node biopsy – the removal of a few lymph nodes situated nearest to the tumour. They were removed during surgery and sent off for testing to see if the cancer had spread into my lymphatic system. I wasn't too worried about this – all my scans had shown my cancer was contained in my left breast only. I was due to see Dr Death in two weeks' time for my results and I was fairly certain they would be all clear.

Removing those few lymph nodes (nine in total) had left me stiff and sore under my arm. It limited my range of movement and made simple tasks such as washing and dressing extremely difficult. Then there was the stiffness in my chest, where I'd been operated on and then glued back together, as well as the drain site adding additional pain to my side. It was no worse than I expected but I did worry how I would manage that amount of pain at home without the morphine handy, so I made good use of it while it was available.

After forcing half a piece of toast into me I decided I wanted a wash. I asked the HCA for a hand over to the bathroom, but my nurse thought it better for me to have a bed bath. Absolutely not! I protested. With some persuasion I convinced her to allow me to walk to the bathroom as long as she and the HCA accompanied me to make sure I didn't fall. When I finally managed to stand I immediately felt dizzy, light-headed and my legs were like jelly. I knew the nurse had been right, but I was too stubborn to admit defeat, so I clung to them both and made it to the bathroom, a little out of puff but still in one piece.

I allowed the young HCA to help wash and dress me. The wound was still well covered, for which I was thankful. Neither she nor I would be getting any sneak peeks of the grisly sight beneath. I shuffled back from the bathroom, amazed how weak I felt from completing such a simple everyday task, and curled back up in the bed with the intention of a long sleep.

I didn't realise that my IV fluids and oxygen needed to run alongside the PCA, and that neither of them was now connected. I carried on pumping at the morphine without giving it a second thought, assuming my nurse would get round to reconnecting me shortly. After all, I wasn't the nurse now; I was the patient and it wasn't my responsibility. I stayed awake long enough to ring Gillian for a quick chat. During the phone call I became aware that my mouth was suddenly very dry, that I was slurring my words as if I was drunk and that I was really sleepy. I don't know if I ended the conversation or drifted off halfway through, but I was disturbed from my morphine slumber by my breast care nurse tapping my shoulder. She'd come up from clinic to check in with me after surgery and go through my aftercare. My face lit up when I saw her – I liked my breast care nurse a lot. She always had a way of cheering me up. I got my usual greeting of *'Hey, girl'* and big smiles as she pulled up a chair. She started to explain what came next for me but I found myself spacing out again. Her lips were moving but I couldn't make out a word she was saying. Everything sounded muffled as though we were both underwater. I gave my head a wobble to snap myself out of my watery trance, but I was just so tired all I could think about was sleep. My eyelids felt as though they were weighted down and I couldn't keep them open any longer. From afar I heard my BCN ask, *'Can I get you anything, Alex?'* I drunkenly asked for some water and mentioned that my tummy was itchy.

My nurse lifted my jammie top and exposed an angry red rash covering my belly. *'Most likely a reaction to the morphine,'* she said. Then she noticed that my fluids weren't running and I didn't have my oxygen in place.

She reconnected me, got me a jug of water and told the ward nurse that I needed an antihistamine for the rash. I gulped down the water and welcomed sleep again. When I woke this time I knew immediately something was wrong. My body felt like it was floating – launching into a drug-induced space. I somehow buzzed for help and the nurse checked my blood pressure, but I was asleep again before she removed the cuff. The next time I woke the same nurse was administering naloxone through my cannula – an opioid antagonist used to reverse opioid overdose.

Suddenly I felt a rush of heat running straight to my heart. My pulse shot through the roof and I was convinced I was having a heart attack. This is it – this is how I'm going to die. Not from cancer, but from a heart attack just like my dad. I started to panic, choking on my own air. They increased my oxygen and reassured me it was a common reaction to naloxone. But I didn't believe them – sure, they had just tried to kill me!

Eventually my heart rate settled and my breathing returned to normal. The PCA machine was removed and my medical records were amended to include an allergy or hypersensitivity to morphine – meaning I would never be offered that pain relief again. I was furious. I knew the machine hadn't been set up right and that I hadn't been monitored properly. And, just to annoy me further, I now had to remain in hospital for an extra night for close observation. I contemplated putting a complaint in but decided against it. I just wanted home as quick as possible with no more drama.

The next morning I was visited by a female doctor who worked alongside Dr Death. She failed to tell me her name or even ask how I was feeling. She waltzed in, closed my curtains, gave me the courtesy of a hello, and went ahead and lifted off my dressing – with no consideration that this was the first time I would see my scar. She muttered that I was healing up nicely – more to herself than to me, while I stared down at the hideous mess where my breast used to be. She covered me back up again and told me I could go home that afternoon.

When the breakfast trolley came round I declined food and just sat letting the tears roll. I was upset after seeing the scar, of course – it was hideous and stretched from underneath my armpit right across to my other breast – but I was more upset at how the doctor had treated me and how dehumanised she made me feel.

To her I was just another body, another girl with cancer, another woman without a breast. In that moment I honestly believed it would have been better to have never woken from surgery.

The next two weeks were difficult but manageable. My brother had flown over the morning I was discharged to see me and my granny. She was unwell and, coincidentally, had been admitted to hospital on the same day I had my surgery. He and Graeme worked around each other to ensure I was never alone, and it was nice to have the help. As always, Gillian was also on standby. It was Gillian, not my husband, who I asked to help me with my first shower. I didn't feel comfortable showing Graeme the scar, not yet at least, so my dear friend had to wash and dress me like a child while trying her best to avoid the eyesore across my chest.

I was still unable to stand up straight and instead hobbled around doubled over in pain. Thankfully, after a few days the pain started to subside, a little at least, and I was able to start my physio exercises, which were crucial to my recovery. My chest and underarm were still very tight – I was sure they would tear as I forcefully yanked my arm into moving again. The exercises were to be done four times a day and I made sure I did them religiously; ignoring the uncomfortable tearing feeling and refusing to let out a single sigh of pain. I was determined I would get my mobility and my independence back before Christmas and I was already dreaming of getting back to the gym and starting my weight training again. Nothing was going to stop me now.

By the end of week two I had managed to regain my full range of movement or thereabouts and I was delighted. I went for my first walk with Bear and embraced the fresh air on my face and the freedom of doing something by myself again. Cancer had taught me to never take such simple acts for granted – even just walking my dog myself, for you never know when that independence will be taken away. It helped that my big black dog had been brilliant since my op. It was almost as if Bear knew he needed to be gentle now. He didn't pull on the lead or jump up at his mummy, not once. Labradors really are the most intelligent beings and Bear is my best friend.

I had successfully showed Graeme the scar and, oddly, he was more accepting of it than me. In fact, he was brilliant about it – emphasising how neat it looked and praising Dr Death's handiwork. Maybe we could learn to live with this after all? I thought. But I remained ambivalent about the scar, refusing to pay it much attention. I was so focused on my physical healing that I wasn't ready to deal with the psychology of it at the same time. I avoided the mirror when possible and kept my eyes firmly glued ahead whenever I was naked or in the shower. Occasionally I would allow myself a sneak peek, just to check for any signs of infection, but other than that I did my best to avoid the surgery site entirely.

I had been given a softie in replacement of my left breast – a little soft cushion that slotted into my post-surgery pocketed bra, but the surgery site was still very raw and sensitive to touch, so I avoided wearing it when I could help it. Instead, I wore baggy jumpers and tried to disguise my one remaining boob underneath. I hated the sight of that one boob possibly more than the scar itself. It just hung there like an ugly freak of nature. I felt it no longer belonged to me. To me, boobs are designed to be a pair. One alone was nearly worse than none at all.

But despite my avoidance of my one breast, I was genuinely happy with my post-surgery progress. I felt that old spark of energy returning – the old Alex was starting to make a comeback. This time bigger and better than ever, I decided. Once I received my biopsy results and got the all clear, I could finally move on with my life.

Both Graeme and I were feeling optimistic when results day came round. I wore make-up for the first time since surgery, accompanied by my beautiful blonde wig. I even forced myself to wear my softie for the occasion. I was sure today was going to be the day – the day I was told I was cancer free. Graeme was adamant too, so much so that, unbeknown to me, he had contacted Jenna and they had arranged a surprise party for me that evening; inviting all my friends and family to celebrate my first day of freedom. But as we took our seats in the breast clinic waiting area, I felt that all too familiar seed of doubt creeping back in – what if this wasn't good news? What if this was only the beginning of more to come?

I searched Dr Death's eyes as I entered the consultation room, looking for a glimmer of hope as he politely shook my hand and motioned for my husband and me to take a seat. I saw his grave face and the darkness in his eyes and I knew. *'I'm sorry,'* I heard for the second time round, and my heart sank. *'Five out of the nine lymph nodes that were removed were cancerous.'* And that was the first time I saw my husband cry. Graeme had been so sure this journey of hell was coming to an end and the prospect of more to come was simply too much for him. His strong facade cracked, and, like me, he finally understood that I might not survive cancer.

Dr Death handed us both tissues as he explained what was to come: he was going to reopen the wound and remove the remaining lymph nodes. I was distraught. I was going to have to go through surgery all over again. All that pain and fear for what? Surely I was going to die now anyway. With the cancer now reaching the lymphatic system, there was a good possibility it had spread outside the primary breast area.
Surely this was the end for me?
He told me my tumour had been 6 cm in length. 6 cm – the size of a lime! My odds weren't looking good. But it's still treatable, my surgeon said. The only thing was, I didn't believe him now.

I feared the worst, that they would test the other nodes and they would all contain the disease too. Then how would they treat it? After all, they couldn't remove my entire lymphatic system! Paris before Christmas was certainly off the cards now – in fact, visiting Paris at all was highly unlikely. I had myself dead and buried before I'd left the hospital.

Graeme and I sat in silence the whole way home. For once Graeme had nothing positive to say and I was glad. I didn't want to hear that power of positivity nonsense any more – it clearly didn't work! And for once Graeme agreed. He contacted Jenna and cancelled the party. There would be no celebrations now. I rang my brother and told him to let Mum and Chloe know; I didn't have the energy to repeat the devastating news. The rest of my friends received a very bleak text message and I ignored their responses. I took to my bed and stayed there until Gillian arrived at my door. She was the only one I allowed in. She cradled me in her arms as I wept, and she wept, and Graeme wept, and we all wept together.

I was scheduled for the auxiliary lymph node clearance in two weeks' time – they really weren't beating about the bush. Surgery would take place on 13 December, only days before Christmas. I was warned that this surgery could be more painful than the last, and there would be no morphine or opioid-based pain relief available this time round. Also, once the wound was reopened I'd be more susceptible to infection and healing could take much longer. What's more, the motion in my arm movements would become more restricted and the limited movement, tightness and possible numbness could be permanent after full node clearance. To top it all off, I would now be at a higher risk of lymphedema – permanent and painful swelling of the arm. Great! I stopped doing the physio exercises after hearing all that. What was the point?

I didn't leave my bed for the next week – I didn't shower, I didn't eat, I didn't speak. I just lay there in my own sweaty smelly despair, completely numb. Even Bear couldn't comfort me now. I morbidly started to plan my funeral. I chose the funeral songs I wanted played, which included Beyoncé's 'I Was Here,' although I didn't feel I had been given the chance to 'be here' in the end. I chose my flowers – my favourite yellow roses. I chose my outfit to be cremated in – my wedding dress with my bridal Minnie Mouse ears, and I wanted everyone else to be wearing mouse ears to commemorate my love of Disney.

I wondered who would show. Would my granny finally make peace with me now that I was gone? Would my friends who had disappeared off the face of the earth have the nerve to show their faces? Would my ex-partners pop along to say their last goodbyes? I was doubtful. I started thinking about who would get what. Although I owned very little, my possessions were still valuable to me. Who would I bestow my porcelain Disney character collection to? Or my favourite painting of my dad and me that I kept on the wall? Or my beautiful wedding rings? Who was worthy of such valued possessions?

Chapter 12

-A Disney Wish-

It was January 2020 and I was still here.

WOW. I had already outlived my expectations. Go, me! Better still, I was in Paris, the city of love. Against all odds I had made it to the French capital, to the second day of our trip. My Disney dream had come true. A dream I had imagined from my chemo sickbed not all that long ago.

Although it hadn't happened at Christmas as originally intended, and it looked a little different than I had pictured, my Disney wish had still been granted. There was no snow on the ground, but there was ice at least. The Christmas parade had ended unfortunately but it had been replaced with Disney's Frozen, which was arguably equally as magical. Sleeping Beauty's castle still towered before my eyes, twinkling in the winter frost. I was wearing my planned outfit paired with my piercing blue Princess Jasmine Minnie ears proudly sitting on top of my silver-grey wig – a special gift from a special friend – and I was holding that warm cup of hot chocolate, the one with the tiny marshmallows melting on top. My Disney manifestation had become a reality, at long last, and I was more than grateful.

I stood directly in front of the castle, after kindly being granted a disability pass because of my cancer. The pass allowed me to get up close and personal to almost everything at Disneyland, including the castle, meaning no one could block my view that evening. At least there was one perk to having cancer.

I had endured two major surgeries and come out the other side, albeit my body felt old and crippled and I suffered with ongoing pain from the trauma caused by both operations. I was still here, I reminded myself, even with my shoulders unnaturally dropping and rolling forwards and their clicking and crunching when I moved my arms; and with my back in constant agony, even more so this evening due to the freezing temperatures.

Graeme stood behind me, gently rubbing my back trying to relieve the pain a little, as the show commenced; starting with the song *'A Dream Is A Wish Your Heart Makes'* from Disney's Cinderella, which was enough to reduce both Graeme and me to heartfelt sobs. As the castle came to life before our eyes, for what I imagined would be my last time seeing it, I wondered could one more dream come true? Just one more? Scenes from Disney movies flashed across the castle walls as fireworks exploded in the night sky in a shower of colour; all in time with the music booming through the park. I whispered along with the lyrics, hoping that if I could manage to keep on believing, just a little longer, the dreams that I had wished for, would come true. Warm tears trickled down my frozen face as I prayed for one last Disney miracle. A miracle of life.

The second surgery had gone much smoother than the first, thankfully, although the aftermath was far worse, as predicted. But what I didn't anticipate was waking up from surgery with my arm stuck to my side as though glued to my ribcage. My left shoulder had dropped significantly, making me appear lopsided, and left me looking like the Hunchback of Notre Dame's twin sister.

Apparently the level of pain I was experiencing wasn't normal either. The nursing staff queried with the doctors whether my drain was touching a nerve ending and requested it be resited but the medical team refused to send me back to surgery. As a result I ended up in hospital for five days – longer than when I'd had my mastectomy, and what should have been a much simpler procedure was more complex because the medical team couldn't manage my pain. Basically I was left to grin and bear the agony until enough fluid had drained from the wound and it was safe to remove the damn drain – with only paracetamol for pain relief.

I lay in the fetal position for the first few days and only left my bed to use the toilet. I faced the wall with my curtains drawn. I feared my arm would remain a mangled mess forever, and once again believed I'd have been better off never waking from surgery at all. Graeme felt my anguish and tried his best to comfort me. He never missed a visit and did everything he could to lift my spirits, but I was too sore to entertain his efforts. When visiting hours ended I'd ask Graeme to close the curtains behind him; happy to be alone in my misery once more.

There were five other ladies in the bay with me, and from what I could gather none of them were cancer patients. There were all much older than me and much chirpier – and why wouldn't they be? They weren't dying like I was. I chose not to engage in their friendly chitter-chatter between the hospital beds and kept myself to myself. The only contact I had with them was when I shuffled past them to get to the toilet. I knew I was a pitiful sight shuffling along with my mangled shoulder hanging lifelessly beside me, one saggy breast swinging, my fuzzy chemo hair on show, and a bag of blood and pus trailing along behind me, but I had no energy to try and hide my cancer any longer. This is it, ladies. This is what death looks like!

I gave the elderly women a quick nod of acknowledgement and then stared at the floor, making sure I didn't give them the opportunity to respond. On the third day I decided I would attempt to get washed and change into a pair of sweats. I struggled to juggle my drain, washbag and toiletries with my one working arm, and the lady in the bed opposite took pity and asked if she should buzz the nurse to help. I politely declined and subsequently spent over an hour in that damn bathroom attempting to yank my left arm away from my body to no avail, all the while biting my tongue to stifle my screams.

Eventually I managed to wash and change my top half, somehow, and gladly shuffled my way back to my pity corner.

The lady opposite smiled as I drew my curtains. *'You look better, dear,'* she managed to sneak in before I slammed them shut. I fought back the urge to cry and muttered a thank you from my hiding spot. After an hour or so I opened my curtains, shuffled into the bedside chair and allowed myself to join the conversation at long last.

I learnt that the lady opposite was called Maureen, or Mo for short. Over the next three days I got to know her very well – maybe a little too well, as a matter of fact. Mo was a very open and honest soul. An admirable trait, I thought. It wasn't long before I was educated on Mo's life story. She sat by my bedside for hours when I was too sore to climb out, chatting as if she had known me her whole life. She talked and I happily listened, grateful to lose myself in someone else's life for a change.

I empathised with her struggles and sensed that her loneliness was similar to my own, although triggered under very different circumstances. We had each other for company now, well, for the next day or two anyway, and it didn't take me long to decide that I liked this lady Mo. I liked her quite a lot.

During one of our lengthy chats Mo asked if I was a person of faith, and I answered her honestly with a no. I told her I had struggled to accept God into my life since my father had passed. Even though I wanted to believe now more than ever, I remained in denial. I had learnt that Mo was a born-again Christian and hoped my honesty hadn't offended her, but she didn't appear to be upset thankfully.

The truth was, after I had been diagnosed with cancer I had become even more resentful towards God. All he seemed to do was punish me, and I felt his punishments were cruel and unjust. I don't know how many times I heard the words *'I'll pray for you'* after I was diagnosed, and how many times I stopped myself replying *'Don't fucking bother!'* I left that part out of my conversation with Mo, though; out of respect, of course.

I was grateful she didn't try and convert me because I wouldn't have been able to help myself in quickly shutting her down. My mother-in-law had already made that mistake once too often by trying to persuade me to come to church with her, which I repeatedly declined and now didn't even bother trying to hide my annoyance. It would go against my morals to turn to God now, and I couldn't force myself to believe out of fear. As much as I really did want God to spare my life, I couldn't bring myself to pray for it.

Although I refused to believe in God I did, however, believe that good people go to heaven and bad people go to hell. The thought of spending an eternity in hell was terrifying, and I feared I was never getting through those pearly white gates to paradise now, which meant I would never see my darling father again (who is surely in heaven because his soul was pure, unlike mine). But even with all that fear, I still couldn't bring myself to ask God for forgiveness. I'd made my bed with God and I would stubbornly lie in it for an eternity, whatever the cost.

Later that evening our local minister, Steven, poked his head around my curtain. I knew his face from local weddings and funerals I had attended but couldn't fathom why he was at my bedside. But on that evening, when I saw his friendly, familiar face poking through my curtain, I felt an odd comfort in his presence. Steven only stayed a few minutes and never mentioned God to me, not once. I knew my mother-in-law had discussed my loss of faith with him and he had cleverly decided against a great push at religion on our first encounter. I did know, however, that he included me in the church's weekly prayer practice, and I knew he would most likely go home and pray for me that evening. On this evening I welcomed his prayers.

I was due to be discharged on the Sunday, a day of worship. Mo had spent the morning in the quiet room reciting her Sunday prayers.

Before she left she handed me a small package and told me to open it while she was praying. Inside was a beautiful pink leather book that I had seen her carrying around, Inspiring Words for Women by Darlene Sala; a collection of biblical scriptures and quotes.

Mo had written on the front page, Especially for you, Alex, to encourage you and help with your healing. From Maureen. She had left a bookmarker on Page 81, which was titled *'I Will Never Forget You.'* The page opened with:

'Sometimes God allows a long period of pain and hardship in our lives, and we begin to wonder if He really cares. He must have given up on me, we think. Perhaps among all the billions of people in the world He has to keep track of, He has forgotten me - or worse yet, forsaken me' I admit I had never felt so abandoned by the Almighty. However, as I read on and finished the final line which read:

"Greater love has no one than this, that he lay down his life for his friends" (John 15:13). *'Jesus did just that for you. You can be sure that the One who died for you. Will never forget you or forsake you. Never.'*

My resistance to faith began to lessen and the tears of belief began to fall.

As I said my goodbyes to my dear Mo, I handed her a tiny scrap of paper with my phone number scribbled on top and a single sentence: *'You are never alone. I'm always just a phone call away.'* It was probably the kindest gesture I had ever given, especially in my current antisocial state, but I felt Mo had come into my life for a reason; just as I believed many other beautiful souls have done. I believed Mo had come to my aid, to give me very particular guidance, to restore my faith in God.

During that second stint in hospital my granny was sadly diagnosed with end-stage COPD. As I was discharged from my ward, she was also discharged from hospital, but sadly with an end-of-life care package in place.

I knew it was now or never to make amends and was pleasantly surprised when I was met with a much warmer reception than I'd anticipated. Old age had been terribly cruel to my granny. She was a shadow of her former self, which was heartbreaking to see. I fought back the urge to cry when I first saw her and gave her a gentle hug; she appeared so fragile I was afraid I might break her.

We never mentioned a word of our fall out, or why she hadn't contacted me after I was diagnosed, or why I hadn't contacted her when I knew she was dying. It didn't matter now. I could see the concern on her face and she could see the concern on mine. She wanted to know everything about my treatment and I barely got a word in to ask her about hers. When I hugged her goodbye I was glad I'd decided to see my granny at long last, but riddled with guilt that it had taken me so long.

I visited again on Christmas Eve. In only a matter of days my granny had deteriorated rapidly and was now entirely bed bound and requiring full nursing care. I held a cup of tea to her mouth with shaking hands and she sipped the hot drink through a straw. I glanced at the syringe driver, which had been increased that morning, pumping continuous morphine into her tiny body and I knew she only had a matter of days. But despite the strong sedatives, my granny remained awake and alert, never wanting to miss out on a thing. I showed her funny pictures of Bear and she laughed at the silly costumes I'd dressed him in. As I said goodbye and wished her a merry Christmas that afternoon, I knew it would be her last. I cried with Graeme the whole way home knowing I had waited too long to make it right with my granny, and I was heartbroken because of it. As Graeme and I drove home I said my first prayer – a prayer for my granny.

* * *

I had been determined to make my last Christmas on earth a special one and it started with the purchase of a new Christmas tree. After sixteen years of grieving I finally let go of my black Christmas tree and insisted Graeme and I picked a new one that year, no expense spared. The theme was to be pink and white. I chose a traditional six-foot dark-green tree with snow-drizzled branches, along with new pink and white baubles, lights and decorations. Never in a million years would I have imagined having a pink Christmas tree – but people do crazy things when they're waiting to die.

Hanging ballerinas, crystal Cinderella shoes, glittering unicorns and fluffy pink peacocks and draping a matching rose-gold garland on the fireplace and placing a shiny rose-gold star as the tree topper, I played old Christmas songs of the past and made my own finger buffet, including the cheese-and-ham cocktail sticks that are only ever served at Christmas.

I decorated the tree meticulously; every decoration had its specific place, including all my Disney decorations collected over the years and a Christmas bauble containing an old photo of my dad holding me as a baby, which took centre stage. I finished off my display with my Christmas Minnie Mouse bears – I purchased a new one every year from the Disney store and they each had a different outfit and design with the year sewn onto their shoes. I positioned them in a circle around the base of the tree in place of the traditional tree skirt.

Meanwhile Graeme watched in silence as I transformed our living room into a Christmas wonderland. He gave me the space to complete a ritual of the past. When I finally finished and took a step back to admire my work, my eyes were teary with the beauty of my creation and the sentimental value the tree held for me. I was intent on making my last Christmas on earth as beautiful and spectacular as this tree.

Christmas morning was spent watching my darling nephews open their Christmas presents. My brother and his family were staying with my mum for the holidays, and Graeme and I arrived early to see the boys' excited faces. Mum was in the kitchen making us a fry while the boys and the third child in the room – my beloved Bear, tore into their presents excitedly. It was the first time the entire family had been together in three long years and everyone was delighted to be reunited. After breakfast I cuddled my nephews on my lap, thanking God for bringing them back into my life – even if it was only to be short-lived, and thanking God I was spending my last Christmas with them.

We spent the afternoon with Graeme's family. Our Christmas dinner was as fabulous as ever – always made by my mother-in-law, and there were two additions at the table this year. Laura and her husband William had been blessed with the most beautiful twins following a difficult IVF journey and two painful miscarriages.

Laura had found out she was pregnant just weeks before I was diagnosed with cancer. My initial delight for her was unfortunately ruined by my sense of impending doom. Although I was incredibly happy that her prayers had finally been answered, I found it difficult to share in her baby joy. Laura and I are the same age, yet our lives couldn't have been further apart. Hers was full of joy and mine full of misery. Knowing I was unlikely to ever carry a child of my own only made it more difficult to share in my sister-in-law's happiness – not to mention I believed I'd be dead by the end of the year! I think that's a difficult situation for any friend to handle, even the best of ones.

At a time when Laura and her family were excitedly preparing for the twins' arrival, Graeme and I were locked in a battle for my life, and the dynamics of our relationship soon turned sour. Naturally my in-laws' focus was on Laura and the twins, not me and my cancer. I tried at first to include myself in the baby prep, but visiting Mamas & Papas and attending a baby shower full of mummies or soon-to-be mummies was just too much in the end. It wasn't long before I isolated myself from my in-laws and began to resent their new-found happiness. As awful as it sounds, I admit I was bitter towards them – not because Laura was expecting, but because I felt so incredibly let down by a family I was so attached to. When I needed their support more than ever, I hadn't received it.

When the twins were born I made my excuses not to visit them in hospital, and when the family arrived home a few days later I had to brace myself before I entered. At first I was reluctant to even hold baby Milo or baby Molly, knowing it would upset me too much, and I was more emotional with Molly because I had so desperately wanted a daughter of my own. When I did visit Laura and her beautiful twins I cried every time my sister-in-law left the room, wishing with all my heart that God would spare my life and bless me with a beautiful daughter just as special as Molly; that somehow I would still get the chance to become a mum. That somehow my life would be *'normal'* like everyone else's.

But on what I believed to be my last Christmas night, I finally let go of the bitterness I'd been holding on to. I let go of the hurt that had been caused by two uncontrollable circumstances and I managed to hold Molly long enough to give her a bottle without breaking down in tears. I had my first picture taken with my beautiful niece and nephew – with a genuine smile on my face; no longer needing to put on a brave face. I hugged my sister Laura and shared a toast with my in-laws to another beautiful Christmas, smiling for our standard family photo and knowing my last Christmas had been a perfect one.

Chapter 13

-The Church On The Hill-

It was New Year's Eve. The end of 2019 was finally here and I had never been gladder to toast the end of a year goodbye – goodbye 2019 and good riddance. I hoped 2020 would be more forgiving and far less painful, starting with my second surgery results.

The evening before judgement day, the second time around, I allowed Steven the minister to come into our home and say a prayer. Graeme and I closed our eyes while the minister spoke the most beautiful words and I broke down in tears. It was the first time I had allowed God into my home and into my heart since the loss of my father. It was the first time I felt the Lord's presence and it was the first time I really, really needed it.

This time when I searched Dr Death's eyes I saw that tiny flicker of light that is hope. Less than half of the lymph nodes removed had been cancerous, and there was no *'I'm sorry'* this time. At last, it was good news. Dr Death remained adamant that my cancer was still treatable, and I was to begin the next stage of treatment – radiotherapy. I wouldn't see Dr Death for another six months, until my annual mammogram. Well, thank God for that!

But it wasn't looking like 2020 was going to be a forgiving year after all. It had only just begun and it was already tainted with sadness. Only days after my promising results and small victory against cancer, my granny lost her battle with COPD. She passed in the early hours with her son and daughters by her side. I drove down as soon as I heard the news, arriving just before the undertakers, which gave me time to say goodbye to her alone. She was lying in the bed as if she were sleeping but her body was now cold to the touch.

Her eyes were closed and her mouth hung open, and the syringe driver was still pumping morphine into her now lifeless body causing her arm to swell. I removed the needle, kissed her forehead and whispered my final goodbye to my grandmother; fighting back my tears as I said my farewells to the women who had given me a home when I had nowhere else to go; the woman who had given me another chance at happiness; the woman who had changed my life. Despite all the pain we had caused each other, I knew she had loved me, and I had loved her. That was all I could hold on to now.

The week after we buried my granny I was to attend my next oncology appointment, this time at the Cancer Centre in Belfast, and I wasn't expecting good news. My brief period of hope had diminished and my instincts were telling me to prepare for the worst. Graeme was working on the day I was scheduled to see Jim's dad, so I brought my friend Vanessa along with me instead. I had purposely told Graeme the date of the appointment late so that he wouldn't have the chance to get it off work because I didn't want him there. I had decided it was best he sit this one out as I intended to ask the question Graeme refused to hear the answer to: '*What is my prognosis?*' Basically, how long have I left?

A cancer prognosis is usually based on the stage of cancer, grade of cancer, how large the tumour was or is, and if there is lymph node involvement. The data is entered into a statistical analysis that generates an estimated figure, which is the likelihood of you experiencing a cancer reoccurrence. In worst-case scenarios this figure is also used to tally how many years you have left to live.

My prognosis was even worse than I had anticipated: I was given less than a fifty per cent chance of survival. I was numb, shocked and numb. The room fell silent, into a long pause that I assume was to give me time to process the heartbreaking news and break down in floods of tears.

But the tears never came. Apparently I had no tears left for cancer. Vanessa sat in shock beside me. There really was nothing left to say!

The medical team still wanted to go ahead with radiotherapy even though I didn't see the point now. But I was set to receive fifteen sessions of radio anyway. One blast a day to keep the cancer away – for a little bit longer, at least. I was to have treatment every day, Monday to Friday, for a three-week period.

I listened to Jim's dad reeling off the possible side effects I could experience: fatigue - often severe, which could continue for months or years after treatment; nausea; vomiting; skin changes to the targeted area – dry, itchy, broken skin; headaches; stiff joints; muscle swelling of the treated area; loss of libido; vaginal dryness; increased risk of depression and anxiety; increased risk of lymphoedema; increased risk of osteoporosis - thinning and weakening of the bones; and increased risk of developing another type of cancer. How delightful!

After enduring three weeks of radio hell I was then to start hormone therapy to prevent my body producing the female hormone oestrogen – the hormone my cancer was driven by. I would receive a monthly implant into my stomach that would temporarily stop my ovaries functioning and put me in medically-induced menopause. I was prewarned that many young women like myself found the menopausal symptoms intolerable and ended up opting against treatment.

I listened to Jim's dad reeling off the next set of side effects, which included hot flushes; vaginal dryness; decreased libido or other sexual side effects; sleep disturbance; memory changes;

mood changes; low mood or anxiety; weight gain; and urinary incontinence. So, basically, my sex life was out the window at twenty-eight years old.

I was given a few days to consider the recommended treatment but my decision was already made.

On my return from Paris, despite all those horrible possible side effects, I would begin radiotherapy and follow it with hormone treatment. The treatment, I was told, could increase my chance of survival by six per cent – hardly worth bothering, you may say, but I didn't have room to gamble; the odds were certainly against me now. I was locked in a fifty-fifty roulette battle for my life: the red numbers on the table represented a tiny chance of survival; the black was certain death. Of course I chose to stick all my chips on the red numbers whatever the cost!

* * *

My obsession with Paris began long before cancer. The beautiful city had been calling out to me for years, or so it seemed. My Paris dreams had begun on a boat trip along the Amalfi Coast in Italy the day before I got married.

We wanted to do something special on our wedding day eve, and had decided to take a boat trip exploring the stunning southern Italian coast. Graeme's parents joined us for the day and the four of us visited the beautiful towns of Positano and Capri before finishing off with a mesmerising rowboat ride through the blue lagoon – a magical blue sea cave illuminated in a soft blue glow. The glow is created by sunlight entering an underwater cave and then reflecting through the seawater, giving a stunning illusion throughout the cavern. It was breathtaking.

But despite my stunning surroundings I was unusually quiet that day; lost in my own train of thoughts. Wedding jitters were getting

the better of me now – such a commitment still scared the life out of me. If I'm honest, I had never imagined myself a married woman and found the whole idea of marriage close to terrifying – which I obviously never shared with Graeme. On my wedding day eve I stood at the edge of the boat thinking to myself that once the ship (more like tiny sailing boat) docked, it would be the last time I stepped onto dry land as a free woman. Dramatic, I know! But in less than twenty-four hours I would sign my life away, and all my aspirations along with it – or so I felt.
I wanted the boat to carry on sailing straight past Sorrento, along the Mediterranean coast and never reach land again.

During my silence Graeme's parents had got talking to an older American couple. They were chatting on one side of the boat, Graeme was tinkering with his drone camera on the other and I sat at the very front quietly contemplating my great escape. Eventually I realised I was being stupid and joined the rest of the party. The American couple knew that tomorrow was the big day and offered us their blessing and well wishes. As we got chatting the American lady, Leisa, asked me if I had ever visited Paris. *'Not since I was a little girl,'* I replied. The couple then told me a story of the most beautiful white church in Montmartre, Paris.

I learnt that Montmartre is well known for its artsy streets and hidden treasures, but the most spectacular treasure of all is this holy white church, Sacré-Coeur, the sacred heart of Jesus. Leisa explained that the church offered the best panoramic views of the city as it was situated high up on a hill and was even more beautiful than Notre Dame herself. I admired her storytelling techniques. The couple had visited the church on their thirtieth wedding anniversary and Leisa's husband had purchased a necklace, in secret, from the sacred church as an anniversary gift for his wife. How romantic.

I was intrigued by their story. I hadn't visited an old church since my dad had passed, and this one definitely sounded worth visiting.

I made a mental note of its name and decided that if I were ever in Paris, I would certainly check it out.

As our boat trip came to an end and I stood staring at the stunning Italian sunset, Leisa approached me, took off her necklace and handed me the pendant. *'A wedding gift and blessing for a long, happy and healthy marriage,'* she whispered.

I stared down at the pendant in my hand. On one side was an image of the Holy Spirit; on the other was an image of a beautiful church perched on top of a hill. Inscribed on the silver pendant were the words *'Sacré-Coeur, the heart of Jesus.'*

I was blown away by this stranger's touching gesture. This necklace obviously held great sentimental value for Leisa, yet she had chosen to give it to me. At first I protested – I couldn't possibly accept such a gift, but she insisted, so I held onto the pendant and promised this stranger I would visit the Sacré-Coeur for myself. I didn't have the heart to tell her I had no faith and refused to believe in God, but still I kept the pendant as a keepsake; not yet knowing what a treasure it truly was.

A few years passed and I hadn't given the pendant much more thought, but my keenness to visit Paris had grown and I asked Graeme to take me there for my thirtieth birthday celebrations. I just felt this strange magnetic pull towards the French capital for some unknown reason. Then one random rainy day during chemotherapy I decided to go into the attic for a snoop around, mainly to give myself something to do. I keep a suitcase filled with old treasures from my childhood up there, and every once in a while I like to go and have a nosy through them. I opened the old dusty suitcase that I had carted over from Blackpool seven years ago and couldn't believe my eyes. There, at the very top of the case, were my dad's old paintings that he had bought in Paris, and the first one was a painting of the Sacré-Coeur.

That painting had hung on our breakfast room wall for years. I had always loved those French-style paintings, so Mum had allowed me to take them with me when I moved, but they had been forgotten in that ancient dusty suitcase in my attic ever since. The Sacré-Coeur had been on display throughout my entire childhood without me ever really noticing it. My intuition, or the universe, or my dad, or God himself, was undoubtably guiding me towards it.

I climbed out of the attic and frantically began the search for the pendant Leisa had given me in Italy. Eventually finding it in my travel purse, I moved it into my everyday purse – now feeling a great need to carry it with me at all times. I knew I couldn't wait till my thirtieth birthday to visit Paris – not any more. Time was of the essence and, like I said, my time was running out.

* * *

That following January Graeme and I were travelling on the hop-on hop-off bus tour in the iconic Parisian village of Montmartre – a village that takes you back in time with its cobbled streets, stunning basilica, artists, bistros and unique charm. I instantly fell in love with this artsy, quaint district in Paris. I had my first glimpse of the towering basilica of Sacré-Coeur from the open-top bus and my skin had tingled with goosebumps. I was nervous – so much emotion was riding on this one experience. I hoped the church would prove my journey worthwhile. I hoped to experience some sort of enlightenment or epiphany as I entered the holy cathedral. I hoped I would finally feel a connection to the Holy Spirit and maybe even the spirit of my father. Once again, I was hoping for a miracle.

From the bottom of the mound that the church rests upon, Graeme and I stood and stared at the conquest above us. The church reaches an impressive eighty-three meters in height and I was understandably daunted by the number of white stone steps winding before me – never mind the further three hundred steps I would have to climb inside to reach the vantage point at the top. I was still very weak and fatigued after chemo and surgery. Cancer had ravished my body and I was worried I wouldn't make it to the top to experience the enchanting views of Paris from above this holy ground. But still I began my ascent.

I climbed the stone steps, stopping occasionally to catch my breath, and finally approached the entrance of a massive bronze door, the entrance to the sanctuary. I held my breath in anticipation as I passed through the grand entrance.

My eyes were immediately drawn to the immense and beautiful mosaic that decorates the ceiling immediately taking my breath away.

After spending an age making my way around the church and lighting a candle for my beloved father, I took my place in the pews in front of the magnificent altar. I bowed my head in prayer but I had no idea how to pray – the concept was completely alien to me. So I began with *'Heavenly Father'* to start my first conversation with God, while Graeme sat in silence beside me saying a quiet prayer of his own. I prayed and the tears just kept pouring as I begged for my life at long last.

Afterwards I made my way up the three hundred narrow winding steps to the top of the basilica. Laying eyes upon Paris in her glory from such a magnificent height had me weeping yet again. I wept out of gratitude for the beautiful view before me and the beautifulness of my life; this one great blessing I had been given, the whole twenty-eight years of it, the good days and the bad. For every waking moment I had been lucky enough to experience, including cancer.

I silently thanked Leisa for giving me her pendant all those years ago and thanked my own intuition for guiding me there that day. As my eyes scanned the city below I couldn't help but ponder how much of my life and how much of myself had changed – just as I had on top of Mount Errigal during chemo.

Again, I felt another shift in my spiritual presence; a feeling of calmness and clarity washed over my battered body and I was finally able to let go of the anger in *'Why me?'* and instead humbly accepted *'Why not me?.'*

Up there on top of Paris I made my peace with myself, made peace with God and made peace with cancer.

Part 3

It is not the mountain we conquer but ourselves.

Sir Edmund Hillary

Chapter 14

-Freedom-

Freedom was in my grasp. The sweet taste of victory was almost upon me as my cancer journey finally drew to a close. I returned from Paris calm and collected and no longer afraid of what was to come. I was ready for radio and it was ready for me. I was on the home stretch now and the finish line was in plain sight. Luckily I had been advised by my fellow cancer survivors that radio was a breeze compared to chemo, which was reassuring. It would be a piece of cake, then.

On day fifteen, and my last blast of treatment, I rang my final bell with my family and friends surrounding me – every one of us teary eyed, signifying that active treatment had officially finished. My radio course was done, and I was free to be on my way. I rang and I wept as my cancer friends clapped and cheered at my long-awaited victory. But there were no mass celebrations planned this time – no dinner parties with my girls or surprise parties with my family. This time I had decided I didn't want a fuss. When I rang the bell this time, I rang it quietly.

My freedom had been exhausting in the end, as I'm sure it is for any human who has been oppressed so cruelly. I had gone to such great lengths to attain it that the sacrifice was difficult to accept. Cancer had been my master for nine long months and I had served it. But now that I was free from such slavery I didn't know how to live without it. I struggled to adjust to my new-found freedom and found myself asking: what happens next?

What happens now that radio has finished and I'm spat out of The Cancer Club back into the cruel world of *'normal'* society? Except I wasn't normal now and didn't belong there.

Not with one weird-looking breast and a wig on top of my head. Not with annual mammograms and MRI scans. Not with the constant worry my evil master would return to enslave me a second time round – this time ensuring I remained in its grasp.

What happens now that my body is forced into a medically-induced menopause that I don't understand and nor does my husband? When the night sweats and hot flushes kick in. When I become irritable and snappy or cry for days on end. When my vagina closes its doors at the age of twenty-eight and physical intimacy with my husband is lost for good. Will my marriage fall apart for the second time round or will it sustain another wicked test?

What happens now when my sick period is over and I'm forced to return to work? To a brand-new hospital that directly faces the Cancer Centre where I had my treatment. How will I cope driving past the heart of my suffering on a daily basis? How will I feel when I return to a new working environment and new staff team who don't understand my torment? How will I feel returning to a clinical setting when the doctors surgery now gives me panic attacks? How will I fit back into my old role as a nurse after being a patient for so long? Will my patient experience make me a better nurse or a worse one?

What happens now when my girlfriends invite me to spa weekends or I book a romantic break with Graeme and I have to wear a mastectomy costume or mastectomy underwear with a fake breast form inside? How will I feel wearing these frumpy swimwear designs that I despise? Surely I would feel like an outcast amongst my bikini-model friends in this unflattering swimwear designed for the over fifties. How will I hide my scar on romantic getaways if my husband attempts to be intimate? How will I feel being naked around him when I still can't look in the mirror at my own naked deformed body? How will he feel when I have to tell him never to touch my remaining nipple or even acknowledge I have a boob at all because it makes me cry?

What happens now that cancer has stolen so much more than just my breast? It has robbed me of my femininity and my womanhood.

* * *

Radiotherapy had been one long, monotonous drag even though it only lasted three weeks in total. Every day was an exact repetition of the one before: I'd arrive at the Cancer Centre early to beat the city traffic. My appointment times were usually early morning or late afternoon, which meant I always hit rush hour either way. Vanessa drove me in and out (I was too drained to drive most days). She'd park her cute little retro Fiat 500 in the multistorey and we'd head over to the coffee shop, fighting at the tills over who was paying. I ordered my usual vanilla latte and she ordered caramel. I liked that coffee shop. It was cosy and warm and decorated nicely. I didn't feel like I was in hospital when I was sitting there. We'd sit for a while enjoying our daily treat. Sometimes the conversation would flow naturally and sometimes we'd sit in complete silence; it depended on my mood that day. I'd watch the clock ticking in front of me and as it approached my allocated time we'd get ready to leave. I didn't want to go, but I had to.

We'd navigate our way along the busy corridors following the signs for radiotherapy and looking out for the familiar black arrows dotted on the floor – my very own yellow brick road to freedom. The end was near. The countdown was on. I handed my appointment card to the receptionists; some of them smiled and struck up a conversation with Vanessa and me, making us feel a little more at ease. Others simply typed in my H&C number and handed the card back to me. My name was now 636 808 6256. Each time I was given a black buzzer and told to take a seat.

I headed for one of the familiar blue plastic armchairs as far away from everyone else as possible. Vanessa followed my lead. I avoided the pitying looks from the elderly folk we walked past. My friend and I sat and listened to the elderly man playing his guitar in the corner.
A sweet old man who gives up his time to entertain those who have been afflicted with this awful disease. Other than that the waiting area was silent.

Our hearts melted as we watched a little girl with no hair smiling from ear-to-ear when she got to ring the big silver bell on the wall. The whole room erupted in claps and cheers as she exited the centre in her toy Ferrari waving goodbye to her friends at the Cancer Centre. I fought back my tears and wondered how life could be so cruel. My eyes were moist for a second time that day when I watched a bald elderly woman shuffle her tired body over to that same bell and give it the quietest of rings. Unlike the little girl she had no family with her, no photos taken, no one to share her joy. She was alone in her battle against cancer. The claps were quieter this time as she exited the hospital, which made me equally sad. Her age doesn't change her suffering.

My buzzer started flashing red and beeping loudly interrupting my angry thoughts. I jumped up quickly, said goodbye to my friend and followed my radiographer, not wanting to draw attention to myself. When I entered the room my radiographers, Amy and Arlene, were usually waiting for me. I liked them – they made me feel less anxious. Amy was young, younger than me, and had a sweet, gentle nature. Arlene was my mum's age and mollycoddled me a little. But I didn't mind; I quite liked her motherly concern. In fact, I needed it.

Sometimes I was greeted by new faces, including men's. I felt uncomfortable at first having to display my lonesome breast to them, but I didn't ask for a swap. It didn't matter when I had no femininity to protect. Sometimes there was a medical student in the room as well, there to learn all about cancer for the day. They asked if I minded them observing. I did mind – I wasn't a project to be observed, but I said no anyway. It didn't matter when I had no pride to protect. I wasn't a person any more. I was just patient number 636 808 6256.

I undressed my top half and removed my wig. (My choice – I could keep it on if I wished.) I climbed onto the machine and the radiographers moved my arms into stirrups above my head. I ignored the pain in my scar as the surgery site stretched. I avoided eye contact with the staff as they drew little red and black dots over my naked chest – the spot where my breast used to be. I was measured up with a ruler like a slab of meat and moved into position in line with the green laser beams directly above my head.

The staff gently moved my body this way and that, apologising for their cold hands. I felt myself tearing up as I was forced to stare at my ugly scar in the reflection of the machine, an image I had long been avoiding, but I refused to cry in front of those strangers. So I switched off – detached myself from the situation as if I was no longer there. My mind remained my own but my body was someone else's. I found a tiny black dot on the all-white ceiling and redirected my gaze. I would not cry – not that day!

I followed the radiographers' instructions and took a deep breath in and held it so that the laser therapy didn't blast and damage my heart. I heard the machine fire up and watched the orange light turn on. The sign on the door now read: *'Do not enter. Radiation in progress.'* I felt nothing while I stared at the tiny black dot on the ceiling – no burning pain or fire irrupting in my flesh. I felt nothing at all. My heart was now numb and had no feeling. I was empty. I continued to hold my breath for what seemed like eternity, so much so that my head was pounding with the pressure of it. *'And release,'* Arlene instructed over the speaker. I let out a deep sigh as the staff exited the radio-free zone to reposition the machine and me ready for blast number two.

Twenty minutes or so had passed before I gladly heard that familiar voice, *'Ok, Alex, that's you all done now.'* I slid off the machine, redressed myself, placed my wig carefully back into position and forced brief small talk with my healthcare professionals. I did it for their benefit not mine. I didn't want them to feel uncomfortable around me.
'See you tomorrow,' I would say with a false smile. I'd find Vanessa in the waiting area and we'd exit the building together. She was the only person who knew not to ask me how it was.

In the car I'd sit and quietly wonder to myself why my dear friend had volunteered herself for that God-awful task. My misery can often be infectious, I know that, but still she dropped me to my door with her usual friendly smile and arranged my pick-up time for the next day. I didn't know who I felt sorrier for, her or me, as I waved goodbye and closed my front door.

I'd collapse on my sofa feeling an overwhelming exhaustion, physically and mentally. Bear cuddled into me. He knew I was sad and tried to comfort me. We'd lie there entwined in my despair until Graeme returned home and I'd have to readjust my mask, not wanting my husband to see me at rock bottom all over again. When my family and friends would phone later that day they'd always ask me the same questions: *'Well, how do you feel?'* and I'd answer, *'Just tired,'* ignoring the persistent headache and the nauseous feeling in my stomach. *'Does it hurt?'* they'd say, and I'd stare down at my red, raw, itchy, burnt skin. *'No,'* I'd reply.

* * *

In the end, radio broke me. It robbed me of my remaining shreds of humanity and the strength I had left. It made me a broken woman. For months I continued my daily business feeling completely detached from myself and my life. I hit an all-time low after active treatment ended, which I learnt was a common experience for many cancer survivors. After the daily grind of a life with cancer comes to a halt and the hospital appointments, scans and treatment finish, survivors are often left with another sense of loss and a new uncertainty of how to proceed with life after cancer.

It's not just a case of picking up where you left off, which many people unaffected with cancer believe. My life had been cancer for the best part of a year now and I no longer knew how to live without it. I was left with no routine, no medical reassurance and no structure to my life. Although my support network was still strong, I didn't require the same attention now that treatment had finished. I found myself not wanting to ask for help any more and not wanting to speak about cancer with my friends and family. To everyone else, that chapter of my life was over and I didn't want to bore them with my cancer journey any longer. But the truth was it wasn't over for me – nor will it ever be. While I recognised that every day after treatment was a blessing, I also saw it as a curse. What I had to do now was learn how to balance the two.

Chapter 15

-The New Me-

I had dabbled in my journey to self-discovery throughout the course of my cancer. When my old hobbies and passions died off, either by choice because they no longer interested me or by force because I simply wasn't able for them any more, the first thing I decided to adopt was the healthy body—healthy mind concept in the hope that it would keep a cancer recurrence at bay. I did my research and explored many different natural health practices, especially to do with diet. There is an abundance of research studies available online that examine diet and its links to cancer, so I figured that nutrition was a good starting point.

Firstly, I decided to go vegan after watching a pile of Netflix documentaries discussing how meat supposedly gives you cancer, especially red meat. I spent a fortune on vegan sausage rolls, vegan meatballs (that gave me the poops), vegan cheeses that tasted like rubber and bottles of oat milk for my coffee that made me heave. I lasted three weeks. I was in hospital after my first surgery when I caved. I had miserably picked my way through two scoops of powdered mash and a spoonful of carrots and peas before deciding I wanted to be a meat eater again. I ordered Graeme to bring me up a foot-long Italian BMT from Subway. It includes a delicious selection of ham, salami, pepperoni, proper cheese and all the trimmings. The first bite of that sandwich was the end of my veganism.

After veganism proved a little too dramatic to maintain I tried the supposedly easier veggie option. At least I could still eat real cheese and full-fat vanilla lattes. I did better with this one. I filled my freezer with meat-free alternatives and managed to make some tasty meat-free dinners that I found rather impressive.

I was even bold enough to order a veggie McDonald's wrap – a cardboard version of their chicken goujon wrap – and that was the end of going veggie!

Ok, so I failed both veganism and vegetarianism. The next best thing was the popular alkaline diet – a diet based on the theory that eating certain foods can change the body's acidic levels. Some studies have shown that acidic environments help cancer cells grow, so a diet high in alkaline foods and low in acidic foods should raise the body's pH levels, making the body more alkaline, and prevent or even cure cancer. But this is a theory tested in a Petri dish; never on a complex cancerous tumour inside the body itself, and these studies are arguably biased. Anyway, the sugar-free concept proved too depressing for my sweet tooth and the alkaline diet soon fell by the wayside as well.

Next I experimented with herbal remedies in the form of multivitamins and powdered wheatgrass that some Irishman from Donegal had drank religiously and claimed cured his cancer. I started taking turmeric capsules daily – basically curry powder in a pill. The anti-inflammatory and antioxidant effects of the herb apparently inhibit cancer induced by the cell cycle. Furthermore, curcumin in turmeric apparently plays an important role in treating several types of cancer, including breast cancer, by promoting cancer cell death, minimising inflammation and slowing tumour growth. Have I lost you yet?

Eventually I had enough of messing about with my diet. My passion after cancer was clearly not to be a diehard vegan and animal rights activist, so who could I be instead? Maybe I could be a pothead like my ex-boyfriends? I'd come across plenty of studies claiming that cannabis in the form of CBD oil was successful in reducing the size of cancer tumours and keeping the disease at bay.

Plus, weed would make me a calmer and collected person, right? I'd heard a lot about the Rick Simpson Cannabis oil (RSO) and decided to give that a try.

I ordered a syringe of the thick black gloopy medicine off a website that had been recommended by a friend of a friend of a friend. It arrived from the Netherlands wrapped in tinfoil to allow it to cleverly go undetected through customs. I was a proper druggy now, it would seem. The website advised that the oil is extremely potent and only a tiny droplet is necessary to begin with – a small drop a day to keep the cancer at bay! I opened the package, squeezed what I thought was a miniscule drop of the black stuff onto my tongue and continued with my day.

Gillian arrived around an hour later to help me with a few things around the house. I told her I had taken the CBD oil so she was prepared if things got a little weird, which they did of course! We had nipped out to get some groceries when the effects began to kick in. I stood at the self-service checkout in Asda and forgot how to use the very straightforward scan-and-go machines. My mind just went blank all of a sudden. My brain was telling me one thing but my body wasn't capable of carrying out the action. When I returned home I could barely string a sentence together. Whenever Gillian tried to talk to me my responses were delayed. I felt like I was on an episode of Who Wants to Be a Millionaire and needed A, B, C or D options to answer any question. Everything slowed down, including my speech and the ability to think rationally. My body felt like it was floating. I kept lifting my hands in front of my face to see if they were still attached; my limbs felt so light and free.

I watched Gillian pottering around my kitchen making us dinner, all in slow motion. She looked like a cartoon in slow-mo. It was comical. In fact, it was hilarious. I began to laugh. I laughed that much I had to go for a lie down on the sofa. I'm not sure how long I lay there, or if I was awake or asleep or floating somewhere in between, but eventually a chicken dinner was placed in front of me. The only thing was, I'd forgotten how to eat it.

My friend had to cut the food up for me, like a child, because I didn't know how to use a knife and fork. The drug was rocket fuel – so potent, and the effects lasted for hours. When they finally did wear off a little I got myself in a panic, paranoid that the syringe hadn't contained CBD oil at all and I had in fact poisoned myself with some wacky drug off the internet. My heart was racing and I thought I was going to have a heart attack – again. I imagined the headlines *'Young girl overdoses on fake CBD oil trying to cure her cancer.'* Of course it was just drug-induced paranoia and once it wore off completely I was fine.

Needless to say, I didn't try the black stuff again out of fear I'd lose my mind entirely. Clearly, I had a very low tolerance to drugs of any kind, but I was still keen to keep going with CBD. After researching its benefits in detail I decided to build my tolerance another way – by eating weed-infused cookies made by a cancer friend from The Cancer Club. The cookies tasted like what I imagine soil and cow poop taste like when mixed together – you would need to be dedicated to the cause to swallow those bad boys.

I ate my first cookie with a cup of coffee sometime after my second surgery and headed out with Bear along our usual river walk, expecting to be home before any unpleasant side effects kicked in. I had Bear in a new harness that Graeme had just bought him – my first time using it. When I got back from the walk I stupidly couldn't figure out how to take the harness off. The effects of the cookie had clearly started to kick in. After a while Bear got frustrated with me and had started to think it was a game, bouncing up at me to play. In fear he'd rip my wound somehow, I decided to go and ask my neighbours for help.

Our neighbours were a young married couple of similar age to Graeme and me, and we had always got on well. When the wife opened the door to me, though, I had forgotten her husband's name and just stood there like a creepy weirdo saying nothing, trying to think of how to ask for her husband's help without using his name.

Eventually I broke the silence by blurting out, *'Is the hubby home and can I borrow him a minute.'* How awkward!

Her husband, who I later remembered was called Kyle, arrived at my front door minutes later and unclipped Bear's harness after noticing a locking mechanism on it. He then asked how my treatment was going, but the full effects of the cookie had kicked in and my mouth was as dry as the Sahara making it impossible for me to get my words out properly. I just grinned my psychotic smile while trying to prop myself upright against the banister, praying good ole Kyle would leave soon. He eventually got the hint and I gladly closed the door behind him, diving straight into my fridge. Everyone knows that weed gives you the munchies but that day I just so happened to be following one of the ridiculous diets I was talking about meaning the only snacks I had in the house were fruit and nuts, so I spent the entire afternoon eating two boxes of grapes and a few packets of nuts while laughing my head off at the commentary on Come Dine with Me. My neighbours and I have never mentioned the harness incident to this day. I don't know if they knew I was stoned or just presumed I'd gone mad with my cancer situation. I suppose, in all honesty, it was a bit of both.

Weed-infused treats became my form of therapy. I found the effects calming and amusing at the same time – and let's face it I needed a little fun in my life. I would take my magic cookies, gummy bears and caramel chews and become lost in a fantasy world where cancer and pain no longer existed. I even brought my magic bears with me on a road trip to Donegal where I and my adventure buddy spent a few nights in the arsehole of nowhere on a random last-minute getaway. Once we realised we really were in the wilderness, we took a gummy bear each with a few drinks to spice things up a little. Unfortunately the home-made bears don't come with any warning labels, and the alcohol elevated their relatively mild and calming side effects turning my friend and me into two full-blown crackpots.

We went for dinner in the hotel restaurant (there was literally nowhere else to go) and laughed our heads off at each other's failed attempts to compose ourselves. The laughter was uncontrollable – once we started we couldn't stop. My friend forgot how to eat, just like I had with the RSO oil, and held a burger in her hands for what seemed like hours while I sat opposite laughing like a maniac. When the waitress came over to take our dessert order my friend couldn't speak, so it was down to me to order two chocolate brownies. But, again, I burst into random fits of laughter and had to ask the waitress to give me a minute. She was clearly unimpressed with my rude and strange behaviour but I couldn't control it. At the end of the meal we managed to walk to the bar to pay. The food had been included with our stay but the wine wasn't. I knew neither one of us was capable of typing in our card numbers correctly, so I asked the barman to charge the bill to our room before I burst into lunatic fits of laughter – again. I didn't know what else to say other than *'I'm sorry, I have a laughing disorder,'* while my friend just stood and stared straight through the barman and the waiter. The poor waiter gave me a thumbs up and said the bill was charged to the room, all the while looking at me with extreme concern. I'm laughing while I write this, by the way – just without the weed this time!

My friend and I hurried up the stairs to hide for the rest of the evening and by 9 p.m. both of us were comatose. We spent the rest of our trip keeping away from the hotel staff, making sure we were out at the crack of dawn and not back till late evening; scurrying in and out of the hotel like two fugitives. Obviously I gave the bears a miss after that, but they were good while they lasted.

Ok, I had had enough of being a pothead, so maybe I could learn to be more spiritual in a less poisonous and more legal way. Maybe I could be like my yoga instructor friend Katrina? She is always calm and collected. I had started going to her yoga classes during chemo but found that the quietness sent me into a panic – there was too much thinking time in my namaste unfortunately. But now that I was past chemo I'd surely be able to find comfort in the silence, so I decided to give meditation a go. I bought a beautiful Buddha backflow burner and some white sage; known for its cleansing properties as well as promoting relaxation and stress relief. To create the perfect mood for my new spiritual practice I started lighting the Buddha at dawn – because I was awake during the early hours and it was a fitting time to train my mind while the rest of the world slept and my street was silent.

I tried to practice mindfulness: to focus my eyes on the flame burning in front of me, the smell of the white sage cone filling my nostrils, the steady rhythm of my heartbeat, the deep breath in through my nose and out through my mouth, but before the sage cone had burned halfway my mind had already started to wander, thinking about what I wanted for breakfast that morning or where I would take Bear for our daily walk that day or if I wanted to watch The Lion King or Aladdin that afternoon. No matter how hard I tried I just couldn't train my mind to shut up!

When I found meditation at home unsuccessful I signed up for a local meditation class instead. The class was held in the evening in a local natural-healing shop after opening hours. I envisioned a cosy back room with nice calming music and fluffy cushions to sit on – something along those lines, but there was no back room or fluffy pillows. The class took place on the shop floor. A hipster woman with super-long red dreadlocks greeted me at the front door, told me to remove my shoes and socks and guided me towards a mat. At 6 p.m. the shop shutters went down and the class began. I was told to close my eyes and repeatedly chant *'uuummmmmmm.'* I tried my best to keep from laughing and stop myself peeking at the rest of the group who were really going for it – fair play to them, they were clearly more mature than I was.

The meditation guru guided us through a visualisation technique. We were told to imagine a golden light shining down from the sky into the tops of our heads, pouring through our bodies and circling each vertebra in our spine ten times (intended to heal any back problems we may have been suffering). Good, this was exactly what I needed. We got to the fourth vertebra before my head started to wonder, thinking back to biology lessons in uni and trying to remember how many vertebrae there were. Ah ha, thirty-three in total. Damn it, we were going to be there all night.

At the end of the class the guru went round the room asking each of us what we had felt and experienced during the meditation. The only answer I could come up with was that I felt cold, and this wasn't because of some great spiritual awakening. The shop was freezing. It was the middle of winter and the underfloor heating was broken. I couldn't have enjoyed the experience even if I wanted to. I had spent the entire hour dreaming of the nice hot bath I was going to have when I returned home.

But still I was determined not to give up on the spiritual element of healing, especially after reading Bernie Siegel's book *Love, Medicine and Miracles*, another gift I had kindly received during cancer. In this complex yet interesting read, Bernie discusses Eastern practices of training our minds to heal physical illness – relaxation, hypnosis, meditation and visualisation. I was fascinated with his findings, particularly after reading about his encounter with a young boy with a brain tumour. The boy practised visualising rocket ships flying around his head shooting at his tumour, like in a video game. After a few months the boy told his father he had taken a rocket trip through his head and could no longer find his cancer. His parents paid for a CAT scan that miraculously showed his cancer was gone! Of course, there is no evidence that the boy's made-up rocket ship cured his cancer, but whatever happened the cancer was no longer there and that's all that matters. If only I still had a child's imagination and could visualise my own rocket ships!

* * *

Eventually I came to realise that I didn't need to create a new identity; I just needed to accept the one I already had – with some adjustments of course. I spent my first year of cancer getting to know myself, investing in myself and feeling worthy of the investment. I tried new things, adapted to new routines and learnt new practices that I would previously have never entertained. In the end I found my own source of calm in practices that suited me.

I learnt belly breathing from a relaxation therapist who advised me to breath in deeply and allow my tummy to inflate like a balloon, then pause for a minute and release. I created my own affirmation as I breathed: *'In with peace. Out with stress,'* I repeated in my mind in time with my breathing. Every time I became overwhelmed with anxiety I stopped what I was doing and used these two techniques and remarkably they worked. The more I practised them, the more I could feel the calm wash over me and my anxiety deflate from within. It was as if by magic.

When my mood was low I pushed myself to get out into nature, which I knew was a natural serotonin boost for me. I had the advantage of living in the countryside, so I had the bonus of country walks right on my doorstep. The little village I had initially hated became my salvation. Every day I went out with Bear to find new routes, not caring if I got lost, trusting my instincts and Bear's nose to find our way home. Some walks were an hour, some two or three, even. I usually ventured out at sunrise – my favourite time of day when the rest of the world remained asleep. I loved to watch the sky changing from a dusky grey to a brilliant burnt orange above a tranquil, sleeping landscape. I'd stop beside a field of sheep or a horse's paddock and watch the beginning of a new day. Grateful to witness another one.

I learnt the art of doing nothing and for once not feeling guilty for it. I allowed myself to sit and read a book – during treatment I restocked an entire bookcase. It had been taken over by nursing textbooks for five years but now I could read books of my own interest. Some were about cancer but most were about life, love and happiness. I allowed myself days to cosy up on the sofa with Bear, light my candles and burners and wrap the two of us in a blanket. With a hot cup of coffee close at hand and some chocolate, I'd read to my heart's content with no alarms set, no time restraints, no gym to run off to, no extra shifts to work. This was my time to do with as I pleased.

If it was sunny, I'd take my books outside or potter in the garden. I painted an old Belfast sink and transformed it into a quirky flower bed. I painted the outside walls and the inside too. I did whatever I pleased, whatever kept me calm. For me calmness is key now. I can't allow stress to feed back into my life and any time it does I remove myself from that situation. I have to put my own health first – physical and mental, and for me that's liberating. Learning to say no, to set boundaries, to do what is right for me without fear of what others may feel towards me. After a lifetime of undervaluing myself and my life, I realised just how valuable and precious it truly was.

In the end I learnt that spirituality doesn't come from being a diehard vegetarian or animal rights activist. It doesn't come from being a yoga fanatic or meditation guru. It comes from within. From whatever allows you to feel connected. To be still, to find peace and clarity, to slow down a little, to live in the present moment and feel comfortable with the unknown.

Chapter 16

-A Bear-

Halfway through chemo my yogi friend Katrina arranged for us to visit a psychic – a palm reader, located in the back of a hairdressing salon in the city centre, who had been highly recommended. I had had my palms read once before and although I had cried the entire way through, believing every word the woman had said, I went home that evening and picked through her predictions and random words with a fine-tooth comb and decided my facial expressions and short answers had led her to such readings. No, I wasn't a great believer in this kind of witchery but decided to go along for the craic anyway.

I chose to wear my jet-black wig as it was the most natural-looking one out of the bunch, and left my wedding ring at home that day, wanting to mislead the psychic and test whether this fortune teller was the real deal. Although I wasn't convinced of her ability to predict my future, I was both excited and fearful of what she might say – even if it was bullshit!

I went in first. The lights were dimmed, the usual fortune-telling trinkets were scattered about the room: a dreamcatcher here, a crystal ball there, and in the corner was a small table where the psychic gestured for me to sit. But this lady certainly didn't come across as Mystic Meg. She was more like your standard Belfast millie – Northern Irish slang for a female chav. Only this millie was older and clearly wiser – charging £30 for a 15-minute palm reading as she was.

I sat down in front of the *'psychic'* and she took my hands in hers and began tracing the lines imprinted on my skin.

'You have a strong lifeline,' she began.

I doubt that.

'You're in a long-term relationship.'

'Yes.' Good guess.

'You'd like to be married.'

Uh-uh, wrong answer. *'I'm already married.'*

'Oh, but you're having problems in your relationship.'

'Perhaps.' Ok, nice recovery.

'You're contemplating leaving your husband.'

'I've thought about it, yes.' But who hasn't?

'He doesn't understand you.'

No, he doesn't understand cancer.

'You think you will be happier without him.'

'Erm, possibly.' But probably not.

'And you will be.'

What! Really?

'But your will also be happy with him if you go to marriage counselling.'

'Right, ok.' Like that is ever going to happen.

'You will have made your decision in six months' time.'

I could be dead in six months' time.

'That's when you should return for another reading.'

Of course! So you can squeeze another £30 out of me for telling me absolutely nothing!

You can't blame me for being cynical. The palm reader hadn't exactly given me much to go on. There had been no life-changing predictions or anything significant to cling to – not as far as I could comprehend anyway. And although I was grateful she hadn't told me I was going to die, she technically isn't allowed to tell clients that.

Katrina, however, seemed to have more luck with her reading and left the hairdressers feeling optimistic rather than conned out of £30 like I did. Her reading had been career focused, which seemed fitting because she had recently started her own yoga business. My friend had also been told that she was going to be led by an Egyptian guide, which we both took to mean me after we'd supped a bottle of wine. I wasn't sure what use my guidance would be when I couldn't even guide myself but the psychic hadn't known we were together when she read our palms or of my origins, so the Egyptian guide comment intrigued us both. It's something we're still trying to figure out now.

The psychic had focused mainly on my relationship but she had also touched on a few other areas of my life – none of which involved cancer, which I found disappointing. The only prediction of interest to me was that I was apparently going to do something creative with my life.

She hadn't elaborated further on what this creative expression would be other than to say it wouldn't become my career but it would be something significant.

At the time I presumed she was referring to the mastectomy underwear I was designing, which was the only creative thing I was working on at that moment. An idea and a few designs that never went any further than my scrapbook unfortunately. But now I sense she was talking about a deeper form of creativity – maybe referring to creative writing, and one piece of writing in particular. Maybe she was referring to the piece of writing you're reading right now. Maybe that psychic wasn't such a phoney after all. Maybe she had known all along that I was going to write.

* * *

I have and always will hate group work. Having to introduce myself to a group of strangers and be forced to carry out uncomfortable icebreakers fills me with dread. I'm not really a people person, as you may have gathered. Despite having a lot of friends I am socially awkward and see myself as more of an introvert. I honestly prefer the company of animals over most human beings, which my family and friends accept, hence my strong attachment to Bear. My husband and I often joke about my love for Bear and how it exceeds my love for Graeme. He is my baby, replacing the baby I am unlikely to have now. He even acts like one.

Every morning, in a ritual that started during chemo, he lies in my arms like a human child. It's a simple routine that goes like this: I come downstairs and Bear's tail starts beating off the sofa as soon as I open the door. I say hello, ensuring I acknowledge him while making my coffee. He waits patiently knowing I'll be with him soon. Coffee in hand, I open the curtains of the double doors leading to my back garden and allow the light to fill the room, and then I join Bear on the window-facing sofa.

He flops into my arms in slow motion, still sleepy and not quite awake, and lies there until I finish my coffee; closing his eyes again and demanding tummy tickles with his paws. Every time I remove my hand he swipes it back into place. Even now, over a year later, I still get up half an hour earlier than I have to for work to ensure we have that time together. It's our time and I enjoy it as much as he does. If I'd planned my life a little better, I'd have chosen to work with animals rather than people. But, hey, there's still time yet for a career change – I hope!

Anyway, I digress. Back to hating group work. So there are a ton of different therapies available to cancer patients provided by local charities or through the NHS. After diagnosis I finally faced my fears and tried out a few of the counselling services. Some of the therapists were good and some were terrible. My first therapist, Joanne, was decent enough and I decided I liked her. But I spent the first five out of the six sessions offered to me, free on the NHS, unearthing the trauma of my childhood instead of discussing the elephant in the room, which was my cancer.

I was with Joanne throughout chemo. I saw her in between each dose, while I was losing my hair, eyebrows, eyelashes and a little piece of my mind. But despite my present hell I chose instead to talk of my previous one. In the comfort of Joanne's warm, cosy, dimly lit therapy room, sitting on fluffy purple cushions close to the ground, with the soothing scents of lavender and AromaTouch dōTERRA oils filling my nostrils and a box of scented tissues close at hand, I was finally able to open Pandora's box.

I unearthed my inner child at long last after years of burying her. I told the truth – a truth I had never spoken of with anyone. The truth about my sense of guilt surrounding my father's death and the abandonment I felt afterwards followed by my self-destructive teenage years and my shameful experiences as a young woman. My turbulent relationship with my family; the hurt and betrayal I felt after my brother, mother and grandmother walked out of my life.

My uncontrollable self-loathing and intense hatred towards my body; the episodes of self-harm, alcohol and drug abuse. And my unmerciful black dog of depression that tortured my soul. I went through boxes of those coconut-scented tissues before I revealed what I had believed all along, ever since I had heard those dreaded words *'I'm sorry, it's cancer.'* That I was a bad person and I deserved to die.

I told my truth and it was now Joanne's job to *'fix'* me, and with intense work on her side and mine, remarkably, she did just that. She rationalised my childhood experiences and negative thoughts, and finally helped me accept that my truth was untrue. After sixteen years of harbouring thoughts that my father's death was somehow my fault, I finally allowed myself to believe it wasn't. After sixteen years of believing I was a bad person, I finally accepted I was actually a good person. After feeling certain that my cancer was my fault, I finally understood that it wasn't. For a while I felt good and my mental state remained stable ... until chemo and counselling sessions with Joanne ended and I was left to my own devices again. This time I was tormented with a new trauma: my scar.

My breast care nurse referred me to a new counsellor at the end of radio after I broke down during a review appointment with her and shared the difficulty I was having accepting my mastectomy scar. But this new counsellor was no Joanne. Her room was a boring, mediocre office that lacked inviting decor and a calming atmosphere. The therapist was much older than me and a little condescending. She just stared at me when I began to cry, offering me no soft coconut tissues, and when I left feeling angrier and more upset than when I went in I decided I wouldn't be returning.

I found it difficult to explain my current dilemma with my *'ugly'* body to a woman three times my age with no understanding of my suffering. A woman who looked down her nose at me and insulted me with ridiculous advice about breathing exercises and a good night's sleep as the solution to my problems.

I knew from the moment I met that woman that I wasn't going to find the help I so desperately needed.

Since my second surgery I had struggled to look at my body without crying. I didn't allow Graeme to see my naked chest, or any of my naked body for that matter. I wore frumpy baggy clothes or polo necks that I hated to hide my prosthetic. I was paranoid that everyone knew I only had one breast, which of course anyone who knew me did know because I had shared my journey openly on social media (a part of me was now regretting my candidness). I was ashamed of the scar and the fake boob with a weird-looking nipple stuck to it, and the one remaining boob that now seemed so out of place. I felt like a freak, which was forced in my face every time I received radiotherapy; staring at the reflection of my scar and my freaky remaining boob for twenty minutes every day for three weeks. It was enough to drive me over the edge. In the midst of the war with my reflection in the mirror, I was also left searching for my missing identity – the woman I was before cancer stole her from me. I was still struggling to adapt to my new normal, and then I found art therapy.

Art was something I've always enjoyed. Although I hadn't created any artwork of my own since my teenage years, I still had a great appreciation for art and design. I stumbled upon this form of therapy in a leaflet sent to me by Action Cancer. The only problem was it happened in groups. I sent an email asking if one-to-one therapy could be accommodated (I may have told a tiny white lie claiming I had social anxiety disorder, which I probably do have undiagnosed). I assumed the answer would be a no anyway but was pleasantly surprised when the therapist replied with a yes.

I arrived for my first session the following Monday, feeling apprehensive and already regretting my email. I was sceptical of how art therapy could help my current situation and had already decided it would most likely be a complete waste of my time, just like the last counselling session. But I was there now, so I decided to see the first session through.

The charity was located, randomly, in the middle of a row of terrace houses in Belfast's city centre. After driving around aimlessly for thirty minutes in search of a parking space, I abandoned my car and entered the building with ten minutes to spare.

I checked in at reception and stood in the waiting area, already feeling too uncomfortable to sit. I glanced at the cool and funky decor. The paintings on the walls were way out of my league and I hoped I wouldn't be expected to create something of that standard. A few minutes later a lady approached me with her hand outstretched. She introduced herself as the art therapist – an older lady, I'd estimate late forties early fifties, dressed in bright orange African-print trousers with her glasses on top of her head, just how real artists wear them. I took one look at her and instantly decided I liked her. I'm going to call her Joan, to protect her privacy and because, shamefully, I don't remember her name. My bad.

Joan took me into her studio and I felt an unfamiliar twitch at the sides of my mouth. For the first time since radio finished I actually smiled – an honest and real, genuine smile, as I eagerly stared around Joan's bright, cheery workshop; soaking up the splashes of colour and intricate designs on every wall. After completing a brief assessment Joan warned me not to be too disheartened if I didn't create any art on my first day. She advised that I took a wander around the studio to get a feel for the place first, but I was instantly drawn to the desk in the far corner. I had already spotted some sketch pencils there that looked oddly familiar. As I got closer I knew they were the exact same set of watercolours my dad had bought me for one of my birthdays. The same set I still had in my drawer at home, untouched for years.

While I sketched Joan shared some of her background with me beginning with her adventures in South America. She spoke of her time living with Native American tribes and what she learnt from their traditions and ancient rituals. It sounded fascinating, strange but fascinating. These were the type of experiences I was craving now – experiences that were unique and life-changing. I had no time for the boring and mundane after cancer. Living an ordinary life was no longer for me, I had decided.

What interested me even more was to learn of Joan's discovery of her totem – a natural object or spirit animal that is meant to represent and guide you in life. Would you believe, Joan's totem is a bear? I got goosebumps. Her totem was a bear, and I was a mother to a Bear – albeit a black Labrador. But surely my choice of name and fascination with real bears wasn't a coincidence. Joan believed so to. She explained that according to Native American lore and mythology, the bear spirit bestows the gift of wholeness and completion of self in its often solitary journey. My journey with cancer had been a lonely one. In fact, my whole life had been a journey of solitude. *'The bear's rugged independence is thought to guide you to self-discovery,'* she added. And self-discovery was exactly what I was seeking. Ever since I watched Eat Pray Love I had been obsessed with finding my true self – even more so after cancer when my old self was no longer visible at all. Self-discovery was what I needed now more than anything.

I have no idea what my spirit animal is, and I'm not really sure how you find out. Google gives you a number of ways, but I doubt any of them are authentic. I would probably have to visit a Native American tribe myself to truly believe it was accurate anyway.

But if I did go to such extreme lengths, I am fairly certain I would discover that my totem is a bear.

Standing in Joan's art studio I suddenly had a feeling I had been drawn to art therapy for a reason and that I was meant to meet this artist in particular. I didn't know why, but I was sure our meeting wasn't a coincidence.

After twenty minutes or so I looked down at my creation. I had arrived that day with no intentions or expectations of what I may or may not produce. I had had no inclination of what I was going to sketch, or that my sketch was going to be of a human body – my body, to be precise. The drawing had come from within – something my mind clearly needed to express but until now hadn't been able to find a way.

I had drawn an image of my torso – no head or legs, just upper body. I had split the torso down the middle with a red dotted line. One side was a fiery red mass where my breast should have been. On the opposite side, across my remaining lonely breast, I had drawn a single wilted red rose. There were giant green flames erupting from my stomach fiercely burning away the red, angry cancerous cells that I had dotted across the torso. I had no idea where the drawing had come from other than that it was a vision I had clearly been holding in my mind. A vision of how I now saw my body. I suppose the drawing was probably quite disturbing – it was most definitely not fit for the walls outside, but as soon as I had scribbled it down on the paper I breathed a sigh of relief.

I asked Joan if I was supposed to explain my drawing to her. *'Only if you want to,'* she replied. Surprisingly, I did want to. I told her it was how I saw my body after cancer. That I imagined my body as broken, split into two sides. A red and dangerous side on the left – the cancerous side, and wilted beauty on the other – the cancer-free zone. I don't know where this description came from either, other than deep within my soul.

Joan asked me what the green fire signified. Without a moment's thought I robotically told her the fire represented the green laser beam during radiotherapy. In the image, I had drawn the green flames burning the cancer away. Maybe I had been using Bernie Siegel's visualisation techniques subconsciously all along. I don't know, but in twenty minutes I had managed to get it all off my chest, quite literally. The fear I had been holding inside up to that moment I hadn't been able to let go of.

I left Joan's art studio and cried the entire way home. I cried out of relief that I had finally discussed how cancer had destroyed my body confidence, and I cried that my body was also ruined for life. Joan had decided we would work on how I viewed my body, and had come up with a clever idea that involved us creating two moulds of my broken torso and joining them together in some fabulous artistic creation. She hoped it would bring me some level of acceptance and healing.

Our next appointment was scheduled for the following Monday. In the meantime I was sent home with homework: Joan had supplied me with my very first journal and had asked me to fill it in however I wished. Over the course of the week I could use drawings, words, magazine cuttings, anything at all to express my thoughts and feelings on that day. I could then choose to share my journal or keep it to myself. It was up to me.

That evening I wrote my first entry. It read:

Who am I?

- I was a nurse
- I was a wife
- I was a friend
- I was a sister
- I was an aunty
- I was a daughter
- I was a woman
- I was attractive
- I was fit and healthy
- I was ambitious
- I was adventurous
- I was young
- I was free
- I was whole

But now I am:

- Broken
- Exhausted
- Alone
- Sad
- Empty
- Ugly
- Freak
- Angry
- Different
- Fake

Beside the entry I stuck a picture of me on the beach in Cannes wearing that gorgeous orange plunging swimsuit, standing at the water's edge on that private stretch of paradise. The photo was taken three weeks after my diagnosis, after I had just received the phone call telling me that the cancer hadn't spread. In that particular photo I am posing – my arms above my head, my hands making a peace sign, and I am smiling. My body is sexy and muscular. I still have two full breasts and no ugly scars. My sun-kissed golden-brown hair is flowing freely just below my shoulders. I have gorgeous long eyelashes and my own eyebrows – not tattooed ones. I look confident and healthy and oddly happy, all things considered. I look beautiful. I stared at this image for hours and I cried. Who was that girl?

The next day I drew a sketch of me on my wedding day. I copied the image from a wedding photograph of Graeme and me that we display on a large canvas in our front room. The canvas I had taken down in disgust on numerous occasions throughout treatment because I couldn't bear to look at that girl any more. I sketched her long curly locks, her beautiful natural curves and two matching perky breasts. I shaded in the sparkle in her eyes, the laughter lines on her beautiful face and her brilliant smile. I cried as I drew the old version of me; staring at the photograph, searching for the girl I once was. Then a random thought popped into my head: what if the new me wasn't so different to the old me?

I looked at my drawing and the canvas on the wall and realised that the only things that had changed were my outward appearance. Suddenly I had a great idea for my journal. I was going to turn it into a scrapbook using photos of the old me and photos of the new me so I could compare the two women, before and now.

I printed hundreds of photos of me before and me after cancer; photos of my life before and after; photos of the people I loved before and after; photos of my Bear, my family and my friends and all the adventures we had taken together before and after cancer. I

sat at my kitchen table and I created a masterpiece. It took me three hours to fill the entire book.
Three hours to come to my final decision: I was still the same me except I was now so much more.

In the pages of that journal I was finally able to see that cancer had been my gift as well as my curse. Thanks to that unexpected gift I was now an aunty again, a sister and a daughter. I was a better wife to my husband, a better friend, a better doggy mummy and a better human being altogether. As I flicked through my creation and examined each and every photo of myself I saw so much more than just a body, whole or broken. I saw passion and creativity. I saw a great thirst for love, life and adventure. I saw everything that makes me me. I discovered that my body is just a vessel. My soul is who I really am. I saw that I was so much more than cancer! I was a survivor.

I couldn't wait to tell Joan my incredible discovery – my life-changing moment, when I discovered me again; the same me, but different. Sadly I never got the chance. In fact, I never saw my bear-loving friend again for reasons totally unrelated to cancer and because of a global pandemic known as Covid-19.

Chapter 17

-The Rona-

I finished radiotherapy a few days after Valentine's Day, which Graeme and I had spent together at the Cancer Centre (how romantic!) while I recovered from another treatment. I used the time to plan my first solo trip to Italy; hopefully at the end of March, giving me a month to recover from radio, regain my strength and then head out to my favourite country – alone! The prospects of flying solo no longer crippled me with fear. I was a big girl now. A big girl who had just conquered cancer. I thought I could manage a journey across Italy all by myself, and I was more than ready for a new adventure. But this time I wouldn't have to please anyone else other than myself and my writing.

The idea of writing a novel first occurred to me during my steroid-fuelled insomnia in my early chemo days. Initially I'd thought about writing a blog to share my experience with breast cancer but the idea fell by the wayside when I became more engrossed in designing mastectomy underwear, completing my chemo bucket list and just trying to get through the day without having a mental breakdown. The thought of then having to sit and write about it all, forcing me to relive each experience, was just too much to handle. The trauma was too fresh at that stage.

Instead I wrote a diary – just snippets of my thoughts and feelings at the end of each evening. Some entries were more significant than others, like the time Graeme surprised me with a hack through the countryside – my very first time on a horse and one of my bucket-list challenges. The experience was a special one. He had planned the activity just after my first chemo when I still had my own hair and was just a *'normal'* girl riding a horse – except I wasn't *'normal'* and neither was the horse.

My horse was pure white and a born leader, I was told. His name was Duke and he liked to stay in front. He knew his path and all I had to do was sit up top and enjoy the view. He needed no guidance or input from me. Duke was a free spirit, and while I was with him I felt free too, just for that short moment in time.

Those special moments found their way into my diary until they didn't any more. Maybe because those freeing moments dwindled off as cancer tightened its noose around my neck. Or maybe I was too distracted with mountain climbing to write any more. Either way the diary was back-burnered, along with the mastectomy swimwear, my blog, my own podcast, a TV interview with Cancer Research, a hair-loss campaign and any other bright ideas I had to change the world. I found I didn't have time for any of it in the end, even though time was all I had.

Active treatment was a busy period of my life. I tried to cram so much living time in with my family and friends, just in case I was actually dying, that there wasn't really any time for me (or for anything else) and there certainly wasn't enough time to write a book. But writing a story wasn't just another random idea that cancer had initiated. Writing a novel had been a lifelong dream of mine since my father had told me I would write one. I still held on to that childhood vision that one day I'd hold a hard copy of my very own book. A book with my name printed across the cover. A book that would somehow change people's lives.

When radio finished I found myself standing at a crossroads unable to turn back on myself but not quite sure how to move forward either. After a few weeks of moping around the house crying continuously and only allowing myself the company of my two black dogs, I decided enough was enough. Until I knew how to move forward I would do something more useful while standing still.

I would use this period of contemplation and uncertainty to write my damn book! And where better a place to write a story than Italy.

By tying in a solo trip to Italy with writing my book I was ticking off two lifelong dreams in one go. I imagined my story coming to life in my favourite spot in Rome, Castel Sant'Angelo – a towering cylindrical building that was once used as a castle and fortress but now serves as a museum with a gorgeous outdoor coffee shop at the very top of its highest tower that provides panoramic views of Vatican City and the Pont Sant'Angelo bridge. If that didn't inspire me to write, I don't know what would. Not to mention the Italian coffee and Italian wine I could count on to keep me motivated. Yes, Italy was the perfect spot to write my first, and most likely last, memoir.

Before I headed to Italy, though, I had promised Chloe I would visit her and her two girls, Pearl and Penny. I had yet to meet Penny and barely knew Pearl, and now seemed a fitting time to finally make the effort to get to know them. Besides, I hadn't been *'home home'* in four years. I suppose I had been avoiding Blackpool, especially after the fall out with my brother, but now I looked forward to the reunion with my old friends and second families. I booked my flights without giving much thought to the news of a deadly virus wreaking havoc in China. China was thousands of miles away. Surely the virus would never find its way over here.

A week before I was due to fly the UK had their first Covid-19 case. Ok, I was a little more worried now but surely it was an isolated incident, right? In a matter of days the cases had gone up to eighteen and were steadily rising. Although Britain still seemed pretty low risk, Italy was another story. I watched in horror as my favourite country was torn apart. Thousands of people were dying. The hospitals were on their knees. Medical staff were losing their lives while trying to treat those who were infected. Morgues were overrun and bodies were piling up with nowhere to bury them.

The army was called in to remove the infected bodies before they caused even more widespread disease.

It was like something from a zombie apocalypse movie. Eventually the Italian government was forced to issue strict lockdown measures across the entire country. Italy became the worst hit European country and the new epicentre of this now global pandemic. That was until the UK overtook Italy with its number of cases and ended up with the largest death toll in the whole of Europe only weeks later.

I wisely decided against my trip to Blackpool just in time, really. Other people were still holidaying across the globe of course with no regard for the growing spread of the disease, lapping up the rapid drop in holiday prices and having a great old time. Unlike them, though, I knew I had to be sensible. I had just finished cancer treatment, my immune system was only just beginning to recover and I was more prone to infection than others. If my damaged body caught this deadly virus, I knew it would be unlikely to recover. I didn't survive cancer to be wiped out by the rona – no way, so with a heavy heart I cancelled my flights *'home home'* and put Italy off for a while too. Or maybe permanently given their current state.

Fourteen days after Italy issued their lockdown, the UK followed suit. In the blink of an eye Brits were forced to stay at home to protect themselves, their families and the NHS from Covid-19. The public's response was varied. Some panic-bought as if the world were coming to an end – you couldn't get loo roll, hand sanitiser, cleaning products, pasta or a tin of baked beans for love nor money. Supermarkets were swamped and it wasn't long before the aisles were completely emptied. It was ridiculous and it was selfish. It would be months before supermarkets could restock essential supplies, leaving some of society's most vulnerable with nothing.

Then there was the rest of the population – those who weren't in a complete state of panic and who ignored the rules entirely. These were the people who flocked to local beaches and national

parks, like they were on their summer holidays, or held lockdown parties in the streets, or worse in their houses, with no regard to the government's pleas for social distancing.
It wasn't until the death toll surged into the thousands that people got scared and heeded advice. Those who were vulnerable were sent letters telling them to shield, to not leave their homes for twelve weeks – no one in, no one out. I, of course, received a shielding letter and was devastated. So much for moving on with my life!

I had been in my own version of lockdown for the last nine months. Yes, my life was on hold long before Covid-19, and now was when I was supposed to be moving on – not forced to stay at home unable to see my family and friends; the people who had carried me through my cancer journey, my support networks, the people I needed in my life to survive pre- and post-cancer (including my brother and my nephews who had recently moved home to Northern Ireland to be close to me and our family. The two young boys had only got used to their Aunty Alex and her fun weekly visits when all of a sudden she disappeared again!

Lockdown also delayed my return to work. I had been out of work for almost a year and the longer I was off the more I feared going back. But work was definitely out of the question now – I couldn't return even if I wanted to; I had to shield and, besides, there were Covid-positive patients on my ward. There was no way I could go back to my old job. Not now – maybe not ever. To top it off I wasn't entitled to the government's eighty per cent furlough scheme, so, unlike everyone else, I wasn't paid to stay at home.
I was bitter and I was angry. Fuck you, Covid-19, and fuck you, cancer!

* * *

Lockdown was a weird time for all. For some it was a time of fear and isolation with only the antics of Donald Trump and Boris

Johnson to entertain or aggravate people. For others it was a time to connect with family and friends via Zoom parties, online bake-offs and the new TikTok craze. For those infected it was a time to fight for their lives on hospital ventilators, alone and afraid.

For our frontline workers it was a time of panic and uncertainty as they faced the unknown – an unknown that threatened to wipe out their patients as well as themselves. For our children it was a time of confusion and frustration when they were pulled out of school and told they weren't allowed to see their friends any more. For me it was a time of quiet solitude. The time I had wanted to avoid but now was forced to accept. The time to reflect on my journey with cancer.

The initial four-week lockdown was extended, lasting three months in total but with further lockdowns and restrictions to follow, making 2020 everyone's worst nightmare. Despite governments' best efforts the virus was untamable and affected each person one way or another.

Mental health suffered tremendously. Anxiety and depressive symptoms heightened due to fear, isolation and limited access to services. Just like the ICU bed crisis caused by the pandemic, mental health inpatient units faced the same capacity strains. Suicide rates soared and are set to continue rising. Reports of domestic violence spiked, thought to be driven by financial stress, crowded homes, movement restrictions and reduced peer support. Alcohol and drug abuse naturally followed suit. Unemployment and redundancies skyrocketed. The whole world was falling apart, and all we could do was stay home and watch the nightmare unfold on our TV screens.

The NHS was halfway through a decade of underfunding when the pandemic hit. It was already dealing with a relatively low level of beds, dangerous staff shortages, stretched A & E and routine surgery waiting times and large cuts to social care, public health and mental health services. Although the NHS rapidly revamped their services on a large scale at the start of 2020 to release capacity for treating patients with Covid-19, all other routine care was put on hold. Thousands of patients were discharged early to free up beds, postponing planned treatment, shifting appointments to online where possible, and redeploying staff to Covid wards.

All routine hospital treatment that wasn't considered a priority or life-saving was postponed, including cancer care, so life-saving chemotherapy and radiotherapy were delayed or cancelled for thousands because it was taken as a given that the risk of a cancer patient contracting the virus outweighed the risks of postponing treatment – and it resulted in thousands of unnecessary deaths. MRIs, CT scans, vital screening and routine mammograms were all suspended, including my own. Shockingly, Macmillan are currently predicting up to 50,000 missed cancer diagnoses in the UK alone because of the pandemic. For once I felt lucky to have been told I had cancer the year previously. If I had been diagnosed during the pandemic, my circumstances may have been very different – not to mention that I would have had to face the disease alone in isolation. What an odd concept to feel lucky to have been diagnosed with cancer when I was.

The majority of my friends are nurses who were on the frontline. I naturally feared for their safety, especially when Gillian was redeployed to a Covid ward and Jenna to a Covid test centre. Our group chat, that had originally been set up to discuss my cancer, was now taken over with photos of my friends' cut faces from dreadful PPE and the daily challenges they were facing. It was hard to comfort my friends – while they were out there saving the world I was sitting at home in my bubble watching the virus wreak havoc in very shape and form and shamefully feeling bitter and resentful that my post-cancer plans weren't unfolding.

It was a bitterness that left me crippled with guilt, coupled with feeling utterly useless. I was a nurse too – or at least I used to be.

I should have been standing alongside my friends fighting the virus and helping save people's lives; not at home feeling sorry for myself as usual. But eventually I accepted that home was exactly where I was meant to be, and that I too could be useful in a very different way.

I decided that the only service I could offer the world at that time was my writing. I was sure someone somewhere, with or without cancer, would benefit from my story, so I removed all distractions, tuned myself out of Covid-19 and tuned myself in to my writing. I switched my phone to airplane mode, I stopped watching the news (that was plagued with death and disease), I stopped checking the daily death tolls online that I had been obsessing over for weeks, I stopped spending mindless hours scrolling through the same negative stories on my social media that only fuelled people's panic and despair. I turned my focus away from the apocalypse outside my front door and focused on the task at hand.

I set up my workstation at the kitchen table. The chairs were uncomfortable as hell and made my back burn even hotter, but the pain kept me alert. There was no beautiful Italian surroundings here to inspire me – just four walls, my kitchen table, coffee on tap (in my special *'like a boss'* mug that Gillian had made for me) and Bear, sitting on the sofa opposite, wondering what the hell I was doing for all those hours. I soon learnt that there is no right or wrong place to write a book. For a book to truly be authentic, the words must come from your heart not from your surroundings.

By the end of week one I had only written seven thousand words – how the hell do people actually write a book? I vented my exasperation to my husband: I wanted to tear my newly grown fluffy hair out the task was so daunting, my sentences didn't flow, the chapters were disjointed and my story didn't make any sense. But Graeme encouraged me to stick with it, and so I did. Determined this would be one thing I wouldn't quit on.

Eventually I found my rhythm. The words started to flow naturally through my fingertips. I soon had so many ideas I became overwhelmed with the number of words I had to get on paper. I wrote like a demon – like a woman possessed, often waking at 3 a.m. bright-eyed and ready to write. Unlike my late-night ventures during chemo, there was no time for sad movies on repeat or depressing soundtracks.
This time round I was a woman on a mission. A woman determined to tell my tale at long last.

Strangely I found my best ideas always came to me at 3 a.m. in the dead of night, and before the sun rose the only sounds were my fingers dancing across my keyboard. I became intrigued by this random 3 a.m. waking and so did a little digging. I found some interesting literature that suggested there's a spiritual meaning behind waking between the hours of three and five on a repeated basis. I was intrigued. Apparently waking at this time is a sign you should move toward your higher purpose in life – a time to connect with your higher self. I had never heard of the term *'higher self'* or *'higher purpose'* before cancer. I had previously employed a very black-and-white trail of thinking: anything that I couldn't see didn't exist. But cancer encouraged me to look beyond what is in plain sight and to examine myself, and life, on a much deeper level; to look within. In doing so I found my purpose, the very thing I'd spent a lifetime searching for: my purpose was to write. To write this book, in particular. The story I'm sharing with you now. The story of my ascent. A story that may one day become someone else's survival guide.

Chapter 18

-The Change Of Life-

A change in any situation forces us into the unknown, and people tend to fear what they are unfamiliar with. As individuals we either thrive on change or we will fall. Whether it be a change in career, a change in marital status, a change in living conditions, a change in politics or changes that affect the entire world. Whatever the circumstances of change may be, it forces us to face a new uncertainty, which can be stressful and destructive.

Although for some change is welcomed as a form of progression, unfortunately for others it is something to be resisted with stubborn determination. For me, the past year was nothing but change – all of which was completely out of my control. Between cancer and Covid, normality was certainly a thing of the past, and to be quite honest I was sick to death of change!

Previously I had used distraction to cope with or avoid change. I used drink and drugs to distract myself from my grief and family issues in my teenage years. I used the gym to avoid my marital issues after Thailand. I used the bucket list to distract myself from cancer during chemotherapy, and now I used my book as a diversion from Covid.

During lockdown I engrossed myself in my writing so deeply that I barely noticed the changes occurring outside my four walls never mind inside my own body until one morning I stood up out of bed and came crashing down to the floor. My ankles had given way from under me, snapping me back to cruel reality. The world was still in chaos – and that now included my body, as another change was forced upon me: the change of life. Almost overnight my body had aged thirty plus years. The hormone tablets I took every morning and the implant inserted in my lower belly every month had finally taken effect. My ovaries were no longer producing the essential hormones my body needed to function and my medically-induced menopause had begun.

Unfortunately the weakness and pain in my ankles were only the start of it. The lack of oestrogen in my body resulted in me losing the natural lubrication in my joints. After my first fall I quickly learnt to take my time in the mornings, shuffling my way from one piece of furniture to the next. Using them for support while gently clicking and grinding my joints awake with every painful step. The debilitation was heartbreaking. I kissed goodbye to ever returning to the gym or hiking up my favourite mountains. My body was no longer fit for it. Within a matter of months my knees followed the same pattern as my ankles, and then my fingers, and then my toes. Every joint, every muscle, every bone was affected, and there was nothing I could do about it other than take painkillers and try and persevere with my life.

My joint pain isn't entirely down to the menopause – I also have radiotherapy to thank for it. My oncologists have suggested I now have arthritis in my joints and possibly osteoporosis in my ankles (I'm waiting on scan results to confirm), but hormone therapy certainly antagonised my joints and made matters worse.

Between the pain in my back from surgery trauma and now the rest of my body shutting down, it was difficult for me to stay upbeat. Since my diagnosis I had tried to focus on the quality of my life rather than the quantity, but the quality of my life was now shattered. Hormone treatment was going against the motto I had sworn to live my life by *'to be happy in being here'* and it wasn't long before I resented the very thing that was keeping me alive. Again I contemplated whether my life was worth such agony, and I found myself facing a new and extremely difficult dilemma: do I want to live? Or do I want to exist?

Prior to experiencing menopause myself, I naively knew very little about it other than what Jim's dad had told me. I mean, it's not exactly part of the school curriculum and until recent years was rarely spoken of publicly. Of course I'd heard of hot flushes, loss of periods and increased irritability that usually occurs in women aged fifty plus, but I wasn't aware that the menopause would have such a crippling impact on all aspects of my life.

I didn't know it was possible to experience ten different moods in the space of a minute. To go from laughing, to crying, to psycho in a single heartbeat. I didn't know that the mood swings could be triggered by something completely irrational like someone crunching crisps too loudly in my ear or someone not washing the dishes. I hadn't heard of the extreme fatigue and lack of motivation that left me completely wiped out and even more irritable, or the relentless insomnia that drove me to anxious sleep-deprived sobs. I didn't know my brain would fog over in an unbreakable mist eating away at my concentration and causing me to lose the ability to string a sentence together. I didn't know menopause went way beyond hot flushes and the end of periods.

The term *'menopause belly'* was also new to me. Yes, I knew women put on weight during *'the change'* but I didn't know it all went to the midsection, creating an unpleasant overhang that left me physically repulsed. In the space of a year I'd gone from having a six-pack I was immensely proud of to a hideous muffin top. My waist vanished, none of my clothes fitted me any more and I went up three dress sizes. As if I wasn't already body conscious enough after being forced to live with only one boob for the rest of my life, I now had weight gain and cellulite to contend with as well. My body no longer felt like my own on the inside or the outside.

I begrudgingly forced myself to the doctors every month to be injected with something that was ruining my life. I held my breath and bit down hard into my lower lip when the oversized needle was inserted into my lower belly, refusing to let out even a whisper of my inner protests. Every morning I involuntarily swallowed my medication. Medication that was preventing me from having a baby. Medication that was making my life a painful misery. Medication that was ruining my marriage. Subconsciously I tried to hold off from taking the tablets for as long as possible. Sometimes it was midday or late afternoon before I opened the medication cupboard. Some days I missed them entirely. Taking my medication was the most strenuous task of the day. Unwillingly swallowing four tiny tablets was incredibly exhausting. It was a daily struggle of me against me: my mind forcing me to swallow my medication while my heart screamed, *'Please, no more!'*

The experience opened my eyes to how my patients must feel when they resist their medications. I now understood why they refuse tablets that cause them to sleep their lives away, or why they refuse medications that quieten their mind when they don't necessarily want it silenced. I now understand why they don't want to take antipsychotics that force them to pile on the pounds, or why they don't want to be force-fed nutritious supplements through a tube because they're genuinely terrified of gaining weight. I now understand my patients' resistance to treatment, resistance against the unknown, resistance against losing control of their own bodies and minds, resistance against medical staff – who postulate that they know what's best for them when they had only just met. I now understand my patients' fears, suspicions and anger. But, more importantly, I understand that their medication is necessary, just as mine is.

Sadly, necessary for my patients and myself doesn't come without sacrifice in some shape or form.

Around four months into menopause I lost my sex drive entirely. Sex become so painful I avoided it at all costs. At first I made my excuses – until excuses were no longer necessary, and my vagina's dry protests were obvious to both Graeme and me. Penetration was impossible and foreplay was no longer enjoyable. I tried a few natural lubricants (all hormone free, of course – I couldn't use standard Durex like *'normal'* people), but it wasn't long before they became a turn off too.

Eventually I withdrew from all sexual activity and physical intimacy. I didn't want to be held or cuddled. I didn't want to cosy up on the sofa in the evenings. I didn't want to be kissed or to hold hands. I just wanted to be left alone! I slowly started shutting down. My body shut down, my mind, my reproductive system and my vagina, until all that was left of me was an emotionless empty shell.

I thought Graeme would eventually leave me. Let's face it, I wasn't really giving him any reason to stick around. I was moody, irritable and no longer fulfilling my husband's needs. Although Graeme never mentioned sex, not once, I had decided he would eventually go looking for it elsewhere. I mean, how could I expect him to be celibate for the next three years whilst I was on Zoladex treatment. I figured the price for my life would, in the end, undoubtably be my marriage.

I soon found myself isolated not only from my husband, but from my family and friends also. I was uncomfortable discussing my situation with my friends. Partly because I was jealous of their *'normal'* happy lives and partly because I knew they couldn't possibly relate. Unlike cancer, which I was incredibly open about, I stayed silent when it came to menopause. I can openly admit I was ashamed and embarrassed of it.

* * *

I returned to work halfway through the pandemic, which proved to be more difficult than I anticipated. The first day I put my blues back on, I tore them off immediately in complete disgust.

Who was I kidding? I wasn't a nurse any more. My working days were exhaustingly painful due to my low mood, irrational anxiety and stubborn joint pain. Not to mention the trauma response it evoked every time I drove past the Cancer Centre on my way in.

I then started to believe my work colleagues hated me and were talking about me behind my back without any evidence of this irrational belief other than I was just certain of it. I found myself hiding in back offices trying to catch a breath, and spending the majority of my day fighting back tears. My mind was tortured with negative thoughts. Even when I was sleeping I couldn't escape my own negativity. Every night I dreamt the same dream: I was trapped in work, all the doors were locked and I couldn't escape. Both patients and staff were pointing at my fake boob, shouting *'freak'* at me, laughing and sneering in my face. I woke most nights in a sweaty breathless panic counting down the dreaded hours until another torturous working day.

I started having panic attacks, usually as I drove in or out of work. They got that bad that I found my chest tightening and I struggled to get a breath, forcing me to pull the car over and carry out my belly breathing techniques before I could drive on. On my days off I moped around in my jammies scrolling through endless job sites, searching for a way out, looking for any occupation that wasn't nursing. But there was nothing that appealed to me. I wished I didn't have to work at all but at twenty-nine retiring isn't an option!

The stress I was under in work naturally projected into my home life – a stress that I had sworn to avoid. After another miserable ten-hour shift I arrived home to an untidy kitchen and Bear still waiting for his daily walk. Pre-menopause I may have let this slide, but now that I was a hormonal mess an untidy kitchen was enough to send me into a fit of rage. Bearing in mind I now suffered with severe fatigue and had gone back to almost full-time hours while dealing with crippling anxiety and facing the pressures of working in a clinical setting that put me at greater risk of catching Covid-19 when I was supposed to be shielding, of course an untidy kitchen and un-walked dog was enough to send me over the edge. A full-blown row erupted in my home that evening. Yes, I may have overreacted by telling my husband to move out because of some unwashed dishes, but I hadn't expected the situation to escalate as far as it did.

Graeme had naturally lost the rag with me and stormed upstairs. After a short cooling-off period I followed him, believing we would laugh this silly row off as we had all the others, and that all would be forgiven. But this time when I entered our bedroom the atmosphere was different. You could cut the tension with a knife and my husband's face was livid. I cautiously sat on the edge of the bed and let my husband speak for a change. He stared at the wall, unable to make eye contact with me, his face turning from anger to sorrow. *'I miss my wife, Alex, and I don't know how to get her back.'*

I sat in stunned silence. I suppose I hadn't given much thought to how my situation affected Graeme. I had been so preoccupied with how cancer affected me, I had selfishly believed I was the only victim in this marriage. I now realised cancer hadn't just robbed me of my former self, it had also robbed my husband of his former wife too. Neither of us had signed up to this on that cliff in Sorrento and it was unfair on both of us. It wasn't just *'why me?'*, it was *'why us?'*.

Graeme told me how ignored he felt. How I barely acknowledged him any more. How I was emotionless around him and how I seemed to have lost all passion for him and for my life. I knew I had begrudgingly accepted my fate and detached myself from pretty much everything and everyone I loved, but I hadn't realised my fate didn't need to destroy my husband's. Or maybe I had but I didn't want to accept it. Graeme still had a bright and healthy future ahead of him, after all. A future that would look much brighter and happier if I and my cancer were no longer a part of it. Maybe it would be kinder to let my husband go? Maybe facing the future alone would be the best solution for both of us?

'What if we separate and just remain friends,' I suggested.

'I can't do that, Alex. It's all or nothing, you know that.'

'I don't want you to stick around out of guilt because I had cancer,' I answered.

'If that was the case, I'd have left long ago.'

The room fell silent.

I don't want to lose you, Graeme. But I don't know how to keep you either.

* * *

After another sleepless night I got up early to take Bear for a long walk and clear my head. Graeme and I had agreed to try and work on things, but we both agreed this would be the last time we would. Divorce was now a very real possibility and I knew something drastic needed to change, although I still felt it was my husband who needed to make all the changes not me. I threw on my oversized coat, plugged my headphones in, squeezed my swollen achy ankles into my walking boots and searched for a podcast.

The podcast world was still relatively new to me. Prior to cancer I wouldn't have thought to tune in – I'd always preferred books or the internet as my go-to sources of information. But since diagnosis I had found them educating, interesting and honest. There was no bullshit on the shows I listened to. Just real people sharing real experiences. I devoured books throughout my treatment and will always have a passion for reading, but it was nice to have a variety of sources of information, especially when I needed to give my eyes and head a rest and just listen.

I have two favourite shows I listen to religiously. The first one is The Melissa Ambrosini Show, where Melissa interviews a series of pretty cool and inspiring thought leaders from around the globe and they describe how they made epic changes in their lives. Each interview has a different focus and Melissa covers a huge variety of content. It's impossible not to learn something new and valuable during each episode. My second is You, Me and the Big C – a cancer-focused podcast led by a group of individuals who either had, still have cancer or have lost a loved one with cancer. This is obviously super close to home for me and although upsetting at times is always relatable.

Both podcasts helped me enormously through my cancer and healing journey and I needed help again, so I typed *'menopause'* into the search bar and hoped to find another useful podcast to add to my toolbox. The top result was titled Menopause: The Good, The Bad & The Downright Sweaty. I scrolled through the episodes and found exactly what I was looking for: *'Menopause and Relationships Part. 1.'*

As I walked with Bear along the familiar country lanes I found myself relating to everything the two relatively young presenters were discussing: how these women both had experienced medically-induced menopause for reasons other than cancer; how they had distanced themselves from their partners; how they both struggled with physical intimacy; how they had suffered with depression, suicidal thoughts and severe anxiety; how they withdrew from their friends and family; how they struggled with constant irritability, hot flushes and panic attacks. I found myself unconsciously nodding my head in agreement with it all!

I extended my walk a little longer, desperate to hear more despite the heavy rain breaking through the trees. I moved on to the next episode: *'Menopause and Relationships: A man's perspective.'* This time it was the husbands' or partners' turn to share.

Surprisingly, hearing the men's experience of menopause saddened me even more than the women's version had. Would you believe the two men used the exact words Graeme had used to describe me – empty, blank and vacant? They also spoke of how they struggled with feeling unwanted and useless. Poor them and poor Graeme. On a brighter note, the podcast did finish with some useful tips on how both couples learnt to adjust in their very different situations, which ultimately made all the difference in helping them remain together. Ok, there's still hope for us yet, then. They concluded that the reason behind their relationships' success was down to one key principle: education.

I realised that Graeme and I had never fully prepared for *'the change'.* Neither of us had researched it or sought advice on how to handle the side effects of menopause. We'd gone into this battle practically blind with a useless medication leaflet (that Jim's dad had given us months ago) as our only weapon. As Bear and I tottered up the drive in a weary, muddy mess, I accepted it wasn't Graeme alone who needed to change – it was both of us, and the way to move forward was by arming ourselves with knowledge and educating ourselves on the menopause.

The following Friday evening I arranged a date night. Bearing in mind Belfast was back in another mini lockdown and my choice of location was therefore limited, I worked it in my favour. I decided we would go for a drive to Tim Hortons drive-through. Customers weren't permitted to sit in, which again suited me better. A French vanilla latte to go would work perfectly. I knew Graeme would pooh-pooh the idea immediately if I told him what I had planned, so I kept it a surprise and successfully managed to trick my husband into spending his Friday evening sitting in Tim Hortons car park with a coffee, a cup of tea and some bite-sized donuts listening to women's problems over the car's sound system. After his initial mortification, even he could admit the date was a success. Graeme related to the men on the podcast just as I had related to the women.

I watched as light-bulb moments fired off in both our heads like a faulty set of Christmas tree lights: so that's the reason I can't remember anything any more! So that's the reason she can't bear to be touched! With understanding came acceptance and a formulated plan on how we could proceed as a couple. The first change we decided to make, right there and then in Tim Hortons car park, was to be kinder to each other.

Over the next few months I worked hard on being nicer to my husband. I held my tongue and paused before starting unnecessary arguments. I apologised on the few occasions I didn't manage to keep my mouth shut, and my apologies were accepted. I made small changes to ensure Graeme felt acknowledged, like stopping at the garage on my way home to buy him his favourite chocolate or remembering to text him when I was at work to ask how his day was going or sending him funny photos of Bear with his tongue hanging out to make him laugh. I wanted to show my husband that I still loved him and wanted him because I did love him, more than anything (except Bear, of course), and I understood he needed to feel my love, not just hear it. If I could only display my affection with a brief cuddle on the sofa in the evening or by placing my hand on top of his in the car or giving him a gentle kiss goodnight, for him that was enough.

Graeme worked on being nicer too. He learnt to be more patient with me and hold his tongue if I snapped. He too apologised on the few occasions he didn't, and his apology was accepted. He understood my obsession over household chores, and we came up with a system that ensured he helped with the workload. He made more time for me to encourage me to do things I previously enjoyed, but to do them together this time round and at a much slower pace. He was more considerate, even if it was only making me a cup of coffee in the mornings or occasionally cooking dinner or running me a hot bath after work. The small gestures made a difference. Our passion between the sheets may have been replaced with tear-stained cuddles instead on the nights when it was all too much for both of us, but I finally quit masking my pain from him.

His reassurance was comforting instead of empty like before because he finally understood how I felt, and for me that was enough.

I am no marriage expert but I certainly know this. In only three short years of marriage ours has faced more turmoil and uncertainty than most marriages sustain in a lifetime, and yet we are still together and still going strong. Our marriage isn't a typical one, but then it never really was. We come from completely opposite worlds – a bit like my own parents did. Me from a busy English seaside town; him a country boy born and bred. Me the ASBO teenager; him the ideal pupil. Me an adrenaline junkie; him cautious and always by the book. Him a home bird, whereas I'm always looking for the next adventure. Yet despite our differences we complement each other. We love each other, and we can't be apart from one another. For me it doesn't get much better than that.

Chapter 19

-I Did It-

I had made it through another Christmas. Like many people in the cancer community, I find Christmas is a significant milestone; one that many of us cannot help but fear may be our last. However, this Christmas, I didn't have the same morbid feelings that had plagued my previous one. Instead I was hopeful.

This Christmas period had been a strange one – even stranger than the last, which was largely spent in hospital fighting for my life. This year the festive holidays were spent in a very different form of isolation, another lockdown. Graeme and I had agreed to spend Christmas with my family this year, at my brother's new house. We bent the rules ever so slightly and mixed three households, inviting my mum and her husband too. It was our first family Christmas since my father had passed – with a few additional members and two very excited little boys. My nephews made Christmas for us all, and I knew our family was one of the lucky ones getting to spend the day together.

There would be many spending Christmas alone – grandparents in nursing homes unable to receive visitors; stranded lorry drivers stuck at European borders unable to make it home for Christmas; thousands in hospital, unsure if they would live to see another one, alongside burnt-out medical staff who sacrificed their family Christmas dinner to nurse the diseased and dying, risking their own lives in the process; people forced into isolation over Christmas and New Year after being in close contact with the virus, many of who lived alone. Not to mention the hundreds of children who would wake up to no presents under the tree this year after their parents had lost their jobs. It was a bleak Christmas for many and I thought of all those people, the old and the young, as I stared at our Christmas feast laid before me, and my family gathered around it, thanking the heavens that we were the lucky ones.

With Christmas being a quiet one, and an even quieter New Year looming, I decided to make New Year's Day a day to remember – kicking the year off as I meant to go on, on a high. Despite the country suffering a depressing low, I was determined Graeme and I would make the day eventful – after all, I may not live to see another one myself!

Luckily for us, there had been a bout of cold weather over the holidays leaving higher ground blanketed in fresh clean snow. My social media had become plastered with photos of the Mourne Mountains covered in the fluffy white stuff and I was itching to take some shots of my own. So I convinced Graeme to join me in toasting the New Year with a cup of hot coffee at the top of those snowy mountains and a view of the first sunrise of 2021. Graeme was surprisingly game for the idea and had the head torches in the backpacks at the ready. And that's why, on New Year's Eve, my husband and I were tucked up and fast asleep by ten, completely sober (a first), with our alarms set for 3.30 a.m.

* * *

I had first reattempted the Mourne Mountains exactly one year previous. Again, on New Year's Day, with Gillian and her friend Gillian. I had stupidly chosen to climb the highest mountain in the region, Slieve Donard. It was a month after my second surgery and my body was still in a lot of pain. I had also been rendered pretty much immobile after having my lymph nodes removed, and for the previous month had done very little physical activity. I knew the journey to the top would be a difficult one but it never crossed my mind that I may not be able to complete it. I had climbed it during chemotherapy, and surely my body was in a worse state back then than it was now. Turns out it wasn't.

The trek to Donard's summit begins in a forest. The trail follows a river and gradually begins to climb more steeply through the woodland before entering a valley between two of the highest peaks of the Mournes. On arrival at the saddle-shaped dip between the two peaks, you then turn left for the final and exceptionally steep ascent to the top, to the summit, which stands 848m above sea level and is the highest point in Northern Ireland. The previous year I only just made it through the forest. We were no more than thirty minutes into the trek when I had to ask my friends to stop while I sat defeated by a large oak tree and tried to catch my breath. My chest was heaving – it had never been the same since that infection at the end of chemo. As I struggled to get air into my lungs, I started to panic, which only made the situation worse. *'It's ok, Alex, we don't have to go any further,'* Gillian reassured me. But we did. I was not a quitter.

I forced myself to the saddle before I caved in to defeat, knowing there was no way my lungs would sustain that final steep ascent. We ate our picnic in silence by the shelter of the Mourne Wall. I was devastated. I had climbed this mountain over and over during my Everest training without batting an eyelid. Flip, I had practically run up and down it! I had continued to climb it during chemo without any real difficulty. Although it exhausted me now, my body had never failed to carry me to the top. Not until that day.

Back in the comfort of my own home I let the tears fall just as I knew they would. Today was the first day cancer had beaten me – the first day it had won, and I was beyond devastated. I wondered if I would ever be able to do the things I loved again. Would I ever be able to do the things I enjoyed? Would I ever stand on the tops of mountains again?

My second attempt ended the same way as the first – I was at the saddle again before I was beaten and had to climb back down; my frustration heightening with yet another defeat. My third attempt I did alone. My first ever solo hike – just me and Bear, of course. Although arguably Bear only made it more difficult because he was badly behaved throughout the entire hike. The mountains tend to make him a little crazy as he loves them as much as I do. I climbed much slower than usual, taking my time, taking it easy. Today was the day I'd reach the summit. I was sure of it. Bear and I stopped at the saddle – the usual picnic spot, and ate our lunch: me, my sandwiches, and him his gravy bones. I sat for a while, daunted by the mighty hill to the left of me, but eventually I stood and began my final ascent with Bear beside me and with sheer determination. I dragged my miserable body to the top of that mountain, refusing to let cancer beat me any more!

* * *

One year later, on another New Year's Day, Graeme and I left the house at 4 a.m. sharp. It was an hour and a half drive and I wanted to ensure we made it to the summit before sunrise at half eight. We drove down the deserted motorways hoping to avoid police vehicles during curfew. The fine if we were caught was £1,000. Thankfully we saw no lights except our own and dodged the hefty bill.

Graeme drove and, as usual, controlled the music from his mobile phone. After half an hour or so of sleepy silence, he turned to me. *'I've wanted to play this song to you for a while now but was waiting for something special. Today seems fitting enough.'* He can be so sentimental at times. I braced myself and listened, already knowing this would be emotional. He played *'Wind Beneath My Wings'* by Bette Midler. We managed to get to the chorus before I burst into tears, and so did he. It was the first time my husband had acknowledged my struggles as well as my strengths. Unable to say the words himself, he played them through the song. I took his hand in mine and stared out the window, lost in my own unspoken words for the rest of the journey.

We arrived at five thirty, parked up, threw our gear on our backs and began our climb. We were the first ones on the mountain that morning. It was pitch-black, with only the moonlight and our head torches to guide the way. A dark silhouette of the mountain peaks loomed before us blanketed in silver stars. It was mesmerising. In fact, I couldn't take my eyes of it.

We couldn't tell if there was snow on the peaks, not yet – it was still too dark, but I was praying there was. For now I had to focus on the difficult task at hand: navigating a mountain in the dark. Having climbed this mountain a handful of times, I knew the way better than my husband, so I stayed out in front.

I had chosen to climb Slieve Binnian, a half-day route that summits one of the seven highest peaks in the Mournes. The trail is usually easy enough to navigate, and if in doubt you can always follow the crowd as it's one of the more popular hikes because of its breathtaking views. But like I said, we were the only ones there in the dark, so following wasn't an option. The trail isn't so much a path but rather a narrow area of flatter ground, that has been repeatedly walked on, snaking its way up the mountain face. Luckily there's always the Mourne Wall to follow – an ancient wall built in 1904 that stretches a whopping twenty-two miles across the mountain region and includes fifteen of its peaks. *'Our next challenge,'* I said, pointing it out to Graeme.

For the first half hour or so the terrain was relatively clear with very little ice. Easy enough, I naively thought, until we reached the start of the rocky ascent, which turned out to be treacherous. The rocks were covered in solid ice and my feet were slipping and sliding all over the show. The ice cracked beneath my boots with every terrifying step. This is it, this is how I'm going to die, I thought to myself. My fear of falling was somewhat justified because I'm more at risk of fractures and breaks than Joe Bloggs after completing radiotherapy, which I had to continuously remind my husband who was starting to lose patience with me. But no matter how I tried, it was impossible to get a grip on the ice. I ended up on my hands and knees in some of the trickier spots to avoid seriously injuring myself.

The black sky was quickly turning a brilliant purple but we were only halfway up. It was now a race against time, and I was slowing us down. I turned to see a trail of head torches behind us catching up, urging me to speed up. My competitive side kicked in – I didn't want to be overtaken, but my legs were heavy and exhausted, my arms were burning from clinging onto the wall so tightly, using it for leverage. Three couples passed me and I was growing ever more frustrated knowing that in my pre-cancer days I'd have beaten every one of them to the summit. But still I climbed.

Finally the ice turned to white fluffy snow (thankfully much easier to walk on), and Graeme and I were able to pick up the pace – full steam ahead. We made it to the top with only ten minutes to spare. A mist had unfortunately crept up on the mountaintop making visibility exceptionally poor. You could see nothing, and I prayed it would clear in time for sunrise. While we waited we took shelter behind an icy rock, drinking our hot tea and coffee and wishing fellow hikers a happy New Year. It was a heart-warming experience to be part of a group of strangers gathered in the freezing snow to watch the first sunrise of 2021.

Ten minutes passed and my hands started trembling with the cold; my gloves insufficient in sub-zero temperatures. I knew I wouldn't be able to wait much longer. When suddenly, low and behold, the mist cleared and the sun rose in a blaze of orange and yellow; shining upon the mountain summit and turning the snow into a bed of glittery diamonds. It was one of the most breathtaking sights I have ever witnessed – and I've seen some wonders in my time. This, however, was something else. I wished we could stay longer but my body temperature was plummeting and I was starting to convulse. I urged Graeme to begin our descent down the opposite, less treacherous, side of the mountain. Once we had made sufficient ground and I had warmed a little, we stopped so Graeme could fly his drone. The snow here was still fresh and untouched; our footprints the only markings on an otherwise blanket of pearly white. The snowy peaks of the surrounding mountaintops were in full view, and this was the perfect spot for some video footage.

Later that evening, in front of our blazing fire and with a scalding cup of coffee in hand, Graeme edited the drone footage and played me the video. I couldn't stop watching it over and over. It was hypnotic. I watched myself slipping, sliding and smiling up that snow-drizzled mountain and felt as though I was seeing myself for the first time. In that picturesque video, made by my talented husband, I saw the beneficiary of cancer, not the victim.

I had been given a gift – a gift that so many are heartbreakingly deprived of – the gift of time, extra time. Time to spend with my husband, family, friends and most importantly my fur baby Bear. Every minute of every day is a gift that I could have otherwise lost. Every morning when I wake I make a point of saying thank you – thank you is always the first words to leave my lips. Some days I repeat it over and over and some days I whisper it only once. But I always make sure I say it and truly mean it. No matter how difficult my day ahead may be, I am still thankful to live another one regardless.

My enormous gratitude for my life would never have existed if I hadn't been forced to face my own mortality. I watched my snowy mountain ascent unfold on our TV screen and saw my journey with cancer in every step of it. A journey I was now grateful for. An epic quest that had led me to myself and the life I was meant to live – a whole one full of love, life, laughter and adventure. I had climbed my very own Everest in the end; an exhausting, heartbreaking cancerous Everest, and I did it with grace, honesty, integrity and superhuman strength. A strength I would have otherwise never known I possessed. I handled it like a true champion. Never letting it wear me down. Never letting it win. No matter how much it threatened me, I remained resilient. Even in the pits of my own abyss I never gave up. Even when I was sure it was the end of the trail for me, I kept climbing, I kept fighting and I kept on with my ascent. Because on the top of those mountains, where the sky is my only limit, I am at peace. Supported and grounded by the earth beneath my feet, free to soak in the beauty of my surroundings, to feel the warmth of the sun on my bare skin, to admire the stunning views below me and the beauty of another sunrise above me. Each one reminding me of my new beginning, my second chance at life. Up there where the air is pure and crisp, I breathe freely without face masks, without fear, without Covid-19, without cancer. Such worries don't exist at those heights for my mind is now as sturdy as the mountains I stand upon. No longer plagued by mental ill health or by a deadly disease, up there at the top of my ascent I am finally free!

* * *

The evening after our moonlit hike, as I rested my exhausted body in our supersized bed, I pulled out my little black journal from my bedside drawer, the journal that my quirky, fellow bear-loving art therapist had given me months ago, and took another look through the pictures I had filled it with. In that same drawer I keep a handful of photos that mean something to me. Not photos of people, but photos of places. Places I wish to visit before I die. Among them was a shot of Mount Everest. I took the photo of the highest mountain on earth in my hands and stuck it on the journal's final page. Underneath I wrote the words: I DID IT.

I did it. I had survived my own Everest and I had benefited from my ascent! As heartbreaking as cancer was, my journey with it allowed me to heal what had long been broken. It healed me. Cancer gifted me with the peace and clarity I had been longing for my whole life. It gave me joy in ways I never could have imagined. It reunited me with my family and solidified friendships that will last for eternity. It opened doors to new opportunities that I would otherwise never have experienced (including the opportunity to live as a patient to become a better nurse). As well as giving me the chance to meet some incredible and inspiring people in a community I am welcomed into and privileged to be part of. A community of survivors who also have a story to tell. Stories that I learnt and grew from.

Finally, cancer gifted me with a new form of creative expression – writing. Cancer had led me to my purpose at long last. My purpose was to write, and to write this story in particular. A personal and emotional memoir of the most difficult and elevating ascent of my life. A story of pain, loss and suffering but also hope, joy and light. A story that transformed me and my life as I wrote it. A story that allowed me to find peace and closure at long last. My story was my gift. A gift that I now pass on to you and whoever else needs to read it.

For months my writing had been at a stalemate. I had been stuck on my final chapter for what felt like infinity, waiting on a miracle to finish with. Perhaps a miracle baby or a dream trip to Italy, India and Bali, a new and marvellous career. Whatever it was, I wanted it to be spectacular. But on the summit of that freezing mountain, in the early hours of that icy-cold New Year morning, I came to an important realisation: my life was the greatest miracle I could ever finish my story on. I didn't need to wait for something extraordinary to happen because my second chance at life was already just that – extraordinary. At long last my story was complete and with it my cancer journey (for now, at least) has come to an end. It has taken me a full year, a year of recovering and a year of writing, to fully grasp the concept of ringing the cancer bell and the poem written above it:

Ring this bell
Three times well
Its toll to clearly say
My treatment is done
This course is run
And I am on my way!

(Inspired by Emma Payton and Maria Watt)

Although I had physically rung the bell that day in the Cancer Centre at the end of active treatment with my family, friends and fellow cancer patients cheering me on, mentally I am only hearing its chimes now. One year later and I can finally say, *'I am on my way.'*

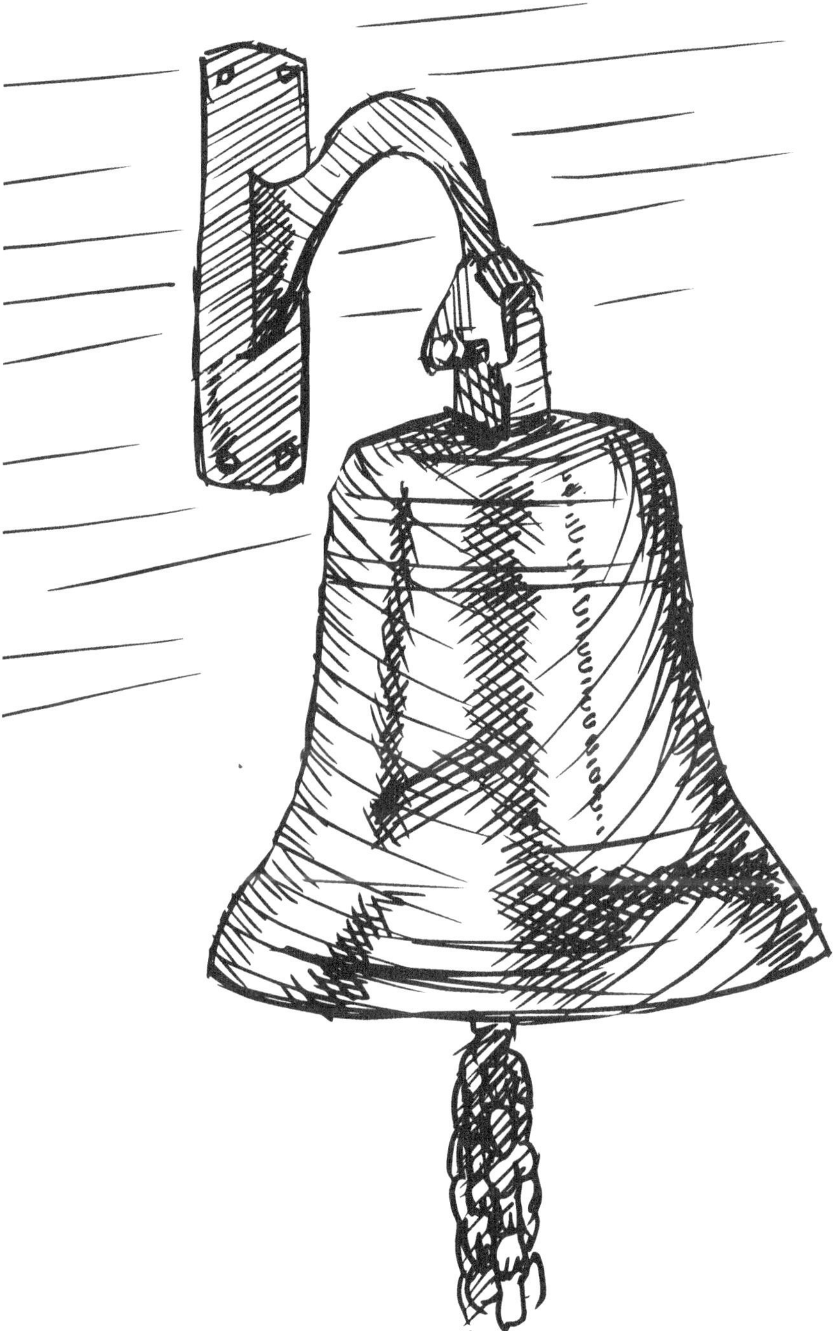

Printed in Great Britain
by Amazon

65787230R00119